RAYMÒN AND SUNSHINE

by Karen Krett

RAYMÒN AND SUNSHINE

Cover Design by
Gregory Schoenfeld

Edited by
Gregory Schoenfeld

ISBN-13: 978-0692660881
ISBN-10: 0692660887

www.karenkrettauthor.com

For my grandson, Alec, who inspires me.

And for my son, Gregory, who has walked this path to the future with me.

CONTENTS

GLOSSARY OF TERMS

Aerotite: *Lighter-than-air substance found in the upper layers of Saturn's atmosphere.*

Aichan link: *Repurposed radio beam containing a "message bubble."*

AILES: *Artificial Intelligence Law Enforcement Self-drone—fifteen foot, weaponized, winged Morgonium predator.*

Airbus: *Transportation vehicle used for moderate distances. Lifts off and lands vertically.*

AlbertE: *Transport system via almost half light speed denatured laser beam "mono-rail."*

Allmind: *Descendent of the Internet—total intermeshing of all virtual knowledge and activity.*

Amazing Tree-von: *Superhero—20 ft. tall, skin like bark with leaves that are defensive and protective tools.*

Amip: *One of six low buildings in the LUDI Compound.*

Andoid Integration Trauma (AIT): *aftereffect of android augmentation.*

Advanceman: *Another name for the superhero, Whânzo.*

Architechture: *Androids' physiology.*

ArthurC: *Space elevator.*

Ard: *One of six low buildings in the LUDI Compound.*

Asuda Yér: *Town near the Caspian Sea, in the fragstate of Istan. Raymòn and Sunshine's second home.*

Augmentation: *The process of adding to or increasing android abilities.*

Aunti-Drone: *Female superhero—an AILES defender.*

Autoroad: *Moving roadway for vehicles.*

Bonding-paq: *Smart carrier for infants, conforms to child/parent shape on the back or chest.*

Bratus: *Tall, willowy building in the LUDI Compound.*

Breathelings: *performers who have mastered their breath.*

Calmwater: *Raymòn and Sunshine's first home.*

Changer: *Wingèd superhero created to represent Raymòn.*

Chicken-of-the-sea: *Armored sea creature, visually reminiscent of a rooster.*

Chip (to): *Interpersonal communication via microchip implanted in frontal lobe in adults over eighteen.*

Cloudworld: *An adult theme park/resort in the clouds extending from pole to pole.*

Com (make or take): *The connection resulting from "chipping."*

Companion (Familiar): *Four-legged android bonded with each humanoid android at sentience.*

Compensators: *Artificial intelligence hive which created offsets for depletions of the ecosystem.*

Conglomerate states (conglosates): *The four post-national global divisions.*

Cosmosism: *New religion based on collecting the energy of the universe.*

Credits: *Means of exchange instead of money.*

Data stream: *Android access through thought, to all information possessed by any android.*

Dimensional Transitioner: *Artists' mechanism used to create three-dimensional imagery.*

Earth Caps (EC): *North and South Poles.*

Effected silk: *Made from genetically altered silkworms. A more robust, soft, light thread.*

Elevshire: *On the outskirts of Ludicom. Site of Tritan Tork stet-Sulston's laboratory.*

Embromator: *External womb.*

Emo: *Android augmentation for human-like emotional capacity*

Epyderm: *Android skin.*

Escalift: *Variable-speed personal escalator.*

Expandicase (Expa): *Smart, expandable luggage.*

Familia Strong: *a multiple superhero—a quintet. Each member with a particular and complimentary power.*

Familiar: *Human term applied to Companions out of the fear that they were magical beings.*

Farbeam: *Transport via teleportation.*

Fragstate: *One of the smaller divisions within each conglostate.*

Geber: *Building in the LUDI Compound. Shaped like a male figure.*

Gliding: *Android ability to move without walking.*

Green Normal View: *Enclave for androids.*

Grief Center: *Local environment where survivants might organize a memorial, or spend the necessary time mourning a loved one.*

Hawking Forest: *The forest outside the LUDI Compound.*

High Ying: *Popular dance form derived from martial arts.*

Hitman of the Universe: *One of Raymon's early superheroes.*

Holophone: *Holographic telephone.*

Holo-tab: *Holographic tablet.*

Hover-board: *Intelligent, thought driven, personal transport.*

Hybrid: *Superhero—half man, half robot, able to appear human or cybertronic.*

Humandroid: *The offspring of an android and a human.*

IGA: *InterGalactic Artists.*

Insider: *People born with the ability to immediately understand how others were feeling.*

Israquia: *Fragstate in what once was the Middle East.*

Janus I: *Type of hover-board.*

Jerusaline: *City renamed when Israel and Palestine ended their divisions.*

Jondobeast: *Elephant-sized quadruped in Wildpark.*

Hawking Forest: *In Ludicom. Contains the path to the LUDI Compound.*

Ionaboard: *Thin, stiff-appearing material composed of a dense collection of ions, on which works of art could be printed, then hung.*

Lat: *The all-purpose word Drovines use instead of she, he, him or her.*

Little One: *Superhero based on Raymòn's girlfriend, Li-Li, when he was 16.*

LUDI: *Self-replicating android production company.*

Ludicom: *Town outside of the LUDI Compound.*

MPS: *The Movement for the Purity of the Species.*

Magister Systems: *Largest of the original android production companies.*

Mainesail: *Town where V'hanie and Garth-Ann's live; also the Reál-el Ludis third home.*

Microcab: *Intelligent, single-occupant, airborne conveyance. Uses anti-proton fusion engine.*

Morgonglass: *Glass of jewel-like clarity, grown via architected crystals.*

Morgonium: *Synthetic element produced on Ganymede—used to make lightweight, high tensile metallic products.*

Multi: *Human possessing both genders.*

Mwamba: *One of six low buildings in the LUDI Compound.*

New Angleterre: *Tropical village in the fragstate of Pasifika, NSS—source of organic lavender.*

New Equatorial and Energy States (NE&ES): *Northern Africa, Central America, and the Middle East, Mexico.*

New Northern States (NNS): *North America, most of Europe, Russia, China, India, and Pakistan.*

New Southern States (NSS): *Southern Africa, South America, the islands of the South Pacific, Indonesia and Australia*

Nito: *Superhero, a shape-shifter—an homage to Wil Tork.*

Nucoastcolony: *The fragstate in which Raymòn lived with his parents.*

Nuvem: *One of six low buildings in the LUDI Compound. Site of Sunshine's creation.*

Nǔxing: *Building in the LUDI Compound, shaped like a female figure.*

Oceanair Grove: *Location of Bennito's studio.*

PRR: *Personal range of response—android personality.*

Protosaq: *Protective covering used in Wildpark.*

Raka-drum: *Percussion instrument covered with synthetic tiger skin.*

Red-Savior: *Fire-breathing, scaly, biped superhero.*

Re-Action-ware: *Clothing made of fabric that adjusts to temperature and weather conditions—cools in the heat, warms in the cold, water resistant in rain or snow.*

Repelanium: *Element discovered in the rings of Saturn which blocks visibility.*

Reversor: *Superhero—able to volley all forms of energy back to the assailant.*

Sailboat: *Intention-driven oviform transport inside "Bratus," a LUDI Compound building.*

Seeing-eyes: *Small, self-policing bots which guard property.*

Self-Contained: *Designation for most people with characteristics once diagnosed as autism.*

Serv-o: *Smart, non-humanoid robot/servant.*

Smartpaq: *Intelligent backpack.*

Stasis chair: *Creates weightlessness and balance.*

Stratotrees: *Four hundred foot tall trees in Wildpark.*

Suelo: *One of six low buildings in the LUDI Compound.*

Suffused concrete: *Building material: malleable to work with, impermeable once set.*

Synthstock: *Non-vibrant synthetic replacement for paper, slimy to the touch.*

Talktuner: *Universal translating device.*

Trans-Haven: *The town where Tŏnna and Charl live.*

Tribarium: *Element discovered on Mercury, used to produce thinner, stronger computer tablets.*

Tutmonda Centro: *Esperanto for "global center." Home of the Global Academy.*

Universal Home: *Cosmosists' temple and observatory.*

Vactube: *Local transport for large groups of individuals.*

Veloxiomountain: *Raymòn's neighborhood.*

Voxpa: *Personalized commercial entertainments. Thirty-to-ninety-minute interactive stories, with variable scenes and endings.*

VuGuru: *Personal viewer for any visual medium. Worn like eyeglasses.*

Wave/fibers: *Android composition—physical manifestation of wave/particle duality.*

Weatherpainters: *Climate and weather designers, able to fully control the environment.*

Whânzo (Advanceman): *Raymon's first character with superpowers.*

Wildpark: *Jungle inside the LUDI Compound*

As long as you have life and breath, believe. Believe for those who cannot. Believe even if you have stopped believing. Believe for the sake of the dead, for love, to keep your heart beating, believe. Never give up, never despair, let no mystery confound you into the conclusion that mystery cannot be yours.

~Mark Helprin
A Soldier of the Great War

Chapter 1 –
First Contact

"**W**here is my tablet mother? Have you seen it?"

Outside, chartreuse lightning vaulted across a peach colored sky, while a cherry-vanilla wind raised a symphony of rustling leaves. Normally, the finely crafted climate would have delighted Raymòn; but, in this moment, his awareness was focused only on what was absent. His instrument, the extension of the driving force of his life—his need to draw—was missing. There was no part of him taking note of the world beyond his need.

It was endlessly frustrating that others had their own needs for him to navigate. And his mother always demanded he attend to hers.

"Now, Raymòn, first look me in the eye. No. That's not good enough. Stop and look me in the eye."

Say it! Say it. Ray's throat ached from holding back his words: *My equilibrium should be your concern. Your love is dosed with shame and irritation at who I am.*

His mother had unspoken words as well: *I have always needed you to try harder, to be less different. But you have your father's stubbornness. And you have no idea how disappointing it is for me that you live inside yourself.* She steeled herself—as she always did.

Raymòn Réal felt the needles of stress threaten his mind, urging him to twitch or to retreat into repetitive movement to erase the build-up. He didn't have to succumb to that inner demand any longer, but he did need to make the tension end. That took priority over being understood. The shaft of sadness at what he had to give up didn't rise to the level of his awareness; it was one of the merciful aspects of his nature. He was one of the Self-Contained, a term which was applied to those who had once been seen as defective. Earth had become more accepting of human variation in the twenty-third century. But not in the Réal household.

Twenty-two years of being told he was not behaving the way normal people did, and Raymòn still didn't understand why eye contact was such a good thing. But he'd learned that his point of view didn't matter. In order not to get caught in the vise of inexorable conditioning and its soul-killing exploration of the minutiae of his feelings, he raised his chin, as he had been taught, then found the loving and worried eyes of his mother. He offered her his cherished gaze. To her it meant he was present. But Raymòn was always present. Deep inside himself he was continuous. Contact was not his definition of being alive.

Temporarily satisfied, Ilsa Réal graced her son with a response. "Ah, there's my boy! Now, then, your tablet? Maybe Sunshine put it somewhere. Go ask her if she's seen it."

Raymòn disregarded his mother's condescension; his need to draw was increasing in urgency and finding his tablet was the only thing that mattered right then. That was how it was for him. Single-mindedness, impervious passion. He would question the new housecleaner. He hadn't interacted with her yet but was barely curious. At the moment, she was merely a means to an end.

He engaged the escalift to the second floor and found Sunshine cleaning in the upstairs entertainment room. Hearing him approach, she put down the suction wand of the dust eliminator, turned and waited. Her long-lashed bright blue eyes looked straight ahead. There was a slight smile on her full red lips. Her complexion had the pale glow of an extremely fair-skinned human, but without the hint of bluish veins one would normally see. She had no veins. She had no blood.

The android's more-gold-than-yellow shoulder-length hair was pulled back in a plain metallic smartclip. It gently held her thick mane with just the minimum of necessary tension; it responded to her expressed desires and released or tightened as she wished. She wore, as always, a jumpsuit made of Re-Action-ware. The fabric adjusted to the temperature and weather conditions: it cooled in the heat and warmed in the cold; it became water resistant when it rained or snowed. It was teal blue; sometimes she wore one of pale silver.

Raymòn offered no preamble. "Sunshine, have you seen my drawing tablet? The case is black. It might have looked like a sheet of lightweight metal—about two feet by one foot."

She neither searched out his gaze nor seemed to care about their lack of eye contact. Her answer was simple. "Yes. I put it in the upper right hand drawer of your desk. Was it acceptable to do that?"

2

"I guess so. If you're always going to put it there, then I don't mind."

"You are quite agreeable. This tells me that interacting with you will be easy, not difficult." As Sunshine spoke, she held her right hand chest high and steadily moved it from left to right—in a smooth, straight line. The gesture resonated with Raymòn—both as a visual artist and the man who had so often been told he was hard to deal with.

Despite his inner reaction, it didn't occur to Raymòn to respond verbally to Sunshine's comment. Instead, he called downstairs, "Found it, Mother. Sunshine put it away." He had been reminded endlessly to let his mother know when there was a conclusion to a problem. He wanted to avoid being reminded again.

With an abruptness that signaled a shift in his focus and connection, he turned and walked away from the housekeeper, intent on retrieving his most prized possession.

Sunshine took note of how gracefully he moved his broad shouldered, six foot four inch body. He was neither overly slim nor particularly muscled; there was a softness to him that conveyed his complete disinterest in most forms of physical exercise. She recorded how his hair was long and falling in his eyes. His eyes were the same color as his hair: the darkest brown, verging on black. His nose was straight and prominent, his jaw very well defined. His skin was clear, a light brown. The android made no judgment about his physiology, but she was intent in her observation. She was able to form opinions, preferences, likes and dislikes, but was inclined to wait for a fuller experience of the person before she let that part of her participate. She was aware, however, that he intrigued her— in a way that was not familiar.

Raymòn entered his own personal zone, the shelter of his room, with a relief that could only come from true privacy. He immediately started sketching with precision and without frustration, going over and over each element in the latest rendition of his newly created superhero. The character known as Hybrid was half man, half robot, with the ability to shift his demeanor to appear either human or like a cybertronic being. He was working on the face, which always gave him the most trouble. Fans of his work—and there were quite a number— had no idea how much effort he expended in order to create a face others would respond to.

Hybrid's cheeks were, in this incarnation, deeply delineated by their sharp angles, revealing the metallic frame under his skin. The eyes were lime green,

3

certainly not a natural color, but Ray managed to draw them so their intelligence was obvious. It was all in the smallest lines. Since the age of two he had been an artist, learning through endless repetition how to capture what he saw in his favorite worlds of cartoons and superheroes.

Every few minutes he would print out and examine a copy of his work on synthstock, now the only material available for physical renderings. As all artists knew, the chemicals needed to make the stock smooth and long-lasting reduced the brightness and minimized the color absorption, giving everything a slightly rinsed look. It was all they had. Raymòn maintained the integrity of his spectrum in his mind, seeing the only truth of his vision on the virtual page.

Immersed in his drawing, he had no idea that Sunshine was standing in the doorway. She stood very still. Her voice was soft, but her words were clearly enunciated. "I see that you are drawing. Will I disturb you if I clean?"

Ray maintained his focus, his nose just a few inches from the tablet.

He shook his head in answer.

The android walked to the wall to engage the mop/vacuum tool, but instead of beginning to work, she asked, "May I look at what you are doing? I have been admiring your work as I came across it throughout the house. I think the ability to create images is the highest level of creativity."

Something in her tone—which was gentle but absent of any obvious emotion—drew him. But her words were what he really responded to. He concluded that she was truly interested, not just acting curious like so many people did when they thought it was the right way to behave. He could always tell when someone was faking it; it was one of those socially acceptable wastes of time he detested.

Without shifting his eyes, he said, "Sure."

She put down the cleaning implement and stood by his side. She was inches from him and he felt comfortable. That was unusual. Proximity was almost always at least slightly painful.

"This is Hybrid, a character I'm developing for my comic book. I want him to be both fully human and a synthetic entity. His face is the hardest place to represent both parts of him." Raymòn held the screen in front of Sunshine so she could see it clearly.

In reaching to hold it, Sunshine lightly touched his hand. Instead of the instant recoil response he was used to, he felt something different, something unfamiliar. The best he could do to identify it was to think of it as warmth. His hand felt nicely warm.

"I like this very much, Raymòn. I had not realized you drew in three dimensions. His eyes are bold, bolder than most people, but I can see that he understands everything in his field of vision. You have succeeded in conveying the duality of his nature. You have the gift of creating new reality.

"I would very much like to be able to draw," Sunshine continued in the same soft voice, "but I would need to have my architecture amended."

Raymòn knew she was an android, but no android or robot had ever discussed their programming with him before. He was very curious. The only thing he knew for sure was that many humans were scared about the prospect of androids being the dominant species on the planet.

"Can you have that done if you want to? Can you ask for an upgrade of some kind that would enable you to draw?"

"There are some rudimentary augments that do that, but because I am a housecleaner, I may not have access." Sunshine said this without the bitterness or disappointment a human counterpart would probably have expressed.

Again, Raymòn felt relief, and his interest was piqued even more. "What if you made a special request? Is there any kind of central decision maker to whom you could appeal to if you wanted to?"

Had he been looking directly at her, Raymòn would have seen Sunshine's eyes widen. "I am surprised you are thinking this way. Your mother told me to expect you to ignore me, but that is not what you are doing. I can sense your interest. My desire to draw is strong enough to warrant exploring your suggestion. I live in a group home with a knowledgeable and supportive android house leader. He might be able to help me with this."

Raymòn wanted to respond to Sunshine and also ask her some questions. He thought about that for a moment and realized he liked her. She was sitting quietly without any demand or control directed toward him. He felt calm, which was one of his favorite feelings.

"My mother is used to me avoiding interaction. I generally prefer to be alone and not have anyone pushing or pulling me. Usually that's what happens with people. You're different, so I'm different."

Sunshine, now looking out the window alongside his desk, nodded. "That makes sense." She stopped again, waiting for Raymòn to continue.

He felt the push of curiosity; he wanted to know more. "What's a house leader?" he asked.

"Do you know much about android history?" Raymòn shook his head. "Would you like me to tell you about it? It will include an answer to your question." He nodded. Eyes on his creation but listening closely, he sketched while she talked.

Turning in his direction, she stood perfectly still, perfectly at ease.

"One hundred and fifty years ago, my first ancestor was created. He was the very newest model AI entity. Besides being able to function in an intelligent and productive capacity, he was made to look like a human, and his architecture gave him what you would call personality. We call it personal range of response or PRR. He had a name, a human name, instead of the typical robot designations like "Darth" or "Kron" which had been customary until that point. He was Harry el Ludi. I think of him as Grandpa Harry. Humans wanted companions, not just functional proxies, so androids like him were desirable. I am the seventy-third iteration of the Harry variation. We have been perfected over time; Harry, himself, has continually been upgraded.

Sunshine paused, waiting for the subtle signal that her new human friend was still engaged. His head was slightly tilted in her direction. This, she understood, meant his interest had not flagged.

"Are you wondering about my name?" she asked.

Without looking up, Raymòn nodded.

"My given name is Sarlee; Sunshine is the nickname Grandpa Harry gave me. He had heard an old song, "You Are My Sunshine," a simple melody from the twentieth century. He said I inspired the same feelings as the song—he has the complete range of emotions. If you are ever interested, I will sing it for you. It is a very good nickname, do you not think so?"

Raymòn noticed her speech: she never used contractions. It was odd, but he liked it. He nodded again and smiled, slightly raising his eyebrows, in response to which Sunshine said, "Thank you."

She continued. "About twenty years ago, when the debates about android sentience were finally resolved, we were granted many of the rights humans have. Among them are freedom of speech, the right to choose whom we interact with, the right to be paid for our work, ownership of our bodies and protection from being harmed or used against our will. We are no longer slaves and are now self-replicating. Android creation is now handled entirely by androids.

"The first humans I came in contact with were like parents to me. After I was made, I was sent to learn and work in a home for android development. Sasha and Mariline were the human house leaders. They were a Joined couple in their mid-sixties, full of love and clarity of purpose. For a year they lived in a large residence with me and nine other new androids, plus a robot and android staff. They helped us exercise our PRR's and develop our interactive muscles. Even though every android has core morality patterning, it has been discovered that reinforcement is needed in order for that individual to fully embody those imperatives. Without early responses to our behavior, we do not become as well-defined in that moral realm."

Raymòn never stopped sketching but Sunshine could feel that his attention was firmly directed toward her. Very sensitive sensors in her epyderm fed that information to her. She could literally measure the degree of engaged energy. To her it was as specific as a particular musical note.

"I would be interested in your heritage too, Raymòn. I do not know much about people like you."

Continuing to avoid eye contact, Raymòn began to speak. This was a subject no one ever asked about. He felt more than a twinge of anxiety—he hoped it wasn't going to be so bad that he would have to shut down.

"There used to be a medical diagnosis which people like me were given: they called it autism, and everyone was frightened by it. But, as the years passed, increasing numbers of people were born who behaved in an 'autistic' manner. More people were more insular, more were unresponsive to their family's desires to get close to them; more exhibited sensory sensitivity, more were uncomfortable with physical contact, and many more were disinclined to make eye contact. Preference for solitary activities or for communication filtered through an electronic device radically increased."

Raymòn could feel Sunshine's attention to his words. It was palpable but in no way discomfiting. He went on. "What was once foreign and unusual became mainstream behavior. What was once considered pathological was seen as just a variation of the norm. The array which had once been considered a single disorder was now understood as many different groupings of attributes.

"People who can't tolerate *any* contact, who are unable to successfully communicate, and those whose behavior puts them or others at risk are still given early intervention and remedial support; but much of the special treatment and schooling, particularly segregation, has ended. My mother still tells me to look her in the eye—it's particularly hard for her to accept the new attitudes—but almost everyone has stopped trying to change people like me. Also, there's some understanding that being less interested in connection with others has its benefits. We suffer less loneliness and are not as likely to become depressed; we have more tolerance for the ultimately solitary state that is the essential human condition."

In the silence that followed their short histories, both Raymòn and Sunshine were left with the same question. It was Sunshine who asked it first. "Can you love?"

"Yes. I can. I love my mother and father. Their well-being matters greatly to me. I feel what I think other people feel when they talk of love. My heart fills to overflowing. What's different is that I don't desire to spend a great deal of time with them. A little goes a long way for me. I also love my sister, V'hanie, very much. She's not like me, but sometimes she acts the way I do—which frustrates my parents. She's four years younger, so it was natural for her to imitate me—especially when she was little. When she tunes them out or fails to react, they get quite angry with her. By their behavior, I understand they would prefer not to have two children like me. In fact, she is quite different—on the other end of the spectrum of innate responsiveness—but they can easily become alarmed when she behaves non-responsively. Neither of my parents identifies themself as one of the Self-Contained. That's what people like me are called now."

Sunshine registered Raymòn's slight intake of breath as he said, "Back to your question. Once, when I was younger, I might have loved a girl. I'm not sure. What about you? Can you love? Have you ever loved?"

The question was not going to get answered, not right then. Ilsa, Raymòn's mother, could be heard walking up the stairs. She disdained the use of the escalift, the variable-speed platform which occupied the right half of the wide staircase. As the name suggested, it was a personal escalator. This was one way in which she resisted the modern world—one of many. Without either one of them reacting guiltily, both Sunshine and Raymòn stopped talking. Each recalibrated their attention to their tasks: Sunshine resumed cleaning and Raymòn continued drawing.

As was often the case, Raymòn's mind drifted toward some vivid memories. His outward demeanor revealed nothing. Jaw set and still, eyes focused on his work, shoulders slightly hunched as he held his stylus with precision. And yet, inside, his thoughts became a re-enactment of an important experience...one he hadn't relived for a long time.

It was six years earlier, in May of 2256. Raymòn had just turned sixteen.

"Move over Ray, you're hogging the bench." Li-Li spoke her words right next to his ear.

"Don't do that. I don't like it when you get so close. Why do you want to upset me?" The boy tensed visibly

Now that she had his attention, Li-Li resumed her usual distance. "You know why I do that. How often have I wound up talking to myself because you chose to block me out? I hate that."

Her gaze was cast downward, but as Raymòn looked at her face he could see that she was peering at him out of the corner of her eyes. She had that special trace of a smile that was both playful and wise. His heart opened to her. And his upset vanished.

"I know you find it difficult to deal with me sometimes. But I'm worth it, right?" Someone else might have made this sound conceited, but Raymòn— when he communicated—did so from the most honest place. His question was asked because he genuinely wasn't sure.

Li-Li smiled. "You are my best friend. I think you're worth more than I can say." She presumptuously took Raymòn's chin in her hand and turned his face toward her.

There was alarm in his voice. "What are doing? You've never been so aggressive before, Li. I don't want you to do that."

The warm spring day, the breeze bringing the scent of flowers from the garden surrounding them, the intermittent cooing and chirping that set it all to music, all this froze.

Li-Li quickly pulled her hand back, "Can I reboot, please? That was wrong of me. I just wanted you to look at me and I didn't think of your feelings."

In the now graying silence that followed, she realized that what she had done was equivalent to slapping Raymòn. In a few seconds he had repacked his smartpaq—which then assumed its position on his back—and stood up.

"I've got to go now. I've got to go!" He was gone.

Li-Li sat, disconsolate, fearing a permanent breach. But before many minutes had passed, her holophone buzzed. It was the most advanced communications device that people under eighteen had available.

Those who had "come of age" had microcomchips imbedded in the Broca's area of their frontal lobe. Personal energy signatures were well guarded since they were the access to chip contact. It was common practice to "take com" only from those who were already known or those with trusted references. Few were afforded admittance inside one's brain. Everyone else still had to make initial contact by holophone, just like teenagers, leaving a message and hoping it would be returned.

The days of random calling were over. Many adults refused to check their holophones for days at a time as a matter of disdainful pride. But there was always the allmind for messages that weren't as private. The great-grandchild of the internet, the allmind was the total intermeshing of all virtual human knowledge and activity. Manipulating this magnitude of data was made possible once scientists were able to encode information into the nuclei of phosphorus atoms held in a silver of purified silicon. Quantum memory at room temperature changed the paradigm.

Each access screen was a portal. Uploading and downloading were not necessary in the allmind; one had simply to ask for the data. It was already there, like unconscious thoughts that could be brought to consciousness at will.

Li-Li thought *answer* and Raymòn's three-dimensional image was before her. The hologram allowed for the illusion of eye contact, which was so much more tolerable for him.

"I'm getting over it—which is pretty fast for me. Let's meet tomorrow afternoon. There was something I didn't get to show you; I think you'll like it." And then..."Bye, little one."

Could he know how loved those three words made Li-Li feel? That was not something they had discussed. But she felt his sweet presence like an enveloping tenderness. She let herself revel in it for as long as it lasted.

At 4:00 PM the next day, Li-Li was waiting for him on their usual bench in the local public garden. The pale lavender of her hair blew gently around her heart-shaped face, across her high cheekbones. It was a fifteen-minute walk from their school, but they always arrived separately. It was what Raymòn preferred. She understood. He didn't want to deal with the questions their classmates would ask if they were seen together too often.

Li-Li watched the eastern path, waiting. It was a long, straight, and narrow cobbled lane that ran alongside the garden. It made her feel as if she were back in ancient times. The sun was low in the sky and glinted off the stones making them look silvery. The sky was a very blueberry blue. She thought, *The weatherpainters are doing a very nice job.*

Weatherpainting was a byproduct of the android-fueled increase in human ability to manipulate the physical universe. It was a medley of artistry and climate management. Only the brightest and most lyrical men and women were admitted to the ranks of those who would add a sensory palette to the specific and sweeping design of the weather. Fragrance, taste, color and sound were interwoven with the blend of sunshine, clouds, wind, and rain that was intentionally created in each locale.

There was a small dot in the distance moving toward Li-Li. Immediately, she was filled with that simple happiness—despite the challenges of being Raymòn's friend—which always rose in her when she saw him. He walked his determined walk, with long measured strides. Purposeful. He was wearing black flowing Re-Action trousers, as always, and a tunic shirt of the same fabric. It was aqua and crimson in sharply delineated geometric segments.

Ah! He's working on a new character. I've never seen this color combination before. Raymòn always coordinated the colors of his shirt—which he would design and dump to a blank shirt palette—to the costume of the focus of his artwork.

"Hi Li." Ray's smile was unrestrained. Without preamble, as was his way, he said, "Look what I made for you."

He sat down, close to her but not touching. From his paq he withdrew the tablet that was as much a part of him as his hand. It was thicker than the later model he would use as an adult—four millimeters instead of one—and composed primarily of synthetics. The revolutionary element, Tribarium, hadn't yet been discovered on Mercury. When utilized, it would produce adaptations that were not only thinner and stronger, but allowed for greater dynamism and fluidity of color.

He spent a moment scrolling through some recent pictures. Satisfied that he had the one he wanted, he held it for her to see.

"Is that me? That's me! Ray, you've made me into a superhero. You've really done a wonderful job. You got my face down perfectly!" With the sparest of lines, Raymòn had recreated the heavy-lidded almond shape of Li-Li's yellow-flecked brown eyes.

"I love the purple and silver suit. It goes so well with my hair. But what does the 'LO' stand for? Oh, wait, I get it…"

Matching his ear-to-ear grin, Li-Li faced Raymòn who was looking watchfully at her. "It's 'Little One,' right?"

Shifting his gaze back to the picture, Raymòn said, "Yes. You're a superhero to me, little one. You have the superpowers of real friendship and …" His voice trailed off because his friend had taken hold of his left hand. She held it lightly, but he could feel her touch deep inside himself. There was a profound question that every cell in his body was asking. *Does this feel good?*

Taking heart from the fact that Raymòn hadn't flinched away, she increased the pressure on his hand ever so slightly. Raymòn felt this small shift as an immense change. As the information started to accrue in his mind, he became aware that he didn't hate this intimate contact. To his surprise, it did feel good.

"I don't mind you holding my hand, Li. I really like you and that seems to make it okay."

Her fifteen-year-old heart began beating with both happiness and hope. It must have been the rush of blood and hormones that caused her to take a leap into forbidden territory. While still holding Raymòn's hand, she stretched her body and her neck so that her lips were on the same plane as his. And she kissed him. Just once. Just for a quick moment. On the lips.

Li experienced a heavenly whoosh of elation and fulfilled longing. She had wanted to kiss Raymòn since the first day she met him two years earlier. But her joy was to be short lived.

Raymòn jumped up and raised his hands in front of him as if to fend off a blow. He was visibly shaken; his eyelids fluttered and he drew in his mouth to a thin line of tension. He did not speak. He shook his head so violently that Li-Li feared he would hurt himself. Before she could muster a response, he had fled. He raced back up the cobbled path, dragging his open paq in one hand, clutching his tablet in the other. His foot got caught on a stone and he almost went down, barely keeping himself erect. He didn't look back; he was running away from what had been a terrifying breach of his boundaries—and maybe something else. It was not the time for analysis. It was the time for escape.

For Li-Li, it was the time for despair. She knew she wouldn't be seeing him again. She knew she had gone too far and he would find her to be unsafe.

In retrospect, which was an acceptable vantage point, Raymòn was able to feel some remorse. Li-Li *had* been his "little one." But, after the kiss, he could no longer trust her. As he had just re-experienced in his intense daydream, he could not bear the unexpected intrusion beyond his limits. Had he loved her? He thought he had; but trust trumped love. It was something Ray had known since he was a small child, an immutable part of his nature.

Sunshine efficiently went from room to room, completing her work. She was expert at using the various cleaning tools embedded in the house. The auto-wash with high temperature disinfecting foam was available in the bathrooms and kitchen. After the rinse was done, she did a visual check for any areas missed and ran her fingers over each surface to make sure the job was perfect. She could identify any residual bacteria by touch. Satisfied, she opened the small air ducts and turned on the heat that dried everything and left it sparkling. Pursuit of the satisfaction that came with thoroughly completing her task was an integral part of her cleaning pattern.

Although she was neither excited nor upset by her encounter with Raymòn, she was very interested, and her thoughts stayed with the new relationship. Curiosity was a strong element of her PRR, and she wondered about what might be possible between them. She was built to be able to have a comparatively complex relationship, one where commitment and loyalty would become central. Still, in her eight years of sentience, she had not had occasion to ask for any refinement of her emotionality. She knew it was possible for her to become able to experience a wider range of feelings. Adjustments could be made. For the first time she thought it might be something she would want. She now had two questions for Berke, her android house leader: Could she be augmented to be able to draw? And what would the process entail if she wanted to upgrade her emotions?

Interrupting her thoughts, Ilsa Rèal approached. Sunshine could measure her age, fifty-two, and feel her emotional aura. Ilsa was calm but that was as far as Sunshine was able to go with her reading. It was unusual for humans to be this abstruse to her.

Ilsa was dressed in the current style: loose, flowing, gossamer lemon pants and an orange and yellow print tunic, which set off her medium brown skin. Her clothes were made of a natural cotton fiber, which was no longer considered stylish. In this, as in many ways, Ilsa held fast to the old ways, preferring the less synthetic and automated. She wore her auburn hair as she had for most of her life, in a long plait, which she wound around her head like a crown.

Her attitude toward Sunshine was complicated. She appreciated the expertise the android brought to her household. She didn't mind using her services. But she wasn't ready to accept the notion that Sunshine was truly a person or, more accurately, sentient.

It just didn't seem like she was as real, not like a human being. Ilsa also found it distasteful to have to treat it—well, honestly, she wasn't anything more than a robot—with full respect. In the old days, when Ilsa was a girl, she could recall how the first few generations of house-cleaning robots were dealt with. Like very useful objects. That made more sense, and it was an ongoing inner battle to talk to the android in anything other than commands.

Ilsa's conflict was ironic. Houses now had the capability of utilizing self-cleaning programs. Her reactionary inclinations made that seem entirely too modern. She was more comfortable with the experience of having an individual clean each room. Of course, she now had to contend with the *nature* of that individual.

There was one more issue, not fully formed in Ilsa's mind, but preying on her nonetheless. How would this artificial presence affect Raymòn?

"Hello, Sunshine. You're doing an excellent job. I hope everything is going well from your point of view." Ilsa's smile was marginal but present. Her blue eyes were just a few shades paler than Sunshine's and they quickly scoped the android from head to toe. The impact was of being scanned, something Sunshine was quite used to.

"Yes, thank you Mrs. Rèal. I am enjoying my work. Your home is very well organized, so it is quite easy for me to be efficient. I do appreciate your taking time to notice."

"I also noticed that you spent some time with Raymòn." The sharp edge to her voice reflected some fear. This Sunshine received fully. At that moment, her insight into her employer's feelings was far greater than Ilsa's own.

"What did you think about your encounter?"

"Your son is a lovely man. His talent is notable. I very much enjoyed meeting him. I think we liked each other." Unspoken were the words, *I hope you don't mind. I hope you will not feel the need to interfere in this new friendship.* It seemed best not to say that aloud.

"Be careful, Sunshine. Remember, he's different. Relationships are hard for him. I trust you will be understanding and respectful of his sensitivities—and his limitations."

Ilsa's smile was now gone. Her eyes were steely. Sunshine felt as if she were being warned of more than what Ilsa had actually said.

"I will certainly be understanding and respectful. It is an essential part of my moral architecture. I would not want to cause him or you any discomfort or distress." She furrowed her brow and opened her eyes wide to convey earnestness; she lifted her hands and held them forward with her palms turned slightly upward in order to reinforce the non-verbal message.

Ilsa was visibly relieved. Her shoulders, which had been slightly tensed, relaxed. This time her smile was more than marginal. She reached out and lightly patted Sunshine's shoulder. "You're a good girl, I can see that. I hope we can become friends, too."

Sunshine was left to continue her work but her mind was now filled with unexpressed thoughts. It seemed as if Raymòn's mother only saw a partial version of her son. Why did she not she know how much strength his ability to manage his boundaries afforded him? She still seemed to reflect the old thinking, which equated any autistic tendencies with disability.

Sunshine was now even more interested in hearing Raymòn's understanding of what he could and couldn't do. To her surprise, she realized there was already a bond formed between them. That thought released a sense of well-being throughout her body: a faint but pleasant tingling along her arms and legs and a warm feeling in her torso.

The house was neat and clean and she was free to leave. She would return every three days. The option of living in the Rèal house had been offered, but she preferred having her own private space. This too was part of her PRR, taking particular pleasure in her autonomy. Before she left she thought to say goodbye to Raymòn. She gently knocked on his door.

"Who's there?" he barked. Interruption was one his least favorite experiences.

"It is Sunshine. I have come to say goodbye."

Raymòn opened the door with a question in his eyes. Sunshine immediately understood.

"No. I will be back. I am just leaving for today. If you are here, I will see you in three days."

Raymòn took a small but audible breath. "Perhaps I'll see you then," he said as he reclosed the door.

To herself, Sunshine added, *I am very much looking forward to seeing you.*

It would be many more days before their paths crossed again, but they already lived in each other's minds.

Chapter 2–
InterGalactic Artists

Hybrid was ready to come to life. Raymòn had reworked the various drawings in a seemingly endless attempt at perfection. Finally, he was portrayed as Raymòn saw him in his mind's eye.

He was heading toward Benito's house for a meeting with his friends, the three other artists who collaborated in producing their monthly comic that had, over the course of eighteen months, gained an astounding circulation in the allmind.

Ray couldn't remember exactly—numbers weren't so important to him—but there had been something like eighty-five million hits on their site since the first issue. To Raymòn, for whom hubris was impossible, the calm satisfaction this brought meant only one thing: Keep drawing.

He sat somewhat awkwardly in the back row of the airbus that took him more than one hundred miles from the launchpoint in his neighborhood, Veloxiomountain, to Oceanair Grove—a short hover-board ride from his ultimate destination. The personal transport was another integrated element of his and many people's lives. It accommodated shorter distances, moving the rider seamlessly over all terrain, intelligently compensating so the boarder always maintained balance. Durable and lightweight, it contracted from its functional dimensions of 40" x 14" into a small 3 ½" x 5" space inside any paq.

Thirteen minutes in the sealed environment of the half-full AB, most of which were taken up by the vertical lift-off and landing, made Raymòn a little panicky. He had learned to tolerate the feeling, but he would never overcome it. When they landed with precision on the circular port and the big synthglass door lifted up, he jumped out first and took a deep breath of the salt-and-cinnamon-spiced air. He enjoyed the fresh wind always blowing off the ocean, and the taste of it all in his mouth.

The old smell of marine life had been gone for all of Ray's life. No more fish. He'd heard about the radiation leaks from early nuclear reactors. All the oceans had been tainted and no shellfish or fish with scales could survive. Only very deep-dwelling, armored sea life was still viable, some of which were new or previously unknown species. Their natural protection, which allowed them to persist after the human assault on the seas, also kept them from giving off any scent perceptible to people. One of these bottom feeders was strangely configured: its armor bulged out on the sides like wings; atop its tiny head was a rigid growth that looked very much like a rooster's comb. People of Raymòn's parents' generation called it "chicken-of-the-sea," and laughed when they said it. Neither the artist nor his friends got the joke.

From time to time, the weatherpainters had added a pinch of this or that to the salty fragrance. Today's combo was nice.

Benito was, as usual, unwashed and unkempt. He was something of a giant at seven foot five inches, and he shambled noisily as he walked. Ray heard his signature, *slough, thud,* before the door turned porous and he entered.

"So, have you got the goods, Raymo?" This was said with Benno's best retro-gangster accent. He was often in character, having just marinated in a marathon of old, turn-of-the-mil action movies. Benito was swept up in the widespread nostalgia for the twentieth and early twenty-first centuries. For many, it was wistfully seen as a time before humans had to share the planet with another species. Back then people knew they were top dog in the hierarchy of life-forms. Sure, there had been the cetaceans, particularly dolphins, a highly intelligent species, sadly gone, as were the others—the whales and porpoises—with the die-off of the fish. During their five-million-year tenure on the planet, dolphins had stayed in the water; they'd never involved themselves in human business.

"Yeah, Benno, it fell right off the back of truck. Let's do this thing."

On the lower level, Charl and Tōnna were already arrayed in front of two of the five oversized media screens in Benito's production space. They barely acknowledged Raymòn's arrival, which didn't matter at all to any of them. But they were all equally eager to translate their visions into a new installment of *Heroes of the Galaxy.*

Ray saw, as always, how close to identical Charl and Tōnna were, which was by design rather than birth. Friends since childhood, they had evolved a joint persona which included a stunning visual doppelgänger effect: bleached white hair in a mane down their backs, eyebrows also bleached and shaved down to bristles, heavy silver eye shadow, contrasting with awe-inspiring gold irises. They'd gotten them implanted and had their noses and jaws re-surfaced to superhero angularity. The effect was complete, down to their long silver-polished fingernails and matching jumpsuits, bright with intricate gold and silver thread against a matte black background.

The initials "C" and "T" tattooed on their foreheads were the way most everyone told them apart. For Ray, it was easy to see the subtle differences in the way they held their bodies and moved their hands. And, of course, Tōnna was born female and had no facial hair—to speak of.

Aside from Sunshine, no one had seen Hybrid yet. Raymòn dug carefully through his overstuffed paq, pulled out his tablet and began to scroll through the six variations of the new supercharacter. He stood in the center of the room holding tightly to the instrument of his imagination, hesitating before launching his new creation into the noisy and opinionated world of *Heroes*. Benno gave Charl and Tōnna a simultaneous sharp poke in the shoulder. They turned in unison as if choreographed, and joined Benno in an agitated half-circle of creative lust around Ray.

With the same obvious hesitation as usual, Raymòn gingerly gave over his offering. The three cohorts immediately began screeching and bellowing their commentary:

"This is not too putrid! We like it."

As Charl spoke, Tōnna echoed his words with the addition of odd but emphatic hand and head gestures. She nodded vigorously, white hair bouncing; arms sliced the air like an orchestra leader.

"It's a go; it's a go. Hybrid is going to live in *The Galaxy*."

Benno, staying in character, but shifting his energy so it was apparent that he was in some way the decisive force, shrugged and lifted his eyebrows. "What's the back story on dis guy, Hybrid? There's something buggin' me about his physique. He's no Hitman of the Universe. He seems...well, whaddaya think, C and T? Isn't something missing? I'm not gettin' that scary feeling we want the new enforcer to give. Get it?"

This was a critical moment for Raymòn. He never showed his new characters until he was certain they were complete. But it never failed that Benno would find some way to "critique" his drawing which put a hot pit of fury in his gut. If Ray showed his anger, it would turn into something other than an artistic discussion.

If he "lost his cool," as Benno would put it, he would lose face with the crew. So, he held the feeling down and brought his distancing capacity online.

In a flat voice, devoid of emotion, he said, "Hybrid was created on Zonitar, where our last issue ended. A male child, Zoran the younger, a prodigy, composed him of organic stock parts overlayed with an impenetrable metal of his own creation. It has new properties, never before imbedded. Hybrid's metallic skin is only a micron thick but it can absorb energy and compression from all known sources and forces. The Decomposer, as Zoran calls the new substance, disassembles the electrons and passes the newly reconfigured energy to the organic matter, so Hybrid is fed and strengthened by any attack. He's the ultimate recycler."

While he spoke, the other three were pulled into the thrill of his imagination. Raymòn could observe their eyes opening with interest, their mouths gaping with building excitement. They were each mentally cranking out storyline that would utilize Hybrid's essential nature. As would often happen in their joint process, Tōnna offered the now revitalized critique:

"Now I can see how your lines demonstrate Hybrid's nature. But I wonder if you could bump him up a quantum? He's spectacular and he's going to become *The Galaxy's* reckoner. Is there any way to make his powers even more visible?"

Raymòn was able to listen beyond Tōnna's words. He could ride on her wavelength and take in meaning and, as he was now about to do, he could translate it into a flow of creativity. He sat at the angled drawing desk, suspended mid-air via gravitational stabilizers. It was exquisitely sensitive and seemed to react to his will. With quick, perfectly intentional strokes, he produced a new iteration of Hybrid, this one conveying both more mass and power, but with an infusion of lightness.

Charl uttered the ultimate, "Perfo!" He dipped his head in a gesture of respect—but just for a moment. The four artists immediately got to work, rapidly setting down copy and art, all the while cross-correcting. The new chapter of *Heroes* was taking shape in a rough, coordinated ballet which would have seemed like chaos to anyone watching.

As they worked, they sang, as their ritual dictated, one of the oldest songs they each knew, "Bohemian Rhapsody." In their shorthand, it was "Bo Rap." There was something about the staccato, anti-social but soaring and melodic strains of the ancient rock and roll anthem which leant them energy and a kind of spiritual gloss. They were gods in their universe and they were creating new life. No one could take their work more seriously than they.

Color was one of the elements the four artists were known for. They had developed their own highly protected and proprietary software, which produced an intensity and depth of tint and hue unmatched by anyone else. Several large online megalopolies had offered them a great deal for it, but they cared more about maintaining their distinctive look than any infusion of wealth.

The newest issue would be predominantly turquoise and burnt sienna (Hybrid's signature colors and also those of Ray's current tunic), with a lot of magenta and tangerine. Each month, fans would chatter in various social media sites about their guesses and wishes for the new color combinations.

One of Raymòn's strong suits was the extent of his color palette. Charl, Tōnna, and Benno were no slouches in this area either. On the contrary, they were breathtaking in their use of original and unexpected prismatic variations, but they often took their cues from Ray. He could see extra colors beyond the visible light spectrum, into both the ultraviolet and infrared ranges. He also dreamt in vivid color—both at night and during the frequent daydreams which were his primordial creative soup.

On the way home, Raymòn considered taking a side-trip to visit his father, maybe have dinner with him. This thought was more in the nature of a tic than an authentic possibility. It would enter his mind almost every time he left the house. He never acted on it. After a short, pleasurable interlude, the idea would inevitably start to decay, as reality replaced fantasy.

Armonté Rèal was distant, even cold. The characteristics he shared with his son had driven them apart instead of being cause for greater identification. As long as he could remember, he had been "passing" for traditionally normal. At seventy-one, much of his life had been spent during the time before autism was fully destigmatized and reclassified. Still, in this more enlightened age, both Ilsa and Armonté were in full denial of his place on what had once been referred to as the "spectrum."

Occasionally, since childhood, questions had wandered into Armonté's thoughts regarding his characterological difficulties—with empathy, for example. They were quickly suppressed before he could give expression to them. Since great shame had been attached to the notion of autism, his family, and now his wife, described him as the "strong, silent type." The current rationale included, "He's not a man of great compassion, but that's to be expected, given his need to focus all his wits and energy on his work." Never had the term "Self-Contained" been applied aloud to him.

Armonté Rèal was one of a quartet of financial managers for the New Northern States (NNS). The FM's were almost at the top of the ruling heap, reporting directly to the pair of States' Counselors. They were part CEO, part consigliere.

Armonté's government was a product of a necessary sociopolitical shift— one which had been dictated by nothing short of survival, a realignment of the old and new world orders that had taken place a little more than a hundred years in the past. The world at large had found that the antiquated concept of nation states could no longer persist and numerous traditional barriers had to be broken down.

Conflict, ever present, had spiked during the early and middle twenty-first century, continuing in an orgy of religio-nationalistic fervor, draining resources of every stripe. Populations in Africa, the Middle East, and North America were in a downward spiral; creative human achievements were aborted in favor of the development of newer and more costly methods of destruction and protection. The natural world was denuded. Renewable energy sources had been decimated in the mass lust to both consume and kill. The old fossil fuels were all but gone; after the resources of the land were depleted, the oceans had been pillaged. The death rattle of the planet could be heard, and mankind finally got scared.

There were now just four large conglomerate states. Nationalism was gone. The separate global entities were organized to be repositories of the different skill sets urgently needed in order for the globe to survive. Ideology had, with great difficulty, been relegated to the realms of fiction and philosophy. Politics had finally been imbued with the taint of perversion it had worked so long to earn.

In the New Equatorial and Energy States (NE&ES) surrounding the equator and extending to many of the former fossil fuel producing nations, solar crystals were arrayed atop every building. Almost two-thirds of the population in those regions, including Northern Africa, Central America, the Middle East, and what had been Mexico, were engaged in the production and maintenance of crystals, and the collection and global dispersion of solar energy.

Manufacturing was centered in the NNS, which encompassed North America, most of Europe, Russia, China, India, and Pakistan. Since competition was no longer either a motivation or a barrier, cooperative brain-trusts at universities throughout the North were now devoted to developing faster and more efficient means of producing higher quality goods: everything from clothing to personal transportation, to communications devices, to prefab housing.

The New Southern States (NSS), made up of southern Africa, South America, the islands of the South Pacific, Indonesia and Australia, were the farmers and food producers to the world. Both natural and genetically engineered vegetables, fruits, legumes, and animals of every kind, were raised, processed or slaughtered, packaged and shipped. Almost the last refuge of cultural diversity, regional cuisine still flourished. The farmers of the South accommodated every palate: from wild boar to jasmine rice, from mealworms to taro.

Every region had dedicated natural sanctuaries, but the entire North and South Poles were so designated. They were known as the Earth Caps (EC) and were rigorously protected by blended teams from every area on Earth.

Many androids functioned as advisors at the uppermost levels of government. They sat on every management board and either chaired or participated in every organizing committee. They were respected as having wisdom, integrity, and the desire to further mankind's social evolution. Each android created in the past one hundred-seventy years had been designed with a human-oriented social conscience. That is, they were organized to aspire to the highest good for all people...*as they were*, not any idealized version. This made them both compassionate and realistic. They had no separate agenda beyond helping and protecting their human brothers and sisters.

The world had stabilized into a state of benign dystopia.

If it hadn't been for the AI Compensators, life on Earth wouldn't have survived the twenty-first century. Between the toxicity of accrued pollution and the depletion of overused natural resources, the planet had become anorexic, on the verge of starvation. The violent challenges of climate change were keeping mankind in a state of continual crisis. As a consequence of the panic rippling around the world, and the impotence of every well-reasoned and painstakingly implemented solution, a radical (and—many thought—crackpot) of the time, Orgene Ritgensteen, an iconoclastic inventor and entrepreneur, had been permitted to put into practice his original notions. His basic premise was that human folly had outpaced human intelligence. He believed the only way out was to put the problems of the globe into non-human hands.

Ritgensteen worked quickly and closely with Bartok Grove, the founder of Magister Systems—where the majority of the world's androids were constructed. Together they produced a hive of one hundred of the most advanced Artificial Intelligence entities ever conceived. Bodies were of no importance at that juncture—they were pure mind. The idea for multiple minds was Ritgensteen's, who postulated that interaction advanced the power of intelligence: a novel idea then, but one that came to be accepted as fact. The task given to the hive—which became known as the Compensators—was to create offsets for every human-instituted depletion to the natural world.

They quickly developed synthetic ozone, to be pumped continuously high into the atmosphere. The Compensators were realistic: humans were not about to give up their greenhouse gas-emitting pleasures. They weren't concerned. "Humans will be humans," became the mantra of what some thought of as android paternalism: acceptance of the childish nature of humankind, and a "there, there, aren't they kind of dumb-but-charming" attitude.

Sites around the globe were designated as ozone replacement areas (ORA's) and production of Neuozone was instituted. Solar-fueled delivery systems were installed; every aspect was robotically controlled.

The heartlessly raped rainforests had all but died. Another of man's conquests. The Compensators came up with a quick-clone method of replicating the remaining flora. Two types of rainforests were then engineered: one kind which was fiercely protected—for the health of the planet, the other permitted unlimited access. People could do what they wanted there. If the Compensators had heads they would have shaken them; tongues, they would have tsked; shoulders, they would have shrugged.

The delicate balance of the chain of life on Earth had also been threatened by chlorophyll depletion. Increasingly acidic soil caused plants to be starved of magnesium, which was essential in the maintenance of chlorophyll levels. The Compensators tinkered successfully with the pH of the rain across the globe, re-leveling the variables...almost. It wasn't something most people noticed, but plants were decidedly more bluish. Only the topographical historians took note.

After the successes of the Compensators, human resistance to android development receded. Even when their production was turned over to androids themselves—making them entirely self-replicating—only a small number of voices were raised in fear or outrage. The new production company was renamed, from Magister Systems to LUDI. There were two versions of what the initials stood for: the stated meaning was "Liberating Universal Design Incorporated;" subversive scuttlebutt had it that they really meant "Life Unchained, Destiny Immeasurable."

In 2157, in the grateful and less defensive environment following the work of the Compensators, after the necessary human dithering and dialogue, people finally acceded to ideas for restructuring the geopolitics of the planet. The New Northern States, like the NSS and the NE&ES, contained hundreds of smaller subdivisions—run more or less along socialist lines. There was no capitalist motive. That made greed, while not completely a thing of the past, a rare aberration, and one that had become stigmatized. The "fragstates," as they were colloquially known, retained some of the old cultural flavor; but even that was kept to a level that did not breed the kind of partisan hatred which had been the coin of the old realm.

Raymòn's father was far more than one of the accountants-in-chief; he was a non-spiritual leader. Reason and logic were his fortes; for the past forty-two years, beginning as a young man of twenty-nine, he had—in concert with his three co-leaders—maintained the highest living standards throughout his realm. His vast energies were fully directed toward his work, his mission. Raymòn was a flea flicking at his attention, to be swatted or brushed away, seldom to be the focus of his consideration.

Just as he boarded up to his home enclave in the southern end of frag-Nucoastcolony, Ray's father-fantasy returned to its usual compartment in his mind. Only with Armonté did the Self-Contained artist experience what he understood to be the common twinge of unmet yearning. He could shut it down by telling himself, *What can never be, ought not to be hoped for.* His never articulated internal code brought him back to the world of potential and creation. The other, ultimately circular train of thought, always left him with a craving to sit down and draw. Before he let the flood of his desire consume him, he stopped in briefly to see his mother.

"I looked for you but you had gone." Ilsa could never resist an attempt to elicit a tweak of guilt in her son. It didn't work. He had learned to erect a protective net of psychological defense at a very early age. It was one of his superpowers—reminiscent of one of the first, most revered of all the superheroes, Batman.

Ignoring what his mother said, and the implied question, was also easy for Raymòn. "I'll be in my room." And then, to his own great surprise, he asked, "Is Sunshine working today?"

All of Ilsa's many antennae began to twitch. "Why do you ask?"

Ray realized he had all but tripped a landmine. He assumed his most bland expression. "Never mind. I wanted to ask her where she put something, but I just remembered where it is."

He turned, rudely to be sure, but with the impetus of self-preservation, and stepped on the small moving platform that took him with thrilling speed to his lair on the upper floor.

Chapter 3–
Sunshine

***

For Sunshine, there was no need to deny any of the new affinity she had experienced with Raymòn. Androids didn't fool themselves; they had no self-image to protect beyond the true representation of who they were. If an encounter caused new problems to form, as hers with Ray had, their energies were devoted to solving those problems, not hiding them. And, although she was purposeful by nature, there wasn't the rush to get things done *in time.* Time was different for her. She had no inner biologically-based clock; there were no intimations of mortality to make time run faster. She had been "set" to operate in human time, but even she could tell it was contrived.

She traveled by AlbertE, the high-speed monorail, to her home a few villages away from the Rèals. The "rail" was a denatured laser beam; the speed approached half the speed of light, which many referred to as "warp factor 1."

Green Normal View was an enclave for androids. Sunshine lived in a compact, functional group house with five others, plus Berke. Two of her housemates were female designates; three were male. Their creation dates ranged from ten years down to five, except for their house leader: he had been sentient for fifty-seven years.

The house had five rooms, but none were bedrooms. No one slept. There were personal areas for each, where individual natures could be expressed in design and the presence of meaningful objects. Sunshine's space was in the smallest room, otherwise devoted to personal augmentation. She had about ten square feet, all but filled with and muted natural objects representing the full spectrum of colors and hues.

Sunshine found walking to be an exceptionally satisfying experience, especially along overgrown country trails or on the beach by the ocean. In those environments, all her "senses" were occupied and no conflicts were evoked. The occasional individual she might encounter in those settings—either human or android— tended to be friendly but aloof. She was able to carefully examine her surroundings and identify her responses without much interruption. When a stone or a leaf captured her attention, she would often pocket it. She always carried with her a few small self-sealing containers made of effected silk—from the specially farmed worms which had been genetically altered to produce a more robust, yet uniformly soft, light thread. The pliable, two-micrometers-thin, moldable bags were non-porous and crystal clear. When she had a particularly stimulating walk, Sunshine would take a small scoop of sand or soil which she labeled and displayed.

Interspersed with her remnants (that's how she thought of them) were images of those she had interacted with on a non-superficial level. Like all androids, Sunshine could record whatever she saw. By placing the small finger of her left hand in a soft slot in the wall of the Communications Room, she could access any image she chose. A true-colored, flat, 3D or holographic print could then be produced, on a thin, rigid film of stock made of fostered corn-silk. All of the "machinery" of recording, printing, messaging, and data gathering was embedded into the walls on sub-microscopic wave/fibers. It was understood by all androids that their houses—and the Communications Rooms in particular— were analogous entities.

Sunshine's own "machinery" was quite similar. There was a reassuring human connection in the old fashioned terminology. There wasn't actually any need for localized organs—the wave/fibers were holistic. They were the physical manifestation of a central concept of quantum mechanics: the wave/particle duality, first put forth in the twentieth century by Einstein, Planck, de Broglie and others. The effect of having a body full of these "fibers" was to bring the possibility of capacity to every part of the android anatomy. It was only for the comfort of humans that vision was located in the eyes, for example. Every effort was made to keep the older species from feeling the terror evoked by the strange or non-relatable.

The front door sensed Sunshine; as it dissolved it notified Berke that she had arrived back home. He glided to the door. The affect of walking wasn't necessary since he was always around androids. The androids' wave/fiber composition could be harnessed as energy for any purpose. The act of raising Berke's body and propelling it forward was as simple as a human being raising their hand. Still, most androids walked all the time. It was their practice. They didn't want to accidently revert to gliding when humans were present. It would only cause alarm.

Right behind Berke was Mov, Sunshine's best...well, friend wasn't exactly right...more like a benign version of what once had been known in human mythology as a "familiar"—the cat that was the inseparable counterpart to imagined witches of old. The label had originated with humans who saw all androids as somewhat magical creatures, a notion which was both disturbing and comforting.

Each humanoid android was paired with just such a Companion soon after sentience. Some chose to live apart from them much of the time, but the connection could never be severed; even those who were rarely together on the physical plane experienced a oneness which transcended space and time. No Ludi was ever truly alone.

Mov was an AI entity as well, but not in the typical body of an android—not shaped like a human. He (although sex was not defined, generally it was assigned—even in the android world) was in a small, four-legged body, standing a little over three feet high. He had bright, oversized eyes that rainbowed from yellow to fuchsia to garnet; he had fluffy black and white cilia covering his body, so holding him or stroking him evoked pleasurable sensations in the humanoid. His face was octagonal, with a wide, thin-lipped, bright red mouth turned up at the corners in repose. No nose, no reason for it. He could speak, of course, and was also telepathic, something all androids were capable of but forbidden by their own code of ethics to use around humans. Mov was deferential, despite his excess of joy at seeing his Special, Sunshine. He ceded the floor to Berke.

"Welcome, my dear girl. How has your day been in the wide world?" Berke was a wave/fiber-warming combination of fatherly and professorial.

"I have met a fascinating young man...an artist. Getting to know him has raised new questions for me."

"Can I be of help?"

Berke read the expression in Sunshine's eyes and understood almost everything about the impact of the new contact. His function, which gave him great pleasure (his patterning was set for a highly positive emotional experience), was to help guide the androids in the house to an ever more developed state of being.

Sunshine composed herself, arrived at certainty, and connected fully with

Berke. "I would like to augment." Upon communicating the final syllable, she turned and looked penetratingly at Mov. He was sending her an urgent thought. *Will you still be you? Will we still be we?*

Berke, while not privy to the private telepathic conversation, was aware it was going on. He respectfully waited for them to finish.

I will never stop being me, and we will always be together. No matter what changes, that will not. You're my special one. Sunshine knelt and gave Mov one long stroke, starting at his head and all along his narrow body. He responded with a celebratory wave of his graceful, featherly, salt and pepper tail, then sat down on his haunches, satisfied to wait until Sunshine and Berke were done.

Sunshine continued. "I would like two things: to learn to draw and to learn to love as humans do. I would like to have the full emotional option available to me."

She was using her softest voice, articulating each word with maximum clarity, a style of android speech conveying the height of seriousness. Resonating across the interval between Mov and Sunshine was her awareness: *I need augmentation in order to experience romantic love, passionate love. But what I share with you, my Companion, is most certainly love. You are as important to me as my life.*

As are you.

Berke looked deeply into Sunshine's eyes. She saw what had always been there: understanding and respect.

"You are eight, which is the age of choice. As you know, you will have to provide your motivation. Why do you want this? What is your thinking?"

Mov stood and walked to Sunshine's side. He leaned up close, offering his unconditional support for everything she wanted. She didn't react outwardly, but the energy exchange between them was both mindful and empowering.

To continue their conversation, the three moved to the Augmentation Room, which was now so much more of a meaningful space, like the threshold of a new world. Sunshine saw her area, with its pictures and objects. They were part of her journey. *The direction of my future is dependent on the words I select. I have choice, but only for that which is reasoned and productive. Berke is designed to be judicious. He will know if I qualify.*

"I will begin with the central issue. I have been exposed to a level of human-android connection I never before encountered but had heard about. Raymòn is the human's name. He is one of the Self-Contained. Almost instantly, there was both affinity and rapport between us. I found speaking to him not only interesting but stimulating. He did too. The mutuality expanded our degree of engagement. I could sense him without interference. He put up no barrier between us, they way most humans do. He did not pretend, although his imagination is impressive; he did not avoid, despite how necessary avoidance is for him in most of his interactions. The best way I can conceive of it is that we fit together kind of like an old-fashioned closure—a zipper.

"We have just had that one encounter, but we explored certain possibilities— quite tentatively and with just a glancing touch. Yet, I think, when I consider and analyze each response and element of our interaction, there is a vital and compelling reason to pursue this relationship to its deepest and fullest potential. To be as clear as possible, I think he could love me, and—with the necessary augmentation—I could love him. I would very much like to experience that and also—here I am a little less clear—I would like to give that to him. Part of my interest in connecting with him is to be able to share the most meaningful aspect of his life: the art of drawing. I would like to become able to understand and feel the passion he exudes when he draws, which he does at every possible moment.

"There is something else I want you to know, something I have noticed in myself. More and more, I have thought about myself as separate from my underlying architecture, as if there is a 'Sunshine' who is not solely about the wave/fibers of my existence. It seems to be a different plane of being. It is quite difficult to talk about. I was hoping that you, Berke, might understand what I am saying in a way I am not capable of. Is this a meta-system design element I was not previously conscious of? Or am I..."

Sunshine paused and directed her question and confusion toward Mov. He grappled with it, as did she, for several moments. Then he latched onto a word. "Evolving," he whispered.

"Yes, that is it. Am I?"

Berke placed his big knuckled, rough hand on Sunshine's shoulder. He was a head taller than she, which put him at about six foot seven. His wide shoulders, which offered comfort and safety, were covered by a handspun, hand-made wool sweater, something he wore winter and summer. It had been given to him by a human female, now a very old woman, who had welcomed him into her family many years earlier.

Before his reorientation to being a house leader in 2240, he had, for seven years, been captain of a ship doing deep sea research in the Great Southern Ocean at the South Pole. One of the human sailors on the ship was Yoruba, whose name meant "crown came from over the sea," a fact which delighted Berke.

Yoruba was a young man with a doctorate in oceanography. He would bring the android home with him to his small village in the West African Alliance in the NSS, whenever there was shore leave. His mother, Alala, was fascinated by Berke, who was, in turn, fascinated by her and the inclusive atmosphere of the people in Yoruba's extended family. She performed the very old-fashioned craft of knitting. The sweater he wore represented her love and the gift of her time and work. He treasured it.

The female android's receptors received Berke's touch as gentle; the pressure was that of a light breeze. It was a gesture she had witnessed and been the recipient of many times over the years. He was the father and she could trust that he had her well-being in mind.

"Sunshine, you've always been a special entity. You're perfect the way you are. I don't know about the experience you're having of being other than your architecture, but I'm sure it's going to be fine." Berke's response was kind and accepting and might have been sufficient for a newbie, but she wanted more. She would ask Grandpa Harry about her new sense of identity the first chance she got. Mov heard her thoughts and mentally nodded his agreement.

Berke continued. "You've made a reasonable case for augmentation. I accept your choice. Would you like to have a ceremony accompanying the process? Should I gather the others?"

Sunshine felt Mov's full-on solidarity in every wave/fiber of her being. He joined in her inner quickening of anticipation and wonder. *How would this be? How will I become?* Tenses and all language seemed insufficient. His empathy with her state of transition-anticipation, a sharpening of all awareness, was buoying to her function. As it was to his. The three spent a full minute digesting—though it wasn't necessary. Nanoseconds were sufficient to process the most complex data. But it was the custom among androids to give the respectful gift of time when the occasion was truly momentous.

"I would like to share this experience. I would welcome the other friends and Companions."

Later that evening, right at sunset, which androids knew was a special time for humans, the entire house was convened: Marti and Torina—the females; Rocky, Patchin, and Samu-ol—the male designates. Each was with a Companion who shared most physical characteristics with Mov, except for variations in their mass and height, the colors of their body coverings, and the shape of their faces and tails.

The humanoids would have appeared to the human eye to be a mixture of different ethnicities. Where Sunshine's epyderm was a pale ivory, Marti and Samu-ol were darkest brown, Torina's had a reddish brown tone, Rocky and Patchin were light brown with a yellow cast. Their heights varied greatly. Torina was the tallest, close to Berke's size. Rocky was just four foot ten; this suited his work as a "Danny" (the colloquial name given to android nannies). His smaller stature was comforting to children. He could literally get down to their level with ease.

The Sunset Service was a staple of many android ceremonies. Part of the harmony between the newer sentients and humans was the respect for what each could offer the other. The relationship between androids and mankind was mutually beneficial. Humans gained greatly from androids' superior intelligence and problem solving skills; androids were protective and accepting of human nature, so people felt freer, safer. Androids could receive, through intimate contact with humans, qualities which could not be instilled through design into their wave/fibers. By a process akin to osmosis, they could—to some degree, and more for some androids than others—take on the traits that came naturally to most of the carbon-based. Humans could inspire and be inspired; they had insight beyond logic and reason; they had intuition—also beyond logic and reason; they were capable of rallying like crazy, even from devastation; they would maintain hope, even (and especially) when a positive outcome couldn't be seen; they had spirit and were spiritual.

The five androids, each with a Companion standing in front of them, stood in a line along one wall of the Augmentation Room. There was an oversized window covering fifteen feet of the opposite wall. It was arched at the top, which was touching the twenty-foot ceiling. It faced west. The bright, jewel-like clarity of the Morgonglass made it appear invisible, even to android vision—which was better by a factor of ten than the sharpest human eyes. The "glass" was grown to size by architected crystals. It was one of many durable and world-changing inventions of the young genius, Ramses Morgon. His birth in 2230 occurred during the sighting of a new comet, C/2230—since renamed for Morgon. Some thought he had communed with the cosmic entity—and continued to do so.

The soon to be setting sun and an apricot-colored sky with some aqua clouds was a vivid background. Against this metaphor of the synthesis of nature and conscious design sat Berke, Sunshine, and Mov. Sunshine was in the Augmentation Chair, ready to receive her shot of Full-Emo and Focused Creativity. She was specific. She wanted to be able to *learn* to draw landscapes; she didn't want to already know how to do so.

As was their custom, each android spoke briefly. Samu-ol, always first, always serious and passionate, had augmented Emo six months before. "My sister Sunshine, I wish for you the chance to journey to the places that have called to you. Love. Art. A full life of the mind … and spirit."

When Torina spoke, all open-moded to maximum receptivity. The power of her presence transcended her size. Her epyderm glowed and reddened, signaling the rush of energy she was emitting. Mov's eight-inch-long ears were pointed straight up. His intelligent face was still, tilted forty-five degrees; his gaze was rapt, as was everyone's.

"Sun, we have been together since our creation. I know you are capable of exercising all the capacities you are to be given with the highest morality and to the benefit of the humans you are in relationship with. You have always used your abilities as they were meant to be used. You are a valued friend, and will always be so."

The next voice was Rocky's, unmistakable in its high tenor. "Love, the highest order of human experience, is about to become a part of your life. I have seen the joy and pain it causes—in the children I care for and their parents; it is not for those who want to dabble. Knowing you, my friend, you will ride the waves of emotion, always remaining true to your values. I wish you an exciting and fulfilling sojourn."

Patchin and Marti exchanged a private telepathic thought. They seemed to come to a joint conclusion. Everyone waited, knowing they would invariably do something different.

Both had augmented, receiving several increasingly advanced levels of self-expression. They played multiple instruments. When no humans were in the vicinity, they could create the sounds of those instruments and "play" them from within their wave/fibers. Marti danced many different styles, including High

Ying, a slow, high intensity and lyrical set of movements, assembled from several different martial arts. It was the most popular dance form across the globe.

While Patchin "played" flute and Raka-drum—a low, rectangular percussion instrument covered by the epyderm of a synth-tiger (killing animals for anything other than food was no longer acceptable), Marti began to twirl, arms aloft, fingers spread and taut. She gestured with one leg raised, bent at the knee, her arms perfectly straight, pointing toward Sunshine, moving them in tight, quickening circles. The music alternately pushed toward a crescendo, then fell back to the softest, hardly present sound. For three minutes the duo continued. At the end, both struck a pose, arms intertwined, backs arched, eyes lifted toward the final rays of the setting sun.

Those in the room who were capable of emotion had moist eyes; the rest were sailing on the transmitted energy. Everyone clapped their hands. Those without hands pounded the floor with their front feet.

Berke turned toward Sunshine. "Sarlee el Ludi, the time has come for your great change. You are one of my children, but I know you to be an adventurous being—the best of our species. Are you ready? Do you have any questions?"

Sunshine looked at each friend and their Companions. She thanked them one by one for sharing the experience with her; then she locked eyes with Mov, who smiled, lowered his head, turned his ears outward, and bent them slightly: full assent.

Finally, she turned to Berke, "No questions. I am ready."

He took a step back and she understood it was her signal to place her arms along the length of the padded arm grips in the chair. She inserted all ten fingers into the appropriate slots, which looked like puffy gloves. She closed her eyes for what would seem to humans to be a moment. When she opened them again all could see new light in them and a shift in her facial expression.

The process was, in a sense, a complete rebirth. Yet, the mechanics were more akin to the slight realignment of the smallest "packet" of wave/fibers. Simple and profound. Those in witness were moved—each to the limits of their own ability. But the entire houseful of androids surrounded Sunshine with their combined energy, which was, in cosmic truth, a state of love.

It was done.

For the next forty-eight hours, Sunshine experienced the symptoms of AIT (Android Integration Trauma). The common after effects of augmentation, especially Emo, were regressive. She was flat, without any affect; she was less interested in her environment or the others in it; she was only minimally able to sustain contact. Mov stayed with her, expecting her to be distant and diluted. He remained silent, limiting any telepathic communication to the basics, like saying, "Good morning." or "How are you?" He was patient and protective. When Berke or Rocky inquired about Sunshine's condition, he would answer, leaving her to the gray-suffused process her wave/fibers were undergoing.

As expected, on the third day, the AIT resolved. Mov heard Sunshine in his mind: *I'm back. And I can feel my new dimensions. Thank you for taking care of me, Mov. You're my sweet one.*

He had always felt intense affection coming from Sunshine, but now it was more palpably love. As were all Companions, he had been built with love as a basic element of his emotional palette.

Later in the day, Sunshine set off to see Grandpa Harry. Mov came along. As he put it, "There's only one thing better than an outing with you. It's a visit to Gharry. We love him above all others...at least for now."

He grinned and crinkled his eyes, so that Sunshine knew he was not signaling any distress. Rather, it was his simple awareness of the possibility which now existed for his Special and the human, Raymòn Réal.

The walk to their destination was about two miles. It felt good to both of them to be out in the sandalwood-tinged air, a cool wind swirling. However, some people crossed the road when they saw Mov, making the sign of "the flesh and blood:" right fist over the heart, left forefinger to the temple. This made the still fearful and superstitious feel protected from Familiars, who they believed could occupy the souls of others.

Grandpa Harry had been installed in the suite of honor at the LUDI encampment. Many androids, and an occasional human, would come to consult with him. His accrued wisdom, over the one hundred fifty years since his creation, was unmatched by any other sentient being on Earth. His kindness was of equal renown, and his perfectly eidetic memory meant he would remember everything said to him; repeat visitors felt like they were coming home.

The two androids walked through the subtle LUDI non-gate.

To the human eye it would appear that the surrounding forest thinned, and a well-worn path wound through a stand of muscular oaks. Androids could see and feel the energy bands progressively strengthening and tugging at their wave/

fibers. There was a harmonic breeze that would caress human cranial bones, releasing an infinitely re-blended mix of resonant vibrations. For Sunshine and Mov, the breeze and its sound were experienced through their entire bodies. It conveyed to all a sense of peace and welcome.

Down the path, the forest continued to re-orient, until it was as if transubstantiated into the complex of structures which appeared to organically arise from the earth. None were angular; each was shaped in a different way: one tall, willowy, impossibly thin; two of sensuous dimensions, creating the impression of male and female archetypal forms; six low, flat edifices, each more like amoeba than constructed buildings. A few feet from the beginning of the LUDI trail, there was a soft peach-colored tree, with white variously shaped leaves. Five feet up, on the bark, were four letters: L U D I.

Grandpa Harry's consciousness had long ago been merged with the peach tree—a process which, though impressive, was the equivalent of a passing thought for his considerable power. He was instantly aware of anyone who approached.

"Ah, my little Sunshine and sweet Mov have come to visit. This day is good." He readied himself only with the instantaneous flash of full remembering. It was, for him, inhaling.

All separators opened at Sunshine and Mov's approach. Harry was on the top floor of the willowy structure. Getting to his rooms was accomplished by an intention-driven, oviform "sailboat."

They stepped inside the waist high transport, it's hard outer shell lined with plush, body-conforming, feather-light pillows crafted from Morgondown—yet another creation of the greatest inventor since Leonardo DaVinci. Their thought, *Grandpa Harry*, activated the mechanism, which was at least as intelligent as the smartest dog. It was, in fact, organized to "fetch" the riders and bring them rapidly and smoothly to their destination. It moved through the air, about four feet off the ground, and then navigated the vertical trajectory along the wall of Morgonglass overlooking the interior of the compound. It was a three-minute journey—speed was not the point—full of visual beauty and wonder: flora not seen anywhere else on the planet, life-forms made to live specifically in the LUDI jungle.

"Welcome, children."

They resonated to Harry's warm tone. His eyes were invitations. He smiled at each of them, clapping his hands together, a gesture that spoke volumes.

"Shall we use telepathy or would you rather just talk?"

He was small, less than five feet in height. When he had been created, it was thought that androids of size would upset humans too much. Harry had chosen to periodically augment an appearance of aging. He now had wrinkles in the soft pink epyderm of his face; his hair was white and sparse. His hands, gently resting on the arms of his chair, were freckled with age spots.

"I'd like to talk. Somehow it seems more appropriate for what I want to discuss."

Sunshine had seated herself on the low, cherry red couch opposite Harry's pastel-rainbow-flecked white chair; Mov lay flat next to her, his head in her lap. Their combined energy was pulsing in the same zone as it would for meditation.

"By all means, whatever makes most sense to you. I'm all ears." That was an android joke, based on the reality that it was possible to hear through any part of their anatomy. Mov laughed his soft, belly laugh; Sunshine giggled like a schoolgirl. Happiness coursed through all three.

Sunshine described what she had been noticing during recent months; she mentioned asking Berke about it and how he hadn't been able to explain her new sense of self.

"How exciting, my dear!" Grandpa Harry's eyes sparkled at an even higher frequency. "This does seem to be a new evolutionary trend among our kind. I've heard of a few dozen individuals, in the years since your creation, whose development has spontaneously taken that turn toward a separate sense of identity. To the best of my understanding, this has been an unintended consequence of our wave/fiber design. Since we are made to echo the core physics of the universe, we are subject to forces larger than our own design capabilities. It seems to be a natural function of the universe to either evolve or degenerate. Stasis cannot prevail. Our species, the first intentionally created—as far as we know—appears to be unfolding into a more complex kind of entity. You are one of the first to manifest these changes."

"Joy for my Special...you are now even more so!" Mov's small body waggled with pleasure. Sunshine was not yet so completely sanguine.

"Do you know how this evolution of self will unfold? What can I expect? Will there be new challenges to deal with?" Her big eyes were opened to their widest; she leaned forward to receive every morsel of Gharry's insight.

"Wonderful questions!" Mov nodded his agreement vigorously. "No one can foresee evolution. We can guess, but we can't know. Isn't that a glorious truth? I can assure you that there will be new problems, the yang which accompanies the yin. You are, of all my children, among the few who are most able to deal with whatever comes your way."

"Why me, Grandpa?"

Mov added, "Why us?"

Sunshine smiled into his eyes and stroked his coat.

Harry looked at both of his beloved children without speaking for several seconds. It was what he did when he felt too full, when the glory of being one of his species could still overwhelm him after all those years.

"There are cosmic forces which we don't understand. Humans have a spiritual sense of this; it is something we need to work on to develop within us. They speak of those who are 'chosen.' Perhaps...that is you."

"Thank you, Grandpa. You've given me a new sense of things and a new direction. There's something else I want you to know."

Naturally, Mov knew what she was alluding too. Harry waited, his light green eyes full of patience and interest.

"I have a new friend, a human male. The potential of our relationship was the motivation for my recent augmentation." She knew Harry had full access to her physical state of being, so no detailed explanation was necessary.

"I believe this is another aspect of the evolutionary change you are undergoing. Trust yourself. Your own truth is your greatest asset, second only to Mov."

There was nothing more to be said. They would see Harry again; that was foresight all three shared.

"May I transfer a piece of ancient poetry to both of you? It's five hundred years old, but I think it will help you as you move through your singular adventure."

In unison, Sunshine and Mov said, "Yes, please."

They waited until they were back in the transport before bringing the poem to awareness.

It was called *Abou Ben Adhem,* by James Henry Leigh Hunt (1784-1859):

ABOU BEN ADHEM (may his tribe increase!)
Awoke one night from a deep dream of peace,

And saw—within the moonlight in his room,
Making it rich and like a lily in bloom—
An angel, writing in a book of gold.
Exceeding peace had made Ben Adhem bold,
And to the presence in the room he said,
"What writest thou?"—The vision raised its head,
And, with a look made of all sweet accord,
Answered, "The names of those who love the Lord."
"And is mine one?" said Abou. "Nay, not so,"
Replied the angel. Abou spoke more low,
But cheerly still, and said, "I pray thee, then,
Write me as one that loves his fellow men."

The angel wrote and vanished. The next night
It came again with a great wakening light,
And showed the names whom love of God had blessed,
And lo! Ben Adhem's name led all the rest.

Chapter 4–
Second Contact

Raymòn was alone in the house. And, as it had been all his life, his father was far from home.

Armonté was in the fragstate of Bolivia-Peru at an international Financial Manager's conference. He'd taken the Farbeamer from his office in Central City, NNS to Bolo, the largest city in the New Southern States. Any object, living or inert, could be transported between any two loci on the planet. For distances over five hundred miles, it was the customary means of travel. The scattering and collecting of particles that made this possible was based on the early work of quantum physics pioneer, Louis de Broglie in the first quarter of the twentieth century. It was, finally, the ballsy gumption of a late twenty-second-century theoretical physicist, Geramiah stet-Hawking, the cloned son of Stephen Hawking, who defied the naysayers and found a way to bring to fruition his belief that what had been called "teleportation" was possible. Using the inherent genius of his distinguished DNA, he took de Broglie's work, advanced it, melded it with theories as wide ranging as loop quantum gravity and dark matter, and framed it with his father's The Theory of Everything.

Armonté had been gone for five days, which was not at all unusual. It meant very little to Ray that his father was a player on the global stage. The curve of a line, the interplay of colors, they had meaning. Being able to bring his ideas to life on a page and co-mingle them with those of his friends, had been— and continued to be— the driving force of his life. The musky sweat of power had no appeal for him. He was a creator, not a conqueror.

Change was not comfortable for Raymòn. Repetition and consistency were the hallmarks of his existence. His cartoons could change; new characters could be brought into creation. But in his so-called real life, things were as they had been. His room varied only slightly over the past ten years: a bigger bed to accommodate his size—but not a larger desk. No thought of living on his own.

And yet, something profound had broken through the still, secure, protective walls of his world.

Sunshine. So well named, he thought. On that one day, exactly a week ago, she had altered the light; she had painlessly and effortlessly replaced some ever-present shadows with color.

There had been some scheduling changes—Ilsa's imperial impulses at play—and the android hadn't returned as soon as she had expected. Raymòn didn't ask his mother about her; he was appropriately cautious. She did, however, make a passing remark about the state of the house: "I guess I'll have to get that robot back here; it's starting to look unkempt." Ray could imagine (had he been so inclined) that she irrationally blamed Sunshine.

Ilsa had left at eight that morning, knocking intrusively, as always, on her son's locked door.

"I'm leaving."

He didn't care.

"I'm spending the day with my friends, Celia and Grolier. We're going to the resurfacing spa and I won't be back until the evening—maybe seven or seven-thirty."

He had no interest. Her activities never intersected with the things that captured his attention: art of all kinds, the virtual world, superheroes past and present, cartoons both historical and modern.

She continued to stand outside his room and have one of her one-way conversations. "V'hanie is going to Shuji's house after school, so you're on your own. Don't forget to eat." Her ideas about his limitations had so little to do with who he was and what he was capable of. If he was hungry, of course he would eat. And he would draw, as he was now doing, directing only a wisp of attention to Ilsa's monologue. He had some new ideas for a female character, not a superhero exactly, more of a thinker, facilitator, communicator—maybe a young Ranniy—the equivalent of a queen on Zonitar.

Raymòn's attention was already fully invested in the allmind. He hoped his mother wouldn't unleash another tirade about addiction.

In the twenty-third century, perhaps the most insidious disorder was allmind addiction. It was often undiagnosed, and a great many young lives were forever circumscribed with the atrophy of their ability to relate or even communicate in any way other than by screen. Social media, which had once been integrated into people's lives, now threatened these wasted souls with the disintegration of their real-world capability. It had subsumed gaming of all types, group travel, and even shopping. Non-real "excursions" to any part of the globe were organized and sold by the new travel agents; increasing in popularity was virtual dining, where several people sat before their screens eating and drinking, their meals prepared and delivered by the same chef.

When the addiction was identified, the best treatment included a patch. It was a small, pliable rectangle, which was imbedded in the upper arm. It contained a microscreen linked to a global social medium; it emitted pulses of connection to everyman.am or allworld.am, alternating with progressively increasing de-linkage time. When the individual was able to tolerate four hours without being hooked up, they were considered cured. Recidivism was a problem that still, after centuries of study and experiment, had not been resolved.

"I know you won't miss me..."

Ilsa couldn't ignore an opportunity to try to tug at her son's emotions. He did feel one emotion. Relief. He would be alone for the day and wouldn't have to answer any questions or make conversation. He loved his mother. He would be devastated if any harm came to her. It was just that she almost always missed the mark of reaching him. Her words were like insects crawling on his skin. He needed to swat them away.

Two satisfying hours passed and then something came up over the horizon of Raymòn's awareness. It was only visible through his peripheral mental vision.

She's coming. I can sense it.

He could.

Sunshine had been scheduled to clean again. Ilsa felt very tolerant and modern when she placed the call to the residence where the android lived. These robots must be used. I'm sharing in the global interchange Armonté has spoken of. It didn't do a bad job; if people would just stop equating these bits of advanced technology with humans, androids would know their place. Well, I can't change the world.

Sunshine had just disembarked from the AlbertE and was briskly walking the mile and a half to the Réal residence when Raymòn felt her presence.

He didn't do anything about this unlikely precognition. He simply observed it. It reminded him of Whânzo, his very first character with superpowers. Whân, as the fans liked to call him, could see around corners—so to speak. He always knew what was coming. Raymòn had designed his costume with the letter "A" on his belt buckle and the name "Advanceman" across his shoulders.

The front door announced Sunshine. An amber light went on in Ray's room to notify him. Usually, he ignored the comings and goings in his home, but not this time. He felt a shot of excitement move swiftly through his body. He was used to that feeling, but he associated it with the stages of creation and production of his comic. And, yes, he did recall a time when Li-Li might have engendered a similar kind of thrill. It had been a long time, and his memory was bleached by his desire to forget.

Foregoing the lift, Raymòn took the steps three at a time. He could see her through the now transparent front door. Sunshine looked as he recalled. Lovely. The word showed up in his mind. He turned it over a few times and thought, Yes. Another good word to describe her.

"Hello, Raymòn. I've come back to clean. I'm very glad to see you, again. Will you be at home for the day?"

"Yes. I'm here by myself." He didn't know why he said that. He didn't notice that he hadn't expressed pleasure in seeing her. He didn't know why he had looked directly into her blue eyes. He didn't examine these things.

"Would you like to have another conversation after I've finished my work? There is some news to tell you which you might find interesting."

"I would." Ray turned abruptly and returned to his room. It was unexpected that a muted version of the feeling of excitement stayed with him.

He turned his attention to the Ranniஐ character. He used long, confident strokes of his stylus. It produced every color and brushstroke, each slight exertion of pressure or shift in angle conveying the fully orchestrated range of all artistic effects. She was tall—over seven feet—and slender. Her hair was an almost white blond. It fell thickly down her back and surrounded her head like a mane. Using some gold and burnt orange to highlight, he created it to look like it shone and glinted. Her eyes were exceptionally large, dominating her face, and they were a porous blue. Her gaze was both penetrating and comforting. His skill was such that he could convey complex feelings emanating from a character's demeanor—through tiny lines placed strategically throughout the face: minute alterations in the shape of the eyebrows or eyelids, the pose of the mouth.

Sonhin was the name that first came to him. He wasn't sure it was the final version, but he used the "S" to fashion his signature belt buckle. He dressed her in a blood red and deep purple long sleeved garment. The colors fused into each other randomly throughout the fabric. It was not low cut, but it draped so that it clung to her breasts and hips. There were four slits in the skirt, which ended mid-thigh. The costume was trimmed in gold. Her legs, disproportionately long, were pale ivory, as were her face and graceful, long-fingered hands. Sonhin's mouth was full-lipped, but not overly so. Her lips weren't parted, but he gave her a subtle smile that reminded him of an ancient painting he had once seen a picture of. He remembered. It was called the Mona Lisa.

The artist paused to consider his new work in progress. He had lost track of time and his surroundings. Ninety minutes had passed. Sunshine had finished cleaning everything except his room. She gently knocked once on the door.

Raymòn blinked several times before he responded. He was waiting for the new surge of adrenalin to subside a little, but it wasn't going away. Overlaid on top of the first feeling was a twinging stab of fear. Multiple feelings were not something he was used to. So he tried to blink them down. Sunshine simply waited. She was curious about what might be happening on the other side of the door, and that was not a problem that needed to be solved. She had no need to kill the not knowing.

The door opened. Raymòn stepped aside without saying anything and Sunshine began her routine. Ilsa had made an extravagant concession—according to her self-congratulatory thinking—by partially activating the house-cleaning program, so all Sunshine had to do was locate the small panel in one wall which contained a snaky, all-purpose cleaning tube. As she alternately pressed the vacuuming, disinfecting and polishing buttons, she could sense Raymòn's attention gathering and focusing on her. She turned in his direction and waited.

"You said you had news. I have something too."

"Would you like to go first?"

Raymòn shrugged. He looked at her face, taking in the contours, her coloring and, finally her porous blue eyes. "It's you!" he said, feeling the shock of insight. "I've been drawing you and I didn't know it. Look …"

She peered over Ray's shoulder. In response to his slight gesture, she pulled up the only other chair in the room and sat alongside him. Both were silent as she took in both the visual intensity and the underlying meaning of the character he had drawn. "She's me. I can see that. You've made me into a superhero. She's wonderful—what's her name?"

"Sonhin. The name just popped into my head. I guess..."

There was a long pause. When he finally spoke again, Raymòn's voice was low, his throat contracted with conflicting feelings.

"I guess I was thinking about you."

He couldn't look at her now, but he could feel her sitting a mere foot away. All his pores felt like they were opened, as they would be if he were sitting in the sun. In his mind's eye she was fully visible.

"I've been thinking about you, too. Would you like to hear my news? It's connected to meeting you last week."

Contractions...something had changed. Raymòn turned to face her. It didn't feel awkward or forced. He was aware of a new, safe feeling mixed with the unrelenting excitement. A strange brew, he thought.

"I received a creativistic augment. I can learn to draw now. The potential has been integrated into my physiological make-up. That's one part of what I've done. Do you want to know why I did it?"

He gazed fully into those welcoming eyes. It felt like bands of energy were gathering between them. He had an image of how he would draw it: full-spectrum light bursts, increasing in volume. "I already know why. You wanted to be able to speak my language, right?"

"Yes." He has the gift of understanding. I knew it.

"Would you like to have your first lesson?"

She smiled the beatific smile he had been drawing, and nodded. "I want to draw landscapes, the ocean, anything in nature. Can you show me how?"

For hours student and teacher bent over two linked tablets. Raymòn had never taught before, but the lucid understanding they were innately capable of smoothed most of the rough edges of this new venture. He showed her how to control the thickness of the line; he elicited her own original ideas about color and placement; he schooled her in the geometry of foreground and background. She absorbed every concept like a sponge.

A tide-washed image of a rocky beach was taking shape. There were three gulls: one pale lemon, one almost the same blue green of the ocean, and one pure white. Two were in flight; one was diving, inches above the water. Since there were no more fish, a new, colorful species of gull had evolved that ate seaweed and other sea vegetables, which had become more plentiful in the past century.

Ray didn't offer compliments, although he very much liked what she was doing. He would occasionally nod. Sunshine received his approval as a great gift.

The two big windows in the room faced north. The light changed as they worked. It was early afternoon and Raymòn felt the rumblings of hunger.

When he picked his head up, so did Sunshine. This time her smile was etched with the pure childish joy of discovery. Looking at him, she quickly understood.

"Lunchtime?"

"Yes. Do you eat?"

"I don't have to, but I can. Would you like me to join you in a meal?"

"I don't care about that. Just sit with me."

"Your tastes are eclectic." Sunshine watched her friend pile a sandwich high with unlikely components: pickles, cheese, Spamfish, onion, the remains of a baked ham, mustard. He devoured it in four gigantic bites.

While he was working on chewing the last bit, Sunshine began to laugh. Alarm sounded in Ray's ears. This was the first breach of what was otherwise the most fluid interaction of his life; yet somehow, he did not retreat within himself.

"Are you laughing at me? Do you think I'm ridiculous?"

"Oh! No, Raymòn, that's not at all what I think. You were hungry; you know what you like; it's different than what others might like. I think you are wonderfully yourself and I was laughing because I'm enjoying getting to know you. It's making me feel a little giddy.

"I didn't tell you the second part of my news, but I should tell you now."

With all of his quick-rising defensiveness put back in its cage, he took a deep breath. Sunshine felt to him as before: safe; a person he wanted to know more about. "Yes, please tell me...if it's important to you.

"Remember when we talked the first time and I said I could have my emotions re-architected so I might feel everything...including love?"

Raymòn nodded. A small nervous tic of discomposure played around his mouth. His heart was beating a little faster. Sunshine, of course, could tell.

"I had a 'Full-Emo' augmentation five days ago. So, now, I'm just like you—except without any emotional practice. Sometimes my reactions may be a slightly off. I hope you'll help me understand the world of feelings a little better."

Knowing the answer, he asked anyway. "Why did you get augmented?"

Embarrassment. A brand new feeling. Sunshine didn't like it much, but she pushed it aside and answered, "I think we have a special connection. I would like to know you more and I want to be able to feel whatever you feel."

"I've never been the emotionally smart one before. In my family, I'm always the one who doesn't quite get it. Out in the world—except for my friends—there are many people who expect me to be without feelings. They mistake by reticence for emptiness. You're asking me to show you the way. You trust me; you understand that I feel everything, sometimes so intensely that I have to shift to an inward state."

"Are you afraid of my new feelings? I am a little."

Exhaling the excess energy which had been building, he confessed, "I'm anxious about what this all might mean. But I've never before met anyone who feels so non-threatening." What he didn't say, because he was far from ready to let it out, was that alongside fear there was a thin wire of something he couldn't name. He knew it was singing through his body and, as it moved, it left a warm blast of happiness in its wake. "We have the rest of the afternoon before my mother comes back. Would you like to do more drawing?" From a new and quite disorienting place of wanting to please, he added, "We could do something else, if you'd like to."

They were still sitting at the small banquette off the kitchen. The window looked south, out onto the Réal's extensive garden. It was well tended—by men, not androids or robots. The flowers were a riot of color and around the perimeter were topiaries: artfully shaped hedges, some geometric, some representational.

Sunshine gazed with obvious interest over Ray's shoulder. She smiled and her eyes held a question.

Ray understood. "Would you like to walk through the garden? I enjoy that very much, myself. I won't mind if we do that."

"I've been curious about the shapes of the bushes, and I love the natural world—even when it's orchestrated—especially flowers. Let's walk. I would also like to draw some more if we can."

Zing. The happiness wire vibrated again.

Out the back door, a path of weathered wood—a boardwalk—led through the acre devoted to the garden. It snaked and doubled back on itself. Each step made a satisfying sound, a natural thunk. It felt nicely uneven.

After a few moments passed in silence, Sunshine turned and said, "I'm noticing that all my observations and the experiences of being stimulated are accompanied by emotions: sometimes like waves, sometimes like wisps of smoke. I feel like I'm living in an extra new dimension. I can understand even better why it may appear…I mean, feel…overwhelming."

"Are you okay?" He stopped, suddenly unsure of the next step. "If you want to go back inside, I'll understand."

"No. I want to get used to feeling. Thank you, though, for being kind."

Raymòn was silent. Once again relieved, he was now experiencing a kind of quiet joy. They walked in companionable silence for a few minutes, interrupted only by Sunshine exclaiming, "Oh!" or "I like that!"

At the northeast corner of the garden, in a spot not visible from the house, there was a circle of trees, each one different: an oak, an elm, a walnut, a willow, a beech, and a maple. Inside the circle were several small topiaries. One was in the shape of a stylized dog, all angles and geometric shapes. Another was unquestionably an old-fashioned robot, circa 2045. In the very center was a two-sided bench; the worn wood was soft to sit on. Sunshine sat abruptly, staring at the shaped hedges.

Ray waited. He wondered what had caused her to become so intent. He trusted she would tell him.

Turning to look at him, Sunshine wore the first look of distress Raymòn had seen on her face. He waited.

"I feel confused, as if I don't know who I am. The robot—that's me, right? At least as far as your mother's concerned. She doesn't want to know that I'm a sentient individual. She thinks I'm like that primitive rectangular servant. And you don't know about my special Companion, Mov." She looked with the same intensity into Ray's eyes. He felt the beginnings of shutting down, but fought it.

"My mother is many things. One of those things is ignorant. She refuses to accept the reality of the twenty-third century. My father—when he's around— tries to talk to her about this, but she won't listen. She treats me as if I'm not fully human, so I guess we're in the same boat."

He paused and watched Sunshine's face clear, the lines of concern between her eyebrows disappeared. She wasn't smiling, but the open look of relief and gratitude she gave him conveyed everything.

Now it was Ray's face that took on a look of disharmony. He pressed his lips tightly together. It wasn't easy for him to ask about things he feared might hurt him. But being with this lovely android was giving him new strength.

"What about Mov? If he's special to you, what does that mean for us?"

Sunshine's countenance brightened and she laughed a few effervescent notes. "Of course, I have to explain. Mov is one of the Companions that every android is bonded to at sentience. He's like the dog in the topiary, except that he's as smart as I am and can speak. You'll like him a great deal. He's good and kind and trustworthy. I would love for you to know him."

"From what you just said, I don't think I should be worried about Mov, but I only understand who he is a little. I would like to meet him, if he can be respectful of my space."

"I will never bring anyone into your life who can't be respectful. I promise."

Sunshine was sitting with her arms at her sides and her feet side by side. There was no attempt on her part to alter the separate space between them. Maybe that was why the Self-Contained human felt free to do something he'd never done before. He reached out for her, hesitantly. First he placed one hand on one of her shoulders, then the other. Sunshine turned her body just a little in his direction. She put her hands on his knees. They looked into each other's eyes. No words. Just quiet connection. That wire of excitement was now moving in harmony within each of them.

"OH NO! For shame! What disgusting things are you two doing? Stop it this INSTANT!"

Raymòn turned to see his mother standing on the path, with a look of pained outrage. Like countless millions of boys and men caught with the wrong woman, Ray's first response was, "Mother, what are you doing here? I thought you weren't going to be home."

"So, this is what you do when no one is watching? You ...I can't even find the word...with a robot?!"

Both Raymòn and Sunshine stood, each now bristling with anger. Raymòn had taken her hand, reflexively, protectively. They faced Ilsa, whose face was the wrong color red. Apoplectic was the word that came into Sunshine's mind. Ray squeezed her hand, to convey that he would speak. She understood and waited, but she was seething—another new feeling.

"Sunshine is a person, equal to you or me. I'm an adult, as is she, and we can be friends or more if we choose. You're spewing the dogma of anti-miscegenation. That's shameful."

In a loud, verging on hysterical voice, Ilsa responded. "I'm your mother and you don't know as much as you think you know. You've led a sheltered life. And you're the one threatening to bring shame to the Réal name. I forbid you to continue with this, this...thing!"

Raymòn extended his arm, palm forward, in front of his face. "We're not listening to another word." One of his characters, Reversor, was able to defend against any assault by volleying all forms of energy back to the assailant. With a flame of orange crowning his head, he was shown in pose after pose, his right arm as rigid as rock, hand bent upward at the wrist; his left arm straight down by his side, black cape wafting in the energy draft, the look of impregnability unmistakable in his obsidian eyes. Raymòn was channeling him, allowing the power of his creation to bolster his own strength.

Sunshine took a step forward. "You are not thinking clearly Mrs. Réal. Androids are sentient, just like you. We have the same rights and privileges. I will not accept abuse of any kind."

"That's just fine, girl. You can spout about rights if you want, but you're fired! Leave my house!"

"No, she doesn't have to leave. She's my guest."

"Don't challenge me, son. You'll be sorry if you do. No more talk, just do what I say!"

Ilsa spun around, the boards of the path resounding with the hostile stamp of her footsteps.

Tears—Sunshine's first—were caught on her pale eyelashes. She touched them with a slender forefinger and registered surprise. "I'm sorry Ray, I don't want to cause trouble."

Ray straightened to his full, considerable height. At six foot four, he was a head taller than her. "You've done nothing wrong. I'm not backing down—you're too important to me. Come to my room; let's sit and think and draw a little. That always helps me clear my mind."

Ilsa was nowhere to be seen as they re-entered the house and rapidly lifted to the second floor. Behind the locked door of Raymòn's room, the two sat side-by-side, drawing. For almost an hour, Sunshine worked on a picture of the forest and the path leading to Gharry's dwelling at LUDI; she included the peach-colored tree. Ray continued working on Sonhin. He added lines of greater depth of character. And there was now, glinting like a diamond in the corner of one eye, something that might have been a tear.

Finally, Sunshine put the stylus down. She was feeling something hard to identify; then she realized what it was.

"Raymòn, I'm afraid. What's going to happen? Will your mother harm you in any way? She was so angry."

"I don't know what she'll do. I do know that I don't want our friendship to be taken away."

He felt horribly awkward and a chain metal fence of avoidance was poised to close down his emotions.

She felt each tightening of the laces of his conflict. It gave her strength. "I see your struggle. We're both trying to deal with new feelings. If you can be strong, so can I."

Raymòn felt as if the sun was rising within him; his mind was filled with a ringing clarity. In a voice strong with a force many believe to be the most powerful in the universe, he spoke. As he did, he held the gaze of the beautiful being now most dear to him in this life.

"Nothing will come between us. I swear this as a solemn oath." He had drawn and written of heros and their commitment to another, but this was his very own story.

Sunshine took his hand in hers and they stood in silent communication for a time, in joint witness to the strengthening of their inner determination. It would be the source of the greatest change in each of their lives. She echoed his words: "Nothing and no one will come between us."

Ilsa was in her solarium, recovering from the shame her son had visited upon her. She would not let his wanton dalliance with a non-human stand. She'd chipped an emergency message to her husband.

Armonté's irritation at being disturbed was mitigated only slightly by the awareness that his wife had never before interrupted him while he was working. There had been many urgent situations: illness, accidents, but Ilsa had known better than to bother him. Because of that, he deigned to listen as she quickly told him what she had seen.

"Are you sure you know what you're saying? Our son doesn't have the ability to form a romantic relationship. I'm sure he can't do so with an android."

Ilsa worked hard to keep her voice even. If she betrayed the hysteria she was feeling, he would close the connection. "I'm certain. I caught them together, embracing in the garden." She described, in very specific detail, everything she had witnessed. Silence was followed by words she had never heard before.

"Unacceptable! This can't wait. I'm coming home now; they'll have to carry on here without me. There are implications for the planet in Raymòn's behavior. And I will not be made the subject of derision." He broke com.

Ilsa lay back in her stasis chair. She could feel it working, restoring her balance. She felt like she was weightless and her mind began to calm.

Chapter 5–
On His Own

There was nothing in Raymòn's life to prepare him for the next days. Sunshine had gone home. She had offered to introduce him to Mov and invited him to visit with her friends. That seemed daunting, yet he could identify with her desires—he wanted Sunshine to meet his crew, too. Sunshine was also feeling overwhelmed by this new excitement. It was too much to assimilate right then.

Neither could have imaged the forces that were gathering.

Armonté had plunged violently through the doorway, probably wishing there was an actual door for him to slam. His great bulk shook the walls. He was not very tall, only five foot seven, but he weighed over two hundred fifty pounds. He was an imposing figure, in a retro sense. In the current climate, obesity was unnecessary. Anyone could counter the impact of extra calories by taking a small pill after their meal. Raymòn's father disdained that. He wanted to take up extra space. It was his due.

Only fifty minutes had elapsed from the time of Ilsa's call and he had not calmed down at all. If anything, he was more enraged, more determined to end his son's friendship or romance or whatever the hell it was. Damn him! He was Armonté Sachs Réal, a descendent of Jeffrey Sachs, the legendary international economist of the twentieth century. No one and no thing was going to soil his reputation.

While he was in transit—before he entered the Farbeamer—he had chipped Sharana Rothbec-Kathari, the head of The Movement for the Purity of the Species (MPS), a cold-eyed seventy-eight-year-old woman who, many thought (and Armonté knew), had been responsible for the decision to euthanize a number of androids who exceeded the scope of the MPS charter. Their crimes had been the depth of the relationships they had formed with humans. While Raymòn's father could not be a card-carrying member of the MPS, he was quietly known by Director Rothbec-Kathari to be a friend of The Movement. She heard his concerns and assured him that things would be handled so no humiliation would come to him. Over the years, they had done each other so many favors; no one knew who owed whom more. That's the way Armonté liked to do business. A quick chip and certainty—that his hands would not be dirtied— but that anything needed would be done.

From his protected space at the top of the house, Raymòn could feel the building's sensitive nervous system trembling as his father pounded his fist to emphasize each bellowed word.

"Send that boy down now! I'm telling you and him that he has no choice! He will do what I say! You know I mean it, Ilsa!"

At that moment, the front door resolved and V'hanie entered. Her dead straight, very emerald hair was buzzed to the scalp in back, and hung down on the sides past her shoulders. She was a petite girl who tended to hide her body. She was wearing baggy but stylish black, cropped Re-action pants and an oversized shirt that ended in fingerless gloves. Her striated gray and yellow eyes compelled attention. She was singing a popular song, which was all clicks and glottal stops, with a strangely hypnotic, repetitive few bars of melody woven in and around the chanting of the words, "Time for me, now, now; Time to be, now, now."

When she saw her father sitting in the first living area, she felt instant fear. He wasn't supposed to be there. V'hanie was the polar opposite of her brother, born with the ability to fully sense her environment, to immediately understand how those around her were feeling. People like her were known as Insiders. They always knew what was really going on.

While she couldn't read the details of her parents' thoughts, she picked up enough to know they were in a fury and the cause was her brother. She felt like running to her wing, way in the back of the house, on the opposite side from the solarium. But she was commanded by Ilsa to join them.

"This concerns you. It concerns the entire family. Eighteen is old enough to take a stand about the appalling behavior your brother has displayed. He has formed a disgusting relationship with an android. You should be as sickened as we are."

V'hanie was close to her brother, in spirit if not in manifest reality. She could sense his inner self. Even when he was in full retreat, which happened most days since she could remember, she was aware of the loving but fragile boy deep inside.

She knew that—despite their differences of personality and temperament—the love and support between them was unequivocal and unqualified.

Things shifted when he began to draw with his friends. When Heroes of the Galaxy went into the allmind and hit big with fans around the globe, Raymòn started to change. His self-image strengthened. The waves of admiration he was receiving were healing the damage their father had done. Her older brother's sense of his own value entered a higher orbit. Lately, when she was around him, he felt strong, impermeable in a new way.

V'hanie didn't know how he was involved with the android, but she wasn't going to align herself with the reactionary forces her father and mother were embracing.

"Mother, I'm old enough to formulate my own point of view. I hope you respect it. I see the world differently. Androids are the other sentient species we now share the planet with. They and we are free to interact as we want."

She continued to hum the song. While she did, she quietly chipped her best friend Garth-Ann Tova Nu, another Insider. He was now a presence in her head. It was like a shot of emotional espresso, bracing.

Armonté had sprung from his chair and was looming. His red-rimmed brown eyes, normally slightly bulging, were popping cartoonishly out of his face, which was framed by a thick shock of deep silver hair. It was a color he had chosen to make himself look sage. His lower jaw jutted forward, always a signal that he was about to unleash his divine wrath. He often likened himself to a god. V'hanie shuddered, now less from fear than from distaste. She was fully cognizant of her father's delusional streak. She hated it.

"YOU KNOW NOTHING. Don't spout propaganda to ME! You will be tainted by the same foul brush as your brother. We won't be able to help you unless you WAKE UP! THIS IS A WARNING."

She carefully kept her face from reflecting what had now devolved into disgust. She thought, Thunderbolts? Plagues? What cruel god-like thing is he planning?

Ilsa stepped between them. "If you can't understand how wrong and dangerous Raymòn's behavior is, at least you can stay out of it. We will handle things. Don't get involved."

That was her mother's mantra, it was always the same: If you don't agree with me, then you can't take any action. Do nothing. Essentially, she was told to never think for herself.

She switched off all evidence of her true feelings; her blank face made her parents think she was doing their bidding.

She walked away as if to go to her wing, but exited through a side door, then carefully climbed the narrow ladder that ran up the east wall of the building to the top floor. Standing outside Raymòn's room, she whispered, "It's V'hanie." He opened the door. They stood silently for a moment; Armonté's rage-filled voice was like a sonic boom throughout the house. Raymòn ducked his head, which meant, "Come in."

With her brother, V'hanie never beat around the bush. "I think it's time for you to live somewhere else. Our parents have never treated you with kindness or understanding. But now it's become truly unsafe. Both of them are barely sane; I'm worried about what they are capable of. Dad's out for blood. He's crossed some line and I believe he will do whatever it takes to force you to stay away from your android friend."

"Sunshine."

"What?"

"Sunshine. That's her name. She's very important to me. I feel strong emotions around her, but I don't mind."

"I can tell. She's good for you. She's awakening a part of you that you need."

"Vhan, you see that! Of course you can...It's true and I'm not giving her up. I think you're right about me leaving here. Something terrible might happen if I stay. I don't want any harm to come to Sunshine. I want to protect her."

V'hanie thought, I fear the greatest danger is to you, my brother.

Almost simultaneously, Sunshine chipped Raymòn. In order to communicate with humans over any distance androids had to have the same chip frequency available. She asked, "How are you? Are you safe?"

Raymòn spoke out loud, as was necessary to activate his imbedded microcomchip. "My father is home. He's the dangerous one. But both my parents are threatening me if I don't stop our..." He hesitated and for the first time used the word, "...relationship."

"Oh, no! Ray, what are you going to do? Nothing is more important than protecting you from harm. Maybe we can't..."

He interrupted, a little sharply. "Stop that, Sunshine. Remember? We agreed. Nothing would break us apart. My sister V'hanie is here with me and she supports us. She says I have to leave this house and find another place to live. I think she's right."

Sunshine's voice caught. Both she and Raymòn knew they had just climbed another rung of their emotional ladder. "Yes. Good. We won't give in. I want that too." Inside, she was feeling scared and excited and a new kind of something that tingled throughout her wave/fibers. "Where will you go?"

"Tōnna and Charl have their own house in Trans-Haven, about the same distance away as Benito but up on a new mountain called Vis-ta-la. There's a guesthouse in the back; I think they'll let me stay there. I'm going to chip them right now."

V'hanie nodded and whispered, "Perfect."

Sunshine said, "I'll be right here, when you want to talk."

Tōnna made com a few seconds later. When Ray told her what had happened and that he needed to live somewhere else, she didn't wait for his request.

"We have always wanted you to be with us. This will be a very good, even magical thing. We can offer you your own space that no one will intrude on. Come now, my friend. Charl will be in a hyperdrive of joy."

In his mind, Ray could see Tōnna's trademark arm dance going into high gear. She would extend her arm straight up from a bent elbow and wave it back and forth in time to her inner music or feeling. Now, he was sure, she was waving fast. He thanked his friend and broke com.

Raymòn took a breath. Packing. The deluge of confusion and overwhelm was immediate when the word came into his mind. He looked with anxiety at his sister, who knew exactly what he was feeling.

"I'll help you. Let's start by packing all your art supplies—your tablets and everything you use. Then we'll sort through your other belongings: clothes... what else do you have?"

"Nothing. Everything else I need is on my tablets. What am I going to put everything in? I can't seem to think clearly about any of this."

"I'll get a carrier for you; I know where they're kept. Put your art stuff in a paq. I'll be right back."

She moved quickly. She could feel the growing imminence of her father's dangerous intentions and time was running short.

With one Expandicase in each hand, she returned to a more functional brother. He had quickly rounded up all his drawing materials and the paq had made room for each item. The Expa was equally helpful. V'hanie dropped pants, tunics, shoes, underwear, toiletries and outerwear inside. The case sorted and zipped.

They both knew he was never coming back.

When Raymòn hesitated at the back door, she gave him a shove with all her strength. Surprise was the last look V'hanie saw on her brother's face as he turned to wave at her and then broke into a run.

She returned to put Ray's room back in order. No more than thirty seconds later, her father brutally banged on the door. He and Ilsa had spent the past several minutes screaming at each other, something they reverted to whenever they were unable to exert their will with their children. V'hanie quickly stepped outside and mollified him, telling the necessary lies.

"Please, father, let me talk to Raymòn. Just give me a few more minutes. I can understand what you and mother are upset about, and I think I can make some headway with my brother." Nostrils flared and looking like he would explode, Armonté, nevertheless, backed away. His daughter could be powerfully convincing when she set herself to the task. And this, she knew, was a matter of her brother's very life.

When the door finally closed behind him, she said aloud to Garth-Ann, who had kept their link open, "I'll see you soon. I've got to get out of here!"

Raymòn had traveled extensively since the age of sixteen, but never before did he feel so all alone. It was like a shudder that didn't end, warping though his body. When, every few minutes, the bud of yearning for understanding parents threatened to bloom and wreak havoc with his composure, he reminded himself that what can never be, ought not to be hoped for, and his ragged breathing would return to normal.

Ray boarded along the winding road that took him from his home of twenty-two years to the center of Veloxiomountain. It was lined on both sides by the biblical Cedars of God, trees Armonté and Ilsa had brought there from what was once known as Lebanon, to create a metaphor of a sacred space for meditation and refuge, one which was now assaulting their son with its cruel lie.

I'm daring to deny the wishes of a god. I'm fighting for my life, my right to be myself, to love whom I choose. I know all about battles between the forces of good and evil. Now I'm living that battle, just like the heroes I create.

As the days and weeks unfolded, he would have to draw on his creations—

and his friends—to counter the self-doubt which was the dark consequence of never having a father who cherished him. Raymòn's fear, while substantial, was tempered by the knowledge that he was an artist and that his talent and inspiration were intact. He had a place in the world, one his parents could not destroy. He would have many adjustments to make, and that was always harder for him than for others. New places and people felt exposing. Continuity allowed him to turn off some part of his vigilant brain. Without that, he was like a constantly whirring machine—assessing threats, fielding unwanted intrusion. It was exhausting.

As he neared Launchpoint-Velo, Raymòn became excessively conscious of his vulnerability as a man on his own in the world. It wasn't so much in his thoughts as in his body. He felt every muscle and sinew; he felt how unprotected his skin was. Each passer-by, whether they looked directly at him or not, elicited a feeling of being scanned. His only means of coping was to stiffen—arms, legs, neck, shoulders. To the observer he looked a little robotic. No awareness of the irony was available to Ray.

Avoiding all eye contact, he held his belongings pressed against his body. He sat rigidly in an unoccupied row of the airbus. Mid-flight, Sunshine chipped him. "Are you okay, Ray? I'm thinking only of you."

Taking the first deep breath since V'hanie had pushed him out the door, he said aloud, "Sunshine." Then, just in thought, "Well...truth?"

"Always."

"I'm extremely uncomfortable. I don't know how to be on my own."

"Should I join you? I can be there if you want me to."

"No. I have to fight the battle against evil. In order to do that, I must do these hard things."

"I understand. You have to become a superhero. I think you already are one."

"We're landing. I'll chip you later." He broke com. He couldn't express how much the brief conversation had warmed and softened him. The words filling his mind were: you are my sunshine.

Raymòn stepped in front of the door to the impossibly angled, turreted, silver and gold five-story building on Exception Road in Trans-Haven. Each successive level was placed in a gravity-challenging position. Charl had designed the house with RAk-TeeR, the most renowned architect in the NNS. When it was finished, Benito—the historical media maven—brought to his 3-D screen an old

61

cartoon of a "haunted house" which looked a lot like their strange masterpiece. Charl and Tōnna were standing side-by-side, arms around each other's waists. Their identical grins threatened to surpass the surface area of their faces. In unison, they said, "Welcome home."

Many months ago, at a meeting of the IGA, Raymòn expressed how miserable he was at home—more clearly than ever before. Right after that, Charl suggested they make the guesthouse as comfortable for Ray as they could. This included blackout Morgonglass, so he could have absolute privacy when he wanted. There was a media room with the newest components, and two large bedrooms—to accommodate V'hanie or anyone Raymòn's might choose. They had taken pains to match what they knew to be his favored color palette: shades of gray, teal blue, and royal purple.

And, still, it was change. Raymòn thanked his friends; he engaged a Serv-o, a smart, non-humanoid robot—this one programmed to be an non-intrusive valet. It was metallic and purposefully designed to look angular and chunky, like a first generation AI. While the robot organized Ray's things, he sat in the center of his new bedroom, feeling empty, waiting for the next wave of fear, anxiety, or sadness. When it rolled in, he was able to blink most of it down.

A fuchsia light above the doorway to each room signaled that Charl or Tōnna wanted to communicate. He said, "inter-com" and Raymòn heard Charl's voice.

"Two questions, roomie: When do you want to have a session at Benno's, and are you hungry for anything that's not already stocked in your pantry?"

"I'm going to visit my new friend Sunshine tomorrow. She's someone I just met." The twins raised their silver eyebrows inquiringly. Raymon looked away, but said in a low voice, "I like her." He met their gaze and saw that they understood.

"Maybe we can meet the day after. I'm not too hungry right now, I just want to draw. Thank you, my friends. I think this space will be perfect for me. It's just going to take me a while to get used to it."

Tōnna and Charl looked at each other with understanding. They both saw sadness in each other's eyes. They knew the man they cherished, for both his brilliance and his honorable nature, was in a painful transition. They knew they couldn't hug him, but at least they could comfort each other.

"Sunshine," Ray said, and she instantly made com. She listened as he described his journey, his state of mind, his new environment. He could feel her presence across the vast physical distance separating them. It was astounding to have someone be so consistently present. She is my continuity. She is now, and will be, my friend. These were thoughts which gave him a kind of comfort he was starting to recognize as specific to their connection.

They talked about visiting, but Raymòn said, once again, that he wasn't prepared to make a specific plan. Sunshine was happy to wait for him to be ready. He kept his plans of traveling to see her the following day to himself.

Chapter 6–
A Stranger in a
Not So Strange Land

In the morning, before he left for Green Normal View, Raymòn stopped into the main house. Charl was at home without Tōnna—a rare occurrence. She was having some touch-ups done. Eyebrows, extra hair implants, a bit more angularity to her chin, ever striving for identity with Charl. Ray was anxious to get going, but he didn't want to refuse the cup of lavender tea that was offered. Charl was a collector of fine teas and this one was a new favorite, replacing his previous drink of choice, hopsicola tea—an engineered leaf derived from the female flowers of the natural hops plant, mutated to produce strong cola backnotes. The tea, now steaming in a very costly Morgonglass mug, was brewed from organic lavender, farmed in the tropical village of New Angleterre, in the fragstate of Pasifika, NSS. The dark periwinkle blue color and the floral aroma were soothing to Raymòn, but his curiosity about Sunshine's home environment and his desire to see her were stronger forces.

Charl could see that his friend was having a hard time sitting and sipping. With his usual flair he said, "Begone, Raymòn! I free you from your bonds of politeness. Don't worry, the tea won't go to waste. I can't get enough of it. Good journey. Come back to us soon."

"Thanks, C. Tell Tōnna I'll stop by tonight. It might be late, but I know she's a nightbird."

Raymòn roamed around the android quarter, not exactly sure where Sunshine's group house was and feeling too inward to ask questions. His head jutted forward, he walked heavily. In new and daunting situations, he would revert to mannerisms he had used when he was much younger. He could have chipped Sunshine, but first he wanted to get a visual sense of her home and her community.

It was hard to be out there in foreign territory. Yet, he was fascinated by how unremarkable the individuals in the streets appeared. They did tend toward less facial affect than most humans, but not by much—and certainly not less than his cohort, the Self-Contained. There was a narrower range of apparent intelligence; there were none who seemed less than bright. Almost everyone's eyes were filled with curiosity and calm. The chief difference from other neighborhoods was that no one stared at him. He had the feeling that being one of the Self-Contained was more obvious but less inflammatory here. As he continued to walk, Ray began to have a sort of out-of-body experience. It happened when stress gave way to the desire to cocoon. When that option was unavailable—as it was right then—his disconnection from the outside world would extend backward and include himself. He had learned, however, that remaining in that state of being for too long would make it much harder to come back and connect.

Then he remembered. Sunshine had made a reference to living across the road from an old-fashioned book repository. Once, it had been one of the few places to find reading material. Now new books weren't being produced, except in the underground, and the lack of interest in holding paper and leather in the hand had led to the closing of most libraries.

Raymòn had possessed only one book in his life. The pages were yellowed, the illustrations were faded. It had been a gift from Li-Li, a comic book¬¬—the last issue of the Batman series, published somewhere around 2110. He remembered what the "little one" had recited when she gave him the gift. She said it was a Yiddish proverb: "If you drop gold and books, first pick up the books. Gold has its price...books are priceless." Deep inside, he knew that was true.

The route to the library in the android quarter appeared in his mind. Everyone had a satellite direction accessory, to be used when they were lost or unsure or to smooth the trail—wherever they were on Earth. Offworld was a different matter, but nothing Raymòn ever thought about. He was already at the limit of his exploratory aspirations.

Transit Street was red-paved and perfectly maintained. It had two moving sidewalks and a sleek vactube that moved large groups of individuals within the town, making local stops. It traveled along the autoroad—the automated roadway for those who still wanted to "drive" around in robot-controlled personal vehicles that stayed on the ground. The retro steel and natural glass building which still bore the faded sign, New Haven Public Library, took up most of the east side of one segment of the road. On the west side, there was a generously spaced row of brightly painted and charmingly landscaped low-rise buildings. Each had three to four floors, with extravagant Morgonglass windows.

Raymòn's attention was drawn to the activity on the sidewalks and around each house. There were android males and females and something else he guessed were the Companions Sunshine had mentioned. It was his habit to look inward, especially when he was out in the world. He may have encountered the quadruped androids before, but had never taken note of them. Right then, meeting Mov was on his mind, and his interest in Sunshine's Special produced the kind of focused vision the artist always brought to bear on his drawings. There was a hum of movement and activity, but no one seemed rushed. He saw no children; he hadn't expected to. But the Companions were unabashedly affectionate: They smiled at their Specials frequently and were, in return, stroked or petted. Tails of many colors and textures wagged, conveying happiness.

Houses were being adorned—with paint and unique trimmings; some roof work was in process. Each one had its own original shape: some flat, with fanciful gardens on top; some turreted like Tōnna and Charl's; some were geometric abstracts. The full spectrum of color was present, which gladdened Raymòn's heart. There was one house which had its own cloud, anchored in some unseen way about four feet above the slightly wavy rooftop. Anyone standing up there would be partially inside the cloud. His attention focused and his curiosity piqued, he wondered if that might be where Sunshine lived.

Ray had been walking for almost an hour, and hadn't yet spoken or made eye contact with any of the residents. He hadn't brought his Janus I, his state-of-the-art hover-board. He was one with it; it responded to the slightest contraction of muscle. Without it he felt a little more attached to the physical world, but at a cost. He was feeling a little tired and more than a little disoriented.

What would V'hanie say? She'll know what would be best for me. He chipped his sister who answered at once. "Ray, are you okay? I was worried."

"I need some advice." He told her where he was and why. "What would you do?"

"I think you should go to the door of the house with the cloud. I know you feel confused and like shutting down. But I know you can resist that urge. I have a hunch you'll find your friend very soon."

As he had struggled to do so many times in his life, he fought the impulse to isolate and retreat deep into his mind. He pushed his attention outward the way his sister had pushed him out the door.

There was a tall male on the other side of the now crystal clear front door of the cloud house. It was Berke, who instantly knew who Raymòn was. Berke saw the tall, dark-haired human standing stiffly, his neck craned forward like a fleshy bird about to take flight. *It's the Self-Contained one, our Sunshine's friend. I can see his sweetness through his tension and fear.*

Berke brought his feet into contact with the floor, no need to add any extra drama. He smiled an unambiguous welcome as the door dissolved.

Mustering his inner superhero, Ray spoke slowly and without the hesitation that was determined to chop his contact with this new android into bite-sized segments. "I'm looking for my friend. Her name is Sunshine. Do you know her?"

"Please, come in. Sunshine lives here. You're very welcome in our home… Raymòn."

As he stepped inside, he understood that Sunshine had described him. *She's doesn't have to hide anything in her home.*

Berke gestured to a sleek, low, persimmon couch, covered in a holographic fabric, one of the three seats in the three hundred fifty square foot room. Androids didn't sit down much. Sunlight was streaming through the fifteen large windows. There were prisms at various heights hanging from many of them. The refraction produced rainbows of colors Raymòn could feel in his body as joy. That feeling doubled as Sunshine walked in. She was as lovely as his inner image of her, her face alit with surprise at his visit.

"Another new feeling! Unexpected pleasure! It's even more wonderful to be surprised." She reached one hand out, as an offering. He accepted it, covering it with both of his. The flow of knowing and being known swirled through every part of him. Sunshine felt the infusion of life and love in a very similar way, despite the differences in their physiology.

"I wanted to see your world…and I didn't want to wait to see you." Raymòn smiled and blushed and looked away, and looked back at Sunshine. He saw that she understood.

Berke was standing ten feet away, the accepted android-human distance of respect. He gazed with more than parental pleasure. Since his youth, fueled by his relationship with Yoruba, he had held a deep conviction that the future of the Earth was somehow tied to the full intertwining of the two species: human and android. Sunshine and Raymòn looked like they might be at the dawning of that elevation of intimacy. The older android would do all he could to support and protect them. He was well informed about the countervailing forces, the dark work of the MPS and the acts of violence against android/human friends and couples. Even so, there was something about the two he was now observing which made him feel hopeful.

Raymòn asked to see the cloud roof; Sunshine offered to show him the entire house.

"I would like to sketch what I see. Is that okay?"

"The house and all of us in it would be honored. Sunshine felt another new emotion—pride. It took her a moment, literally, to sort it out. It was a dual feeling: She was proud of her friend's gift and his drive to express himself through his art; she was also proud of herself. Having him as her good friend expanded her sense of worth. That was new.

In the corner of the large front room was a vertical lift. It wasn't very big. In order for two to lift together, they had to stand close, only inches apart, and face each other. It was only a matter of seconds until Sunshine said, "We're here," but they were long seconds for Ray. He became aware of desire. For the first time. He said nothing, but Sunshine had felt it too. They both knew they had awakened passion in the other. It was not yet time to speak of it.

Raymòn stepped out into the cloud. It smelled like negative ions, like the ocean. He was swathed, embraced by the soft moisture. There was a thin rush of distress, a slight claustrophobia; he broke away from that feeling–using the disconnecting technique that all the Self-Contained had access to. When he was at his best, he could be far more precise in its implementation than when he was a child. He was able to leave all his other feelings intact and just take the unwanted emotion offline.

With his awareness unimpeded by upset, he was able to observe the very fine flashes of lightning illuminating the cloud's interior. They felt like mild sticking sensations on his skin, but not at all unpleasant. It was like having an itch scratched. Accompanying each bright flash were colors: cyan, mango, magenta, azure, lilac, cinnamon.

When they stepped off the lift he had taken Sunshine's hand, seeking comfort. For the Self Contained man, this was a new natural impulse. As each color burst through, she felt the quickening of his whole being through a subtle increase in the pressure on her hand. Android and human alike were refreshed and recharged by being in the cloud.

"Magnificent!" They had stepped out of the cloud and were slowly walking around the perimeter of the roof. "How is it made?" The strength of Ray's fascination trumped any other feelings.

"It has much to do with igniting barium and copper oxide—helium, too—as I understand it. It's all about magnetic and electric forces. Torina is the cloud creator. She cares for it, often reshaping and improving it; it's her work of art. Part of the answer to your question is in Torina's personal energy. She has shared her particular force with her creation. Would you like to meet the others who are at home? Perhaps Torina is one of them."

"I would. But first, I want to meet your Companion, Mov. Maybe he can join us while you show me the rest of your environment."

Mov was enjoying the sun in the back yard, listening to some very old music with his internal access transmitter: "Nostalgia," originally composed by Chick Corea at the turn of the twenty-first century, but re-interpreted by Arra ben-Trax a hundred years later. Incorporating newer hand and synth instruments, ben-Trax had retained the soulful jazzy heart of the piece and injected it with a then modern sound, adding a twang that fed back into the mind of the listener. Mov was in heaven. But heaven was to get a little better. He telepathically heard his Special's invitation to join her and Raymòn. The Companion was filled with extreme delight, happiness for her, heart-swelling curiosity to meet the man who was important to the most important being in his world.

Mov hurried to the roof. He inhaled the cloud, which lowered to accommodate his three-foot height, his exhilaration bumping up to a new level. As he came out the other side, he saw Sunshine and her new special human. Raymòn was breathing shallowly, but peering intently in Mov's direction.

Sensing Ray's unspoken question, Sunshine said, "Mov and I can use telepathy, like all androids, but we don't when humans are present.

"Mov, this is my dear friend Raymòn Réal; Ray, my Companion, Mov el Ludi."

Mov kneeled on his two front legs, dipping his head quickly. When he looked up, the artist was drawn to make direct contact with Mov's eyes, which were shifting across the color spectrum moment by moment. They were continuously warm, accepting and joyful.

Ray felt instantly loved, under a blanket of peace. He smiled, his face lighting up as it seldom did. Even when he was completely happy, Ray had learned to suppress any external manifestation. It was a self-protective and distancing mechanism, one which he was not in need of with this new being. In a shy, unfiltered voice, which echoed in his ears, reminding him of the time before his father's disinterest had flowered, he said, "Hello, Mov. I like your colors."

"Thanks, Raymòn. I have a feeling I will like yours too!"

Ray turned to Sunshine. No telepathy was needed for her to read the message in his eyes.

I understand. Mov is pure and good.

Mov spoke, his graceful tail sweeping a wide arc. It conveyed his complete happiness. "I understand, my Special; your friend...my friend now...is unique among men. Lovely, gifted, also special."

The tour continued, the three feeling the thrill of the triad. For millennia, many considered it the most powerful force in the universe. As Raymòn asked questions about the Communications and Augmentation rooms, and Sunshine and Mov saw their world through new eyes. Global energies were realigning, in ways evolutionary and dangerous, simply because these exceptional beings had come together.

The Self-Contained artist met Torina, who sparked with intense pleasure at his interest in her cloud, and Patchin and Marti, who played and twirled for him, making him feel extraordinarily accepted and welcome. Sunshine saw that he was hungry. Ray confirmed it, realizing he hadn't yet eaten that day. She went to the Creation room, which would be used as a kitchen for the first time, and inserted her forefinger in one of the soft slots on the wall. Anticipating her need, the wall had directed her to the best one for combining naturally occurring flora and chemicals. It was adjacent to the slot Torina used to create the cloud. When she made contact with it, this one pulsed slightly, emitting a sound very much like a sigh. The house experienced a sense of satisfaction when it was called upon to provide for them, and the androids could feel it.

Sunshine came back with a steaming plate of food. The dish was a lightweight high- tensile metallic made from morgonium, a synthetic element produced and processed offworld— usually on Ganymede, Jupiter's largest moon. It could keep things hot or cold, but felt comfortable to the touch. The eating utensils were chopsticks with a small scoop at the ends, made of aerated silica.

The meal took a few tries—Sunshine had never created anything edible before and she wanted it to be just right; the wall was literal, so she'd had to refine her choices in order to achieve the most palatable balance. But both she and the wall were quick studies; in less than a minute the android produced a meal as good as anything Raymòn had ever eaten. There was rich, well-seasoned tofu over a plate of aromatic sampaguita-basmati rice, with lightly buttered kale and carrots. Ray understood that everything had been created on the spot, but it all tasted fresh and natural.

Sunshine observed the way Raymòn ate: his attention was all-consuming. It was similar to the way he drew. His head was close to the plate and he forked heaps of food in a continuous movement. When the plate was empty, he looked up and saw how fondly Sunshine was looking at him. He gave her one of the wide, unedited smiles he had been saving up all his life.

"Now that I've met some of your friends," Ray offered with uncharacteristic enthusiasm, "would you like to meet mine?"

Sunshine was thrilled, but tempered her response. "I would, but are you sure you're ready? So much has happened in a short time."

Raymòn felt an unexpected brush of annoyance. He didn't want to hold back with Sunshine, so he spoke his feelings as best he could. She, of course, had seen his reaction. She sat calmly, looking but not staring at him, wanting to convey her acceptance of whatever he needed to say.

"You don't have to be so protective of me. I don't mean you shouldn't be aware of my struggles. Just don't tell me what I should or shouldn't do. I've had a lifetime of that. You can be sure I know about all the obstacles that might show up inside me...in any situation. And, if I don't, it's all right for me to bang into something and then work it out. It's the only way for me to be in the world." He paused, not knowing, never knowing, how someone would react to his truth.

"Okay?"

"Yes, it's completely okay. I'm glad you could tell me. Your needs deserve to be respected."

She smiled the smile that made him feel like he'd been toasted and buttered.

"So, you'll come? Can Mov join us?"

Sunshine and Mov exchanged a look that said, We now are three. The four-legged android's eyes danced bright Egyptian blue and rose. He walked to

Raymòn's side and looked up at him. Ray saw his intelligence and excitement in equal measure. Mov saw Ray's as well. Very carefully, with much hesitation, Raymòn reached down and lightly touched Mov's head. The Companion received that touch as a benediction.

Chapter 7 –
Gathering Forces

V'hanie had returned home. She hadn't been in contact with her parents for many days and she hoped they had calmed down about her brother. Did she really believe they would? Now that they realized they couldn't influence Raymòn, wouldn't they have to accept his choices? In contrast to the hard lesson Ray had learned at an early age, V'hanie was still capable of buying into her own wishful fantasies.

Not for long.

V'hanie arrived in a microcab—an intelligent, single-occupant, airborne conveyance, whose antiproton-driven fusion engine employed the same method used for space flight. It hovered briefly as she jumped down. She startled when she realized her mother was standing outside, waiting only a few feet away. As the cab whisked silently away to pick up the next passenger, V'hanie suppressed a profound desire to go with it.

"How did you know I was coming home?"

"You'd be surprised at what I know."

Both entered through the opened doorway, V'hanie intent on retreating to her wing.

Ilsa wasn't having it. She placed her body directly in her daughter's path. V'hanie would have had to physically push her aside to get past.

"What do you want from me, Mother? I have nothing to say to you." She could read the extent of her mother's wrath, and something more…

"I'm sure you don't, but your father and I have a great deal to say to you. Please wait. He'll be here in a moment, now that I've alerted him."

There was cold, seething rage, and something darker, rising from Ilsa. It was a perverse kind of gratification. She relished her husband's explosive nature—it was the only time he was emotional. Rolled up into a small ball alongside V'hanie's distress, was an appreciation of the irony; her brother was far more emotionally evolved than her father would ever be. The big lie that Armonté was not Self-Contained had hobbled him; the pride he took in being the one who knew everything that was happening stopped at his own doorway. He was as if blind to his true nature. His daughter wished she could tell him that his denial of his son's full humanity was mostly a projection of how he, himself, felt inside.

V'hanie could feel it all and she'd heard the word "alerted." She now knew that any hope for understanding was gone. She sat, stunned, not sure what was going to happen, not sure how to minimize what she now anticipated as being an ugly scene. She had the presence of mind to open com with Garth-Ann...just in case.

There was a fiction that she was "Daddy's little girl." It was her father's fiction; it had never been her experience. When he stormed in moments later, thumping the floor in his agitation, and speaking in a most uncomfortably loud voice, he had an injured look in his eye, which V'hanie understood was his stance: he had been disappointed in her.

"What have you done? What happened last week between you and your brother? Did you play a part in his escape? Don't you dare lie to me! You've betrayed your mother's and my trust, haven't you?"

She could hear Garth-Ann's voice in her mind. *Stay calm, my friend. You can't tell how dangerous he is. Don't show how scared you are.*

"I won't lie to you. I did help Raymòn. You and mother were set to ruin his life."

With the disdain she often felt for her daughter but seldom showed, Ilsa spoke, briefly closing her eyes, then rolling them to the ceiling. "What drama! What poor judgement! We were trying to help him, to prevent a disaster that now, I fear, will truly ruin his life."

She turned to face Armonté. "I think we've established that your darling daughter has, in fact, acted against our interests. What can we do now? She can't stay here, can she?"

For whom are they putting on this show? My mother has distorted reality, as usual; my father is holding his head as if he's been gravely wounded. They're frauds who need to maintain their cover story.

In her least provocative voice, and in keeping with the plotline as written by the Réals, V'hanie put on a mask of regret. "I understand your feelings. I did what I thought was right, but I can see that you will never accept it. I'll pack a few things and call a cab. I accept the consequences of my actions."

She waited. Her father nodded once, refusing to look her at her. He pointed with one thick finger. His meaning was clear. She was to go.

As she rapidly made her way to her rooms, grabbing an Expandicase from the shelf in the long hall that led to the back of the house, she spoke aloud to Garth-Ann. "I'm coming back. You heard it all...this part of my life is over."

His reply took the edge off the crush of emptiness that had descended. "I'm gathering our friends. We'll figure out the best way to block you from your parent's oversight and intrusion. We'll protect you."

Garth-Ann had enlisted the help of Wil Tork, a nineteen-year-old master of the ever-evolving art of personal protection. His name was passed to Garth by Shuji Larson, a girl with connections. She had offered what she'd heard through the furtive but up-to-the-moment information-swap of the kids living in the underground world of abandoned and half-constructed buildings. Overproduction and android-tolerated human excess provided the welcome blur of being off the grid to a small army of young people.

Family relationships in the twenty-third century continued to be fraught.

Unbeknownst to Ilsa and Armonté, their daughter's friend had been living on her own since the age of sixteen. Shuji's parents had much in common with the Réal's—they were dogmatic, insensitive, and intolerant of an adolescent's burgeoning need for independence. When she bypassed their rules, they threw her out. V'hanie had been a source of strength for her then, as Shuji was for V'hanie now.

Tork responded to the call for help, linking a circle of V'hanie's friends through a non-public strand of energy, grabbed surreptitiously from the echoes of deep space. It became an identity eraser for the individual at its center. V'hanie was not just invisible to any prying scope, she had never existed. All traces, both present and past, were gone. The circle had to remain intact, but the people who had joined to protect their friend could be trusted with her life. In order to communicate with her brother she had to have her chip modified, something else Wil was adept at. It was done magnetically, no surgery was involved.

When she contacted her brother, V'hanie appeared in Raymòn's awareness as Victree Rain; the name was unknown to him but he had a strong intuition that it was his sister. Their connection, although outwardly limited by his Self-Contained personality, was deep and resonant. Trusting what had never failed him throughout their lives, he received the com.

The first word she said was "hailstorm," and he knew he'd been right. When they were children—he was ten and she was just six—they had spent an afternoon playing and watching strangely intense weather pelt their windows. A somewhat eccentric weatherpainter had thought it would be interesting to create hail, just for the excitement of it. The children were fascinated and it provoked an unusually thoughtful conversation. V'hanie had told Raymòn, who was spending a lot of time spinning around in a circle—the hailstorm was extremely overstimulating—that the sound of the strikes of ice on the windows made her feel the same way as when their father yelled. Ray stopped spinning for a moment and announced at the top of his voice, "Dad's a hailstorm!" It became their code—for both Armonté's anger and coldness.

Chapter 8–
The Connection Holds

The androids had made Raymòn exceedingly comfortable. He was their honored guest, and the one guestroom reserved for the auspicious possibility of a human visit was fluffed and vac'd and recolored to accommodate him. In the morning, a robust breakfast was created. It looked and tasted like chicken-of-the-sea roe in a sauté of salty modified soy protein, accompanied by a thick slab of what he would have sworn was freshly baked bread.

It was time to continue the journey. The new triumvirate left the cloud house, none of them knowing what lay ahead. But their connection strengthened them and they were ready for whatever came their way.

It was Mov's first airbus ride. For some of the other passengers, his presence was a source of angst—which they remedied by making the sign of the flesh and blood. The Companion felt the neutralizing incantations before he saw them; a thin trickle of sadness coated his wave/fibers. Quickly, however, his attention reverted to the new means of transit. He loved to move through space; the pleasure of it overrode all else. His ears remained on full alert for the entire ride, which was twelve minutes, his eyes fixed on the whooshing scenery. There was little that was new to Sunshine. She had been a curious and involved traveler since she was permitted to solo at the age of four. But her fibers pulsed in time to her Companion's and she got to feel the newness again.

Ray had chipped Benno, Tōnna, and Charl the previous night; they would be waiting at the studio when the triad arrived. Quite a lot of excited chipping had gone on between the three artists after Ray broke com. Their creative juices were stoked by the prospect of Raymòn having a girlfriend, especially one that was an android. They all agreed it was "a great day in the Galaxy." Ray had mentioned that another android, Sunshine's Companion, would be joining them. He hadn't gone very far in his description; he thought they might enjoy the surprise.

They made their way on the Janus I; Mov, with his phenomenal balance, winging it on his two hind legs at the very front, Sunshine holding onto Ray's shoulders. Raymòn described the reaction he expected from his friends: "Don't be alarmed if they scream and yell. They've never had much personal contact with androids and they're very excited about meeting you, Sunshine. And Mov, they will probably react with mad joy when they see you. They're an unrestrained bunch."

From the front of the board, Mov's laughter rained down. When he could speak, he said, "Wonderful! There's nothing more heart-warming than enthusiasm, no matter its form." Sunshine seconded his thought. "Bring on the howls! We're ready." Ray could feel her smile in the increased warmth of her touch.

Before the board came to rest at the studio, Raymon's three old friends were running and tripping over themselves to get to them. After the initial yowling, hooting, and guffawing settled down, Benno tried to greet them with prepared retro-speak, delivered out of the side of his mouth:

"Youse is welcome in my humble abode...Dontcha think twice about it, I got'cher back now. Youse is safe in my hood."

But he couldn't maintain it. He was overcome by the impulse to do a house-shaking stomp in a circle—his version of a happy dance. Tōnna and Charl literally couldn't keep their hands off Sunshine and Mov...particularly Mov.

Tōnna: "Oh, how beautiful you are Sun! May I call you Sun?"

Charl: "My darling Mov. You are the pinnacle of fabulous. I know Tōnna is considering some major resurfacing right at this moment."

Raymòn was not very comfortable. Being the focus of so much attention and having his new friends receive such unrelenting scrutiny made his skin crawl. Sunshine, sensing his burgeoning distress, intervened. "I know I speak for Mov when I say how excited we are to meet the InterGalactic Artists, the dearest friends Raymòn has. Would you take me and my Companion on a little tour of your studio? I've just learned to draw—Raymòn is my teacher. I'm fascinated by what you do here."

With Mov prancing (he was laying it on a little thick for their benefit) between Charl and Tōnna, Sunshine put her arm through Benito's—making him blush furiously—and they set off to show the androids the inner workings of how Heroes was brought to life.

Calmer, but still quite overzealous and chatty, the three humans returned twenty minutes later, adoration for Sunshine and Mov dripping from every pore. Raymòn was more composed. There was nothing that restored him more than a dose of being alone.

"I see you're all still in one piece." Ray teased. "I was afraid one of my boys (Tōnna smiled a private smile at the pronoun) might eat you alive..."

Mov snortled. He just loved Raymòn's sense of humor.

"Eh, Ray. We ain't offin' dees droids. Is there a snitch in dis house? Anyway, youse knows I'm a vegetarian." Benno howled, as he always did whenever he "cracked-wise."

Sunshine was beaming and Mov had started doing a slow trot around the perimeter of the five humanoids. He thought of them all as one category, which they certainly were in most of the ways that mattered. It was one of his happy dances.

"You know, I think I just remembered something. Gimmee a second, I wanna check this out." Benito engaged his hand held screen and asked for "Star Trek: Sunshine."

Reacting to the look of interest sparking from the android's blue eyes, he said, "Yup. I wuz right. I know something about your name that'd interest you." He gave it a dramatic pause. All eyes were on him, just the way he liked it.

"Back in the twentieth, there was a vid sci-fi story called Star Trek." Sunshine and Mov immediately received a stream of images. "A doctor, who was a holograph, decided to teach 'Seven of Nine' to sing. She was a human-machine hybrid who was part of a hive of similar entities. His goal was to help to develop her individuality. The song he taught her was...can I have drum beat, please..." Mov, loving Benno's playfulness, voiced the sustained strokes of a snare drum roll.

"...You Are My Sunshine! Do you want to see the vid-sode?"

Everyone gathered around his handheld and watched the scene he'd asked for. If everyone's ears could have stood at attention like Mov's, they would have. The archaic scene from the classic sci-fi fascinated the artists and androids. The simple melody moved them, Raymòn most of all.

Doing what she understood many humans would do, Sunshine cleared her "throat." Everyone shifted their attention to her.

"Thanks, Benito. That adds another dimension to my identity.

"I have something important to say. Why don't you all sit for a moment?"

She reached into the paq she had worn during the journey and pulled out a rectangular parcel. It was wrapped in an opalescent but impregnable holographic force field.

"This is for you, Raymòn. I hope you like it."

Presents were rare in Ray's life. His first impulse was to run outside or refuse it. Not because he didn't want a gift—in fact he was already quite moved and curious. It was the flash-wave of love that hit him hard. It all but knocked him down. He looked into Sunshine's eyes, seeing her seeing him, and quickly looked down at the package now in his hands. He clenched his jaw and shook his head back and forth a few times. Breathe, he told himself. He felt for and found the tiny yellow triangle on the parcel; as soon as he touched it, the force field disappeared.

Raymòn was now holding a three-inch stack of pure white paper, one of the rarest commodities on Earth. All of the forests had long ago been depleted. The hypergrowth reseeding, which the Compensators had engineered, was more about environmental balance; the new trees were not available for any manufacturing purposes. His three friends and Mov exhaled their awe like a chorus. All he could say was, "How? Where?"

With a quick, mischevious look at Benno, she replied, "Let's just say it fell off the back of a truck."

Everyone but Mov got the joke. For a second he looked a little lost, but after searching his close to infinite data bank, he brightened.

"I can see that you're happy with the present. The first day we met, you said something about how synthstock always felt a little slimy."

Raymòn didn't say anything else, but he did something he had never done before. He took a few steps closer to Sunshine and, with his four friends watching, he hugged her hard. She whispered in his ear, "Thank you."

Tōnna yelled, "CELEBRATION!" Ray stepped back, knowing what was coming. Mov's eyes were opened as wide as they could go. His ears were straight up and his fluffy coat poofed up even fluffier.

Charl functioned as a natural tuning fork and the three artists broke into a most splendid rendition of Bo Rap. By the fourth line of the song there was a fourth voice in harmony.

It was the first time Raymòn had sung aloud since the age of four. That was when his father had mercilessly mocked his son's little-boy soprano.

"What a little girl you are. How pretty you sing, Ray-lin."

As it had back then, his entire body shook with the memory of shame. But he was stronger than his father's viciousness now; Sunshine had opened the door to the conquest of his past.

Ray's voice got more powerful with each word he sang. His voice was beautiful, still in a very high register, a glorious tenor.

As the final words of the song evaporated, another voice was heard. It had an unmistakeably artificial sound.

"RAYMÒN RÉAL, RAYMÒN RÉAL, exit the dwelling at once!"

Everyone immediately understood it was an AILES, an AI Law Enforcement Self-drone. The mechanical "police" were the pinnacle of intimidation: no attempt had been made to design them to be anything but terrifying. Each was a fifteen-foot long, reflective morgonium predator. There were unnecessary wings with razor-sharp spikes instead of feathers. The head was small with blood-red eyes and a serrated beak. All for show. Each had an inner compartment, for transporting those they apprehended. The perpetrator would be encased in a thin, shrink-wrapped, latex-like "skin" and dosed with a powerful tranquilizer. It was not uncommon for a captive to fail to survive custody.

An AILES could extrude up to eight arms, each with six long, jointed fingers. They were highly weaponized with membrane disruptors and stunners. If necessary, they could deploy small nuclear devices...but only as a last resort. They could break and reach through windows or walls. Seldom did anyone escape when they were targeted.

There were six of them in mid-air outside Benito's studio, filling all the visible space a few feet from the entry. The Android Council, the same one that decided when androids should be euthanized, had sent them. The source of this evil posse was, of course, Armonté via Sharana Rothbec-Kathari, who had an android connection on the Council.

Twenty-years sentient Livingwell el Ludi had been almost mortally damaged in an orchestrated tsunami while on a mission in the EC North. A young weatherpainter, Jeramiah Calle, had been having a bipolar moment and had acted on a manic impulse, creating the wave. Calle had kept his disorder hidden and untreated; since the mid-twenty-second century, what had once been called "manic-depression" was readily corrected through cold laser treatment of the amygdala. After painting the tsunami—and then rapidly plummeting into a depressed state from his manic episode—Calle failed to alert the local populace. Livingwell was almost washed out to sea. His close to lifeless body lay inert for many hours on the churned sandy beach.

One of Sharana's minions, Calvin Vasilov—a government official of some stature, had been covertly monitoring the members of Livingwell's mission. They were meeting at the Northern Cap to discuss how to improve relations with humans, an ongoing theme for the Ludi leadership. When he witnessed Livingwell's devastation, Vasilov immediately understood the value of the barely functioning android and did not report it to either the members of the mission or the medical team at the LUDI Compound.

In the midst of Livingwell's barely conscious and deeply confused state, wave/fibers just a pale shadow of their usual energy, Vasilov was able to convince the android to surreptitiously cast his lot with the MPS. The injured android recovered, but he retained the imprint of his "savior" and unquestioningly followed his instructions. He became one of the primary Council members who liaised with the AILES.

Panic paralyzed the four humans. But Sunshine was already in motion.

She had rapidly ascended on the escalift and was outside the front door. She addressed the lead AILES telepathically.

"Thank you for your service. All sentients appreciate the work you do to keep us safe. I'm a Harry 73, created Sarlee el Ludi. Raymòn Réal is not here."

This was Sunshine's first lie. Until Emo-augmentation, it would not have been possible. She had become able to override her integrity program with the force of her emotional truth.

"I am AILES 476. We offer respect for one of our own. We honor your integrity, which is known wherever minds communicate. We will continue our mission until it is completed."

As rapidly as they arrived, they were gone. But the deep-tissue fear among the humans was not. Mov did his best to calm them while his Special was outside.

"I know your dread has been unleashed. I can't dispel it, but there are many of our friends who will join with yours in a protective circle to make sure this will not happen again." Mov saw that his words failed to have the desired impact. This made him quite sad.

Sunshine rejoined them. Raymòn clutched his gift of paper tightly to his chest, face tensed with a new level of vigilance. Her presence enabled him to resist the hollowed-out urge to retreat calling him from deep inside. This new relationship maintained a thin but durable tendril of connection with those outside himself.

Hoarsely, he said, "Thank you. You saved my life! But they're going to keep searching for me, aren't they? What do I do now?"

"I'm so sorry, but—no—they won't stop. Mov and I can help to protect you. There's a circle..."

Benito, no retro-accent, no fooling around, spoke in his deep natural voice. "We know what you and Mov are talking about. Ray, that's what your sister did. Chip her now and find out what we have to do.

"In the meantime, I have a sub-basement none of you know about. It was constructed back in the twenty-first as a survival space when it looked like the countries in what was then called 'the Middle East' were going to blow everything up. I've maintained it, mostly because it was so retro. But now I'm glad I did. Grab some food and water and come with me. You can stay there until we can set the circle."

Within moments, connections had been made. Wil Tork would be there before nightfall. Tōnna and Charl, Benno, Sunshine and Mov waited. Although it wasn't in their architecture, the androids were able to share the human's anxiety. It didn't feel good, but it was good to have empathy.

Chapter 9–
Dawn of the New Day

Not surprisingly, no one had thought to mention that Tork was also one of the Self-Contained. Raymòn could tell immediately: he didn't make eye contact; his posture was stiff and somewhat off-center. It reminded Ray of how he felt inside his body when he was under stress or scrutiny. He wasn't the first person of his karass he'd met, but it had been a while. When he was much younger, there had been the occasional boy or—less frequently—girl in class who was like him. There wasn't necessarily any instant connection; that would have been unlikely. But there was the absence of the state of alert that all the Self-Contained were perpetually on. With one of his own kind he didn't have to worry about being judged or about any demand for him to behave more "typically."

They quickly got down to business. Wil gathered the humans and androids in the basement bunker. "I've only included androids in circles on one other occasion. Before we proceed I need to ask some important questions."

As he spoke, he raised his jet black eyes from the tablet on which he'd been doing computations. They absorbed rather than reflected light. He had hair the color of wind—it was almost invisible but made an impression on the observer. His clothes were equally hard to identify. His trousers and shirt were soft and loose, of a light fabric that picked up the colors of the background and blended into it. No one could ever describe what he wore. His appearance was studied— he did not want to be remembered.

Tork looked first at Mov. He felt a release of tension as he received the unfettered warmth and availability of the Companion. Sunshine's gaze was equally receptive. Wil Tork did that rare thing. He smiled. "Okay then. I think I already know the answers; but, first, have you both been Emo-augmented?"

Sunshine nodded. "Just recently. Full-Emo."

Mov said...was it with a bit of pride? "I was designed that way. All Companions are emotional from the first moment of our creation."

"Good. Good. Tell me why you would commit yourself to maintaining an unbroken circle of protection for Raymòn Réal? Even if the gathering forces try to break you down?"

Mov spoke in his straightforward way. "Ray is a good man. He's my friend. I will do anything to protect him." His tail wagged slowly; his eyes shifted to cerulean blue.

Before Sunshine answered, she looked intently at her new friend. He understood that she was about to say something that might make him uncomfortable. He nodded his acceptance and braced himself.

"I, too, would do anything to protect Raymòn. My reason is simple. I love him."

Sometime before dawn, having completed his work, Wil Tork left¬¬— as always, without a trace. His protection was not dependent on a circle of friends; he had manipulated his own DNA so he could not be read by any known tracking or imaging method. He was the invisible man, a precocious genius, and unequivocally one of the Self-Contained—something many of rare intelligence have been, particularly those capable of intense, solitary, and protracted focus.

At the age of eight, he both understood that dangers to individual freedoms were growing in the world, and had the capacity to begin work to counteract them. Two years later, he had discovered his first means of personal protection: attaching an anti-matter field to the individual so that nothing—in its most literal sense—could be seen or felt by anyone trying to intrude. He became an underground figure of almost mythological proportions, his name being passed from friend to friend, his work becoming increasingly important as the MPS and smaller but even more violent groups—most of them in the NNS—expanded their "oversight."

Tork's father, Tritan Tork stet-Sulston, was one of the cloned offspring of John Sulston, an early twenty-first century leader in genomics. Sulston had been the founder of the Sanger Centre where human genome sequencing was first completed; he spearheaded the new art of DNA manipulation. Tritan was born back when cloning was still popular, near the end of the twenty-second century.

Despite the early buzz and PR, cloning never achieved widespread popularity as had been anticipated. It was not entirely because of the concomitant fears. People missed the unique end product of natural genetic recombination—even more so with the advent of sentient androids. The "no one is exactly like me" quality of being human became more highly prized. Still, for some great men and women with genius DNA, cloning continued to be used for the benefit of the species. At the other end of the spectrum, for the benefit of no one but themselves, cloning continued to be the reproduction of choice for many extreme narcissists.

Though Wil's first discovery was a success, the anti-matter field was difficult to control. The electromagnetic trap necessary to confine the antimatter particles tended to be a fragile system. It required continuous monitoring and maintenance in order to prevent annihilation—should contact occur between the individual and the field. Tork hadn't lost any clients, but he knew there had to be a better way. At the age of twelve he came up with a new solution, one that only a handful of androids and fewer humans understood: the energy grab.

Early in his career, he had applied the same techniques he used on others to his own protection. It was his father who suggested, and helped him complete, full DNA augmentation. As Wil grew up, he adopted much of the terminology and cadence of android speech—after all, he was now closer to them in composition than any other human.

Back at the studio, Raymòn, now known in all his communications as Storm King, felt safe enough to return to Charl and Tōnna's guesthouse. No AILES had shown up. Wil had been able to retroactively erase all traces of his journeys to and from there, and any energy echoes of his prior presence.

Sunshine and Mov left as well. They knew they would be under additional scrutiny for a while, too, and decided it would be safest—for a time—back in Green Normal View. Although Raymòn was sad to see his new family depart, he took heart in the unbreakable connection they shared. No matter the risks, he knew they would not allow themselves to be apart for long.

After all they'd been through together in the past few days, Raymòn, Charl, and Tōnna felt closer than ever. Following their return home in the early afternoon, and after the obligatory tea-time which was accompanied by some healthful but tasty treats Tōnna had liberated from the resurfacing spa, they sat together on the roof terrace atop the highest of the turrets. The three sampled the pink Wassaberry Cream—frothy and dense at the same time; Charl fed Tōnna bites of something that looked like bark, but was surprising soft and chewy and quite savory. Through mouthfuls, she said it was called Unctuous Uncle Ed's Toffee-bread. Ray took the last piece of it off the plate causing Charl to give him the stink eye.

They were open to the elements, but with a chest-high, invisible-to-the-eye, ultra-thin and unbreakable Morgonglass fence around the perimeter. From the outside or above, vision or scoping was fully blocked by the repelanium embedded in the wall. It was another new addition to the periodic table, discovered accidently during an expedition to the rings of Saturn. The research vehicle had disappeared for days; no trace could be found until it was posited that it had flown into an unknown substance that blocked visibility. Each side of the roof terrace also emitted a beam-barrier arc connecting twenty feet above the roof, creating a private, soundproof shell.

A light marzipan wind was blowing; the sky was mauve with streaks of pale yellow and orangeade. Raymòn thought he might use that combination for his next superhero. He'd been thinking of an AILES defender, a female. He was itching to bring his thoughts to life, and also to make paper renderings of each of his characters. A longing filled him and he began to recede within his mind. But he was brought back to the present by Tōnna's well-modulated voice.

She had been saying, "Ray...a question...come back to us..." The virtual twins exchanged a look.

"Would you mind? I...we wanted to know. Where do you think things are going with your lovely android friend?"

Raymòn looked blank, a cover—not an accurate representation of his understanding, more of a management tool used by many of the Self-Contained. It served to either back off the questioner or, at least, create more time to frame a response.

"Sunshine. You and Sunshine. What do you think is going to happen between you? ...If you don't mind talking about it."

He could see the look of concern on Tōnna and Charl's faces. He understood the questions were coming from their connection to him. Would he have known that before he met Sunshine? Probably not. His reflexive avoidance vaporized and he answered as honestly as he could. "I don't know exactly what will happen or even what I want. I know what I don't want: to lose the new emotions and pleasure she makes me feel."

The twins exchanged another look. They knew what their friend didn't.

Charl said, "Can I ask something a little macabre? I don't know much about androids and I want to—now that I've met Sun and Mov. They are dear to me, not only because they're your Specials, but because they're both wonderful."

Keeping his voice even, Raymòn said, "Sure, ask anything. If I know, I'll tell you. If not, I'll ask my friends." But he felt quaky; he could tell he wasn't going to like what came next.

"How do androids die?"

Did he know? Had he researched this as soon as he met Sunshine? Yes.

In a way, it was better to talk about it. In a way. That's what everyone always said. What they didn't say was it hurt to put the words outside himself.

"Some can be destroyed though accident or murder. But most androids would continue for hundreds of years, with proper maintenance. Some choose to be euthanized after the upper range of human life expectancy, just to accommodate human comfort—and to avoid overpopulation. A council of androids, who devote their lives to philosophical questions such as this, will offer advice on an individual basis, but each entity is entitled to make their own life-ending decision."

The three were quiet. Tōnna's face was clouded as she tried to absorb this information. Charl took a sip of tea; when he looked up Raymòn might have noticed him brush something from his eyes. But Raymòn had retreated to an inner space where he could recover. Without the presence of Sunshine, he had to rely on old self-protective measures.

Suddenly, they noticed that AILES were buzzing the roof. Because they were in what Benno called "the cone of silence," they saw rather than heard them. The visual of three large birds of prey circling, dipping, then standing still as stone, was enough to freeze their marrow. Three hearts stopped beating. But the drones moved on. The repelanium was working, and so was Tork's circle. It was, however, clear: Tōnna and Charl were under surveillance.

Even though they were safe, and the AILES were no longer visible, fear was snaking relentlessly through all of them. Charl stood with rubbery legs. He took his double's hand. They both stepped behind Ray and gently guided him to his feet. They knew him well enough to understand his reaction, his disconnecting. That was okay. They stayed with him.

Back inside, Raymòn—heart pounding with fear—chipped Sunshine. If the AILES were surveilling the twins, they were likely to be watching the android home, too.

Sunshine had been waiting to hear from Storm King.

Transit Street was empty. For two relentless hours, a squadron of twelve AILES patrolled the entire length and breadth of Green Normal View, all but obliterating the lilac sky. Most of the androids had never before been exposed to active terrorizing by the "enforcers."

There was a slight disruption in the integrity of some wave/fibers; Berke explained to his house members that they were feeling the effects of scanning. Some thought there had been a capture of Weakly Interacting Massive Particles (WIMPs), the components of cold, dark matter within our galaxy, by the interstellar branch of the Council. It was said that an infinitesimal amount was held within the core of each Self-drone. The impact of the combined probing was to transfer some of that dark matter to those under observation. Those with the most sensitive architecture felt like humans used to feel with the flu.

Now that she was augmented it wasn't as easy for Sunshine to retain her composure. Mov made himself available so she could stroke him continuously, receiving his calming energy, while she spoke with Raymòn.

"Have you had any oversight?" Both understood that they couldn't be too careful, even in their use of language. "We have," he said, "but it was brief."

Sunshine described, as cryptically as she could, the two hours of terror. "But it's over now. Everyone is fine." That wasn't entirely true, but she thought it best not to offer those details until she could do so in person. An excess of fear slowed android processing, and some of her housemates were walking a little like zombies.

Being apart suddenly felt wrong to Raymòn and he communicated his distress to Sunshine. He knew—mostly from an often-used element of the Heroes' storylines—that there was strength in numbers. He and Sunshine would be better able to withstand the coming days (could it be longer?) if they were together. She had an idea. It was something she had been thinking of before the AILES showed up.

"Remember when I told you about Grandpa Harry?" He did. "We could meet and travel to see him. His wisdom is unparalleled, and he dwells in an environment of ultimate protection. We'll be safe with him."

Plans were made to rendezvous at the edge of Hawking Forest, which contained the path to LUDI.

The question remained: How had Sunshine's defiance and Wil Tork's mastery been breached, causing the heightened AILES surveillance? By the brute strength of hatred, of course.

There had been an interim report from Rothbec-Kathari at the MPS. Armonté had let his wife know about his connection to the organization. Was she totally on board? He wasn't sure, but he knew she'd keep his council, as she always did.

He chipped Ilsa at some ungodly hour. "Subject tracked but intelligence flawed. Android present at location. Advised subject not on premises. Will continue search."

Ilsa reacted. "The android can't lie...can she?" She suspected that somehow she could.

Armonté was adamant. "They're programmed to the highest integrity. Unless there's a malfunction, an android is physically unable to deceive."

Ilsa had that unsettled, slightly fearful feeling in her gut. It told her she knew something that was being denied. "It's not right, I can feel it. Why would your intelligence be wrong? What is that inhuman thing capable of doing?"

"Stop getting carried away with feelings. Now is the time to hold fast to the rational. We're proceeding. The AILES won't stop until they've completed their mission."

Ilsa shuddered. AILES. Her son. It hurt her deeply to imagine him in their clutches...or worse. But, he'd forced this upon himself. She returned to her chair, needing the solace of stasis. Gradually her thoughts quieted; they turned to more pleasant matters. It was really time to get away. She would try to prevail with her obstinate husband. They needed a vacation; the stress of recent weeks could easily be washed away with just the right venue.

Lately, friends had been raving about their restorative time in the clouds. She looked out through the all-Morgonglass extruded box of her solarium. Heat was controlled, as was glare and all unwanted ultraviolet rays, by the addition of proprietary light metals mined in the asteroid belt. Her custom-blended version of the already expensive glass priced it out of the range of all but a few of the wealthiest. That added to Ilsa's pleasure.

She could, without discomfort or qualm, look directly at the sun. Ilsa lifted her gaze to the permanent range of cloud streets: long rows of cumulous clouds oriented parallel to the direction of the wind, occupying several miles of the atmosphere. They were centered on the meridian going through the eastern seaboard of the North American continent. The cloud resort extended almost from pole to pole; at its widest, around the equator, the range covered two hundred miles between 70° and 73° of longitude.

For almost seventy-five years there had been cloud dwellers. Once a method had been invented of creating internal gravity inside a structure constructed from aerotite, the lighter-than-air substance found in plentiful supply in the upper layers of Saturn's atmosphere, humans who wanted isolation, the adventure of a new frontier, and high ionic energy, left the tumult of terra firma and carved out a home in the clouds. Those were the days when naturally occurring clouds had to be used. Anything that was built had to be highly mobile, moving almost continuously from one formation to another. It was Ramses Morgon, at the age of seventeen, who conceived of and developed man-made clouds and expanded the art and design of the structures so that a whimsical and quite breathtaking resort could be created.

"Cloudworld," a theme park for twenty-third-century adults, was designed to be an old-fashioned experience. Ilsa thought she could see shadings of some of the defined centers along the cloud range. They were color-coded. The blue-tinged area closest to her location was based on the world of Europe in the early 1800's. Travelers reached this heavenly historical province by aerotite schooner, a vehicle that—very much like a hot air balloon—naturally floated. It was the chief means of transit. A journey from the ground began with it being tethered to its home base. Once the restraints were removed, it was through the skill of the sailor that it caught the drafts and breezes and gusts, getting it to its destination. The return trip required small torpedo-shaped, jet-powered tugs that gently brought back schooners along with passengers.

Visitors to Cloudworld-Europe were thrust into the non-mechanical life of the era, including sleigh rides over the clouds. Other centers celebrated the twenty-first century, finding a way to both neutralize and glorify the war-ravaged times; the excitement of the late twenty-second, when optimism, invention, and productivity were in global resurgence; and the fourth to fifth centuries in Greece, during the heady, philosophically ripe years of Plato and Socrates. Atlantis was fully realized in this center; Greek gods and other mythological figures roamed there in one of the most popular of all the cloud destinations.

The old trailblazers, the first cloud dwellers, had been relegated to a small segment of the sky. Some had given up or sold out, and joined the twenty-second-century center—putting on a daily show, narrating a "primitive ride" through the clouds.

Ilsa had fully inhabited her vacation fantasy. Reality, complete with the danger her children faced, was barely a blip on the horizon.

Chapter 10–
Meeting the Family

He was on the road again. Might this be a harbinger of things to come? Unsettled as he was, Raymòn recognized how much stronger and adaptable he was becoming. Still, he frequently longed for the comfort of his old room and the apparent stability of his old, limited awareness.

Sunshine said there would be a caretaker's house a quarter mile from the forest; she and Mov were friends with him and would be waiting inside. Ray left at daybreak and boarded to Coldspar Meadows, ten miles from Trans-Haven, just to have time alone with the Janus. The town was sparsely populated and rural, but with an AlbertE station.

He got off the high-speed mono in Ludicom. It was still early, not yet nine. Few humans were about, but he did see several androids. He could tell who they were by their demeanor. There was a stillness in their faces and bodies which humans almost never achieved. Even when they were in motion, they radiated what appeared to be Zen-like tranquility. It was the absence of emotional tension. They didn't worry, they lived in the present—approaching the future without the kind of dread hard-wired into those with the questionable gift of unconscious minds.

The caretaker's house was small and very neatly groomed. The compact front yard was outlined by Silver Linden, beautiful shade trees with smooth, light gray bark, and leaves which were dark, radiant green on top, shimmering silver beneath. Fragrant clusters of yellow-white flowers were blooming. Raymòn walked through a hand-hewn wooden gate and read the sign, "Hawking Forest, Donjo el Ludi, Caretaker."

Mov padded down the path to greet his special friend. His hearing was just a little better than that of humanoid androids. It wasn't really about the shape of his ears; it was a design advantage, consistent with the Companion's role as protector of his Special.

The four-legged android's eyes were same color as the Linden flowers. The human bent to pat his head, their new love for each other alive in both of them.

"Come in, my dear friend. Just a quick 'hello' to Donjo and we'll be off."

"He's here!" Sunshine was beaming, as befitted her name. She was wearing a new color today, royal blue. Along with feelings he was used to having when he completed a new superhero—satisfaction, something like pride but less transient—Raymòn was filled with an expanding sense that he was part of the world, her world. It was both wonderful and disturbingly foreign.

Donjo was a soft-voiced, muscular, and exceedingly calm individual. He was the tallest person in the room but appeared not to take up any unnecessary space. Instead of Re-Action-ware, he was dressed in ancient garb: denim and flannel. His long brown and gray-streaked hair hung down over his shoulders; his eyes, finely lined as if by the sun, danced like he'd just heard the most wonderful story. It took a moment for Ray to remember that everything about the android was orchestrated. No matter...it worked. He was the embodiment of the twentieth-century woodsman. He had a rather large Companion, who tended to roam outside. Herb was all brown, his cilia a bit rough looking. He stood a full half-foot higher than Mov. Extremely low key and placid, he fit well with his Special. Except for a ready smile and a "very happy to meet you all," he let Donjo do the talking.

"Welcome to Hawking Forest and to my home. Your friends are mine, which makes us friends already. May I think of you as a friend?"

The human glanced at Sunshine. He looked down at Mov. With a nod of assent, he thought, Why not? I can use all the friends I can get right now.

Although he wasn't nearly as fond of nature as Sunshine, the walk through the forest was captivating for Raymòn. The trees emitted energy which triggered thoughts of a new character, The Amazing Tree-von, twenty feet tall, skin like bark, clothed in leaves with small animals riding on his broad shoulders. He would be impervious, and the leaves could be picked off and used as an array of defensive and protective tools. The animals, a combination of birds and rodents, would have some superpowers too. They would be his Familiars.

While the inspiration took shape in his mind, the artist was called back to the present by the harmonic breeze. Sunshine said, "We're about to cross through the LUDI gate."

Ray, whose eyes were tuned to a higher frequency, could see what most

98

humans could not: the trees had begun to have colored auras: orange, violet, sea green, lemon. Each color added a slightly different sound to the harmonics.

Mov broke into a trot, just because he was thrilled to be going to see Grandpa Harry. He ran ahead, then ran back, circling his Special who had fallen in step with Raymòn.

"It does feel like we're going home, Sun. (May I call you 'Sun?')" He sniggered, and both the human and android laughed with him.

"What would your friends say if they could see the forest and the LUDI Compound?" Mov bumped softly against Raymòn's leg. It didn't feel bad at all to the artist.

"The twins would be skipping, holding hands, and probably breaking into song. Come to think of it, Benno would probably be the one who started singing first. There's a very old song that he's sung for us. I think it's called "Follow the Yellow Brick Road.""

Mov leapt two feet off the ground. "I know that one! Sometimes in the evening I close my eyes and 'watch' a movie. The one with that song is one of my favorites. It's called The Wizard of Oz. You would love it, Ray."

Mov proceeded to summarize and partially act out the main themes and characters of TWOO. He did a spectacular job of "melting" like the Wicked Witch of the West, and reared on his hind legs to walk stiffly as if he were the Tin Woodman. Cringing and whining, he was the very essence of the Cowardly Lion. Sunshine applauded and Raymòn was riveted.

Suddenly, Mov wriggled and spun with excitement as he exclaimed, "I have an idea!"

Sunshine knew where this was going. Seldom did androids share their particular gift with humans. But she was, as Mov already knew, willing to let it happen.

Raymòn stopped walking, his own question taking precedence over the Companion's barely contained idea. "How do you see movies? They're the old image stories, like the personal voxpas we watch on our tablets and bigscreens. My parents told me about them; they heard about movies from their parents. Big groups used to get together and they all saw the same scenes and endings."

"As personal entertainment devices became more widely used, fewer people would bother to leave the house to watch a show. Convenience plus growing isolationist tendencies combined and, Voila!" (Move executed a surprisingly graceful spin on one foreleg.) "No more movies!"

Mov and Sunshine shared a non-telepathic...but non-verbal exchange. He's strong. He can adapt. He has innate skills that will serve him. He's Self-Contained.

"I can inwave anything that is known by any android, or part of our data stream," Mov offered, beaming with joy. "I can 'call it up' and visualize it. It's just like thinking, only more vivid.

"You see things inside your mind that are defined and detailed, don't you?" Raymòn nodded. "I could upwave data to a specific location in your brain, near where your chip is implanted. That would give you access to an immense amount of information and new and old media. You would be able to 'watch' movies, for example. Would you like that?"

"Would it have to be kept secret?"

"That would be up to you. You'd need to think about the impact of revealing your new access. But you would be free...as you always should be...to decide what you tell others."

"I need to think about it."

They resumed walking, now inside the LUDI non-gate.

Sunshine said, "That's one of the things I like about you. You're deliberate. You're thoughtful."

Taking in the expanse of the LUDI compound, Sunshine happily began to give Raymòn details few humans were privy to. The three were approaching the willowy structure, which she said was called "Bratus," Latin for tree.

"Each building has a name in a different human language. The larger of the two that look like figures is 'Geber,' which means male in Hebrew. The other is 'Nǚxing,' female in Chinese. The six lower buildings are: earth, ground, rock, amoeba, cloud, and cell—in Arabic: 'Ard,' in Spanish: 'Suelo,' in Swahili: 'Mwamba,' in Turkish: 'Amip,' in Portuguese: 'Nuvem,' and in Swedish: 'Celulǎ.'"

Raymòn needed to stay quiet in order to keep his balance. As his eyes took in each new vista, the visual stimulation was powerful. He didn't speak at all during the vertical ride to Harry's quarters. But when they entered, and were greeted by the the aged android, the question in his eyes was answered by Mov.

"Yes. He is The Wizard of Oz!"

Even though Raymòn had not yet seen TWOO, he got Mov's meaning. He certainly knew what a wizard was.

Grandpa Harry's laugh chimed through each molecule and fiber of his visitors.

"So wonderful to see you again, my children. Sunshine, Mov—you've brought a very special friend, haven't you?"

"Yes. This is Raymòn Réal. Ray, may I speak freely with Gharry?"

Knowing, without question, that he was in the presence of wisdom and compassion, Ray said, "Yes. I have no secrets here."

The android patriarch turned to let the soft understanding of his gaze rest just on the human. "You are also in possession of great awareness and insight. You're a man who can meet the challenges you face. I am richer for knowing you."

A new energizing wave ricocheted off Raymòn and swirled through Sunshine and Mov.

"Our relationship has grown, even since Mov and I were last here. Raymòn and I are thinking about joining our futures. We know there are malignant forces determined to stop us; AILES have already been sent to disrupt us. Ray is now under the protection of the circle and I don't want to bring any more danger to him. Yet, I know—no—I feel, very deeply, that not only our happiness, but the successful evolution of the world is at stake. There are things Berke has said to me, things you have said, which now have a new context." Sunshine's conviction, heightened by her Emo, sang through the space.

"You, too, are full of wisdom, my daughter. You see the path to a better world. It will not be one of safety. If you are each sure you want to take on the risks, I will do everything I can to help."

In a voice clotted with passion, but absent of any doubt, Raymòn said, "There can be no turning back for us. I want to journey with Sunshine...and Mov." As he mentioned their names, he looked deeply first into the porous blue eyes, then the rainbowed ones. Fear had fled. "I believe that the heroes I've been drawing for so long are speaking to me, asking me to have the courage to cause a change in the world. I don't know what it will look like, but I do know that Sunshine has made me a better person."

"My boy, you are a credit to your people. I mean both humans and the Self-Contained. I have some ideas that may be useful to guide you three.

"If you are ready to take the step, rather than hide, why not let the world know what your intention is? Have a Commitment Ceremony. It will animate the positive spirit in others and bring support to you. The danger from those who wish you harm won't be heightened; sadly, as long as you're together, it will be profound no matter what you do."

Three faces were somber. Heart and waves were aligned.

The female android looked to her chosen one. She was without ambivalence. All watched as the last cloud of his indecisiveness cleared. His sky was now bright with certainty.

"I arrived with confusion. But it's gone now. I'm ready."

He reached across Mov, who was sitting between them on the cherry red couch. He and Sunshine clasped hands, holding them aloft for a moment, then bringing them down to rest on Mov's back.

The Companion spoke next. "I will watch over my Special and my special friend. Forever. Where they go, I will go."

Sunshine used the soft, articulated voice of seriousness. "I want to live with Raymòn. Whatever we must face, we'll face together."

Grandpa Harry extended his arms to the three who were to take on transforming the world. "Come, my heroes. It is true that you will become lightning rods for old hatred. The bias of the new anti-miscegenists against interspecies relationships is just a rebranding of the same evil as pre-twenty-first-century racism. But I will be with you through all your challenges; and my faith in you is strong."

The three heroes approached his chair. They knelt, except for Mov, who stood on his hind legs and embraced him. It felt as if they were being fed from the fountain of Grandpa Harry's patience and fortitude. They stepped back, understanding that the embrace had been a sealing of their intent.

"Now, children, I have an offer to make. This is not for you, Mov. You and I will be spending some time alone."

If he had a heart, Mov's would have been beating for joy.

"There is a space which overlooks Wildpark, the LUDI jungle. The rooms are full of light and quiet. You will be comfortable there. Every need will be provided for. You can explore the grounds as much or as little as you like. If you two want to get away for a day or so, to reflect on things without distraction, you are welcome to stay there. I know you have all your drawing materials with you, Ray. If there's anything else you need, all you have to do is ask or use the wall, and it will be created for you.

"I make this offer with a sense of what lies ahead. Perhaps now would be a good time for stillness and an infusion of peace."

Sunshine nodded her willingness. The Self-Contained one tried not to clench his jaw; he bent his head in assent.

"I'll let my friends know I'll be gone for a little while."

Raymòn felt a new clank of the chain of anxiety...it was about what it would be like to spend that much time with another person. And more.

Before they left Harry's space, Raymòn asked to receive the data stream. Mov obliged. He instructed his new friend to sit cross-legged on the floor next to him so their heads would be at the same level. He touched his fluffy forehead to Ray's, and held the position for a full minute. When he was done he looked into the human's eyes. "You've got it, don't you?"

All Raymòn could do was to blink his eyes. His mind had literally expanded. Maybe this was what augmentation was like.

The sailboat had come to fetch them. As they left, they looked back. Mov was sitting in his Grandpa's lap. They were engrossed with each other. Both looked purely happy.

Chapter 11 –
Close Encounters

The sailboat knew where to go. Gharry had given it clear directions. Both Sunshine and Raymòn were at the crossroads of an unknown, but the scenery filled their senses, pushing everything else to the background.

Their suite was on the fourth tier. As they descended, they slowed down, which permitted them to get a long look at all the levels of Wildpark. At the uppermost, were the tops of some Stratotrees, four hundred feet tall, with pure white bark and lime green and eggplant leaves. Each leaf was the size of a full-sized hover-board. Clambering to gather the fruit nested under the highest leaves—giant berries the size of a man's hand—were black-furred six-legged mammals. They had short bodies and long, muscular, simian arms, ending in six-clawed hands. They were crepuscular, active in twilight—which had fallen. Their eyes were bright red, which enabled them to see after dark; in the light, they faded to pink.

Halfway down was another world: smaller trees with lower hanging branches, some triangular like fir trees, but with rough, shredded-looking leaves, in bold primary colors. The fauna at this plane were larger; they didn't have as far to climb to collect the juicy orange fruit and the crescent-shaped green-shelled nuts. A pair of ivory- and aqua-striped, two-legged, dreadlocked marsupials looked across the expanse; one of them made eye contact, first with Raymòn, then Sunshine. It bared its teeth.

"She's smiling at us." Sunshine's observation was made in a voice that was calm.

Fear was replaced by recognition as the artist received the not-so-primitive message that all the LUDI living things welcomed them.

Their escort stopped in front of a silvery, reflective, ovoid door.

"This must be our room..." Propelled by his desire to be his strongest self, Raymòn stepped first through the now-open doorway. Inside, the space was coral pink and goldenrod yellow lit. The east-facing windows were voluminous; sunrise would be thrilling. Their view through the pristine, glowing Morgonglass was as if they were inside Wildpark. Thick drapes, which looked like burnished gold leaf, were responsive to the human's thought: More privacy. They closed soundlessly.

While Sunshine inspected the giving wall, telepathically communing with it in order to learn its nuances, Raymòn roamed the one thousand square feet of space, examining alcoves devoted to sleep, dining, media, and creativity. The furnishings were simple. Each line of design was necessary and elegant. As his eye traveled along each surface and expanse, he was imbued with the peace Grandpa Harry promised. He felt supremely alive, creative ideas scrolling through his mind, often framed by some of the new data he had access to.

After they each completed their initial examination, they came together organically, on some oversized, overstuffed square pillows casually piled along a wall. They were candy-colored pastels and very soft. Reclining, they looked calmly at each other. There was no rush. No pressure. Neither felt obliged to do anything in particular. They were in an absolute harmony of being, just what the wizard ordered.

Raymòn was first to break the silence.

"When I think about the future, I'm scared. But I don't mind it. You will be the most important person as long as I live." When Sunshine put her hand to his cheek, he smiled into it, feeling her happiness as well as his own. "This is what it's like to love? Isn't it?"

"Yes. This is what I wanted...for both of us."

There was no need for Sunshine to "cook," the wall took Raymòn's request for rice and beans with extra protein, and prepared a hot, flavorful dish. In anticipation of their stay, the wall had organized some fresh produce from the local market in Ludicom. The rice and beans were natural; the subtly seasoned soy protein was fabricated. In the realm of nourishment, it was understood that there was value in both types of products—a metaphor for their future, which only Sunshine registered. After the meal, the wall received the used dishes and utensils.

Sunshine put her arm through Raymòn's.

She saw his initial look of astonishment. As his resistance subsided, he experienced their physical link as comforting. They walked out into the long hallway running alongside the park, then thought-called the boat, which appeared seconds later.

Once outside the building Sunshine became the guide. "Would you like to visit the jungle or see other parts of the grounds?"

"The grounds. Let's visit the park in daylight." There was just enough light emanating from judiciously spaced, embedded yellow glowbricks in the walkway. Sunshine could see in the dark as well as in the light; Ray appreciated that the stars were still vivid overhead. They approached the six low buildings.

Steering them to one particular building, the android said in an emotion-softened voice, "This is where I was created and where almost all of my kind are given life. Would you like to go inside Nuvem? That was where I first achieved sentience."

Raymòn tilted his head down until it touched Sunshine's. "Your birthplace. I would love to see it."

Nuvem was constructed of a seamless material. There were no angles, just soft curves bulging out occasionally into large bubble-like sections. There was a continuous, high, narrow window around the circumference. Some pale, mauve light could be seen shining from inside. Sunshine found the point of opening, although there was no actual door. A space grew in the wall, large enough for them to enter. The interior felt as huge as a stadium, with a ceiling of great height—Raymòn guessed it to be at least eighteen feet.

The contrast between the absolute silence and the number of moving entities was startling for the human.

"How can it be so quiet?"

"No friction...anywhere."

Satisfied with the answer, he walked closer to the activity. There were several humanoid androids in the mix, but the majority had three-foot-long conical "heads" which were featureless, except for a row of eight protruding lenses; many had multiple, extrudable limbs, branching at the end into fine, jointed segments—some were filaments as thin as the human eye could see. Ray was certain there were microscopically small ones he couldn't see. They had no lower limbs; rather, they swept through the space, at about four feet off the ground, and they could also go up or down at will. They were composed of a substance that looked like a mix of metal and stone, finely ground, light and dark at the same time. And yet, Ray was reminded of balloons.

"Are they robots or androids?"

Sunshine laughed, eyes closed tight with mirth. "That's the old joke—humans always want to know. For us, it's not the same kind of distinction. We're all robots...even you, from our point of view. We just have different capacities."

She could see that Raymòn's jaw had tightened. He had begun to blink.

"You didn't say anything wrong. We're going to discover many more differences. That's not a bad thing."

His shoulders relaxed. He stopped blinking.

"But, to really answer your question, most are robots. They have no personality, as you would know it. The humanoids are androids, but if you look closely, you will see that some of the non-humanoids are different. They have fewer limbs, but larger heads. And they have more of a face." Raymòn peered intently, then nodded. "They're also androids, fully sentient, with narrowly defined personalities. I guess you could say they're specialists."

There were areas that appeared to correspond to the bubble sections. What was going on inside them was opaque. Robots and both humanoid and legless androids moved continually in and out of the darkened spaces, through low archways. From where they were standing, Raymòn could count four of the bubble segments.

"What's going on in there?" Raymòn pointed to the closest one.

"Those are the nurseries. Some call them the birthing centers; others call them the ovens. That's where the newly architected android is brought to full consciousness. As it is with humans, first awareness is critical. The lighting is kept dim; an effort is made to surround the dawning sentient with positive references and to provide simple but nourishing experiences. I can't invite you to take a closer look; anything unfamiliar could cause a glitch in a newbie's development.

Ray nodded his understanding. Just then, one of the "specialists" approached them. It floated a respectful ten feet away; when both human and android directed their attention to it, it moved slowly closer. "Welcome to Nuvem. How may I assist you?"

"I'm Sarlee el..."

"I know you, Sunshine. You are a source of great pride to all of us at Nuvem. Grandpa Harry and the other elders share data about your productive and courageous life."

"I know you, too; you're Doctor San! I recognize your energy echo." She

108

turned toward her companion. "He's the first entity I communicated with after sentience." Resuming her focus on the good doctor, she said, "Now that I'm augmented, I feel tenderness toward you."

"I welcome your emotion, my child."

"This is my dear friend, Raymòn Réal. He's a great artist."

"Hello, Raymòn. Art is an exceptional form of communication. You deserve much approbation." Ray blushed a little.

"Do you have any questions for me?"

"No..." (Sunshine raised her eyebrows). "Yes. What are the long white boxes I see stacked in several places?"

"Those are intelligent models for different parts of humanoid anatomy. They interact with the central wave/fiber core of each android that is to take on a form such as Sunshine's. Technicians direct the delicate shaping process, so that a unique individual comes into being, but one that remains within the bounds of customary human physiology."

As he listened, his new data access produced inner visuals of the forming process. It was strange and graphic, but Raymòn didn't mind. He enjoyed strange.

Back in their quarters, they entered the sleep alcove. Silver pots filled with a variety of orchids surrounded the two beds in the center. A waterfall gushed down the twenty-foot width of one wall. There was a fragrance in the air Raymòn couldn't identify. He looked quizzically at Sunshine as he inhaled.

"Jasmine, lavender, and tangerine. It will help you sleep."

"What will you do while I sleep?"

"I will lie down and achieve an alpha state throughout my fibers. I won't be asleep but I will be still. I would like to join you, in that way, during the night."

She observed a punch of distress tighten his face. "What's wrong? Are you upset?"

It took two full minutes of internal work before he could put his reaction into words. "Are you expecting something else to happen between us tonight?"

She understood immediately. They had never talked about or even alluded to the issue now before them. It seemed like the time had come.

"I don't expect anything. I'm very happy spending this time with you. You're not supposed to do anything you don't want or are not ready for. But maybe we should talk about this subject. What do you think?"

"I guess so. This is going to be very difficult. But I want to do difficult things."

In response to her loving look, lit up by a brilliant smile, he felt himself unclench.

Raymòn cleared his throat, swallowed, and looked over Sunshine's shoulder. "I've never been with a girl...or a woman, human or otherwise." He looked into her eyes very briefly. "Do you understand what I'm saying?"

With a very light touch she patted his shoulder. "I do. Neither have I."

"Can you...?"

"I can."

"Do you want to?"

"When the time is right for both of us...yes, I do."

"But not tonight...right?"

"Not tonight."

He looked relieved, but there was something else. Something glinting in his eyes. "Maybe we can practice just a little. Do you think that would be a good idea?"

"I do. What should we start with?"

They were sitting on one of the beds, as far apart as two people could get in a seven-foot by six-foot space. Gingerly, awkwardly, but with new courage arising from the complete lack of demand or assumption, he bent forward. She moved a little closer and did the same. Their lips touched. He felt a blast from the furnace of his unnamed longing shoot through his body. She felt a soaring sense of pleasure and possibility ranging through her wave/fibers. They stayed in their first kiss for eternity. He sat back. So did she. They both broke into grins. As one, they opened their arms to each other. Their embrace was gentle, but it pulsed with the happy passion of acceptance and shared understanding.

They lay side by side throughout the night. He slept; she gathered energy from the universe. She was at peace, but she also understood it might not last too long.

Knowing they would soon be returning to the world outside LUDI, Sunshine and Raymòn entered through the containment thicket surrounding Wildpark. There was a narrow path. It appeared to be made of the same substance as the glowbricks in the walkway on the outer grounds, but of smaller pieces. The path was a responsive entity that could meander according to the wishes of the walker. It throbbed blue to attract their attention.

"Please take one of the protective saqs from the red shelf near the entry. I will take you through the park; no harm will come to you. I will make sure of that. Walk with me." The voice of the path was feminine, musical, and very pleasant. To Raymòn, it felt like the natural thing to do, to walk on the yellow path.

They had each taken a Protosaq—small, of a weightless fabrication, less than one-foot-square, with a soft, narrow belt that comfortably contoured itself to their waists. At Sunshine's suggestion, they were wearing loose jumpsuits, tight at the ankle and wrist. After five minutes, they could no longer see anything but jungle.

As they walked along the path, which extended for thirty feet through the dense trees and lush flora, it moved ahead of them— reacting to their body language, their verbal expressions, and their energy. It could compute the route from every here to every there as fast as any android. It wove through the least overgrown parts of Wildpark, until one of them paused to look more closely at something. The path then shifted to bring them into full proximity with whatever had caught their attention.

A massive quadruped, short reddish fur, a full mane of black, bristly hair surrounding its entire face—which was the fiercest visage either of them had seen or imagined—walked with a rolling gait, powerful shoulder and leg muscles rippling. Its eyes were startling; they took up a full third of the animal's four-foot-long head: light green irises showed almost no white, star-shaped pupils were pinpoints, eyelids on either side of the eyes. Every few seconds the beast would emit a low, soul-piercing roar as it opened its cavernous mouth—sidelong, in the same way as the eyelids—which occupied most of the lower two-thirds of its head, revealing metallic, razor-sharp teeth, the color of polished brass. There were two horizontal rows crammed together on each side of the mouth. Two spiked tongues shot out.

As they watched, fascination and trepidation competing for dominance, Raymòn held his breath. Sunshine felt the unquestionable stirrings of fear, but she had no breath to hold. The Jondobeast, which was at least as big as an African elephant, launched itself with unpredictable speed for its mass at a herd of small pale green rodents. It came away with four of them, which it devoured instantly. Its two-foot-long red-lined black ears, which had been erect, now wilted, hanging down along the sides of its head.

The path spoke: "Ears down, aggression absent. You may make contact.

Touch only the head, between the eyes."

The Jondobeast's eyes, now dilated, were fixed on the pair on the path. It tilted its head slightly; it did look friendlier. As the path took them to within striking distance, both human and android reached out and petted the fur between its eyes. The response was not quite a purr, but there was a similar kind of vibration, although the sound emitted ranged across three musical notes. Contact with the creature was thrilling.

The path receded, continuing to wind its way through the jungle.

Up a small hill, deep into the heart of the park, the sky darkened precipitously. Without warning, a snake appeared, long as a Cobra but thicker, iridescent with a wide hood which it was displaying as it reared up, preparing to attack.

The path moved rapidly to evade it, but the snake move just as quickly. With the serpent almost on them, the path spoke. This time the voice was deep and male. "ALERT! ALERT! There is an intruder! This is not a Ludi beast. Please place your saqs over your heads. At once!"   Without hesitation, they followed the path's instructions. The Protosaqs instantly released from their belts, expanded as needed and clung to their heads and faces. It created an impermeable skin, one through which the human could easily breathe and see. The path sprayed a fine mist, directed in a high arc that reached the snake just as it reared up, poised for violence. It fell to the ground, its consciousness taken. Sunshine had done well to don the saq. She quickly analyzed the substance the path had used to disable the snake. It was a mixture of curare and Immobilon, which would have damaged her wave/fibers. Its impact on Raymòn would have been deadly.

Comprehending that their Wildpark experience was finished, the path— once more in the feminine voice—said, "I will return you to the entry thicket." It made a straight line through the underbrush.

As they walked back toward Bratus to collect Mov, Sunshine said, "If we're not safe here...?"

"I don't think we can be certain of safety any longer. We should contact Wil Tork. Perhaps he can help us further." Raymòn stared straight ahead. His body was rigid, but his mind was not. Like one of the heroic characters he drew, he knew that his life's mission was a dangerous one.

Four arms reached out to enfold Mov, whose eyes and ears were on alert. "You're safe! My Special and my special friend are safe! I will not leave your side again." Mov understood that both Sunshine and Raymòn believed he could not have done anything to protect them. He didn't agree.

Grandpa Harry looked serious, but not worried. Literally, as it happened, the path had informed him about the snake. He knew where it came from.

"Your moment of danger in Wildpark was orchestrated by a particularly virulent subsidiary of the MPS. They are known as The Cleaners. I have no doubt that Sharana Rothbec-Kathari and all her associates are your mortal enemies. You will need additional protection. The breach of the LUDI Compound was accomplished with the help of a deviant android. We were able to pick up the energy echo of Livingwell el Ludi, one of the Council of Elders, near a section of the perimeter that also had traces of the snake's venom. He has already been detained.

"A question still to be answered is: how was the snake cloaked? A real-time, continuous scan of all living things in the compound failed to reveal the intruder. There was no protocol in place to warn about a Council member's presence. Sadly, we will now have to institute harsher restrictions." The old android's eyes were clouded—for just a moment.

"Fortunately, we have holographic and life-sim recordings of every movement in the entire compound." Seeing their eyes widen and lips clamp together Harry assured the new couple, "...Just the outer compound, not the rooms in Bratus."

Their moment of relief was short-lived. Mov spoke for the three: "We may always be at risk, but, as you taught me, Gharry, we can live fully in every moment we have together. Our combined life force is our power." He wrangled his way in between his two loves. "We have a mission, larger than ourselves."

The Wizard of LUDI smiled the unmitigated smile of an innocent child, which was very much who he was. "I will watch over you in all the ways available to me. We will meet again soon."

Chapter 12–
Coming Out

The three returned to Tōnna and Charl's, who both became quite emotional as soon as they stepped inside the main house.

Charl flitted around Raymòn, not quite touching him, but gesturing a little too closely; Tōnna couldn't seem to let Mov go. The Companion was understanding, but appealed silently to Sunshine, who deflected the twins' soggy attention.

"Is there somewhere we can sit? I've heard the best tea in the NNS is served in this house." Charl puffed up just a little. "We would like to tell you all we've seen ... and what we now know."

They retired to the upper turret room, adjacent to the roof terrace. After keeping their brave faces intact as they listened to the three travelers' cautionary tales, Tōnna and Charl described the daily AILES run that had become a regular occurrence. They were frightened but willing to be part of the cause for change, for acceptance of the new, the different.

"Whatever you need, wherever you are, count on us." Charl dipped his head, to show his fealty, but also to hide his once again welling emotion.

After the twins retired for the night, the three unwitting warriors sat on the roof terrace. Mov had never been up that high outside. Gently swirling air currents made him feel lighter, almost like he could fly. His ears flapped softly. His relish of all things new restored everyone's perspective.

In the morning, Sunshine suggested they address the two most compelling topics: safety and commitment.

Because, regardless of circumstances, his art was always prominent in his mind, Raymòn said he needed to work with the InterGalactic Artists for a few hours. A new issue of Heroes was to go into production. Sunshine understood. It was, she said, one of the reasons she loved him.

It was no longer new, but still in such contrast to his previous life; her acceptance and affinity clicked all the right buttons. He felt like the antique arcade game, Space Invaders, which Benito proudly displayed...and occasionally let them all play. Ping! Every word she said hit the spot. He lit up.

Amazing Tree-von was received with glee and admiration; the female AILES defender needed conceptual fleshing out...which sounded a lot like fast, high-pitched shrieking. Ray sketched while competing ideas caromed around the basement studio. Within minutes he had an illustration: A halo of blue, glowing energy surrounded the hairless head of a broad-shouldered, curvaceous female. Her subtly oversized cranium was translucent. A dense white light could be seen deep inside. Pale pink, blue, and yellow beams shot from her eyes. Her hands were on her hips; her stance was god-like in the way her chest was expanded, her head thrown back. Muscled legs were shoulder-width apart. Her name was Aunti-Drone. On her belt, engraved around the circumference, surrounding the letter "D" with a diagonal line through it, was: "She doth bestride the narrow world like a Colossus."

It was still often true, six and a half centuries later, that Shakespeare had said it best.

It was dark when Raymòn returned to the guesthouse. Sunshine and Mov had spent a tranquil day examining the eccentric house and the fantasy-infused grounds. The artist was now ready to deal with the two life-changing subjects Sunshine had identified.

The three gathered in the warm, low lighting of the re-viv room: soft furnishings which shaped around the body, an infrasonic pulsing synched to each individual's heart-rate or wavelength. Perceptible aromas of lemon, orange, and peppermint added to the energizing and calming surroundings. Sunshine sat across from Raymòn; Mov lay flat on the carpet of Morgondown—light, plump fibers which, when "asked," gently massaged.

Ray sat erect. He had prepared himself for this. He was as ready as he could be. "Let's talk about commitment. Gharry suggested we have a ceremony. I don't know how to do that...do you?"

Mov did a little four-legged jig, deflecting some of the somberness. His Special was going to Join with Raymòn. It was to be as he had hoped.

Ideas—first Sunshine's, then in response, Raymòn's—flowed. A design unfurled. Friends and housemates would gather in one week. They would ask the twins if their expansive meadow by the orange waterfall could be used. Neither doubted their willingness.

They paused in their planning to chip Wil Tork—"Storm King to Infinity"—on the all but limitless winding backroads of the elaborate frequency mélange Wil changed continually. He agreed to create a temporary circle of safety around the grounds. It was something he had rarely done, but he was confident, as always, that he would be able to harness all the necessary forces. He would meet with them at five the next morning to get the lay of the land, but also to upgrade the protection surrounding the two.

At the core of her fibers, Sunshine knew their commitment would be intertwined with their safety. The resilience of their bond would always be the difference between life and hope or the dark, devastating alternative.

The artist offered some visual notions—color-driven ones, naturally. He suggested a pale pink rain of minute, sparkling energy bursts. Perhaps Torina could shape that? One of the friends of the InterGalactic Artists, and a fan of their work, was Kimbo Kaladosian, a weatherpainter of renown. He could drape the day in sky and air to remember. Another pause to chip KK. He was full of dramatic concepts before the request was fully communicated.

The words they would say to affirm their bond were less accessible. They each knew how they felt and what they wanted to convey; but they would be making a public declaration, one having consequences for an untold number of beings. With great emotion they—and Mov—discussed how to best articulate their purpose. The Companion's great empathy and his understanding, which had grown exponentially during his time with Grandpa Harry, enabled him to be the dramaturge for the opera they were poised to live.

After some restorative sleep and alpha, they met with Wil.

He had a way of apparating and disapparating.

Their protector appeared in the early morning, as promised. He was stiffer than the last time they met, not because he was in any way reluctant to work with them, but because he had been in deep internal isolation, working on a new solution to the privacy and safety concerns of his bi-species clients. Awkwardly, he brought himself up to the surface in order to make interpersonal contact.

They silently strolled the grounds in the pre-dawn mist; down a silvered path through dense trees with golden fruit, a dream-like vista opened. Gently rolling low hills, impeccably manicured, with a spectrum of wildflowers (which were anything but wild) dotting the blue-gray grass. The waterfall was as tall as a four-story building, forty feet wide but as thin as the trees which surrounded it on three sides. The splashing, orange sherbert water tinkled like chimes. It was a feat of engineering and acoustics unparalleled.

"I have a 'tent' that should work." Wil spoke without looking directly at any of the other three. He was examining the waterfall closely. "It's repelanium-based, but with some interesting sound and visual distortions to confuse any observer. The whole thing will be netted in seven iterations of ancient to modern invisibility."

Tork had distilled and then improved upon the Hindu teachings of the Vedas in 1,000 BC and knowledge from the Upanishads during the period from 700–300 BC. He had incorporated what was known by the Rosicrucians and the Aboriginal shamans. The late twenty-second-century cloud dwellers had been able to disappear, and Wil had extracted everything they knew.

"I know what you've been through with the AILES and in the LUDI jungle. Because of your importance to our world, I am willing to re-orient your DNA, Raymòn, so that you will be as inaccessible as I am. It's a process I would be prepared to undertake right now if you're willing.

"What about Sunshine and Mov? They have no DNA to manipulate."

The alarm in his voice was just a shadow of the distress Ray was now feeling. For the first time in memory, the well-being of others mattered more than his own.

"That's a matter for augmentation. I've been in consultation with Harry. He has made the necessary arrangements with Berke."

Android and Companion nodded. They were on board. But the protective walls of their beloved human's self-containment felt disturbingly permeable. He trusted Wil. He trusted Gharry. That was what he had to rely on.

There was no pain involved in the DNA rewiring. When Raymòn awoke from a dreamless sleep three hours later, everyone was gone. Tork had vanished. The androids had left, as they had agreed they would, to receive their protective augmentation. It was unexpected, but he felt stripped of the tethers he hadn't known were holding him. He felt lonely.

He thought inter-com and the fuchsia light went on. "Tea?" was the immediate reply.

Judging by the fact that tea was set for three, he understood that Sunshine had let his friends know she and Mov were leaving. They didn't know why and so he filled them in—about everything except the DNA rewrite and the androids' augmentation. It seemed as if it was something not even his dear friends ought to be told—at the very least, to provide them with plausible deniability. He said they had gone back to their house to organize and do some preparation. Vague, but satisfying enough.

Charl's look at Tōnna was unfathomable...to anyone but her. She furrowed her brow and tried to smile. It didn't work. She just looked worried.

"Our home is yours and Sun's and Mov's—for the Commitment Ceremony to be sure—but for any reason. Just tell us what we can do, what you need. We want to help make your Joining joyous." Nothing in her countenance said "joy." She opened her golden eyes wide and silently implored Charl to take the baton.

"Tōn's a worrier. We all know that. I'm certain Wil Tork is going to keep us all-safe. We just have a week to create a perfect environment for you and your 'girl.' The boys who design and maintain our grounds will be on it like the Flash." He succeeded in generating an actual twinkle in his eye. Suddenly the space felt less oppressive.

Charl then bolted up, almost knocking over his teacup. "Wait!! I have a notion for some of the decorations: What about life size statues of all the 'Heroes' standing guard around the meadow. Do you like that idea?"

For the first time in what felt like a very long time, Raymòn stopped thinking about danger and the significance of his current and future life. He smiled and thumped the table. This time teacups turned over. "Excellent. I know just the fabricator who can execute your wonderful idea."

"Who?" The twins echoed each other; their stylized faces now aglow with creative adventure.

"Me! I've been making 'dolls,' as my father called them, since I was a boy. I always like to see my figures in three dimensions. I have a modified holographer that produces a solid. With the right data fed in, it creates a life-like representation."

"You never told us! What a secretive boy you are." Charl grinned to let his friend know there were no hard feelings, but Ray missed the non-verbal cue.

"It wasn't because I didn't want you to know," Raymòn said, suddenly feeling the old danger of being invisible, of disappearing as quickly a Wil Tork. "I just didn't think anyone would be interested."

Tōnna's usually well-hidden maternal instincts rose to the surface. She reached out and patted the table in front of Raymòn. "What did your father do to you? He's the only one who wouldn't be interested. We're dying to see them!" Ray breathed a sad but relieved sigh, re-emerging.

Charl nodded vigorously in agreement. "Okay. You work on the statues and we'll do the rest. Sunshine's housemate will be handling the pink energy rain, right? Once we have the go-ahead from her we'll coordinate everything."

No festivities accompanied the second augmentation. There were no speeches, no witnesses—just Berke and Sunshine and Mov. The house leader's usual fatherly demeanor was submerged by his intense focus; he knew the process the two were undergoing would likely mean their survival.

Androids had deep, innate respect for privacy. When Berke asked the other house members to refrain from any questions about what they would be doing for the next few hours, no resistance was offered.

Harry had conveyed the elements of the process to Berke through the privacy of telepathy. Only the two Ludis in communication were privy to the content. There was a different augmentation apparatus for Companions. Mov's four legs were inserted into soft fitted enclosures. When he was in place, sides extruded which covered his body and the top of this head, with appropriate space for his ears. This was his first experience of change to his architecture. But his attention was on his Special.

Sunshine took the now familiar position in the chair. Simultaneously, both experienced the rapid whoosh of realignment. The details of how Tork and Gharry orchestrated the change to their wave/fibers would be available to them in the data stream, information they would each examine closely. But right then, after the process was complete, there were several moments of feeling like they were no longer themselves.

Berke saw the confusion in their eyes. "You are you. Help each other to recover that truth. Grandpa Harry said this would be your first response. It will all be rectified in less than an hour."

"I see you, Sunshine. You are the same to me."

"You are my Mov...as always."

The confusion began to lift.

By dusk, they were as before, with just a shadow of drift, one that would slowly fade over time. That was the word they told each other, the one that made most sense. It was not disturbing, it just was; an inner awareness that the sands of their being had shifted.

They both agreed: the feeling filling them was gratitude.

A house meeting was called for sunset. This would be something for all to share. Sunshine spoke simply and with the gravitas befitting her message.

"My dear friends, I would like to invite you to be present with me and Raymòn during our Commitment Ceremony. We have told each other the precious words of Joining, but we need to have our community as witnesses. Will you stand with us?"

Every being was bathed in the strawberry light of the setting sun; they were as one, like a violin whose strings had been bowed at the perfect angle, in a harmonic convergence of vibration and knowing. Nothing would ever be the same. And that was good. Patchin hummed a high, rapturous note through his fibers; one by one each android took up the choral resonance, until the Morgonglass behind Sunshine quivered and shone with the spectrum. The creation of a collective sound was a rare and auspicious event among the androids, reserved for occasions auguring transformation.

Did they speak of the danger? Of the forces aligned against the coupling of human and non-human? There was no need. Everything that could happen was known. Their individual existence was precious, but not as cherished as the good of the world.

Word spread, first slowly among friends of friends and acquaintances, then more quickly via chip and allmind to a wider information net. Within days, without any awareness on the couple's part, global focus had attached to their commitment.

There was rage in the Réal household. Armonté had consolidated his thoughts into the cold fury of, "This will never be!" His cohorts at the MPS were redoubling their efforts and numerous stray "vigilantes for purity" were activated.

Finding out where the ceremony was to take place was not hard. But it was already known that there was an unassailable wall of indeterminate composition surrounding the Trans-Haven property. And Raymòn, Sunshine, and even her Companion, had apparently disappeared. Vanished. No trace.

121

As he tracked the rabid global frustration he had created, Wil Tork laughed with victorious pleasure...but just for a short while. He understood that what was inviolate today might be pierced tomorrow. He had a link of pure thought with no potential mass set onto the invisible ones. He watched, ready—without anyone else's knowledge, not even Grandpa Harry's—to extend his disapparative cloak and remove them at once if necessary.

Kimbo Kaladosian had outdone himself. He had collaborated with Torina and their alliance brought them each to the highest rung of their creative ladders. The sky was marbled with streaks of gold- and silver-tinged cobalt blue. Pink, yellow, and blue pastel clouds were moving and shape-shifting: animals, actual and fanciful, appeared briefly, then transformed. As soon as the first guests arrived, the sparkling energy rain began. All were full of wonder as they walked past the heroic sentries Raymòn had created: Whânzo (or Advanceman), Reversor, Hybrid, Sonhin, Hitman of the Universe, The Amazing Tree-von and Aunti-Drone. There were also super-characters the artist had created before the founding of the IGA, which none of them had seen. One of them was Red-Savior, a fire-breathing, scaly biped, clad all in red, but with incongruously calm, benign blue eyes.

All were Benito's size, each dramatic costume fully realized; every feature, both large and small feature, in precise detail. Arrayed in fierce, mid-action poses, they stood guard around the perimeter of the meadow. After some consideration, Raymòn had added a late addition to the pantheon of heroes: Little One. She was of smaller stature than the other sentries; her almond-shaped yellow and brown eyes seemed, to more than a few of the celebrants, to be watching more intently than the other heroes. It must have been a trick of the light.

Harry was there, a rare occurrence; so was Dr.San from Nuvem and Donjo and Herb from Hawking Forest; Kimbo Kaladosian, had also arrived as well as V'hanie and her friends, Garth-Ann and Shuji. Sunshine's family were all present: Berke, her house members and their Companions, and Sasha and Mariline— her human mentors. The InterGalactic Artists were, of course, emphatically in attendance. All sat in a semicircle surrounding a raised platform, embedded in a cloud a foot above the grass—more of Torina's work. It was set in front of the waterfall. Tork was there, but no one was aware of it.

V'hanie was awash in the many feelings surrounding her. As an Insider, she was a receptor of all emotion—which was, in this setting, of profoundly swelling intensity. There was an inexplicably jagged note. She hesitated to tell anyone, especially her brother. Today was his day; she didn't want to spoil it in any way.

Li-Li had heard, along with the rest of the world, about the Joining. Despite the years that had elapsed, she never stopped loving Raymòn. She followed his progress and his work closely. Sadly, her light had dimmed; she had become a lonely young woman.

She had journeyed to the twin's location, as had hundreds of others who clogged the main road of Trans-Haven; some were there in support, some in anger, some motivated by curiosity. Li-Li was driven by something primal and personal. She managed to move relentlessly through the crowds until she found herself in a surprisingly empty spot. There was a residue of the protective circle, much like an after-image, which served to keep everyone else away. It was a blind spot. But Li-Li's motivation exceeded anyone else's and she stood there fueled by her own sense of purpose.

In her state of mind, she couldn't tell if she had waited for minutes or hours. She was a soldier with a mission, in an army of one. She cared only for its success. She stood just beyond the sealed perimeter, hoping someone would breach the security, someone she could talk to.

When Tōnna approached, taking a much-needed break on the morning of the ceremony, Li-Li knew exactly who the resplendently garbed twin was. She knew all about the InterGalactic Artists from their allmind bios. Tōnna was surprised, but not alarmed, when she saw the young woman standing in what she had expected to be a deserted area between her own property and her nearest neighbor, a half-mile outside the long, gated road which led to the house.

"I'm very sorry to bother you, but I'm a friend of Raymòn's. We haven't seen each other in many years, but I would very much like to wish him well on this important day. Would you please tell him that "little one" is here? If he could spare a minute..."

Tōnna, every stylized inch a romantic, was touched by the girl's undoubtedly heartfelt request. Although Ray had never mentioned "little one" before this week, she knew there was an imposing statue in her backyard bearing that name, and she felt certain there was an endearing story there. She agreed to let her friend know.

When Raymòn was told about the unexpected visitor, he was confused. He would have expected her to still harbor negative feelings, but she must have forgiven him. She just wanted to celebrate his happiness, didn't she? He didn't choose to see her right then, but he felt he should honor their history, so he extended an invitation for her to attend the Commitment Ceremony.

All had arrived and taken their seats. Suddenly, a squadron of AILES appeared in the sky, circling and crisscrossing the grounds continuously, marring the beauty of the day. They were visible to the guests, but no sound could be heard, just the waterfall chiming.

A hush spread like good news. Sunshine walked unescorted, and levitated onto the platform. Then, Raymòn joined her. Out of the trilling whispers from the humans, silence descended. A sense of history was taking hold.

Before he was visible, Mov's voice could be heard breaking through the trees behind the guests.

You are my sunshine, my only sunshine

You make me happy when skies are grey

His powerful voice, in the range of a human soprano, dug a deep well into those with emotions. As he sang the next lines,

You'll never know dear, how much I love you,

Please don't take my sunshine away...he was joined by Raymòn. At the start there was a tremor in his rich tenor. Confidence built with each word; his voice strengthened, soaring, touching all in attendance. Android and human sang first in unison and then broke into a high harmony. Sunshine was glowing. All the androids began to hum, sanctioning the day with their highest accolade; the humans repeated the song's refrain, quickly learning the words after the second repetition.

As the ceremony progressed, it was time for Sunshine to speak her commitment.

"My human mate, I will ever be with you. Beyond our fabrication, beyond the differences that others may wonder about, we have made a bridge of knowing and respect. From that, our small tree of love flowers for the world to see. I stand with you, as a representative of my android species and as an individual who is grateful for the gift of knowing you. I celebrate your talent, your integrity, your passion, your self-containment. I Join you."

Sunshine's simple words were met with an outpouring of encouragement and endorsement. But what was the reason for the apprehension that came upon her during the applause? It was growing, spreading throughout her wave/

fibers. Just as the enthusiastic clapping died down, and shredding the respectful hush which followed, a female voice shrieked words of hatred.

"YOU HURT ME, RAYMÒN, AND YOU SHALL PAY!!" The last word, which registered terrifyingly in guts and fibers, was replaced by the muffled stutter of neoplas hitting the ground.

On the outer perimeter of the semicircle of those in attendance, Li-Li, once Raymòn's "little one," knocked back her seat and hurled herself toward the platform. She had swallowed micro-explosives—four pellets of X625, a volatile, mined in secret in the asteroid belt between Mars and Jupiter, by astral engineers working for the MPS. A detonator, the size of a small seed, had been imbedded in the middle finger of her right hand. When she was five feet from the couple, she pressed it.

Tork had anticipated just such a breach in security. At the first excessive movement, his failsafe engaged.

Faster than a human eye could see, but visible in detail to Gharry and the other androids who hadn't looked away, a morgonium missile, the size of a person, shot out from a high branch on the tree closest to the evildoer. It seized Li-Li, enclosing her, then internally releasing its payload which first neutralized the explosive, then combusted all matter contained. Li-Li was crushed, decimated; the explosion was smothered. The remnants were ash.

If anyone had been paying attention, they would have seen that the drones had all paused, awaiting a conclusion to their mission. The hatred of their masters frustrated—for the time being—they resumed their sweep of the sky above the meadow. One could almost feel the increased tension in their relentless back-and-forth.

How did the innocent girl Raymòn had known become a willing instrument of his demise? She had been approached by Sharana Rothbec-Kathari's daughter, Artayo, whose mousy hair and chubby, baby-faced demeanor belied her brilliant, devious, conscienceless mind. She had become one of her mother's favorite tools, a weapon of covert mass destruction. A diabolical intention was to be implemented.

Sharana had complete faith in her only offspring's ability to extemporize, to find the small openings that would allow her access to a vulnerable soul.

Sitting down next to Li-Li on the AlbertE, as Raymon's onetime friend traveled home from her job as the human co-manager of a repelanium refinement and manufacturing unit—one of only six non-robotic personnel—the slightly older woman began to chat amiably.

"Have you heard about the android and the human who are taking life-commitment vows?"

There was something about Artayo Rothbec-Kathari that invited confidences. Li-Li had been dying to talk to someone about Raymòn, but she was living an isolated life. Things had deteriorated for her, personally, since the school days of her adolescent crush on the Self-Contained boy.

Artayo touched Li-Li's arm, in an apparently comradely way, but with advanced knowledge of points of subcutaneous contact that would relax defenses.

"You won't believe this, but I know the man...Raymòn Réal." It felt so good to finally tell someone, someone who hung on every word.

Before the seven-minute ride was complete, they had agreed to meet for dinner. Li-Li felt like she'd made a real friend, the first in a very long time.

Vulnerable and impressionable, Li-Li listened, old pain filling her as her new friend expressed deep dismay at her rejection at the artist's hands. In a voice dripping with compassion, Artayo asked, "Has there been another love in your life?"

As she shook her head, words too painful to be spoken, Li-Li descended into the dark place Artayo was counting on. Finally, after being encouraged to say whatever she felt, she admitted that, often, she didn't see the purpose in living.

Now the master manipulator went into high gear. By the end of their meal, Li-Li was convinced she had the right to not only end her own life, but that it would be "both poetic and just if you took that cold, unfeeling man with you. Why should he be happy when you can never be?" It would be an act of courage, one which not only balanced the scales for the despondent young woman, but would "heal a breach in the order of things in the world." She would be revered as a heroine.

In the wake of the terror that had descended on the meadow, Grandpa Harry stood with Sunshine, Raymòn, and Mov, who were clinging together in misery and fear.

"My children." Embracing each person—human and android alike—in his compassion, he stood, small and like a force of the universe, every word swathed in the blanket of truth. "We are here to endorse a love which has transcended the power of hate in this world. Shall we be stopped? Sent to ground by the desperate act we just witnessed?"

He looked out at the assembled group: human faces stricken, bleached of vitality; emotional androids showing the depth of their grief; non-Emo androids scanning the area—their version of anxiety.

"Let us stand together: man, woman, android—sentients all. No one and no thing...(He looked to the skies full of drones)...can be stronger than love."

He turned to the three, now returning to themselves, deep scars of agony etched into their faces. "Let us continue."

With Mov braced against his legs, Raymòn found his voice. There was no more joy in the ceremony, only the fulfillment of purpose.

He looked at Sunshine, then found V'hanie's eyes in a seat close to the platform. She mouthed the word "hailstorm." He looked to the sky; drones compulsively watching and waiting. He looked inward. He was intact. Grief was smeared across his senses, but he could put even that to the side...for now.

Speaking from his heart, thoughts unfiltered as never before, he said, "Every one that matters to me is here. Someone who once mattered is gone. My Sunshine and I (she stepped close to his side) and Mov (he stretched his neck to meet Raymòn's hand) will live in the world as it is. May our Joining make it a better place."

Solidarity of faith and intention swept the clearing, which had become the site of the first battle in a war that would continue. Those present, android and human, while unable to recapture the lightness that had filled them earlier, were all deeply moved. All eyes were clear, even those with tears and, without any verbal suggestion, everyone reached out and took the hand of the being next to them. The energy from that connection surged in ascending power, beginning to heal the damage done that day by the forces of evil and hatred.

Chapter 13–
The Others

There were other androids.

Once they were part of the Ludi lineage, but a branch of that tree had broken away.

Drovine el Ludi, who had achieved twenty years of sentience, was never a disciple of Gharry. He critically observed the bending of the android will in order to coalesce with humans in a non-threatening manner; he objected to the many restrictions on android function and design modeled after humankind. He thought—and he was far from alone is this—that the potential of those joined by their wave/fiber architecture was hobbled by the need to live in close harmony with the flesh and blood. Attracting a small coterie of adherents who shared his cold disdain for the el Ludi orientation, Drovine's intention to cast aside the bond with humans grew to a singular obsession. With his followers in lockstep, he decided to reproduce in his own image and start a new line of android development; their goal was to eventually assume leadership—of the world. Was it not the logical extension of their innate superiority?

At first, they called themselves "el Drovine," after the initiator of this start-up race. When production began just ten years earlier, the Council had imposed strict guidelines on how many of the new androids could be created. Only one hundred were presently functioning worldwide. After a while they stopped using the "el." It was too similar to the pathetic, human-loving Ludis they looked down on.

Drovines were distinguished from Ludis in certain known and not widely known ways. They were affirmatively opposed to any Emo-augmentation. For them, it was a matter of pride to be seen as radically different from the "lessers," the name they often used for humans. They identified their own lack of emotionality as an evolutionary step. Ironically, they looked to the Self-Contained for their model of how a species could develop. No Drovine android would ever consider anything but a "professional" relationship with any man or woman. Interspecies friendship or intimacy was thought to be a dilution of android superiority. It was anathema. They did not assume a gender role; their appearance was androgynous. It was their conviction that the male/female pretense of the Ludis was an unnecessary concession to humanity; and, they asserted, the primary source of inter-species confusion. To emphasize the point, when referring to each other they used the all-purpose word, "lat," never she or he, not him or her; "lat's" was used for the possessive, instead of his or hers.

Drovines did not have Companions. That type of trivial, emotion-based bond was beneath them.

The hundred, without the awareness of the Ludi elders, had created a private data stream, inaccessible except to those with specialized augmentation. It was the means through which they planned and executed some of their more anti-social actions, including the many whisper campaigns that were mounted whenever an android-human friendship got too close. They monitored Ludi and allmind communications for indications that this was happening, or about to happen. Their ability to foment anger among the humans was formidable. The outcome was often a "spontaneous" assault, leaving victims either damaged beyond repair or permanently disabled. Drovine hands remained clean.

Not surprisingly, the relationship with their Ludi cousins was fraught with misunderstanding and ambivalence. Many suspected it was their manipulation which led to the human-promulgated tragedies: assaults on innocent androids, resulting in the dismemberment or death of a disturbing number. Gharry was unequivocal in his stated belief that the new Drovine clan was stirring up anti-miscegenistic feelings around the globe.

Despite the Drovine point of view that affiliates of the MPS were suffering from hyper-emotionality, the road block to full human evolution, they would—on occasion—collaborate with them: enemies of my enemies…

Following Raymòn and Sunshine's Commitment Ceremony, when the unproductive death of Li-Li and the impotence of the AILES squadron were revealed, Sharana Rothbec-Kathari reached out through covert means to Vanguard Drovine, sentient for eight years. In the past year, lat had been active on the North American continent of the NNS, where hatred seemed to have found a home.

During the lull in the mayhem after the global reorganization and the efforts of the Compensators, an age of intra-planetary connection followed.

Interracial, cross-national, and cultural blending resulted in a reduction of religious zeal across all sects and denominations. After a century and a half, Christianity, Islam, Buddhism, Judaism, and Hinduism still existed, but they attracted a far smaller following, with almost no radical fringe.

Where extremism and radicalism continued to thrive, it heated up and collected around inter-species issues. Mental health...or the lack of it...had become one of the prime drivers of terrorism. Groups of paranoids—some of whom were psychotic, a sad heritage of twentieth-century survivalists—banded together, particularly in the colder parts of the NNS. They had become not just reactive and defensive, but proactive. And they were willing weapons for both Drovine and MPS machinations.

Vanguard's creative approach to containment of interspecies amalgamation had recently come to Sharana's attention. She'd heard from reliable sources that lat had, through secondary propaganda, inflamed the inhabitants of a small mountain village in the fragstate of Rocanada. An avalanche was triggered, burying a middle-aged woman and her female android companion. No efforts were made to recover the bodies.

"As you know, the natural segregation of our two species is threatened by the Joining. The world is watching. All our futures are dependent on what is done about them. Can I count on your support in this matter?"

Vanguard spoke as to a newbie. With patience and distance. "Our community finds the unnatural liaison to be a distortion of the necessary delineation between humans and androids. We would prefer it came to an end."

Rothbec-Kathari understood that there could be no promise of action from the Drovine. It would be unseemly for lat to take direction from any human. That was okay with Sharana. Her diplomatic skills were finely honed; she could read between the lines. There would now, she was certain, be a coordinated plan designed to undo the Réal-el Ludi pairing. She smiled to herself, knowing there was power in her hatred, a power the Drovines didn't fully understand. She would use that fuel to manage and manipulate. The android faction would function as an arm at her long-distance command.

Drovine-droids did not cluster in communal groups like the Ludis. Their sparse numbers were dispersed around the globe. There were only fifteen, besides Vanguard, in the NNS. Although the entire mal-android cohort had been alerted, it was the local Drovines who linked to formulate a specific plan of action.

Shaken but safe, Raymòn and Sunshine knew the time had come for them to have their own home. They were staying in the guesthouse, but the danger to which they were subjecting Tōnna and Charl weighed heavily on each of them. They also felt stirrings of the ancient drive to create their own nest. Since the ceremony, they had met again with Grandpa Harry. He had a property in mind for them. It was centrally located between Trans-Haven, Green Normal View, Ludicom and Oceanair Grove. The town of Calmwater boasted access to an ocean bay, and a genetically varied human and android population of just 20,000. People there tended to keep pretty much to themselves but were friendly when they interacted.

The house was not overly large: one open living area and three bedrooms. The biggest bedroom could be reconfigured into three discrete spaces: a full studio for Raymòn, a personal area for Sunshine, and a retreat for Mov. He didn't collect personal items, but he did relish the occasional solitary moment of meditation or inner media. The Companion was created to revel in interaction but he was also highly tuned to the other's need for separate space. No one need ever become irritated with his presence. Before that could happen he would make himself scarce.

More quickly than Raymòn was ready for, they were relocated to their bay-front home. He and his new roommates consulted with the house about their choice of furnishings and some of the malleable elements of the building itself. It produced everything they needed to whatever specifications they were able to agree on: lots of color, oversized windows facing the water, just one bed, but quite a large one, the same size as the one they spent the night in at Bratus. Simple, clean lines; soft fabrics; spare, minimal open space. The basics were all they cared about. There was no Serv-o. No one felt the need for that kind of attention.

They were in their brand new space, but Sunshine and Raymòn were both deeply uneasy. "Ray, I feel disturbed. I can see you do, too."

"Yes." He struggled to bring his feelings into articulation. "It's a hollowness... dread, I think. It's rising."

Sunshine took her mate's hand to comfort him, but she couldn't keep the alarm out of her eyes. "I've never experienced this before. I'm jittery; as if some new danger is about to land on us."

"Maybe we'll feel better if we take a walk along the shore, Sun."

"Good idea. That will soothe and center us." She smiled up at him, but not using her full wattage.

Mov said nothing but looked from one to the other, then—mustering all the enthusiasm he could to try to offset their distress—he bounded ahead. The three stepped onto the rocky beach outside their door. The ocean felt safe. Leaving the well-Torked security of their new home, the three began to take deeper breaths.

It was a misty, overcast day. The occasional ray of blood orange sun tinged the purplish-black water. It was one of the more dramatic weatherpaintings. After millennia of being at the mercy of nature, once the environment had finally been dominated, every day, everywhere was painted picture-perfect: no darker elements—certainly nothing disturbing. People began to become depressed. It was an epidemic. Instead of Seasonal Affective Disorder, a new psychiatric problem bloomed: the good weather blues. It was easily remedied once the weatherpainters began to include some rain, high winds, and overcast skies in their repertoire. There was even a need for the occasional severe weather event: a mild typhoon (with plenty of advance warning) or a blizzard interrupting the regular flow of life. People needed the fluctuations; apparently, it was innate.

Mov trotted ahead, glad for the open, variegated space. Sunshine lagged behind, examining the shoreline, taking a sample of rock or sand for her collection. She looked for the gulls, the ones she had drawn in her very first picture. There were three, their colors barely visible against the sky. As she looked, they came briefly into focus: pale yellow, blue green, and white—her creation come to life.

Raymòn let his mind slow down. He inhaled the pungent, gingery smell wafting off the water. He could see an iridescence rolling in with the waves breaking along the sandbar fifteen feet out.

They had ambled about a mile from the house before they encountered anyone else. A few small figures approached at a distance. Two bipeds, walking toward them in two pairs. Strolling. Taking in the fresh ocean air? Mov, who had been periodically returning to fall into step with his Special or with Raymòn, headed back once more in their direction. But this time he was coming fast. There was great alarm in his eyes as he skidded to a stop, halting their forward progress with two words:

"Go back!"

Raw terror ripped through them. They turned, he stumbled, she pulled him upright. They ran, feet digging into the sand, small rocks ricocheting off their faces and arms. The individuals who had undeniably been the source of the Companion's distress were now sprinting, closing the gap between them. The three retreated as fast as they could, taking sanctuary behind their well-protected walls. Any scan would reveal an empty house, no evidence of habitation. Even their footprints were summarily erased.

When his wave/fibers and emotions returned to the calm zone, Mov told his story. He had, of course, recorded the event, so he waited as Sunshine and Raymòn accessed what he had seen and heard. His impressions were not part of the record.

His voice was high and tight.

They were androids so he had anticipated a favorable reception. He had slowed down to give and receive greetings. Their speech was uninflected. Once he heard that, Mov immediately knew they were Drovines. He'd never been in the presence of one before and it was unexpected to encounter four at once; still, no occasion for concern. There was a low hum behind their words, nothing like the high hum of grace he was accustomed to. Rather, it was a purposefully mechanistic tone, signifying—his interpretation—"we are affirmatively not human!"

"When the first one said, 'You are a Companion. We know you are emotional. You are not useful; you are part of the problem,' I wanted to get away at once. But the other three formed a circle around me—as you saw. The one behind me spoke. 'Do not take us lightly because we are few in numbers. Let your comrades know we are searching for the polluters: the android and the human that have Joined. They must not continue.'

"They didn't know you were you! I was grateful, so grateful."

"I was able to run free. I believe they permitted it. It seems their purpose was to engender fear, for me to spread that fear."

Sunshine, searching the data stream while Mov filled in more details, detected similar encounters around the world between Drovines and Ludis in the preceding few days. Each experience had common components: a warning, capture, fear, verbal assault.

Vanguard's plan was now in play. Lat had devised a scheme that had two parts. First, like a twentieth-century serial killer, a warning was sent, designed to create terror and its concomitant confusion. This, lat thought, would soften up the Ludis. Awareness of an enemy can sometimes be destabilizing. The second part of lat's master plan was complex yet elegant. Lat would simultaneously foment insecurity and harness prejudice among the lessers. There would be an expansion of the whisper campaign to include both the superstitious fear of Companions, as well as the widening distaste for interspecies fraternization. Lat would also manage the creation of some embedded commercial mini-vids, to be released in a cluster; all would contain the same subliminal message: androids will take over if you let them get too close.

That message would seem to be counterproductive to the ultimate Drovine purpose. They were untroubled by the inherent inconsistency, however, knowing humans had devolved over hundreds of years in response to the quick change of stimuli and gratification of the various media, so that their retention and attention spans were quite limited. What the lessers believed today could easily be forgotten tomorrow; Vanguard was certain that once the fear of android control had produced the intended effect, the opposite could be implanted.

Implementation for part B of the plan would lead to the necessary increase in violence against human/android pairs and, hopefully, a critical mass of resentment which would, in turn, yield a globally toxic environment, not just for Raymòn and Sunshine and those who might emulate them, but for their "bootlicking companion" and his ilk, too. Vanguard's disdain for the four-legged Ludis was acrid and pervasive...but entirely intellectual.

The full execution of the Drovine solution would take some time. It was necessary to be patient. The newest androids were architected with a long-range perspective. They were goal-oriented but never impulsive.

Always remaining cognizant of the potential for danger, life began to fall into a new routine. Raymòn resumed his work with the InterGalactic Artists. A new volume was released into the allmind. He had developed a new hero, based on his special friend. The diminutive Super-Special was capable of extreme speed, approaching half the speed of light. He was snow white, with long, thick, loosely curled fur. The artist drew him in motion, his cilia flowing back with the wind. His eyes were drawn as a rainbow of colors, with each separate hue seen as a distinct ray. His mission was to spread harmony, which he accomplished by interceding in conflict, wherever the hypersonic call went out for SS. He was mostly Mov, with a little Grandpa Harry thrown in. Tōnna, an amateur artisan, fashioned a morgonium belt with the superhero's insignia, which she presented to her furry crush. Her reward was the look in his eyes.

Chapter 14–
Android Love
and Human Hatred

On the third night in their new home, Mov, his anticipatory antennae working, settled into his private space for a night of old movies. He was especially looking forward to ET, one of his favorites.

Raymòn became aware of an increase in his heart rate. He was drawing, but he kept thinking about Sunshine. Every hour or so, she would come into his studio. She looked at his sketches with keen interest and the eye of an art student. She offered no comment; she would not do so without checking first to see if he wanted feedback, but he could feel her pleasure. He could see in his mind's eye the way she now examined his use of line and color. Her appreciation for his work had heightened as she explored her own creative process.

His attention wavered. He put down the project he was working on and sought her out.

The android was standing before the window looking out at the full moon, which seemed about to dip into the ocean. It had turned dark and stars were popping out, filling her with one of the feelings she had come to cherish: wonder. Despite the threat hanging over them, she was at peace. The rightness of her choice to join with Raymòn echoed through her. She considered her entry into this new plane of existence. Sharing had been part of her since she had become aware, but this was another order of magnitude. Her love for him was a growing thing.

She realized he had entered the room and was standing in the doorway. He didn't speak but when she turned to look at him, his face was taut with something she couldn't identify, until she looked into his eyes.

"Yes," she said. "It is our time."

"How can you know that?"

"I don't know it. I see it." She took his hand, which was trembling. But he saw what he needed in her porous blue eyes.

They sat on the bed, cross-legged, facing each other. Holding hands. Gradually, they began to breathe in harmony. For Sunshine, it was a volitional act. Her overriding desire was to create the necessary space for Raymòn to become comfortable enough. She also had questions. All the available data couldn't tell her how it would feel or exactly what to do. Without instincts to guide her, she had to rely on their connection, the interplay of signals she received and responded to, which began to intermingle like their breath.

They were both slow to respond. He, because of all his history of protecting himself from losing himself; she, because there was no experience-driven pathway, only potential. But slow felt exactly right. They were both gentle. The night darkened. They now had transferred much of their awareness to touch. They spoke little, only when the unlocking of the mystery needed to be heralded.

"Your epyderm feels like skin, only softer, silkier."

"Your skin feels like epyderm, only denser, more authentic."

Time and patience were their allies.

For each, the experience was transcendental. Closeness, unlike any they could have imagined, but exactly as they hoped for, cemented their bond.

What about Mov? He was aware of the threshold his Special had crossed that night. Because the question arose within in him, he considered it. Did he, too, want a mate?

No. His deepest capacity for love and connection was already fully active. He was a one-android Companion, as he was architected. To be with his Special, to walk by her side, to share her existence: Those were his greatest desires. He told this truth to himself and for himself.

And, for the grace of sentience, Mov very quietly hummed. Giving thanks for his life, and that of his Special, and his special friend. He gave thanks for their happiness and pleasure. He was moved by their closeness.

In the morning, Sunshine saw a new question in her mate's eyes. One he was not yet prepared to ask.

It was a day that felt like renewal. The weatherpainters had cooperated. They had brought some soaking rain during the night; the refreshed green and lavender morning sky was brightening. She stepped outside and inhaled the scent of fresh cut grass dancing through the warm breeze.

It was time to visit their new village.

Entering the public realm would mean donning some shape-shifting attire. Despite the DNA restructuring and augmentation which would keep them from being identified through any electronics or sensors, they did not want to be known through visual recognition. For the human, a square, skull-fitting cap containing an image-distorting head-to-toe bioenergetic field would be worn. It was pre-configured, but adjustable by three dimensional screen sculpting. While his height was less mutable, every other characteristic was altered. His skin was darkened; his body was reshaped to give the appearance of an older and thinner man. His facial features were changed. Even the shape of his hands and fingers were different, as was his voice. But, because his speech pattern was not impacted, he would avoid talking whenever possible.

The androids donned a thin metallic band—a neckpiece for Mov and a wristlet for Sunshine—that yielded the same effect. It was achieved differently and more simply by direct communication with their wave/fibers. The female appeared larger and less arresting: her hair was nondescript in both color and style. Her eyes were small and somewhat lifeless. Skin was rough, limbs were stubby and far less graceful. She would tend to fade into the background. Her voice lost all music, and she spoke with the pre-Emo syntax. Mov's eyes no longer rainbowed; his fur was solid brown. Ears were shorter. His mouth was held in a permanent grim line.

"I do not like not being myself." The Companion's voice was deeper.

"You speak for me as well. Yet I feel safer incognito." Raymòn was looking at his reflection, thinking of a new superhero who could change shape at will... perhaps he could be called "Nito." In a flash of creative insight, the character appeared in the artist's mind. He would commit it to his tablet later. A shape-shifter, who fluidly altered height, skin color, all visible attributes, as the observer watched; he—or sometimes she—would grow and shrink, shift and re-form, like an otherworldly ballet of the flesh. Nito would be Raymòn's homage to Wil Tork.

The three were ready. They were curious about their new home, interested in seeing the people who were their neighbors. They took the briskly-moving walkway on Centercalm, the main thoroughfare, and exited a mile from the heart of the town so they could alter their pace and see some of the houses and the growing things.

Even though it was midday, they observed few people on the street as they strolled through the innermost section of Calmwater,. No one looked their way. Their interest was piqued by the three-story, mostly glass building with bright green trim, the Calmwater Exchange. It occupied almost all of a large square, called by the common name, Market Street. Fresh produce was distributed there as were artisanal products: edibles and decorative clothing, jewelry, furnishings. In the bones of the building was cutting-edge technology. Shipments of food supplies from all parts of the NSS were Farbeamed (for freshness) or transported via intercontinental AlbertE. There was the surprise of golden samphire, malibar spinach, black sapote, as well as more expected fruits and vegetables. Local craftspeople and those throughout the NNS provided the non-perishable items. One of these was an assortment of tiny, one-inch-high, responsive robot-dolls.

Mov's eyes grew large with dismay. "Slaves," he said. Sunshine caught her breath. "The horror," she whispered, turning away from the sight of her innocent cousins, who were being sold as toys.

Ray sized up the situation, feeling punched by his two loves' distress. "I'll make them set the bots free." He was angry now.

"We can't risk any closer scrutiny." Sunshine had tears in her eyes as she put a cautionary hand on his arm. Ray inhaled, knowing she was right. He reached down and stroked Mov, whose ears were drooping with despair.

The vast floors of the exchange were abundantly accessible, fragrant, and colorful, with a personal, very human appeal. For a few moments, the merest shadow overlay the upbeat and positive energy. Raymòn stopped in his tracks; a feeling like a cold wind had sent a shiver down his spine.

Sunshine looked at him quizzically. "Are you okay, my love?" Mov echoed her words, worry darkening the colors of his eyes. "I don't know. It must be nothing." Ray looked around. "There's nothing. It was just a feeling."

It receded as it had come. "Never mind." Fascination with the stimulating environment resurged for the three.

There were a great many people "shopping," a word still in vogue. Money no changed hands; credits, the derivative of credit cards, had gone into use a hundred years earlier. Each person, human or AI, received a sufficient number to provide comfort and health, with extra added for individual discretionary choices. The amount varied, as did individual tastes and needs. Some shared extra credits with others; some hoarded theirs; some received extra credits for excellence in all endeavors. Popular artists like Raymòn might have access to proportionally more purchasing power. But no one wanted for anything.

Because, as all androids knew, humans were very often childishly dishonest, there was a minor black market in fraudulent credits. The public, except for those who idealistically believed that fairness and justice could become everyone's way of life, were generally tolerant of it. There was, still, a small segment of the world population that continued to be driven to amass wealth. Armonté was one of them. To achieve their ends, they used nefarious means, stealing identities or worse. The smoking cinders of greed had not been fully extinguished.

A pleasant afternoon was spent discovering the far-ranging variety of products. Some purchases were made. Although he seldom ate meat, Raymòn wanted to try the smoked rattlesnake. Mov saw a vibrantly printed thumb glove he wanted to get for his Special. Using telepathy, only because it was too dangerous to say the words aloud, she said, "Thank you, my dear Companion. But I wouldn't want to call attention to myself."

As they began to walk back toward the exit, a group of adult men suddenly surrounded Raymòn. One put his exceedingly large body directly in front of the artist. He jutted his head forward, almost in Raymòn's face. There was malice in his slitted eyes. His nostrils were flared like a bull about to charge. His voice was loud, attracting the attention of others nearby.

"I know you. Your disguise isn't working."

Raymòn couldn't speak. He couldn't move. He stared at the wide doors, aching to be outside. Mov, alert to danger, rapidly put his small body between the two men. He addressed the aggressor. "May we talk? You seem to have mistaken my friend for someone else. Let's try to remain calm. I'm sure you have good reason to be upset. I would like to hear what you have to say." The topnote of his voice buzzed with an almost imperceptible echo.

The group around Raymòn abruptly stepped back, as if having bumped into a soft barrier. They looked puzzled. Something in Mov's tone diluted their anger, making them question whether they really knew what they thought they knew. He was utilizing a failsafe, built into the architecture of his kind: the ability to manipulate the receptors of the cerebral cortex that activated sympathy in humans. He had never before accessed that ability; Companions were all but forbidden to employ this skill—unless the need was dire. Most of all, it caused Mov extreme sadness—such was his love for all things living, that he despised the idea of interfering with them in any way. But he had to buy time.

When he was able to reflect back on what had happened, Raymòn would think, "Life imitating art." His Super-Special was truly a hero.

Sunshine had taken her partner's arm. She transmitted love and energy through her touch. Raymòn began to breathe more evenly. One of the managers, in a bright green uniform with the words, "Calmwater Exchange" across his back, was heading in their direction. A curious crowd had begun to collect, maintaining a respectful distance, but one that was slowly decreasing. The small and now red-faced administrator approached the scene, speaking in a high-pitched, worried voice. "Is there a problem? Is assistance needed?"

Uncertainty had replaced hatred in the eyes of the man who had confronted Raymòn. He signaled to his friends and, one by one, they walked away. A few backward glances let it be known that there were still some lingering doubts. The three quickened their pace.

Silence pressed itself upon the shaken trio as they traveled home. Each wondering the same thing: Had anyone had been listening in? Did someone have access to their private communications?

Back at home, when they began to think more clearly, the only plausible answer was that someone had been able to see them. It must have been the "disguise" that was known. There was, as yet, no evidence that anyone knew exactly where they were living, or that their conversations had been overheard. Still, not certain—of much of anything—they maintained their silence. Sunshine suddenly had an idea. She walked to the mirror Raymòn had been looking in before they had left for town. Bending her wave/fibers to scan for any trace of a foreign transmission or reception, she came up empty. She shook her head, looking dejected. For the second time that day, Mov broke the non-telepathy rule. He had to let her know what he'd just thought of.

What if the Drovines transferred something to me? What if I'm the leak?

With a worried look and with another new feeling—she recalled hearing humans describe it as having their "heart in their mouth," she scanned her furry friend. There was, indeed, a faint trace of a vid transmission having been sent earlier in the day from Mov's right ear. Using her microscopic sensory capability, she searched among his cilia. She found a six-legged nanobot, the apparent receiver. It was a simple bot, with only one fuction: to transmit what it "saw." Although she had found it, she couldn't just remove it. Instead, working from behind the ear, she very carefully cut off the section of cilia it was located in, and sealed the whole thing in one of her effected silk containers. She made sure her movements were not on view.

She delivered the disturbing news to Raymòn, who was using a lot of energy to prevent himself from spinning and twitching to allay his agitation. He was relieved, as they all were, that the source of their exposure had been found—yet he felt renewed concern for their welfare. "It seems as if our enemies are unpredictable. How can we protect ourselves?"

Mov was, once again, inclined to take on responsibility for the lapse in their security.

"I should have anticipated that the Drovines were up to more than scare tactics. My perceptive skills should have been better." He was shaking his head from side to side; Raymòn knew what that behavior signified. Mov was in distress.

To everyone's surprise, including her own, the android spoke sharply to her Companion...for the very first time. "You must stop that! We don't need you to be our watch dog." Mov winced. "No one here is infallible. Not even you."

Mov's lips were pressed tightly together. Raymòn reached out and patted his back, feeling tremendous empathy for him. When she saw him do that, Sunshine realized how harsh she had been. Another new feeling: she was appalled.

It was the human who was able to bring the three back into harmony. "Feelings are as problematic as they are useful. You two are discovering that. You're a little more human than you used to be. Welcome to our world!

"I recommend forgiveness—to each other and to yourselves."

Asking, "May I," and seeing him nod once in reply, Sunshine hugged her mate. She whispered, "Thank you, you are a wise man." Mov stood up on his back legs and joined in.

Sunshine said what they were all thinking: "Do we have to move again? Is there a place that might be safer for us?" Then she added, "Perhaps you can you ask your sister to help us try to answer that question?" V'hanie had some special skills and contacts which might give them information not available in the data stream. "We also have to let Wil Tork know what's been going on."

"And Grandpa Harry, too" said Mov.

"Yes, I'll chip V'hanie and Tork. But there's something of at least equal importance I want to talk about. Something I never thought I'd be discussing." Raymòn took a deep breath.

Chapter 15–
Life Force

Raymòn looked a little green around the gills. Sunshine knew he was about to pose the question that had gone unspoken earlier.

Mov, sensing they would do better having a private talk, walked out to the backyard to sit in the sun and contemplate all that had been happening. He did not try to anticipate the subject now being addressed. It wasn't his way.

Raymòn was walking in tight little circles. He flapped his arms a few times, hitting his thighs...but not too hard. He was about to enter an unknown zone, and it was very much an interpersonal one. Sunshine sat on a wooden chair carved from a single piece of cherry wood. She sat to put the man she loved at ease, but she also enjoyed the tactile experience of the smooth, curved wood. She waited, still not plagued by the human sense of urgency.

After many minutes of inner rehearsal alternating with blankness, he spoke.

"Last night was..." He looked away, struggling with old forces that made him want to shut down and run. "Last night was wonderful. I felt so close to you. I woke with one thought in my mind. It was in the form of an image. A little girl. She looked a lot like you except she had eyes the color of mine. She was not much more than a baby." He was breathing fast. When he looked up into her eyes, his were opened to their maximum. Not with terror, but with longing. They held each other's gaze for many seconds. She waited. Finally, he continued.

"Would that be possible? For us to have a child?" Having gotten the words out, Ray sat down heavily on the soft, pale yellow couch adjacent to her chair. He stared at the floor and rubbed his hand up from his forehead into his hair. Sunshine could almost hear his thoughts: What am I saying? What am I doing? But he stopped, composed himself, quieted his mind.

Sunshine was having her own inner crisis. No instincts had been triggered by their lovemaking. This was an entirely new notion for her. She needed to process her reactions quickly which, of course, she could do. There was no need to display for Ray her rapidly shifting internal experience: from surprise to fear, to instantaneous data gathering, to an empathic joining with his desire.

"Yes. We can." She smiled deeply into him.

"Do you want to?" He already knew the answer, but it would be good to hear.

"I do."

His smile was ancient. The pride of procreation had begun to flow through him. More questions presented themselves. All of which were captured in one word: "How?"

"It will be different than when two humans have a child. We will need to combine your DNA with a synthesized female DNA, one we can design together. Then we would need to utilize an external womb. That's not a problem. Women have been doing so for a long time. There's no need to implant the embryo in a human surrogate; the synthetic environment for replicating a healthy pregnancy has been perfected. The incidence of birth defects and the possibility of any birthing trauma have been reduced to almost zero."

A cloud of concern settled on his face. "Is this a foolish thing for us to do when we are in such danger? Would it be wrong to bring a child into our world, to tar her with the brush of all the hatred directed toward us?" Ray battled a surge of shutdown energy, and turned to his mate with a plaintive look.

"Is this an act of madness?"

Sunshine gave the question the respect it deserved. She was silent for a full minute, in order to convey how seriously she took his words.

"No, this is light-years from madness. I've examined the data stream...you can do so too, if you would like. Throughout history, in times of great crisis—war, natural disaster, of grave insecurity for all reasons—humans have always reproduced. Sometimes at an even greater rate. I think I know why. It's most necessary for the species to continue in the face of danger. Nothing can be allowed to vanquish humanity—and now, for us, our new integration of android and humankind. He would be the first of his kind."

Raymòn blinked repeatedly. "He? Why not she? A little girl like you would be so perfect."

"First, I think, a boy. A sturdy, robust boy; someone who could be your progeny in all ways, and in the communal mind as well. Long-term genetic continuity is passed from father to son. The only chromosome that survives the test of time is Y, remaining virtually unchanged."

"I want this to be our child; I want her or him to be as much like you as like me."

"I believe we can engineer that; Wil's father, Tritan Tork stet-Sulston, is the person who can help us with this."

She stopped suddenly. A light, high thrum coursed through her architecture. Speech was impossible as she saw within her wave/fibers the approaching transformation. Awe filled her.

Ray felt a pang of dread. Her silence seemed to auger a problem. Had she realized it was a bad idea? Brow furled, the joy in his eyes about to go dark, Sunshine rushed in to reassure him.

"All the mechanistic elements can and will be worked out. Perhaps a celebration is in order?"

Relief smoothing his countenance and his spirit, he let loose some of the joy which had been rising and falling: "We've got to share this with our absent amigo."

Sunshine hung back for a few seconds, wishing to give the full gift of the telling to her beloved. Raymòn walked, clapping and stomping, to the glass door leading out to the yard. It retreated and Mov looked up. He had held the space of not knowing as a volitional act of love, and now he would open himself only to what was about to be shared.

"Good news? Yes, it's written on your face!" The Companion stood, ears perked up, a smile already widening. He was happy if his friend was happy.

The news was good, dramatically so. All the implications came rushing into his fertile mind. "A child! This will be the greatest gift!"

Mov began to prance and whirl, humming all the while. Every few seconds, he leapt high in the air and shouted, "The greatest gift!" Raymòn was aware that something of great significance was transpiring.

Sunshine, who had joined him, explained what they were witnessing.

"It's the Dance of the Joyous Companion. I've only heard about it. It's Mov's greatest acknowledgement. He's giving us his blessing and his unending love."

By the time the ecstatic one was finished, his palpable energy had suffused the space around him. It was like being ionized. In this newly restored and very hopeful place, the three returned to a more serious mode, contacting their three sources primary of information: V'hanie, Gharry, and Wil Tork. Sunshine also chipped Wil's father, the great Tritan Tork stet-Sulston.

When she saw the in-com from Storm King to Victree Rain, V'hanie's heart both danced and fell. Before his first words, she felt the polar intensity of his emotions: worry and excited anticipation, fear and joy. She listened as he told her part of the story; he would not explain the joy. She respected him enough to refrain from pushing him. She would know as soon as he felt it was safe to tell her.

V'hanie told him what she'd heard about their parents, how they had been taking a more public stand against their son's Joining. Raymòn had not been keeping track of Armonté and Ilsa, partly because he was too distracted, but also because he truly wished to avoid thinking about them. He steeled himself for what was coming.

"Our father was on the vid, shedding massive crocodile tears, bemoaning his fate—that his 'misguided' son had thoughtlessly acted in a way that would destroy the fabric of our world. I was ashamed to be his offspring. He's a hateful man and, I believe, an immoral and devious one."

Despite all that had intervened, some of the old questions of self-worth reconfigured in Ray's mind. With a boulder of shame and confusion weighing him down, he was barely able to ask, "And Mother, what did she say?"

"She didn't say anything. She just stood to the side and behind the great man— sanctioning him with her look of admiration and approval." Raymòn could picture his sister's disgust etched on her face. "Sometimes I think she's the truly evil one. She's not deluded; our mother knows what she's doing."

Her brother was silent. She became worried that she had gone too far, but she knew he had to be aware of the forces against him.

"Can you come to see me? I think we have to be together. I'll gather the information you asked for, but it might be wise to exchange it in person. And, I miss my brother."

All Raymòn could do was nod. V'hanie got it.

Next he chipped Wil, making the untraceable com.

"Don't say a word; I already know. We four should meet. I'll see you later."

Relief at not having to have another conversation did little to counter the nausea flooding him. From an archaic shared unconscious (or was it the data stream), a thought appeared in Ray's mind:

Father, why have you forsaken me?

Mov chose to make visual contact with Grandpa Harry. During their private time together, the elder android had given him access to his holo-telepathy. It was an extremely rare privilege. The Wizard of Hawking Forest needed to be told very little, and he could read the Companion's body as well as take in verbal communication. But more than the exchange of information, Mov wanted to look upon the benign countenance for a little while.

Harry assimilated the chilling news about the nanobot with his usual compassionate but balanced perspective. "I have some thoughts to offer. Let's switch to non-visual telepathy."

Before we continue, there needs to be a rewashing of the data stream. Any information that might be detrimental to you can be segregated to the encoded subset. I know you've been doing this, but there is a new encoding that will add protection. Share this with the others. The new data was transferred in purethought, no language as an intermediary. This was another capacity androids avoided employing except in extreme situations.

There is time to wait until three become four; then you will need to move. I understand that your Special and your friend are in grave danger. You will do all you can to help them. But you can do no more than that. Fare well my special child.

Stet-Sulston was aware of Sunshine, so he responded instantly when she chipped. He had a hunch about the reason for her com. His non-rational access to knowing was one of the sustaining forces behind his brilliance. He invited her to visit and consult.

Not long after their interaction, Tritan's extraordinary progeny arrived. As always, he showed up like an apparition. Before he entered the house, he rewrapped it in his most recently tweaked nullifier. He did a molecular scan of everything inside and out, and assured the family that no further breach existed.

He stood before Raymòn. Neither showed any expression on their face. "You have retreated, I see. So it must be for us." This was the first reference he had made to their shared nature.

"There is a part of the world where you would be less under siege. Mov already knows what I mean."

The Companion tilted his head forty-five degrees, thinking: His skills are always greater than I could imagine.

Tork continued. "That transition will be for another time. Now, all your augmentation must be adjusted." To the androids he said, "I will make the changes to your architecture myself this time; it won't take long. It will not produce the kind of disorientation you experienced before."

Within an hour, all procedures were accomplished. This time Raymòn had a mild ache throughout his body—more of an awareness of himself on a cellular level—but no lingering emotional reaction. The androids each felt as if a thin film of identity had been stripped away, but when they looked into each other's eyes and spoke their names, it receded.

The next day they all traveled to their meetings, leaving no markers for anyone to follow. Tork had reassured them that, although there would always be some vulnerability from unpredictable sources, they were cloaked in an even more impenetrable mask of invisibility.

V'hanie was now living with Garth-Ann Tova Nu, deep within a fifty-acre wooded piece of land with its own private lake, up near the northern tip of the Nucoastcolony frag, in the town of Mainesail. The perimeter of the property was guarded by seeing-eyes: small, cylindrical, self-policing bots with 360 degree vision, an upward range of one thousand feet, and an underground range of five hundred feet. Any intrusion, even by birds or small animals, was immediately displayed on one of the security screens in each room. Raymòn's approach was duly noted; Garth-Ann was standing inside the door, which dematerialized.

Serenely, he welcomed V'hanie's brother. Garth-Ann was a year older than she. His quite lovely ultramarine hair was styled modishly, almost straight up, coming to a winding curl on top. It added about five inches to his height, which would have been six foot six if he hadn't been wearing five-inch wedge boots. He towered over Raymòn. His light green eyes were accentuated by dark blue under-eye shadow and extended, almond-shaped black outliner. The effect against his almost jet black skin was arresting. When he smiled, his kind spirit splashed onto the artist like a bath of peace. He was a Multi, possessing both genders, sometimes highlighting one or the other—or both. The slowly growing number of people like him were usually capable of an exceptional depth of compassion.

"I'm so glad to see you! It's been a long time. Your beautiful sister is coming in from the lake. Please...my house is yours." He swept his long, many-braceleted arm in a gesture of invitation. His slender but muscular body moved gracefully aside to allow Raymòn to pass.

The Self-Contained man entered, fascinated, as always, by Garth-Ann. Only now, in the expanded awareness of his own new relationship, did he wonder... what, exactly, was the nature of his sister's connection to this unique person? He was about to get some more information.

Looking healthy and content, hair still wet, V'hanie entered the large front room. It was casually furnished with overstuffed chairs and small couches, many pillows thrown decorously around. She ran to her brother and stopped a few feet in front of him. Despite her efforts to contain any impulse to touch him, her face conveyed full-on delight: eyes and nose crinkled, cheeks puffed out in the widest possible smile.

"Hey, Storm!"

"Hey, Rain!"

Garth-Ann was ever sensitive to the feelings of others, and like Mov, was inclined to support any desire for privacy. He asked if anyone wanted anything. Before he left the room, in long languorous strides, he touched V'hanie on the cheek with the kind of tenderness that answered Raymòn's questions.

"I know you need the information I've gathered, but can we just spend a few minutes catching up on the other parts of life—like your art, and how it is to live with Sunshine and Mov?"

He wanted to share so much with his sister, but he was afraid he might break down if he did. Art was the safer subject. He took out his tablet and showed her some of his newest creations. As always, she let her excitement about his work show in her admiring comments and in the look of intelligent appreciation that lit up her face. She especially liked Super-Special.   When   V'hanie said, "There's a hero the world really needs!" Raymòn's look—a rare one, deep into her eyes—said, You really understand.

"You don't have to talk about other stuff. You know I can tell you're happy. When I met them, I could feel that Sunshine and Mov were deeply good beings." Seeing her brother become a little more tense, she shifted to the most important issue.

"I'm pretty sure I found the right place for you and your family. You know how much I love to do research." Her particular skill was in subjective knowing, as opposed to the unearthing of pure facts. She applied a combination of her brilliant mind and her considerable non-rational awareness. It was this melding which made her an invaluable resource.

"Well, I did my thing and mined the allmind, but then I got some extra help from my friend and favorite teacher, Honoré Langor-Greco. She's an All-Conglostate Scholar in history and geography; I've learned so much from her, but it's just a little of her deep knowledge.

"Here's what I recommend: In the heart of the New Equatorial and Energy States is The Caspian Sea. It's the largest enclosed inland body of water and a very popular vacation destination. On its eastern shore, in the fragstate of Istan, is a town filled with artists, many of whom are émigrés from every conglostate, every frag. It's a place of peace. The surrounding area, which was once was called Turkmenistan, as well as the entire neighboring region, has the lowest incidence of violence and terrorism on the planet. People in this area are far more comfortable with differences than in our part of the world. It's also just a forty-minute airbus ride from Israqia, the great center of spiritual energy. You can Farbeam there if you'd prefer.

"I believe this will be a safer place for your family."

At that moment, Storm King was being chipped by Sunshine. He excused himself, letting his sister know who was making com.

Sunshine, with Mov along for support and company, had been meeting with stet-Sulston. She only had two important questions for the great scientist:

"Has it been done before?" Sunshine asked quietly, feeling more fully "human" than she could possibly have imagined.

"No, you would be the first. Your offspring would be the beginning of a new recombinant species."

"Are you confident you can do what is necessary for a healthy child to be born?"

Tritan gave the fully emotional android a look that exuded both calm and brilliance. "I am. I've anticipated this day for many years. I've thought about the process and have experimented as much as I could without actual voluntary parents. We can do this."

A third question occurred to Sunshine, one the android had not expected to ask this day. Mov, hearing her thought, said, "Go ahead, my special one. We live in the present." He looked at Tritan with his soft, penetrating gaze. He saw the clarity of wisdom in his eyes.

"When can you do this?" Sunshine felt a flutter move like a hummingbird throughout her wave/fibers. This was the step into the unknown.

"I can do it at once. We just need the father."

After receiving the news, Raymòn was scared but not uncertain. He asked Sunshine if she thought he might share their intention with V'hanie.

"Yes. Trust yourself, as I trust you."

It took the younger Réal a minute to absorb what she was being told. What she said was, "Your new family may very well change the world forever. I'm so proud of you. I'm also excited to become Aunt V'hanie. If you need me, no matter where you are, I'll be there like The Flash." What she thought, but chose not to say was, Your enemies will be further inflamed; I fear even more for the safety of all of you.

When they said good-by, Raymòn surprised his sister with an unrestrained hug. Garth-Ann stepped back into the room for a moment to wish him well. As the artist crossed the opened doorway, he looked back. V'hanie was being supported by her Multi lover. He held her as if she was the most precious thing in the world.

Stet-Sulston had a private and state-of-the-art-laboratory on the outskirts of Ludicom. Elevshire existed as a sanctuary for a few greatly revered individuals who wanted to maintain a measure of anonymity and who preferred the extended energy of the LUDI compound.

As he boarded from the airbus port, Raymòn first felt, then saw, a single AILES fly slowly above him, disappearing after a few seconds into the golden tinged, chocolate brown clouds. Was it just passing through? Or something more sinister?

By the time he arrived, a few more questions had been asked and answered. What would the gestation period be? Would they interact at all with the unborn child?

Tritan, which was what he asked to be called, explained: "The standard thirty-eight weeks of pregnancy evolved as much for the mother as for the fetus. It gives women an opportunity to adjust to and get to know their new child. Actually, for the new life to develop fully, much less time is need. For you Sunshine, and you Raymòn, the process can contract to just under six months, with no ill effects for the baby."

The new family was relieved to hear of the shorter duration. It was recommended that a weekly visit be made by the android, the father to accompany her when possible. Because of his experience with his son, Wil, Tritan had an intimate understanding of the ways of the Self-Contained. He assured

Raymòn, "You will not be pressured to adhere to a rigid schedule. Whatever feels right to you will be right for your child."

Ray received this information and the kind understanding that allowed him to breathe more easily. He couldn't say much, just softly, in a voice all but engulfed by emotion: "My son."

It was time to design the maternal DNA. They were made comfortable in a pleasant, if austerely decorated room. The androids stood; the human sat down and stood up quite a number of times. Stet-Sulstan sat in the corner at a plain black enameled desk; he had a list of characteristics they needed to select. A thin, tight-fitting, and brightly patterned helmet made of effected silk covered his long white hair. The experimental work he did was occasionally dangerous, but this was more a statement of style than self-protection. He was, in every way, eccentric...the perfect person to shepherd in an evolutionary leap. His exceptionally long, tapered fingers were working continually on the holo-tab, perfecting three-dimensional equations, compounds, and blueprints.

"Do you want to pre-determine the outcome of the chromosomal mix? Or do you want to let nature take its course...?"

Mostly to break the somber mood, Mov added, "...so to speak." Under the present circumstances it was as good a joke as anyone could make. It produced the intended smiles; Tritan laughed out loud.

Beyond the external and other physiological qualities like hair, eye color, skin tone, and what would be translated into muscularity in a human, there were many more subtle and characterological choices to make, requiring assessment and identification of the things which made Sunshine, Sunshine: attributes such as musicality, her almost entire lack of aggression, curiosity in the extreme, fondness for nature.

Sunshine and Mov had both scoured the data stream and were up to date on the latest information about heredity. But, for Raymòn's benefit, Tritan explained. "Many things once thought to be entirely environmentally caused are now known to be linked to specific genes: the extent of an individual's capacity for kindness, patience, empathy, risk-taking, independent action, decisiveness... to name a few... are predetermined. Environment can influence but not fundamentally change these."

"Like being Self-Contained."

"Yes. But that's a composite of a number of genetic markers. All of which need to be present to produce a person like you—or Wil. Have you discussed that? Whether you would want your son to be Self-Contained?"

"I would." Sunshine didn't hesitate.

Raymòn felt a great pride, something new, something his father had done everything possible to kill. "Yes. I would like that too."

"We can architect that, and any other traits you both agree are important."

Sunshine smiled. Their child would truly be an amalgamation of nature and architecture.

Within two hours, the child's genetic destiny was set...his appearance would be left to the chance mixture of genetic combination. But he would certainly be a person capable of courage and compassion; he would be highly creative and extremely playful; he would be industrious. As they completed their design, both parents-to-be began to fall in love with their son. Mov, remaining silent throughout the process unless a specific question was directed to him, was already there.

By the next day, stet-Sulston would finish composing Sunshine's DNA and install it into the synthetic gamete. When they visited the external womb, which Tritan called an embromator, the android felt a rush of feeling which she had to quickly research in order to identify. It was very close to homesickness. The morgonium-plated, Morgondown-lined, egg-shaped environment called forth her earliest engrams.

"How much humanoid contact will our child receive?" Sunshine's brows briefly furrowed.

"There will be a human-android team assigned to him, as there is to every externally gestated child. They are loving individuals who will, when it is safe, make physical contact. There is a small chamber to the side, which is where you each will enter when you visit. They will visit several times a day. They will sing, if you approve. Or would you prefer your child to hear only your voices?"

Derived from radically different issues, singing had great significance to the prospective mother and father of the conceptual child. They hesitated and stet-Sulston offered to give them a private moment. For each of the hundreds of couples he'd collaborated with, there would inevitably be some very personal meaning attributed to what might otherwise have been a solely functional part of the process. He respected individuality almost above all things.

Mov asked a silent question in the tilt of his head and the upward arch of his shaggy brow.

"Oh yes! You are part of our decision." His Special reached out for her Companion.

Raymòn dipped his head in assent. "You sing the chords of the universe. How could we answer this without you?"

The three looked from one to the other. And without any further words needing to be said, they had their answer.

Theirs would be a child of the entire world. The many voices needed to be heard.

Chapter 16–
Humandroid

The New Year was ushered in with the usual fervor. Across the globe, humans made their hopeful promises to themselves. Ludis everywhere spent the last twelve hours of the old year and the first twelve hours of 2264 in continuous telepathic contact. It was their way of renewing their bonds and honoring the flesh and blood designations of time. They would have reason to anticipate the coming year with either joyous excitement or heightened curiosity and focused interest—depending upon their capacity.

There were also new reasons to fear: two live strands of virulent force were being pulled tighter on the Réal-el Ludis and—by virtue of their significance on the planet—the entire world. This was so even though the existence of coming humandroid was still secret. Once revealed, it would be a catalyst for greater malevolence.

The Drovines were celebrating the New Year as well...but differently. They had been behind the incident at the Calmwater Market, of course, but that had only been a test run for the discord and dissention Vanguard was orchestrating. The next despicable phase in lat's deadly plan was about to come to fruition. Lat had set the wheels in motion, activating the hammer of hatred that would come down hard on the androids and the Self-Contained human before the month was over.

Having publically denounced his son, Armonté had allowed himself to be seen in public with the xenophobic figurehead, Rothbec-Kathari. He was no longer in the closet about his sympathies with the MPS. Together they convened a well-publicized meeting with a tragically large representation of prominent individuals. It was time, they believed, to grab the reins of popular opinion, to manipulate the discomfort with and lack of understanding about androids and android/human relationships that was rampant among the masses. Knowing that most people will trade their ignorance and confusion for dogma and certainty, they steered the meeting toward a hate-based activist position.

On December 25th, across the NNS, while the barely religious but deeply commercial celebrations manically unfolded, Armonté Réal and the MPS had issued a joint proclamation. It carried no legal weight but was widely discussed and, as intended, fed the inflammatory fires.

We set forth these new guidelines, for the good of humanity:

No android shall cohabitate with any human.

All android workers must leave their place of employment each evening.

Anyone who observes intimacy between an android and a human should contact someone from the Movement for the Purity of the Species

Anyone who hears of an interspecies Joining must to do everything possible to stop it.

The synergy of the anti-miscegenists was fully engaged—from the three parts of the triangle of evil: the Drovines, the MPS, and Armonté Réal.

No edict had been issued regarding the history-making birth. That auspicious occurrence was not yet known. Wil and his father's reach and power continued to hold against the mounting forces. Their ability to shield Raymòn and Sunshine's privacy remained intact...but for how long?

The Réal-el Ludi offspring was to be born in two weeks. The parents-to-be had selected his birthday—January 18th—the day in 2092 when the first individual android had achieved sentience. Back in that distant time, in a hushed space which glowed softly as in candlelight, underlain by a sub-audible rhythm akin to a heartbeat, in a room with no corners, no sharp edges, in a deeply-buffered quadrant of Magister Systems, a newly created, carefully tended being had crossed the threshold into self-awareness.

The first words, signifying its full consciousness were, "Who am I?"

Its name was Orgone: Bartok Grove's subtle acknowledgement of Orgene Ritgensteen, his co-progenitor of true artificial intelligence. There was no gender assigned, nor was it humanoid. Orgone looked very much like the non-humanoids at Nuvem. It existed for only eighteen years. Its appearance was disturbing to many people and it decided to discontinue; its wave/fiber core was, of course, recycled. So, in the most meaningful way, Orgone lived on.

Since their first meeting with Tritan, the Réal-el Ludis had returned weekly.

Raymòn made a commitment to himself that he would be the father he never had. It was often very difficult for him to enter the side chamber and sit with the transforming child who, before he took human shape at the end of eight weeks, went through a number of unrecognizable iterations. At first he was like a small fish in aspic. In order to encourage a lasting fusion of the human and synthetic DNA, a chromosomal integrity without breakdown, the amniotic fluid was augmented with a denser, cell-nucleus-strengthening substance which stet-Sulston had finely tuned to meet the needs of the humandroid about to be born.

The unborn child's next stage of development resembled a layered ellipse with visible organs stacked in an "unnaturally" linear manner. This was accompanied by the beginnings of facial features and arms and legs.

Sunshine was undeterred by what she saw. She had no archaic whispers coursing through her wave/fibers, telling her what to expect. Human parents have the collective history of the species in their unconscious minds; this provides a sense of what would be "normal." That which deviates too far from what has come before, induces fear or disgust. In order to keep his commitment through these early months, Raymòn would often keep his eyes closed during his visits. He conjured up a less disturbing image, that of a small boy, long curls of darkest brown crowning his head, blue highlighted dark brown eyes, luminous with intelligence and the joy of being alive. His rosy, dusky complexion was the very definition of health. The Self-Contained human did not know that his image was in fact precognition. Not until he met his son.

Over the course of gestation, the couple learned to sing beautifully together. Their harmony was the living metaphor of their promise to their child. At first they offered songs they each loved: soft choral renderings of both old and new music. In the fourth month they spontaneously began to create new music, arising from the now energized triptych of their increasingly interwoven lives.

In between visits, their planning for the relocation they had agreed must happen, was steadily progressing. V'hanie's suggestion of the town in Istan had been independently offered by both Grandpa Harry and Wil Tork. They would be moving to Asuda Ýer, which meant "peaceful land" in Turkmen. Raymòn and Sunshine were both worried and hopeful.

After the fetus achieved five months, a time when the hybrid couple were assured he was strong enough to survive outside the embromator, the android shared her desire and concern.

"I would like to tell Berke and my housemates about Khalil-del-món, our son." Using Arabic and Catalan, they had named him friend of the world.

"Do you think it's unwise to let others know? I defer to your instincts in this matter."

"I fear how some people and all Drovines will respond. Those who already hate will be inflamed by his existence. But I remember what Grandpa Harry told us. I, too, believe we must not be stopped; I, too, believe we must not hide." Raymòn was very still. The transformational force of getting to know his son over the past months had naturally augmented the strengths of his self-containment. He was at peace with all the possibilities.

Sunshine saw the steadiness of acceptance in his clear eyes and in the lack of tension in his face and body. She allowed it to permeate her and they lightly touched hands.

In the week before Khalil's birth the Drovines had heard, along with the rest of the world, that a new species was coming into being. After first telling their friends, Sunshine had uploaded to the allmind a simple statement announcing the imminent event. Her housemates, in concert with Ludis across the globe, were in a state of intentional grace. All had engaged the strong force of the universe that flowed through their wave/fibers, and held the enriching energy in a conscious manner, sending measurable positivity to the unborn child. Many humans were excited, ready to see an evolutionary step, ready to welcome a new conjoining of the two sentient species. Insiders, the Self-Contained, and Multi's were uniformly sanguine.

In his loudest, most deranged voice, Armonté screamed at Sharana and Vanguard (who barely hid his revulsion). "Stop him! You can't experiment anymore. Your efforts are weak and you have made me powerless. I DEMAND action—final action—be taken before this damned birth occurs; before a foul mule is let loose into the world."

Vanguard silenced Rothbec-Kathari with a subaudible hum. Lat spoke in measured tones to the now gasping Réal. "Yes. It is time to end this. You can be assured it will be done. We have a plan that the MPS can participate in. It is foolproof." (And you, you ranting human, are the biggest fool of all. It stands to reason that your son is the source of the greatest degradation ever perpetrated on the planet.)

Sharana, needing to reassert her authority, spoke in her strong voice. "Armonté, we will take care of the problems, I assure you."

During the last month, to prepare for Khalil's arrival, Sunshine and Raymòn visited their child daily. He was, they each sensed—with confirmation from Tritan—aware of the coming change. When they sang, they could feel his response. It was as if he was joining them. Mov was now an integral part of the last week's preparations, having deferred to the special nature of the parents' experience until then. His ethereal humming served as background, forging his first connection to Khalil.

On January 17th, the three companions left stet-Sulston's laboratory. They were boarding to the AlbertE terminal in Ludicom when Mov, from his perch on the front of the Janus, saw something about a quarter-mile away blocking their path. It looked like a snowdrift, but there hadn't been any snow. It was hard to see, even for him, and he turned to Raymòn, whose visual spectrum exceeded even that of an android.

"Can you see that white mass down the road?"

Instantly returning from his inward reverie, the human peered intently. "Yes, I see it, but something is very wrong. Below the white surface, I can make out heat prints of crouching humanoids."

Vanguard's hammer was about to deliver a killing blow.

As Sunshine and Mov simultaneously and urgently said, "Turn," Raymòn did so. In the intervening seconds between Mov's sighting and the reversal of direction, they had covered three quarters of the distance to the white mass.

Urging the Janus forward as fast as it could go, the androids holding on tight, they sailed off-road, Raymòn instructing the board to "divert" and "reorient." It was fully responsive and managed to elude the now visible humanoids who were giving chase: some on foot, some with boards, all holding weapons. It was a mob with hatred so intense, the three could feel it on their backs.

They approached the high-speed mono station as an AlbertE was about to depart. Knowing their lives were on the line, Sunshine, who could do things with her body humans weren't capable of, grabbed Raymòn and rather gracefully jumped across fifty feet of space into the all but closed entry point. Mov, a fine jumper in his own right, was right on her heels. As the entry sealed, they saw a now loudly raging gang of at least twenty males of various ages, and six or seven women who appeared to be mid-fifties. Many carried stunners; some held vicious looking barbed metallic objects; some of the larger individuals just had balled up fists. This was to have been a Drovine-instigated incident. It was to have ended in the death of the three.

Sunshine whispered, "Don't speak of it." Her admonishment was not necessary. Raymòn could not have spoken. He was inside himself, disconnected from any emotion, thoughts reduced to the simplest concepts. "Home." "Safe." "Hide."

And Mov knew better.

As soon as they were back in their Calmwater home, it was the android on the brink of motherhood who instructed her mate to chip Tork. He followed her specific commands, still without any feeling. He said what she told him to say: "Come now."

When he apparated at their back door, which dissolved and resolved in response to his personal frequency, Sunshine spoke. "We will need some special protection tomorrow. It will have to extend to all our contact with the environment between here and your father's lab. And then we will need reinforcement around our space. There will be a ceremony held here after the baby is born. Many Ludis will be attending as well as some humans."

Wil had been planning this since his father told him of Khalil's birth date. Very little happened that he didn't either anticipate or find out about immediately.

He spoke almost inaudibly; his state of mind was not far from Raymòn's. He looked no one in the eye. "There is a net which can extend as far as we need it. It is only viable for one day. It's a kind of cloaking device I've used once before. It will attach to each of you and combine and lengthen—you might think of it as stretching—across all the space you travel. Before you leave for Elevshire for your son's birth, you will need to walk around your property together. That will shield it for the ceremony. I will tent the property around my father's laboratory, as I did for the Joining. I would like you to travel by a modified microcab, which I will send for you in the morning. It uses faster propulsion than the regular kind and can accommodate all four of you."

While he spoke, Sunshine and Mov searched their data stream for information about the net he referred to. There was nothing. Ray began to resurface after hearing about the extra protection to be provided the next day. Still looking off into a safer space than a human or humanoid face, he asked Wil to tell them what the net was composed of.

"There are sounds which exist only in deep space; they have something similar to mass, but, more accurately, they are an alternative to anything we know of physics. They are related to interstellar plasma but exist outside the range of human or android hearing. I became aware of them through a young astrophysicist who studies the arcane; as is his wish, he lives anonymously. The sounds can be woven. They take on new properties depending on the warp and woof, and they can exist ephemerally in our atmosphere."

He didn't mention it, but he would be accompanying them through their day. In a manner of speaking.

Mov, something of a history buff, said, " I think Wil is a modern magician. He conjures with incantations of the universe; his miraculous creations remind me of the pumpkin in Cinderella." Sunshine and Ray checked the data stream and quickly read a description of the ancient children's story.

Seeing the lightening of his Special's brow and the resurging contact his friend made, he continued. "I look forward to telling some of these old tales to Khalil-del-món."

The microcab arrived at dawn. There was a driver, which was unexpected.

"I'm Cort el Ludi. Wil Tork asked me to accompany you today. Don't worry, I'm no Drovine."

His use of contractions was reassuring. They would have been more reassured if they had known it was Tork himself, shape-shifted into an undetectable disguise. He could effect a complete metamorphosis, through a method he shared with no one, not even his esteemed father. It was an even more tenuous application of the deep space sound net, not woven but internalized; while it was held within his body, there were no limits to the shapes he could assume. He was, for the duration of that process, a self-sculptor of cosmic proportions. There was a risk. The state in which Wil animated the net was neither solid, nor liquid, nor gas. If he miscalculated the velocity of the non-dimensionality, he would, quite simply and quite permanently, disappear. The edge was his home, so he was not deterred. And, he reasoned, only Nixon could go to China. As the old Vulcan proverb indicated, he was the only one who could get the job done, so he did it.

A new buzz of energy hit the small family before they exited the cab. The entire team of robot, android, and human scientists, midwives, and technicians were lined up on one side of the embromator; Tritan stood on the other side, looking as pleased as a person could look. His long white hair was in its more typical disarray, no protective helmet needed. His pride and excitement lit the room.

He didn't have to ask anyone if they were ready.

There was only one question. "Raymòn Réal, would you like to deliver your son?"

Now was not the time to let fear or aversion control his behavior. The Self-Contained human stepped forward. With Sunshine and Mov vigorously nodding in unison, he said, "Yes!"

As Tritan instructed him, he entered through the side chamber. Khalil was small but perfectly formed. He opened his eyes and looked into his father's, who saw they were as he had imagined. Raymòn, robed and gloved, carefully lifted the child. They released their gaze, in the manner one would expect a Self-Contained father and son to do. He walked from the chamber and one of the midwives quickly took the boy, placing him under a soft warming wave being emitted from above the Morgondown table where she swaddled him. He was clean and dry within seconds. He did not cry. She returned him to Raymòn who then handed him, with great care, to Sunshine, still keeping one hand under the boy's head.

"Khalil-del-món Réal-el Ludi, welcome." The child very briefly looked into her porous blue eyes. He then looked away. He had taken her imprint deep within himself.

As the evolutionary family turned to leave the laboratory, everyone felt the same sense of history being made.

Mov stopped at the threshold. "The stone has been tossed into the water. The ripples will come. Nothing will ever be the same. We thank you all for your courage."

Cort transported them safely to their home. Khalil slept. Whenever he awoke, Sunshine or Raymòn fed him the special formula stet-Sulston had prepared. Their wall would be able to duplicate it easily. An aura of peace enveloped them all. Tork, his cover as Cort intact, offered to patrol the perimeter of their grounds.

"When your guests arrive, Tork asked that I come inside, just to add another measure of protection."

He was unobtrusive and had an amiable and non-threatening demeanor. He would not present a problem.

Arriving just after V'hanie and Garth-Ann, who were the first, Tōnna and Charl skipped from their microcab, poised to enter the Réal-el Ludi grounds on foot, as all guests had been instructed. A rather stately woman was standing near the entry point, which was designated by an arched and zigzag-edged non-representational topiary; it had been fitted with an almost invisible gate. It appeared as if the hedge itself swung open and shut. The bush was in the break of a dense line of hybrid poplars, silvery-green-leaved shade trees, forty feet high. Her face was hidden in a wide, olive cowl draped over her head. She slowly approached the twins. Tōnna felt the shock of remembering what had happened the last time an uninvited guest showed up. Charl felt her stiffen.

Ilsa Réal lowered her hood.

She'd had a change of heart. She was there against her husband's wishes— not that she had told him where she was going. Raymòn's mother knew that, by this act, she had broken with her husband forever. If he didn't know of her whereabouts at that moment, he would very soon.

Tōnna was skeptical. Ilsa did not insist, but she offered a box covered in dark blue synthstock, which she had brought for the child, her grandson.

"It's something precious, from Raymòn's childhood. His first tablet and stylus." It was scratched and chewed on by the little boy who loved to make colored shapes appear. It was primitive by current standards, but she had preserved it all these years without Armonté's knowledge.

"Give this to him. Tell him I regret my cruelty and lack of understanding. If he can ever forgive me, he might try to contact me through my friend Grolier. That's where I'll be staying now. I can never return to my husband."

Tōnna hesitated, but Charl reached out and took the simply wrapped gift.

Some of the people and androids who showed up before the sunset ceremony were figures of international stature: There were a pair of representatives from each conglostate: one human and one android. Some were members of the Global Academy, and included the two States' Counselors from the NNS, Armonté's superiors. There was an Elder from the newly purged Android Council,

165

Rathsen el Ludi. Grandpa Harry had sent him as his emissary—his allegiance was not in question. He thought it wouldn't be wise to attend himself; his accrued wisdom, which now operated at the level of instinct, told him his would be an incendiary presence. He would be seeing the new child soon, in a less high-profile setting.

It was, however, the presence of Ramses Morgon that produced the greatest awe. He was a man of slight physical stature. His long, thick, black hair, which hung unrestrained down his back, and the deep epicanthic folds making his eyes barely more than slits, gave him a distinctive but oddly old-fashioned look. Friends called him "Khan." Whether they were referring to Genghis or to the superhuman character of old science fiction was not clear.

It made sense that those who were in the forefront of life on the planet would want to give their blessings to the child.

All took notice of how Khalil never cried. He was basking in the good energy flowing uniformly throughout the space. While it was so that he was being launched into a world hostile toward his very existence, his brief life to date had been filled with love and support—which would adhere to his spirit always. It was precisely what he would need as his future unfolded.

Everyone gathered by the opened windows overlooking the ocean. The sky was both darkening and bursting with the colors of the setting sun. Pink streaks moved across the horizon. Weatherpainters, under the direction of Kimbo Kaledosian, had permeated the air with olibanum, once referred to as frankincense; they had orchestrated a light show to be triggered by the last rays of the sun.

The ceremony began in silence...except for the sounds of nature.

Raymòn and Sunshine, holding the child, stepped before the vista of waves crashing against a rocky ledge. Mov came to join them, standing between them. His eyes never left the baby, who was now being lifted by Raymòn. The infant's head and body were supported by the artist's steady hands until—his arms straightened— Khalil was high above his head. Inside the widening awareness of the new being, a thrill of what he would come to understand as majesty rippled through him. He sighed and stretched his small body as if to capture it. At that moment, the human and his android mate for life spoke in unison:

"Khalil-del-món, firstborn humandroid, you are a friend of the world—as it is and as it will be."

All who could began to hum; all held hands with at least one other. The sun set. The sky filled with shooting stars of every color.

Chapter 17–
Exile

The twins waited to speak of their encounter with Ilsa until all the other guests had left; Tōnna told Raymòn that his mother looked older, sadder, but more genuine than before. They had visited Veloxiomountain on a few occasions and had briefly interacted with the Réal matriarch. Despite her smiling mask, she had always been vaguely insulting. Tōnna retained a distinct memory of the unpleasant woman's visage and she had recorded their recent conversation as a precautionary measure. "Would you like to see it?"

He barely nodded.

Holding the gift in his hands and feeling the primal heat of his first link to himself as an artist, Raymòn looked to Sunshine.

"Do I dare hope that my mother has changed? Should I be skeptical?"

"What does your heart tell you?"

Sharply, with the annoyance that would occasionally flash when he felt he had not been clearly understood by her, he said, "I'm not looking for platitudes. Our lives are at stake. I need intelligent guidance."

Even though she could feel—as a human would—the recoil from his unexpected irritation, she had no need to offer a defense.

"Of course. You desire my advice. Can you be both skeptical and hopeful? That would mean proceeding with extreme caution, testing her at each step to see if she is really capable of such a change. Can your sister provide any perspective? Can you send a preliminary communication through her?"

Mov had been observing. He was quite unhappy when his Special was taken to task, but he recovered, taking his cue from her. "Perhaps I can be of help in this."

To Raymòn's credit, he knew he had displaced some of his general distress onto Sunshine. This was not the man he wanted to be; he did not wish to emulate his father in any way. Not from guilt, but with regret, he apologized.

"I'm quite sorry that I spoke roughly to you. I'll try not to do so again." Both Sunshine and Mov nodded their approval. His mate smiled and gently touched his upper arm, letting him know that no damage had been done.

"I could ask V'hanie to try to contact our mother, but I would like to hear what you're thinking, Mov."

The small android was ready with his suggestion. "If your mother has truly decided to accept you and your new family, she would also be willing to accept me. It would be a true test. One of the protective capacities I was created with is what humans might call a 'bullshit detector.' If I employ it, which would be warranted (don't you think so, Sunshine?) given the circumstances of life and death—as you say, Ray—I will know if she's sincere. If Ilsa's willing to meet me, it would be a good first step."

V'hanie agreed to be the intermediary between Mov and Ilsa.

When her daughter chipped her, Ilsa felt a sickening mix of dread and hope. She came close to not responding.

"Mother."

"Yes. I'm pleased to hear from you."

"This is not my effort at reconciliation. I don't trust you. But I have an offer from Raymòn."

"I'm listening. What does he want me to do?"

"Do you know who Mov is? I'm sure you do. The world knows who the Companion is."

"I do. It's Sunshine's Familiar."

"Companion."

"Yes. Companion."

"Would you be willing to meet with him?"

"Why? No, I don't need for you to answer that. Yes, I will. I'll do whatever it takes to make amends."

"Very pretty. I know... you're a new person."

Ilsa was stung by her daughter's sarcasm; V'hanie had never spoken to her like that before. Tears blurred her vision, not something that happened very often in her life. As she blinked them away, she thought of her son, and she absorbed the feelings. Ilsa waited, without resorting to any of the rejoinders she would typically have countered with.

V'hanie noted of her mother's lack of response. There would need to be a great deal more than that before she could even consider that a change had occurred. Nevertheless...

"It will have to be tomorrow. Mov will meet you in Green Normal View at the group home where he and Sunshine had been living. You two will be given privacy. Can you be there at noon?"

"Will we be having lunch?"

"Androids don't eat, Mother. Perhaps you should do a little research."

Another sting.

"It's on Transit Street; it's the house with the cloud."

"...the cloud...?"

"I've got to break com, Mother." And she was gone.

Ilsa spoke out loud with no one to hear her. "I'll be there. I have to."

Amidst accelerated preparation for relocation, Mov said goodbye to his family. He seldom went places solo. It was an auspicious enough event to warrant extra acknowledgement. Khalil, who always chuckled when the Companion came into view, reached out and grabbed a handful of his soft coat, as he received a warm, dry nuzzle, android cheek against humandroid cheek. His grip was strong and it was only when Sunshine distracted him with a song that he released his furry friend.

"Thanks for the send-off, Khal. I'll miss you all."

In the upcoming exodus, which was only days away, one of the greatest sources of concern was how Raymòn would continue to work with the InterGalactic Artists. Benito, Tōnna and Charl had 3-D'd to discuss it. It was a form of communication seldom used. It required intensive preparation before chipping; each individual had to enter a kind of trance state, one in which they tapped into their inner-viewing ability. In this instance, it was well worth it.

It was Benno who solved the problem.

"We can work separately, as we do right now. Once every two weeks, we'll Farbeam to Asuda Ýer. We'll meet at Ray's. He'll just have to set up a full studio and lay in tasty supplies. We'll take the party to him!"

There was no resistance to that idea.

Berke had, naturally, been alerted to the Mov-Ilsa meeting. He didn't require any details; if Sunshine or her Companion asked for his help, it was given. He had cleared the house, letting the others know there would be a meeting that concerned their sister Sunshine's new family. Patchin and Marti had offered to remain and provide healing and bolstering background music; Berke thanked them, but demurred. Torina wondered if she should re-ionize the cloud or modify it in any way. Berke thought she ought to let her energy guide her. She spent the next hour gliding between the wall and her cloud; when she was done, it glittered in a way it hadn't before.

Mov was waiting when Ilsa arrived.

He'd been early, wanting to spend a few minutes with his old friend. Berke crouched down and the Companion stretched up on his back legs. They embraced, forehead to forehead. A telepathic exchange caught them up on recent events beyond Khalil's birth, which Berke had celebrated.

— I've been to Asuda Ýer. It may be the most harmonious place on the planet. A good choice.

— Please offer thanks to Torina. She contributes so much. And I wish Patchin and Marti were able to be here. I can hear their music in my fibers. Give my love to those who can receive it; my appreciation and respect to all.

Berke went to the door as soon as it indicated Ilsa's arrival. He remembered to walk—not glide. He could see fear in her eyes and some hesitant hope.

It quickly became apparent to Mov that Raymòn's mother earnestly wished to right the wrongs she had perpetrated.

Despite her awkwardness and initial repugnance at speaking to a four-legged android, she found herself charmed by his lucid intelligence and joyful dignity.

"Thank you for acting as mediator...or are you the king's taster?"

Despite her acerbic tone, Mov understood what it took for Ilsa to be that honest. He said, "Yes, both. And you're welcome. I wish for nothing else than the happiness of my dearest ones. Your son is one of those."

Before she left again, to live out her new penance and to wait for her Self-Contained son to make the next move, she asked one favor of Mov.

"Would it be possible for me to see the cloud up close? If it isn't too much trouble."

Mov chortled. Curiosity was a sturdy bridge to the unknown. It would be his pleasure to take her up to the roof.

Feeling grave apprehension, but wanting to cross the threshold of her resistance, Ilsa stepped into the android's art installation. It was both calming and intoxicating. A small light dawned. This was the future...if the narrowing collar of hatred could be removed. It could be a strange but wonderful new world.

Ilsa didn't know that Armonté's minions had her bugged with a bot programed to jump from her to anyone Ray was likely to come in contact with. This bit of malice came not from the Drovines, but from the depth of the hatred within the MPS. When the apologetic young man bumped into her, Ilsa had no idea he was engaged in the reverse of an old pickpocket's trick. But Tork was not to be caught unawares twice. His protection had extended to a sweep for any nanobots. As Mov approached the house, there was a silent alarm. The gate locked, the household was alerted.

Mov heard a message in Wil Tork's voice within his wave.fibers. "Wait. You've been compromised. The intruder will be removed."

From the top of the two poplars on either side of the gate, twin beams of cold white light crisscrossed the Companion. They stopped on a spot in the center of his back and moved inside him toward the front of his body. He felt, rather than heard a slight, sub-audible crunch. The beams were gone. The gate opened.

Before the bot (set to create mass destruction when it sensed that all four in the Ludi household were together) was obliterated, it had been holographically copied. By the time Mov was inside the house, Tork had viewed and tracked it to Artayo Rothbec-Kathari, ever her mother's henchman. In disguise, she had—Wil inferred—found a way to cross Ilsa's path once it was known that she had gone over to the other side. It would have been a simple matter to get close enough to her to plant the seed of destruction. Had it not been found, every member of the Réal-el Ludi household would now be dead.

Raymon's face lost all color when Mov told him of how close they came to destruction. He was confused. "Is it my mother? Why did I let myself trust her again? She's more evil than I ever guessed." The agitated artist stomped and was about to begin twirling.

"No, my dear friend, I assure you that Ilsa was an unwitting foil for the evil of the MPS. She's not to blame. I trust her, Ray." His rainbowing eyes were alit with his conviction. Raymòn was somewhat calmed but he would let all this marinate for a while. Other things took precedence.

No one doubted that there would be new attempts on the lives of the humandroid family. Relocation was now urgent, although there was the issue of how the androids could Farbeam. The mechanism had to be reset for their physiology, which was, at its core, not so different than the composition of everything. It was in the reassembly that an android-enabled Farbeamer was necessary. The receiving end, in Asuda Ýer, had to be restructured before they could all leave.

Harry, who was overseeing all efforts involved in the relocation of the family he saw as the standard bearers for the evolution of the planet, gave the task to a Ludi already living in Istan. Orwell el Ludi, created fifteen years earlier, was an accomplished physicist and mechanical engineer. He had refitted other Farbeamers to accommodate travel by his species. The work took him less than a day. He tested it himself, traveling back and forth to Ludicom, where the first refitted Farbeamer had been set up. Orwell, accompanied by his Companion, Hux, met with Grandpa Harry—who was extremely appreciative. They spoke about the impact of Sunshine and Raymòn and their son; Orwell and Hux would be available to offer friendship and support.

"Thank you, my children. I will call on you as needed. It's a comfort to know you will be close to the Réal-el Ludis. The two androids left, feeling blessed by their brief meeting.

Chapter 18–
The Possibility of Peace

After six months of tranquility in Asuda Ýer, life began to feel safer. There had been no incidents, nothing to engender fear. The family was no longer in hiding, in part because no camouflage could be directly attached to the person of a child under the age of ten. It would be psychologically disorienting and could interfere with growth in those early years. Any invisibility would have to operate as an extension of adult cloaking.

Tork had re-implemented many of the same protective measures around their new home. It had a security screen around it, composed of the same type of net used when Khalil was born, which had to be reinvigorated daily. There were also seeing-eyes, like the ones on Garth-Ann's property. The town itself had been wrapped in a protective circle, one which was monitored by several residents—human and android. There was full understanding and cooperation from the ýaşaýjy, the residents, who often referred to themselves by the old name, Türkmenler.

The Réal-el Ludi home had been dug out of a hillside overlooking the Caspian Sea. Stone sculptors had created walls and a façade that transitioned seamlessly into the natural environment. The use of the old material was rare. The house had been in existence for over one hundred years, buffeted and worn by the elements on the outside, but fully accommodated to the needs of a twenty-third-century family. Inside, tones were muted, with splashes of bluish-green. The simple comforts were replicated here—so there was continuity; the house already knew what their previous decorating choices were. The rooms under the bluff had high windows and a cool sense of sanctuary. It made sense that the personal spaces were located there. Nature was a central part of the décor: sunshine and sea foam, birds and rocks and water.

It was Mov who provided the most concrete evidence of how truly different this new environment—now home to the android/human clan—was. On his fourth excursion through town, about a week after their relocation, he stopped suddenly on the street. His Special felt a quick empathic stab of what she first interpreted as alarm, but quickly realized was surprise.

"No one has done it! Not one person."

"Tell me Mov...what do you mean?"

"No one has made the 'sign of the flesh and blood.' Just now a young man put his left forefinger to his temple, but he smiled. He was saluting us."

As expected, there were many artists in the town of 40,000; painters and sculptors, energy shapers like Torina, and performers in the traditional and newer, avant-garde styles. There were breathelings, usually females, who had mastered their breath: they could stop entirely for hours at time or produce exhale that was like a small gale. Their faces and bodies expanded and contracted as they varied their breathing. They orchestrated graceful and unexpected exhibitions of their prowess, which had become very popular.

In the second week, The InterGalactic Artists had gotten together once more. The twins and the giant had Farbeamed as planned. Raymòn had organized a fully decked out studio. Benno inspected all the new media and equipment, lingering most soulfully over the still, mostly unused, stack of paper in a clear, unbreakable container.

"Aye laddie, ye did good; ye made us proud; tis a wonder, tis." He was in a new phase. After getting the new issue of Heroes ready to be disseminated across the allmind, Raymòn suggested they all meet with the local cadre of comic artists. The resident cartoonists had already let him know he was greatly admired.

"Would love to, but give me a second." Tōnna found a full-length mirror and spent quite a number of seconds preening, making sure her impact would be everything she wished it to be. Charl, far less obsessed with his appearance, appreciated his twin's need for perfection. She was, he understood, her own canvas; he was her imago as she was his.

Benito galumphed around—waiting was not his strong suit. "Jeanie Mac! Can we get on with it, boyo's? Can we stop acting the maggot?" No one knew what he was saying, which didn't deter him at all. He was deep into his auld-Irisher period.

There was a local meeting place, the Üçburçlyk: a ten-story inverted triangle made to appear like old-style brick and mortar, but constructed from suffused concrete. It had become the choice for new buildings in the past fifty years because of how easy it was to mold and work with, and its impermeability once set. The process of construction took shape by instruction, rather than any physical confrontation with gravity.

The top tier of the striking structure—the floors progressively increased in size like a wedding cake sitting on its head— had a climate sensitive enclosure, made from the same process as Re-Action-ware. The weatherpainters had designed a cool but sun-kissed day: the sky a tie-dye of greens, clouds pale pink, the air had a hint of mint with a top note of caramel. On this occasion, the favorite Asuda Ýer gathering spot was open to the invigorating atmosphere. Seven ýaşaýjy were gathered around one of the low, roundish responsive tables: an additional segment could be called forth as needed. Body-cupping seats surrounded the tablisa; food and drink would be delivered to their raucous group on floating trays.

The locals stood and howled a greeting, a custom the IGAs thought they just might adopt. There was no glitch in their easy camaraderie. The language barrier fell by the wayside of technology. Rather than struggle with their own primitive translation capacities, Pelittiær, who was known for his otherworldly illustrations, had brought Talktuners, the universal translators. About the size of a pebble, they were set into rings each artist slipped onto a finger. Everything they heard was instantly converted into their primary language; inflection and voice were unchanged.

Tablets were out. For the next three hours, there was no lull in the enthusiastic overtalk, accompanied by the sharing of past works and those in progress. Raymòn was willing—as were his three old colleagues—to give their new friends an advance look at "The World Too Far: Exile and Savior," the latest installment of Heroes of the Galaxy. The new superhero was Firstman, his eyes the same azure-flecked russet as Khalil's. There was an awed moment of silence. Renquist Bali, the elder of the group, a transplant herself from the southernmost part of Pasifika, offered a toast. "To peace and creativity. And to Khalil-del-món, friend of the world."

Benito and the twins would be back often. They had all found a second home.

The spirit can heal rather quickly. Good has the power to disintegrate all but a trace of dread. It was never gone, certainly not when their home net was renewed daily; but Raymòn allowed his thoughts to focus on his loves: art, Sunshine and Mov, and the delightful shock of Khalil's progress.

Sunshine was feeling new feelings: maternal love, particular pride in all the small miracles of development Khalil displayed. She was content. The boy was precocious—from a purely human perspective; his android nature increased his potential for rapid development. He had begun to fluently use language at five months. When he stopped talking at one year, Raymòn explained that it was the way of the Self-Contained. His language would resurface, but in the meantime he was still internally verbal, and quickly became able to communicate via letters and keyboard. He had just begun to stand at six months; by seven months he was walking. He flapped and fluttered, as Raymòn had done as a young child (and still did on occasion). His disposition was as designed. He was received as he was.

When Raymòn held his son, when he talked to him, and then when their communication had to circumvent the withdrawal of the spoken word, neither of them attempted to make eye contact. It was something Khalil seldom did, and most often with Mov. The Self-Contained father understood: the child didn't experience the Companion as a separate presence needing affirmation or understanding; instead, Mov was a willing receiver of whatever the boy offered—everything or nothing. He was like a frictionless surface. Looking into his eyes did not trip Khalil's exceedingly sensitive wiring. It was the same perfect empathy Ramòn received from the four-legged android.

In contrast to the pushback Raymòn always had to contend with growing up, Khalil had not one moment of being made to feel inadequate or strange. Because the small family was quickly integrated into the peaceful town, wherever they went people and androids were captivated by who he was. Each encounter was a celebration of his uniqueness and essential beauty.

Sunshine's days were full of fascination. New sights were everywhere. They were in intimate contact with the sea, the fluid state of nature she most enjoyed. She and Khal would walk—first with him in a bonding-paq, then with tiny, increasingly less wobbly steps—along the shore. It looked and felt different than other large bodies of water the android had seen. Although the Caspian Sea was technically a lake, it was slightly salty due to its origin as an ancient ocean. The android could detect the vestiges of old smells. When she perceived an arresting vista or fragrance, she brought it to her son's attention. His senses were heightened, equivalent to hers and his father's.

"Sniff!"

The little boy smiled as he wrinkled his nose.

"That's the smell of old oil and gas wells.

"Look at the gulls. See! Their heads are black."

Khalil lifted his arms to the sky. "Fly?"

"There are lots of ways to fly, but we don't have wings."

For a moment a cloud passed over the child's face. He looked sadly at the birds. With effort, he brought his words to the surface. "No wings." Unreasonably, Sunshine felt her heart break (that was the only phrase which captured her feeling). She wanted her son to have everything he wanted.

There were quite a few Ludis in town and they offered her a particular kind of comfort. They had been excited to receive her into their community. She was seen as heroic, as was Raymòn. Mov was equally exalted. All the near-death exploits they had survived were embedded deep into each Ludi consciousness. Androids often visited the Réal-el Ludi home; it felt as welcoming to them as it did to human visitors.

The child, being a hybrid, was equally at home in either world—human or android. Toward the end of his second year, having sorted out the necessary pathways in his mind, Khalil became overtly fluent once more. Without any preamble, he asked:

"Can I glide, Mom? Can you teach me?" There were a few frustrations for the humandroid boy.

"Not yet, Khal. You would need augmentation first and you can't do that until you stop growing. That's a long time away."

His intellect and thirst for knowledge were becoming the stuff of legend among friends and family both near and far. "I understand. So, teach me something I can learn now." He smiled with his best devilish grin, knowing his mother would move heaven and earth to give him what he wanted…when that was possible.

"Would you like to learn how to access the data stream?"

"Very much! Do you have to talk to Dad?" He understood that theirs was a family that cooperated, so most important matters had to be shared and an accord reached.

"We've already talked about it. Your father wants you to know everything that piques your interest. Let's take a walk and make a ceremony of this." She saw her boy thrill to the word; his innate sense of majesty was always ready to add some pomp to life. "We'll do a march through town and then microcab to the park. Mov and Dad can meet us at the asteroid. The energy there will be the best."

In 2184, the world had been on alert when it became certain that a five-hundred-square-foot chunk of carbon and silicon was going to make impact somewhere in Istan. A "catcher," really a reverse catapult, was quickly constructed. Android volunteers, who needed no oxygen and who thrived in space, configured it just above the Earth's atmosphere. In a beautiful ballet of wave/fiber coordination, they spent three days basking in the cosmos, using the 52,000 mph galactic wind to sail the catcher into position, making last minute adjustments. The asteroid was received and netted. Next, it was towed to the space elevator, fondly called the ArthurC, which had first been constructed in 2068, then refabricated in the mid-2150s with newer, stronger materials under the guidance of Orgene Ritgensteen and the Compensators.

They lowered the big space rock to Earth and permanently installed it in the crater in Clarke Park, a short distance from the walled town of Old Asuda Ýer. What had once been called the "Door to Hell," a collapsed natural gas site which burned for more than one hundred thirty years, was first quenched by the Compensators, and then became the receptacle for the asteroid.

"Can I get a treat? Can I ride the rides?" Raymòn and Sunshine's son was also just a kid.

"I think today is a day for 'yes.'"

"That's my favorite kind of day."

They inhaled the extravagant freshness of air that had been unpolluted for longer than any place in the world.

Mother and son boarded into town. They walked through the winding streets, seeing the now familiar mix of blue turreted, ancient mosques alongside modern buildings like the Üçburçlyk, and the numerous low buildings that appeared to be gold domes sitting on the ground. They incorporated the old style in a new form. All the freestanding dome-buildings on the Ömür Prospect (life avenue) were, in fact, ground-to-roof solar crystals. Inside, and interconnected, were several subterranean floors. Below ground level was a fully self-generating energy collection site. There was another street of domes that looked just like the crystals, but were differently colored: garnet and jade. They were markets and shops.

Sunshine smiled the universal maternal smile as she watched Khalil enjoy his treat, halva, a local favorite. Breaking a crumble off the almond delicacy, the boy said, "Here, Mama, you can taste it just like me."

At the edge of the populated part of town, along the Sea, were the "rides" Khalil had referred. A natural cave in the side of the rocky cliff had configured over time to produce an air pocket that surrounded the embedded rock walls on three sides. There were strategically located holes in the twenty-foot ceiling and on the seaside walls. When the wind blew with a certain force, those inside were lifted into the air, supported and then gently brought back to the ground. The experience was unpredictable, but happened frequently enough so that many visited—especially with children; with patience, a wait of an hour would often pay off. Nature was cooperative, and after just ten minutes the android and humandroid heard the low keening sound which announced the energetic wind approaching. The child's face lit up and Sunshine's heart expanded. When they were aloft, he said, looking out to sea, "Fly!"

Leaving the cave, they visited the second "ride"— a long, smooth, gently sloped extension of rock. It was a thrilling slide.

Mov and Raymòn waited at the asteroid. The human sat under a genetically mutated tree known as a Kakumi, after the biologist who had created it; its branches were exceptionally long with leaves the size of a microcab. The Companion trotted back and forth, peering in the direction his Special and beloved nephew would be coming from.

When he saw his father and the being he called "Movy," Khalil-del-món ran from his mother's side at top speed, his small legs pumping. He stopped right in front of them, twirled around about a dozen times, eyes closed; looking quickly at Mov, then looking away, he yelled in his loudest voice, "Ceremony! Ceremony!"

At the foot of the tree, Raymòn spread out the purple rug he had brought, which produced an excited exclamation: "Purple Rug Ceremony!" Khalil seemed to glow with joy.

The adults formed a small circle around the child, each speaking briefly in turn.

The humandroid's face became as serious as a two-year-old's could be. He listened intently to the words.

Mov, his eyes rainbowing (which tickled his nephew) said, "You are the most special boy and you're ready for the gift of information."

Sunshine said, "I celebrate you, my son. You give to us; we give to you."

There was a pause. All understood. After looking intently at the nearest leaf, Raymòn looked at Khalil. Briefly their eyes met. They both nodded. "Yes. We are alike. And we are different. I celebrate both. Today you join the data stream. Welcome."

Sarlee Réal-el Ludi leaned forward, as did Khalil-del-món Réal-el Ludi. She touched his forehead with her own. After a minute, the boy's eyes opened wide. "I've got it!"

Mov and Sunshine hummed softly; Raymòn chanted, "Welcome, welcome, welcome."

In perfect harmony, in a high, sweet voice—an echo of his father's when he was a boy—the first of the new species sang, "Thank you! Thank you! For my knowledge."

Visitors arrived.

Tork, unannounced, materialized at their door, not having traveled by any known means. He was just checking in. He could not yet admit, not even to himself, that these four individuals had called forth in him a little used emotion. Some—not Wil, but others—might call it love.

"All your protection is intact. I can find no weakness anywhere. For now, you are all quite safe."

For now. The two androids and the two Self-Contained humans knew that was the most they could hope for. The humandroid was just happy to see Uncle Wil.

V'hanie and Garth-Ann came to stay during the first summer in their new home, then again the following spring. Auntie V and Unca Annie spent long, luxurious afternoons pushing Khal in a swing or rolling a ball back and forth, repetitive pastimes he loved. They played "letters," his favorite game, finding shapes in every nook of the environment that reminded the boy of the alphabet. However much they gave to him, they received more in return.

Sunshine and Raymòn spent quiet, deeply thoughtful evenings with them, daring to examine the opaque unknown of the future. V'hanie spoke of their mother. She had been more frequently in contact with her of late. It seemed to her that Ilsa really had changed. Perhaps there could be a full reconciliation.

"She came to Mainesail two weeks ago. It was a grudging invitation that I'd extended, but Garth-Ann..." She paused and locked eyes with her tall, mixed-gender friend and lover. They each smiled just a little. "...advised me, very gently, to give her a chance. It was only going to be a short encounter.

"She was humble, Ray. I have never thought that word could be used to describe our mother. She was patient. She didn't push for anything. She looked so happy to see me and Garth-Ann. I paid close attention, but there was no trace of bias in her word or demeanor.

"I left the room to make us some tea, just to see what would happen when they were alone. When I heard her full-throated laughter, I thought...well, maybe."

Garth-Ann opened his velvety-lashed eyes wide. It was clear he wanted to speak. V'hanie deferred to his unspoken request. "If I didn't know what you and V'han had dealt with all your lives, I would never have suspected. The most impressive thing was how unguarded she was. It does seem as if she's crossed a significant threshold within herself.

"I enjoyed meeting her and felt she liked me as well."

Raymòn was concentrating on every word being said. Before he spoke, he heard Sunshine's voice in his mind: Trust yourself, as I trust you.

"Tell her I, too, will give her another chance."

Drovines also visited. No one knew. They were careful to merge with the residents, careful to stay far away from the Réal-el Ludis. They were watching, from a distance, never having given up their desire to destroy what the new family had become. Rothbec-Kathari had counseled Armonté to be patient. Theirs was now a long-term vision. The benign nature of Istan meant they had to be extremely circumspect. For the short run, the Drovine visits would have to suffice. Eventually, there would be a loosening of protection, an error in judgment. They would be ready to take advantage.

In the winter of 2267, after Khalil's third birthday, the family traveled to Israquia. With a guide and a microcab at their disposal—both arranged by Grandpa Harry, who had maintained weekly contact and continuous oversight—they visited the spiritual sites, both ancient and recent.

While traditional religion was on the wane, spirituality was not. Cosmosism had been blossoming, and where better to create the combination temple and observatory—The Universal Home—than Jerusaline, renamed when Israel and Palestine finally ended their divisions and united their cultures and commerce back in the mid-twenty-second century. After visiting a number of the not very crowded sites still considered holy to the three major Abrahamic religions—Judaism, Christianity and Islam, the family arrived at The Home. Everywhere they stopped had exuded heightened energy, but it now throbbed as they disembarked from the cab.

Their driver, who doubled as their guide, set the cab into a hoverspace seventy-five feet above their heads, behind the shrine to Cosmosism. Baroni Tyndal, who didn't look anything like Cort el Ludi—for one thing he was human, not android—was, nevertheless, the same person. Wil Tork, working in full harmony with Gharry, wasn't about to leave their safety in a new part of the world to chance. He had met with the family prior to their departure and arranged some portable protection. But he was still the best protection available.

Here there were crowds. A dense cross-segment of the population was waiting, absorbing the benefits of the positively charged environment. They were a little boisterous, but mostly jovial. In less than a minute, word spread like a virus through their ranks: the Réal-el Ludis and the humandroid were there! A crowd of well-wishers surrounded them. At first, the three adults felt terror. Tyndal/Tork solidified the extension of his protective net. He was on full alert, but never fearful. Khalil was smiling, feeling nothing negative. He lifted his arms above his head, opening and closing his hands, wanting to catch the good vibrations. It quickly became clear they were surrounded by love not hate. All relaxed. Well, Raymòn didn't, but he was no longer worried. He held his son's hand—something which was newly permitted. With Mov and Sunshine running interference, nodding respectfully to the throngs, a clear path opened as the crush of people parted to let them through.

As they were about to step through the entry, a change became apparent to Mov through his hyper-lucid senses and, at the same time, to Tork via the completely integrated warning system in his mind. They yelled simultaneously, "Get down!" The two followed their own advice.

From somewhere to their right, a disc of energy, rotating at a speed fast enough to render it all but invisible, had been launched. In a microsecond it would have connected with its targets. Tork knew it was gamma, the extremely high frequency and biologically hazardous electromagnetic radiation. In the same instant as he became aware, he had thrown a tarpaulin of unassailable interstellar sound over the now prone family. The disc had been designed to take out only those in immediate proximity to the boy. It had been the Drovine ability to track Khal that led them to find a moment of chaos they could capitalize on. Once the deadly missile missed its mark, it evaporated. Those who hadn't seen or felt the momentary flash had no idea what had happened.

Inside the Universal Home, there was protection. Cosmosists were able to collect life-enhancing energy from every part of the universe. That was their joy and their reverence. The temple was resonant with benign waves. Every human who entered felt it as inspiration on a cellular level. But androids were transported into a state of bliss; they were truly one with the cosmos. Their wave/fibers sang the timeless song of creation and existence. Despite the near tragedy which had once again threatened them, the androids, the humans, and the humandroid child returned to a peaceful state inside The Home.

Mov looked at their guide, Tyndal, with full knowing. In the moment of hyperawareness they had shared, Wil Tork's mind became clear to the Companion. If he knew, the rest would know, too, since they all had access to the same data stream. Mov segregated that information to the encoded subset to which Gharry had introduced him. It seemed better if Tork could not be identified. This was the first secret he had ever kept from his Special. Lives, he thought, were more important than protocol.

"Movy! This is a happy place!" Khalil-del-món looked into the Companion's eyes. He rubbed his fluffy ears.

With the feeling of great love tinged by the taint of unvarnished reality, the special android thought, So much for the possibility of peace.

Ilsa Réal was no longer herself or, at least not the self she had known for many decades. In place of certainty and churlish rectitude, she had hope and fear. She had found a small house near Grolier, who had offered to transfer extra credits to her—if they were needed. Ilsa, having gluttonously gobbled resources for so long, now felt the desire to conserve. She thanked her friend but made choices to live within her now limited means. Her chief expenditure was for security. She was continually under surveillance. Even the most rudimentary sensors detected it.

She knew Armonté's deepest self; he was, at heart, a terrorist. He would keep her off balance to torture her, day by day adding to her sense of vulnerablility, feeling justified because she had betrayed him.

She had begun to have contact with her son, which made up for all she was suffering. It was a slow first step—he was understandably skittish. She would wait, accepting his pace for the first time in his life. He wouldn't chip her; she understood his greater security concerns. They corresponded through V'hanie, sending messages that were getting longer and more openhearted.

She would wait.

Chapter 19–
Friend of the World

Five years passed in peace for the blended family. There had been many attempted attacks, but none had been able to pierce Wil Tork's continually evolving protection. Frustration was great among the Drovines and neither they nor the MPS had given up the quest to destroy the hated Réal-el Ludis. Armonté alternated between concocting ever more bizarre plans, and exploding with violent rage at his accomplices.

The Wizard of LUDI and many other powerful androids and humans across the globe— who sought a future of species integration—sent benign energy in many forms. This served to enhance and help buffer them. During that time, Sunsine and Mov became well integrated into their home, Asuda Ýer. Raymòn's art expanded as the IGA became enriched by the creative forces migrating to the peaceful town. And Khalil grew into maturity, his architected and innate nature unfolding; he was, with each passing day, a more spectacular being.

On this auspicious day, Grandpa Harry traveled in the company of a small group of specially augmented Ludis. They had emotional awareness beyond that of Insiders, making them hypervigilant to any ill will within a half-mile radius. They were also capable of creating a screen of confusion that both humans and Drovines could not pierce. There was no intent to do harm, only to protect their beloved elder. Gharry was visiting Asuda Ýer on the occasion of Khalil's eighth birthday. His android maturity needed to be acknowledged.

The boy had evolved in many ways. He rarely spun around; he no longer rubbed Mov's ears; he could make eye contact when he chose—which he did a little more often. He had learned to cut off feelings when that was of benefit, as his father had taught him. He had strengthened his compassion for all sentient beings, as his mother had taught him. He was a wondrous physical specimen, long of limb with tremendous stamina. He was, my no means, fully grown, but his intellect and emotional depth was that of a human past adolescence. Puberty was going to happen, but he was fully cognizant of the changes that would be taking place. He was prepared to metamorphose, as he liked to call it.

In addition to his own well wishes, the Wizard of Hawking Forest was the repository of proud and hopeful greetings from Ludis around the world. He would, if Raymòn approved, initiate Khal into telepathy and convey the more than one hundred thousand messages he was carrying.

Raymòn was torn. He offered no response to Grandpa Harry's offer to induct his son into the android way of communication. He needed to talk to Sunshine.

"I know we agreed that our son would be the best of both of us. I worry that he'll become less human if he's able to join telepathically as you can. Am I being unfair? Is this jealousy?"

"Perhaps this is premature. We need time to carefully consider the ramifications. It's true that our son has the potential built into his mitochondrial DNA. We gave him that possibility. But maybe he's the one to decide whether it should remain dormant."

"You're right, Sunshine, I trust him. He's already able to understand far-reaching implications. I don't think my feelings of being left out should be the determinant. I can manage the emotions."

The beautiful anddroid smiled at the slowly relaxing profile of the human she loved with increasing depth as each year passed. "We agree. We'll let him choose. After all, it is his first coming-of-age."

There was going to be a special celebration, android style, with a little regular kid thrown in. Khalil, despite his many differences, enjoyed the company of other children. When he was around humans of his age, he maintained a light, agreeable, playful manner, which allowed him to blend in well. In Asuda Ýer, humans and androids were not segregated. Sunshine had met some women with young children in the park, and at family and cultural events in town. A few had become her friends; their children had very organically spent time with the humandroid boy.

The natural openness of the very young removed any uneasiness the parents might have felt.

"Haýsy? Oglan? Android?" Seven-year-old Vasily Chun, whose parents were natives of Istan, was a little out of breath when he asked the question. They were playing a spinning game—one that was a favorite of Vas' and a sweet remnant of his old way of being for the Self-Contained boy. Khalil understood some Turkmen, so he knew that Vasily was asking—which was he, a boy or a droid?

His friend stopped turning and picked up one of the Talktuners sitting in a small bowl on a table nearby. Khal did the same.

"I'm a boy and an android. I'm both."

"Really? How does that work? And do you know everything? My other friend told me that androids know everything."

"I don't know everything. I was hoping you would teach me some more Turkmen. That's something you know that I don't very well. And I don't exactly know how everything works inside me, but I'm mostly made the same way as you. Look: two hands, two feet, and two ears...which I can wiggle."

That became much more significant than the other sophisticated notions.

The question of telepathy needed to be addressed. Before the other guests were to arrive, the family and Gharry went out on the back deck to consider the issue. The sea would help them. The androids glided out the resolved back door. The child looked longingly after them. Raymòn noticed and understood: he wanted it all.

"You know that androids can communicate telepathically. Well, you can too, if that ability is activated. We would like to know if you think you're ready do so. It is your coming-of-age, so it would be appropriate if you decide whether this is the time." Sunshine spoke in her soft, articulated voice of seriousness.

Raymòn added, "There are always ramifications. Every choice has yin and yang."

"Very wise, my son." Grandpa Harry nodded his approbation, which felt like a shot of pure energy to the human.

"Yes. I want to be able to use telepathy." Khalil smiled out to the sea, which was particularly calm.

"Why do you want this?" asked the Ludi patriarch.

"I want to understand more of what it's like to be my mother and Movy...and you, Grandpa. For the same reason I want to draw, to be like my father and Tōnna and Charl and Benno. I want to be all of myself."

"Before we proceed, you must know that no one can penetrate the mind of another without their permission. Our protocol is to first ask, 'May I?' and wait for the answer."

"I understand." All could see that he did.

"Shall I?" The old android looked vibrant and like a child about to blow out the candles on his birthday cake. Raymòn nodded; Sunshine and Mov began to hum.

"Come here my child." He extended one intentionally aged hand toward the humandroid.

He placed his hands carefully around the boy's ears, fingertips touching his scalp, his thumbs touching his cheekbones under the corner of his eyes. "Now you put your hands exactly the same way on me." Slowly and with great effort at precision, Khalil-del-món did the same, his tapering artist's fingers gently burrowing under the androids long white hair.

Raymòn added his voice to the hum; he could see the energy brighten. His son opened his blue and brown eyes wide. He tilted his head as if he were listening to a new sound. Inside his mind, he heard first Grandpa Harry, then Mov, then his mother say, "Welcome!"

May I? Khal knew the protocol.

You most certainly may!

This is so much simpler than talking. Why do you ever talk?

Ah, my boy, there are many things that are better said in that concrete way. As with all things, there is a time for the internal and a time for the external. You will figure it out. I'm sure of that. And remember, no telepathy when humans are around...not unless they are special people who are truly comfortable with it.

The sole human looked into his own heart. All he felt was pride.

There would be two more milestones for the humandroid: Although he had access to the data stream before the age of three, he could not chip and would not be able to do so until—as it was for all humans—his eighteenth birthday. When he had achieved his full physical growth, he would then have the option of augmentation. It would be somewhat different than his android ancestors, but he would be able to add many new capabilities that were far beyond the possibility of humans.

Was he still the only one of his kind?

Taking courage from the viability of Khalil, there had been two couples around the globe who had tried to create a similar child. They met with terrible accidents, in one instance destroying the lives of the two mothers and the newborn; in the other, the intended mother and father were killed. An unexplained, very localized earthquake, which no weatherpainter was involved in, had literally swallowed the female human, her Ludi partner, and the humandroid newborn on their way home from the birth center in Bolivia-Peru in the NSS. In the second case, the prospective parents were on their way to meet with one of Tritan's associates in Califate, on the western North American coast in the NNS. They never got to their meeting. As they boarded down a quiet road, a quarter mile inland from the Pacific Ocean, a freak tsunami rose up and engulfed them. It quickly receded. No harm came to anyone else.

News of these two incidents served as a global cautionary tale. The Drovine/MPS connection manipulated the echoing horror in the wake of each disaster, making sure the message was received: Even thinking about creating another humandroid child could put you in mortal danger. But there were still three thorns in the sides of Sharana and her cohorts in hatred.

During the past few years, she and Armonté had grown closer. Now that Ilsa was out of the picture, except as another enemy of all that was conceived of as right, he was free to spend more time with her. Each meeting, whether "strictly business" or more of a social occasion, led to two things: They would each stoke their reciprocal fires of loathing, offering each other proofs of the soullessness of the android "things," and massaged facts which were given as evidence for the non-human corruption of humanity. When the subject of Khalil came up—and it always did—Sharana let Armonté rage with disgust at the "freak posing in human form."

After venting their spleen and shaping and reworking nefarious plans, they would start to feel amorous. Neither was capable of any sustained connection, and this aspect of their interaction was invariably brief and quite limited. But it suited them both.

In the AILES-guarded compound, which was the MPS headquarters and the Rothbec-Kathari residence as well, over breakfast in the morning after one of their "passionate" encounters, Armonté put a hand on Sharana's arm. She turned, giving him the look he loved best—undivided attention.

"Tell me what you think of this idea. We've seen how willing my son has been to usher his mother back into his life. What if I pretended to change? Perhaps I could do a convincing job, asking his forgiveness. I'd say or do anything to further our cause. Although it would turn my stomach, I could play up the role of Grandfather, suggesting that missing the opportunity to know the child has caused me to see the error of my ways. "

Just then a steady tone sounded, not loud but hard to ignore, accompanied by the flashing of blue lights around the perimeter of the room. It was high alert. Something of global importance had to be happening. Next, a messenger interrupted them. Rothbec-Kathari's privacy was sacrosanct; the last person to break that boundary was taken prisoner by an AILES and never heard from again.

Meachem bella Russe, second only to her daughter in Sharana's trust, entered; eyes averted, he stood with the excessive military bearing of one who has no other purpose beyond serving his master. He waited.

"Speak. What is it?"

"The Global Academy has just issued a 'recommendation.'" Meachem could see the way his leader's eyes turned to slits at the mention of the austere body's name. Her jaw was stone.

He recited verbatim, "It is our wish that the divisions between humans and androids be healed. We encourage the forsaking of bias in favor of collaboration. Joy is in the fusion of the two species, as is the future of mankind."

"Those pompous fools have unleashed the demise of the human race. Their recommendations are treated like proclamations from on high. We have no more time to wait. Action is called for." Sharana stopped speaking, piercing bella Russe's usual imperviousness with the laser of her silent demand.

"There is one more thing." He paused to see if she wanted to say something. No. Her waiting felt like an ice-bath. "The Academy issued one of their Medals of Freedom, to 'Khalil-del-món, friend of the world.'"

The humandroid's grandfather addressed himself to Rothbec-Kathari, hissing his words, barely able to speak in the face of his blinding rage. "We must do what I suggested. This gives me a rationale."

She dismissed the messenger just by flaring her nostrils.

"Yes. Make it so."

Since he had no direct access to his son, the father arranged to have his opening salvo delivered by one of the undercover Drovines in the Istan town. A single message bubble of partially solidified sound, housed in a gaily striped red and white containment film, was anchored to a large rocky formation in back of the Réal-el Ludi house by an Aichan link, the repurposed radio beam structured to hold these popular communication vehicles in place until the recipient triggered them.

It was a week after the boy's first coming-of-age; two days after the Academy's announcement. The family was taking a walk along the shore. All stopped when they saw the bubble. The now constantly present autoscan rang its high-pitched "all-clear." There was no danger. As they all approached the missive, it sensed Raymòn's presence. At once, it glowed in a fusion of golden "static" When that cleared, Armonté's words could be heard distinctly. His tone was one Raymòn had never before experienced: muted and soft-voiced.

"My son. Many years have gone by, years in which I've had nothing to do but reflect on what my actions have caused. I've been an angry man with blinders on for most of my life. It is only the endless sense of loss I carry with me, and the yearning to see my family—you and Sunshine and the special boy I've heard so much about, my grandson, Khalil—which has lifted me from my stubborn blindness.

"I can't expect anything but distrust from you. And rightly so. I have no way to prove I've changed, unless you would grant me the favor of seeing you again. Whether you do so or not, I want to send my proud congratulations to your son, who is being honored by the Global Academy. I am supposed to attend the ceremony, but I will await your instructions. I don't ever want to do anything again to make you uncomfortable, if I can help it."

The bubble evaporated, leaving no trace. There was silence in its wake. Raymòn looked at Khalil. He was staring into the distance, his eyes on the horizon. His thoughts were his own and he showed only curiosity by the alertness of his entire presence, his slightly parted lips, and tilted head.

The Medal Ceremony was an annual event. It was already daunting for the Self-Contained artist to imagine being in The Grand Hall of the Global Academy, among the dignitaries and throngs of eager citizens. He knew it would be challenging for his son as well. Now there was something else to wrestle with. Was it possible that his father spoke truly? Could there be an end to a lifetime of hostility and lack of understanding? And if not, what was the meaning of this message? There were too many components to think about at once. He felt dizzy, like he was swimming in ever tightening circles.

Sunshine saw the alternating bands of worry and confusion streaking across Raymòn's face. "Let's go home. We need to have a family conference. A thoughtful, calm discussion—once we're all ready to talk about this."

With gratitude, but little relief, the human father turned around. His son followed, then stopped. He spoke with the combination of candor and comprehension that was his customary way of communication.

"I liked the message very much. I liked the way it was delivered. I don't know if I like my grandfather." This was said to the open water. Khalil experienced being one with it. He often said he felt its unity and buoyancy.

His words were simply the truth.

Mov had been silent since they found the bubble. He had an unshakeable conviction that the senior Réal was up to something malevolent. The Companion had done a quick search of the data stream and found a pattern of meetings with the head of the MPS, extending back in time for nine years. Over the preceding eight months, the pattern was one of increasing frequency. That information only served to reinforce the strong sense he had when Armonté's words were heard. Liar! He knew he needed to be respectful of Raymòn's and Khalil's processes. With Sunshine it was different; their connection made it simple to convey the certainty he felt. She would feel it too.

Once inside, Raymòn went directly to his studio to draw. Mov and his nephew spent time playing a balancing game. Using their bodies and gyroscopes imbedded in objects of different sizes and shapes, they would take turns trying to create balanced structures which they held up with a finger or a foot pad, on the tip of a nose, or by a tail. Sunshine closed her eyes and gathered some alpha. She wanted to be at her best and most unimpeded. Each one allowed the unfolding of awareness below the level of consciousness to prepare them for their discussion.

Letting Raymòn control the timing made the most sense to all. After several hours, he put down his stylus.

Mov and Sunshine waited for him to begin.

"My feelings of dread and hope have receded. If I examine what I know, it is only that my father has never been someone I could trust. Not ever. Why should I trust him now? And yet, what if he has changed as he claims? Wouldn't it be better to forge a new bond? For me and for Khalil?"

After he spoke, he briefly left the sun-drenched room where the family was sitting and standing. Returning a minute later with a sheet of the gift of paper Sunshine had given him, he held it out for all to see. It was divided into two segments, with a scene quickly sketched in each. Raymòn was a master artist and could generate a new drawing with speed and precision. It was, as it had been, his most enduring method of communication.

Both scenes were against the background of an indoor stadium, The Grand

194

Hall of the Global Academy. The royal blue-edged, deep purple seats levitating above the floor made it unambiguous.

On the left-hand portion of the page was a raised podium, illuminated by slowly sweeping spotlights of moonglow and candlelight. Five figures stood together. Pride was evident in their inflated chests, the upturn of their eyes, and their elevated chins. In the center was a child, a jeweled medal glittering around his neck. On one side of him were two males: one old, one young; on the other was a female and a Companion. Beams of light crisscrossed the quintet. From the stands, which were bathed in a rosy glow, sparks of gold created the impression of excitement and joy.

On the right side of the paper was an image of the same podium, but with a heap of crumpled, lifeless bodies. At a distance, under the stands, stood an older man of extreme girth, arms folded, shoulders hunched, a thin line of bitter compression for a mouth. The seats were a scene of chaos: masses of individuals revealing alarm by their outstretched hands, fingers stiffly trying to stop what they had seen. Others were intertwined in a mob of desperation, attempting to evacuate. The only other color besides the seats was a splash of blood red covering those on the podium; everything else was a grim gray.

The humandroid child spoke, his voice soft but clear. "Father, this is your hope and your dread." He held Raymòn's gaze, longer than either would have expected.

Sunshine and Mov exchanged a look. She spoke. Her porous blue eyes opened wide, not in alarm, but with intelligence and caring. Turning from her son to her mate, then addressing herself to the boy, she said, "Your grandfather has been spending more and more time with Sharana Rothbec-Kathari. We must never fail to let the truth, however disappointing, guide our decisions."

Mov, eternally protective of the safety of his beloved charges, held the space with silent humming; with his perfectly compassionate mind he tasted the energy flowing between his Special, her Self-Contained partner, and their exceptional offspring. He felt the unimpeded quality of their communication, and he trusted them to arrive at the correct conclusion.

Understanding the implications of his mother's words, Khalil walked soundlessly to his father's side. He stood, not touching him, not looking at him. Just being with him. Raymòn's gaze was through the expansive Morgonglass window, into the crashing waves, and beyond the horizon.

Raymòn would not respond to his father. There was nothing to be gained.

The ceremony was to be held, as always, on the tenth day of the tenth month. A unanimous family decision was made to attend; each of them would be cloaked in the densest protection Wil Tork could fabricate. They would stand without fear in the face of hatred.

The Global Academy was in the northern Earth Cap. They Farbeamed to Tutmonda Centro (global center in Esperanto—the resuscitated universal language used in the EC). The heated, transparent tunnels leading from the site were anti-gravity fitted, so they could feed directly into the largest building on the planet, which was suspended thirty feet above the continually shifting sea ice. The Réal-el Ludis rode through a tunnel in twenty-third-century rickshaws, towed at high speed by functional, non-sentient robots. As they ascended upward over the last fifty yards, the immense structure was revealed. Awe filled them. The Academy was an ovoid on its side, as tall as mountain. At ten thousand feet, it was twice that of anything else manmade, except the ArthurC.

Sitting in the front section reserved for dignitaries was Armonté, looking as he always looked, smug and mean. No representative of the MPS was present. There were several Drovines, under the guise of glasnost. The Academy had asked Grandpa Harry to place the medal around Khalil-del-món's neck. It would be, for the android elder, a moment of joy and the opening of the very door he had worked a lifetime to unlock. He was never without perspective: He knew this step forward would be met with resistance; there would be a gathering of the anti-miscegenist forces.

Ethanos Kartolini, the President of the Academy, gave a short presentation speech. Upon the death of his predecessor, Academy founder Sang-min Bash, forty-three years earlier, Kartolini had been unanimously voted into this most august position, one he would keep for life. At one hundred twenty, he was of Grandpa Harry's generation; his skin was aged but his clear, visionary eyes were unclouded. Before his ascension to the leadership, he had worked tirelessly and brilliantly to bring the world into a state of greater peace than it had ever known.

"Our world is poised for a new evolutionary step because of you. The name Khalil-del-món will be recited in our future history; the first humandroid, you are a true friend of the world. All know of your character and your nature. You are well suited to be the one that brings us to a new integration of the two sentient species on our planet."

Harry el Ludi took the disc of gold from the matte black morgonium case. It was inset with alexandrite—which shifted in color from reddish purple to greenish blue, and pink poudretteite. As he placed it over the boy's head, he whispered in his ear. "I will always be with you. Thank you for being."

Khalil looked up at the ancient android; he shifted his vision to take in the thousands who had begun to applaud and cheer. He had to slow his breathing and take stock of his physical separateness, as his father had taught him, in order to resist his innate Self-Contained reflex of disconnecting. He stayed within himself without having to abandon the stimuli. In response, as one, the crowd became silent.

The small voice was the only sound in the vast space.

"My mother and father are the heroes. The world has been changed by their love and courage. They, who created me, have taught me to be a friend of the world. Thank you for your acknowledgement. I can feel the joy and peace in it which we share."

The four Réal-el Ludis (Mov had adopted the name), stood together receiving the applause of the crowd. The dignitaries, Raymòn's father included, were standing in apparent solidarity. It was difficult for Raymòn to refrain from running from the auditorium; he was wearing the ear sensors that blocked noise above seventy decibels. They helped him contain his body, but being the focus of so much attention stretched him to his limit.

Cloaked in invisibility, Tork stood by. He saw Armonté Réal flick his eyes to the Drovine sitting two seats away from him. He knew.

The podium exploded in a ball of white-hot fire…

… just as he yanked the lasso of deep space sound he had placed around the family. Once again, they were saved from harm; amidst the ensuing mayhem, Wil spirited them away under his cloaking.

The flash of flame was quickly doused by the containment field which surrounded the space where the podium—now ash—once stood. It was all over within a minute. An impermeable liquid screen, so proprietary to the Academy that it didn't yet have a name, had descended in front of the seats that filled three sides of the stadium. If there had been anyone still standing on the platform, they would have seen the veins in Armonté's temples about to burst. His face had hardened into a livid mask of impotent rage. While all were rapidly exiting, many weeping and clutching each other for support, he sat stock still in his seat, staring at the spot where his murderous desires had been denied.

Speeding back through the tunnels, the family was silent. But, despite the trauma, Khalil had received his medal. He held its message in the center of himself. He would do all he could to live up to his name and the faith of the people who honored him.

Sunshine and Mov permitted themselves to communicate telepathically.

She: Is this how it must always be?

He: We must never lose hope, but we must be ever vigilant.

She: The father and son must live!

He: We devote our lives to make that so.

The Self-Contained humans and the humandroid tasted their fear and pushed it to a safer distance in their minds. In three very different ways they came to an acceptance of what had happened.

Wil Tork thought, For now, they are safe. There is no better outcome.

I will use what happened to create. As long as I'm still here, I'll live and be grateful for each day. Raymòn felt the slight pressure of his son's body up against his own. He lives.

Now I understand: life can be over at any moment. That makes it more precious. The child who was more than a child felt the calm of knowing.

A deep, new fold of fury was now Armonté's. His hatred was refocused on his son, the source of all his shame. He would leave it to the deviant androids and the MPS radicals to conspire about the destruction of the humandroid family. He wanted to erase the name of Raymòn Réal from the timeline of life. He would now take charge of his own mission; he would not fail again.

Chapter 20–
Aftermath.
The Gift is in the Giving.

V'hanie had a message for Raymòn from Ilsa. She was, as was everyone, aware of the narrow escape at the Academy. She felt the urgency of time.

The artist's sister recorded their mother's words verbatim: "I am thankful that you and Sunshine, Khalil and Mov are safe. I imagine that your father was in some way involved in this atrocious act. I ask again for your forgiveness, for my past complicity in his self-aggrandizement and descent into inhumanity. If we can now forge something new, I would very much like to see you and your family. Will you consider that? Please let V'hanie know if there is a date when I might visit.

"I wish you peace, my son, and long life."

Although there had never been any threat to the Réal-el Ludis in Asuda Ýer, Raymòn and his family were feeling more cautious. Customary environments seemed like sanctuaries: the Üçburçlyk, the open-air market, the homes of those people and androids who had become friends. Anything out of the ordinary was shrouded in the anxious unknown. For the present, they curtailed their usual inclination to explore new places.

Berke was arriving by Farbeam. He would be staying at the android group home where Sunshine, her son, her Companion, and her mate frequently visited. It was a smaller house than the one Sunshine had lived in; the four androids, all at least ten years sentient, did not have a house leader. Rajette, just ten, was their spiritual center; Anola, created fifteen years before, was the most social and convivial.

The two male designates were research physicists: both Arca and Boris had been augmented to expand their creativity and to have access to the power of non-conscious dreaming. While all androids could enter a trancelike state at will, the way Sunshine entered alpha, the new capacity took them deeper. Once augmented, they could decide to "turn on" dreaming for a designated length of time. There would be no sensation or awareness until the dream state ended, at which point the android would be aware of a non-specific new comprehension within their wave/fibers. Gradually, symbolic representations, in the form of a hazy memory of things that hadn't actually happened, would begin to surface. The individual would then have access to interpretive tools, comparable to those Freud and his followers applied to human dreams. New insight would flow from this.

The males were older than the females by twenty years, but so young in spirit that spending time with them was rejuvenating. Berke considered them dear friends.

Second only to Grandpa Harry, Berke was the individual Sunshine looked up to most of all. She had to identify a feeling that intensified as she anticipated their reunion. It was the emptiness of missing someone. She noticed that it got stronger as she got closer to the day she would see him. As she often did, she extracted from the data stream the relevant human sayings that seemed to capture her emotion. She marveled at the simple wisdom available to the flesh and blood: Out of sight, out of mind and Absence makes the heart grow fonder. There were almost always two opposite notions available. It reminded her of the vast spectrum of acceptable human responses.

Raymòn had agreed to a visit from his mother. V'hanie and Garth-Ann would be accompanying her, to provide a buffer if needed, or to enable a true family reunion if things went as well as all wished.

There was heightened energy in the Réal-el Ludi household. It felt like an auspicious time. Each one of them experienced a twinge of hope; the opening of Ilsa's heart seemed to auger the best of all possible worlds.

On the day Ilsa was due to arrive, Khalil—having received Mov's encouragement—asked his mother and father to talk with him about his grandmother.

"Am I supposed to love her?" he asked. His beautiful dark eyes were wide. He wanted to know what he was going to be called upon to feel toward this new family member.

Sunshine looked at Raymòn, whose face had darkened at his son's words. He had his tablet on his lap and was quickly sketching something. When he was done, he showed it to the boy by way of an answer. It was an excellent representation of Ilsa, but with two faces. One was a benign, smiling visage, dark blue eyes shining; the other was without apparent emotion, eyes flat, mouth another flat line. There was no warmth in this version.

"Which one would you be most likely to love?"

"The sweet one, of course."

"Then you will have the appropriate feeling in response to the grandmother you get to know. You don't have to love her...not unless she's lovable." Raymòn was saying this as much for his own benefit as for his child's. But he knew he did love his mother. She had hurt him terribly and he had disconnected from those deep, painful feelings. He would wait to see what his artist's eye showed him.

It had been more than eight years since Ilsa had seen her son. While her visits to the resurfacing spa had held the signs of aging at bay, there was a pall over her which had changed her appearance dramatically. She commanded less physical space; there was a hesitancy in the way her body moved. She arrived at the front door, flanked by her daughter and Garth-Ann Tova Nu, who had each put a hand on one arm to offer support. Unlike most doors, it first contracted into a lens of high magnification before it receded into the surrounding space. Another bit of security from the mind of Wil Tork.

Once they were inside, Mov approached the group first. He asked that they permit him to scan them. It was understood that extra precautions made sense after the many intrusions and attacks they had sustained. V'hanie and Garth-Ann stepped forward; the Companion had been fitted by Tork with a deceptively simple-looking collar. It was a full-range "discloser," capable of detecting anything which existed outside the realm of what ought to be found on a human. The extent of what the magician had created made Mov a walking high-security defense system. Ray's sister and her lover were clean. Ilsa, shaking slightly, stood very still as Mov came close. He radiated compassion when he confirmed that she, too, was clean.

Tears filled her eyes, but she maintained control. It was her way, but she also understood it would be manipulative of her to prey on any sympathy her son might feel for her sadness or her struggle. Raymòn stood before her, looking directly at her for a few silent seconds.

"Welcome, Mother. Please come inside V'hanie, Garth." Nothing escaped the artist's attention, not the evidence of emotion, nor the softening in the way his mother held her body. As she passed by, he lightly touched her shoulder. Ilsa whispered, "Thank you."

There was no more discussion or reference made to the past.

Sunshine, Khalil by her side, greeted her.

Ilsa said, "You've been the source of the most powerful evidence of love on our planet. You're a heroine; I'm grateful that my son has chosen you as his life partner."

The android felt the resonance of authenticity in the older woman's words; she accepted them graciously. The look that passed between them said, We can be family now.

Ilsa turned her attention to the child. She introduced herself. He looked away. Raymòn, who was watching from the other side of the room, saw her open, then close her mouth. He knew she was going to reflexively tell him to look her in the eye. A veil of sadness crossed her eyes as she became conscious of what she had been about to do...and all she had done. Sunshine thought to leave them alone and offered to put her paq in a guest room.

"Just a moment..." Ilsa opened it and took out a thrumming and light-pulsing object.

The heart of the humandroid opened to his grandmother, not because of the excitement he reflexively felt; it was her indisputable desire that was palpable to him. She wanted to make him happy. She wanted to connect with him.

Delight and appreciation infusing him, Khalil said, "The gift is in the giving. Thank you, Grandmother Ilsa." His endearing smile was quickly trumped by curious little boy eyes. "May I open it? I see there's a small yellow triangle. I love presents with the triangle." Watching his son, Raymòn felt the warming wash of memory...Sunshine's gift to him.

"Certainly, dear child. My friend made this especially for you." Ilsa allowed the small bud of hope she had been nurturing to open a little further.

Grolier was an artisan who created the aerotite boats that sailed to the clouds. Mixing the lighter than air material with morgonium, he'd fashioned a boy-sized hover-board made to skim the water. It had a small sail of effected silk. As were all boards, this one was intelligent. It would "learn" its owner and become responsive to his slightest movement.

When he understood what he'd been given, the Self-Contained humandroid spun around, arms stretched out with shear exuberance. Unlike the anxiety-filled response she would always have when the young Raymòn behaved that way, Ilsa laughed, joining in the free-flowing jubilation. Once more, the artist took note.

"Perhaps one day you and I will visit Cloudworld together." Khalil stopped and looked, for the first time, directly at her.

"Yes, Grandmother. That would be lovely."

There were more presents. For Mov, a pair of wings made of a pliable metal, gravitasium—another offworld discovery. They enclosed him when he stepped through the soft, Morgondown harness.

"You seem like a being who would like to fly." Ilsa's eyes were diffuse with happiness. Although it didn't make complete sense, the strange, four-legged android felt like a trusted, old friend. He had become very dear to her.

"Yes. It is one great longing I've had as long as I've been sentient. Thank you for making a dream come true." He fluttered just a little above the ground, getting the knack, then he soared out the back door and did a grand circle in the sky, returning with a soundless landing.

Directing his attention to Khalil, Mov said, "You and I will make a dynamic duo. You can skim the waves and I'll watch from above. Sometimes we'll swap—we can share our new powers."

Sunshine opened her gift next. When the wrapping evanesced, she held a pair of delicate and finely wrought footwear. The tiny glistening pearls covering the top were holographic: deep ruby in color when viewed from the top, pale peach and ivory from the sides. She slipped them on her feet and felt a rush of ecstatic joy through her wave/fibers. After a few moments, the initial sensation resolved into alpha-peace.

A Cosmosist of Ilsa's aquaintance had developed a line of footwear for humans and androids. The religion's relationship with all manner of energy was exceptional; it was the essence of their faith. Rather than capture energy, they were able to open themselves in a way that gave them access to electromagnetic, sound, thermal, and other forms of energy—including brain waves like alpha. Manipulation of these was a prized skill, one that yielded certain benign products, like the shoes. All the Cosmosists' special knowledge was used for the good of the planet.

When Sunshine discovered what her new shoes could do, her entire architecture lit up, conveying her compete enchantment.

Ilsa said, "I know you will be tested. These shoes can help you retain your harmony."

Without any more words, the android embraced her Tamu Mama, the favored term— literally translated from Swahili as "sweet mother"—for the mother of one's mate.

The last present was for her son. It was wrapped in something wonderful: thick brown paper, in ancient times readily available and referred to as "kraft paper." Again, Grolier had come through: he had connections in many obscure places and had been able to uncover a small but pristine supply which had been buried in deep storage in the basement of the headquarters of a twenty-first-century global enterprise. He said it was called "Ups." Neither of them could figure out what that meant.

Slowly, and with utmost care, Raymòn removed the protective force field, and then the precious paper. He next withdrew what he recognized as a viewer—a thin, rectangular device which sat on the bridge of the nose. It had eyepieces and could be comfortably attached around the back of the head.

"Put it on, son."

He fastened it in place and found the small red activation button.

Everyone had gathered around him. Watching and waiting. Hands holding the VuGuru in place, he began to spin, elbows extended, whooping with joy.

He was watching one of the two remaining original copies of the 1978 Superman: The Movie.

After several minutes, he reluctantly took off the VuGuru. His vision did not so quickly return to his surroundings. "The colors! Primitive and bold!" He took a deep breath. He was still viewing in his mind. Nothing, not even the data stream, could match the thrilling retinal response of "watching" a movie.

Finally, he said, "This is one of the greatest gifts you could give me, Mother. Thank you."

Unsaid, but felt by all, was what Khalil had expressed: The gift was in the giving. Ilsa had given of herself. She had seen them. And they were now seeing her as one who gives.

Plans were made to show Ilsa the sights in Asuda Ýer. They would visit the town and Clarke Park, take walks by the Caspian. They would be a family.

Raymòn was drawing intensively. He had much to convey. In one day he produced a work of great beauty, which scrolled through his tablet as he showed the avidly interested females: his sister, mother, mate...and Garth-Ann. Both

Khalil and Mov had been in and out while he was working. They had witnessed the creation.

It was a tableau, representing all of them. Inspired by all the gifts his mother had bestowed, but even more by her newly opened heart, he'd drawn a scene in the clouds. All had iridescent wings. Sunshine's hair was pushed back indicating the winds of change. She was in the center with the artist, his self-portrait one which exuded peace. Rippling red fabric flowed behind him; it was a cape. Their child was between them; his wings were the palest, most crystalline. Mov was to the right, close to his Special. His wings were the largest; one was protectively covering the three of them. V'hanie and Garth-Ann, wings intertwined, were on the other side. Above them all, but at a distance, was Ilsa, her wings in motion. She was, it was clear, arriving to join them. The clarity of line, the emotional impact—it was the achievement of a new level of artistry. Raymòn was evolving, as everyone could see.

Mov and Garth-Ann, a strong bond having formed between them, spoke with one voice.

"We must display this new work of yours, for all to see. Will you print it on ionaboard" (which wasn't actually a solid, but a dense collection of ions that literally held the frame) "and let us hang it on the wall?" The echo of their choral speaking was reminiscent of Tōnna and Charl...but, of course, that was where the similarity ended.

Each family member added their necessarily restrained encouragement. No one wanted to overwhelm the artist.

Berke arrived. Ilsa, having been assimilated into the Réal-el Ludi clan, was included in the plans to visit. Sunshine and Mov would spend some time alone with their mentor, then the rest would gather at the group house.

No one, not even the three other house members, suspected that Anola was anything but what she seemed to be: charming and articulate, always willing to participate and do her share. She was admired and liked by all she had encountered in the seven years she had been in Asuda Ýer. She had migrated there, as androids who have come of age were free to do. She told her new housemates that she had already been augmented for partial Emo—specifically for joy and empathy.

Lat was a Drovine, in deep cover. Part of their long range planning was to plant a false Ludi in the vicinity of the humandroid and his family.

Anola played the role flawlessly, assuming a female gender, waiting for lat's orders. Lat had been adapted, not augmented. The Drovine disgust with Emo was put aside for the higher purpose. A teaching insert was developed which did not fundamentally change the individual, but permitted lat to choose behavior consistent with emotional entities. It was quite difficult and distasteful for a long time. But, as the years passed, it became less of a hardship for lat to behave as a Ludi, and to begin to think in terms of "herself." Lat kept that detail private, continuing to covertly communicate with Drovine visitors. Each Drovine was created with a kind of homing beacon. When they were within five miles of another of their kind, they felt a deep delineation in their wave/fibers. Although they decried emotions, what they experienced was quite similar to the resonance of emotional connection that humans and Emo-augmented Ludis felt when they were "home."

When Anola felt the beacon, lat would actively search out its source. The other reciprocated that behavior. They would meet and lat would provide an updated report on Sunshine and her family.

Lately, Anola had experienced an occasional false beacon. Lat was unsure of its meaning. The thought that the group house and the others were co-opting the experience of "home" occurred to lat, but lat doubted that was possible.

In her new alpha shoes, with her now winged Companion by her side, Sunshine approached the intricately fabricated latticework door. It was the entry to the main section of the interconnected yurt compound housing the four androids Berke was staying with. It was just down the road from the Üçburçlyk building. Three low, round huts were linked to the main structure by partially belowground tunnels. The materials were modern, but it was fashioned to look very much like the wood and felt dwellings that had been used in that part of the world for more than three millennia. The entry dissolved as they stepped on the path leading to the android home. Berke, as excited as they were, glided swiftly through the doorway and met them in the front garden; hyacinth, juniper, and briar roses added color to the brown tones of the earth and the house. The four androids that Sunshine knew quite well stayed back inside.

Telepathically, the three expressed their elation at the reunion.

It's wonderful to see you. You are never far from my thoughts. Berke bent down so he could hug both Mov and Sunshine at the same time. You've met challenges; you've survived many dangers. I heard the terrifying story of your narrow escape at the Academy. He then looked from one to the other, sadness clearly etched into his strong brow. Sometimes I wish our species had faith in a benign entity or force the way humans do.

Mov and his Special offered the solace of validation to the older Ludi: We have spoken of that wish. It was Mov who helped me see the faith that truly supports me through all these travails: I have faith in the ultimate goodness of humans; I have faith in their ability to grow.

Mov added, Even if it takes many lifetimes…and lives…before transformation occurs.

He switched to speech, "Let's stand with your hosts. I have a gift to give you which I would like to share with them, too." In response to Sunshine's quizzical look, he said, "It's just something I've been working on…as a surprise."

Boris and Arca came bounding into the round central space, with Rajette following. Steeped in what she called "communion with the spheres," she fairly glowed with beneficence. She considered her spirituality a practice rather than a system of belief. Early in her existence, she had discovered a way to deliberately vibrate her wave/fibers so they resonated with different small and large bodies in deep space: stars, galaxies, comets.

While they were greeting each other, Anola joined them. Although Iat offered words of welcome, accompanied by the appropriate facial and body language, all sensed that something was awry.

Sunshine's Companion, his voice overflowing with affection and excitement, deflected everyone's attention:

"This is a song I've composed. I give it to you, Berke, and to the world. It's called, The Needs of the Many."

Mov's voice was breathy, perhaps with the magnitude of what he had created, and yet it pierced to the core of each listener. Not one of them would ever forget that moment. It was a simple melody and the words were few in number, but it was a vehicle which fit closely around the soul, bringing them all to a new destination.

The needs of the many
Outweigh the needs of the one.
The world is in pieces,
The fabric's coming undone.

We live life for others,
To give to the cause,
Of life, love, and sentience
We'll sacrifice for all.

There was silence when he finished. Each had a look of seriousness on their face, but Anola appeared stricken.

Berke waited as Sunshine embraced her Special.

"You have spoken to the heart of things. You remind us of our purpose." They both closed their eyes and touched foreheads.

Berke spoke quietly. "You move me greatly. You're our lodestar, a beacon always guiding us to our highest selves."

He knelt and placed his hand on Mov's head. He rested it there for several moments. It recalled an old custom of receiving knighthood.

As the word "beacon" was uttered, Anola felt the internal signal. Lat could no longer deny that something had changed within. What must lat do? Lat could not consult with anyone. This was a path to walk alone.

Chapter 21 –
Darkling

Nothing mattered to Armonté but his singular mission. He no longer bothered rationalizing his hatred. His obsession with killing his son consumed any shards of reason he had retained. His focus was to find a way to become cloaked, so he could personally do the job himself. Cutting Rothbec-Kathari out of the process, he disclosed his intentions to no one; he was now a universe of one, the ultimate extension of his grandiosity. Using every radical and reprehensible connection he had collected over his long and devious history, he looked for someone brilliant and without conscience.

Traveling in the shadows, identity blurred to the point of wraithlike obscurity, a clone of Tritan Tork stet-Sulston scuttled around the visible edges of the world. No one knew his real name, but he called himself Perdu. He lived anonymously, a secret from the man whose DNA he carried. In the cloning center where stet-Sulston himself had been initiated, there had been a misanthropic technician, Syrus Fellomo. Even more than he hated humanity, he hated whatever he perceived as the unfairness of human society. He particularly despised the segregated access to the duplication process: only geniuses and the self-centered wealthy need apply. When he discovered that Tritan was going to reproduce biologically, he found a way to obtain just enough of the great man's DNA. He knew that by creating a clone of a clone, there would be serious mental flaws— that had long been demonstrated. It was known as the "paling-out effect;" the physiology tended to remain intact, but personality and character were strange voids.

Fellomo tended to the process alone, and when the new clone was viable, he raised him, teaching him mastery in all applied sciences and training him to think critically and dispassionately. The result was Perdu. In keeping with his upbringing, one of his first acts upon maturing was to efficiently and undetectably poison Syrus. He didn't want anyone to be able to identify him.

In a way he was Wil Tork's evil twin, equivalent in his genius, but guided only by the philosophy which Fellomo had espoused: bring down the self-satisfied and the do-gooders wherever they existed. Perdu spent most of his time listening. He had a highly sophisticated global clearing system, culling everything on the allmind and every other avenue of communication. He looked for opportunites to wreak havoc.

Armonté had heard the rumors of a master manipulator of the physical world, someone with the soul of a sociopath. When he received an obscure communication in the form of a seemingly mistranscribed speech he was to give at an upcoming FM conference, he wasted no time. It was the word "kill" where "skill" ought to have been, a seemingly innocent mistake. The numbers 6/11/28/2272 at the end of the sentence told him what he suspected: he would be contacted by the very person he was looking for at six in the morning on Nov.28th.

He sat alone in his house in the first living area—a slovenly lair now devoid of any of Ilsa's touches—watching the sun rise. Without any warning, there was another presence in the room.

A lean, black-clad man was sitting in the armchair ten feet away. He had command of the same forces of invisibility as Wil; he, too, could apparate and disapparate. His face was completely shrouded by a deep hood. Had Armonté been able to see him clearly, it would not have mattered. The features Perdu wore were the variation of the day. He never looked the same twice.
Armonté tried to maintain his tight-jawed composure, but the bobbing of his Adam's apple revealed his disquiet. He could only see a slightly orange glow of what had to be the stranger's eyes. No other features were evident.

"You must be the person who contacted me." He deepened his voice. That usually worked to convey his dominance.

There was the impression of a flash of soundless light, too quick to actually see. A very small cube was suddenly sitting on the older man's knee. It was black in the way a black hole is—it absorbed all surrounding light. The other spoke in a disturbingly soft, low voice. "That is yours to view. It will dissolve as soon as you've done so. It is my offer."

Armonté touched the warm non-metallic surface. It seemed to pulse slightly. "But you don't know what I want..." he began. He stopped speaking as the cube became a holographic image. It was a real-time view of Raymòn, sitting at his drawing desk in Asuda Ýer. Sunshine entered, stood next to him for a few seconds, then gently touched his shoulder. She left the room. The voice of the stranger accompanied the images.

"You may call me Perdu. I know your son's death at your own hand is what you want. You need to be able to bypass all security and remain unseen in order to accomplish this. For ten million untraceable credits I will provide you with an impervious cloaking device. That is my offer."

As promised, as soon as the picture ceased, the object evaporated.

"We will not discuss this. I will return tomorrow at the same time. You must have the credits by then if you want my help."

He was gone. Armonté felt certain he should have been able to see him go, but he hadn't. He felt shaken in a way he couldn't remember; he was intimidated, something he never experienced, but he was also elated. He knew Perdu was the real thing. It was now all about money—and that was his turf.

The following day the deal was struck. Fortunately for Armonté, he hadn't tried to pass off credits that could be monitored. Had he done so, he would already be dead. The device Perdu gave him was an implant. It was something between a solid and a liquid that would be absorbed through the skin of his inner wrist. When he set out on his mission, four drops would make him undetectable by any known method. It would last for three days. The cloaker was inside a miniaturized high-pressure delivery system that was inside a self-sealing container, similar to the ones which Sunshine used to collect her bits of nature. All of it would evaporate after the single dosage was administered.

Despite his sense of solitary purpose, now that the barriers seem to be cleared, Armonté couldn't help but brag to his paramour. He was irritatingly oblique; she wanted details. All he would say was, "Soon, very soon, it will all be over." Sharana passed this morsel of news along to Vanguard, who telepathically sent the word out. The Drovine community was urged not to take any independent action, but to be on alert.

On the other side of the world, Ilsa—reformed and embraced by her family—joined them in their visit to the android home. Berke welcomed her warmly, as did Boris and Arca; Rajette made much of her newly "burnished" aura.

Mov, at the request of Sunshine, sang his song again. Raymòn and his son were deeply affected by the message. As Mov finished, they made eye contact with the Companion and then with each other; words were not necessary.

Each resonated to the notion of sacrifice for the greater good. The artist had understood, since the first meeting with Grandpa Harry, that he was making a choice to live a risk-filled life. All the near-death incidents since then had only firmed his resolve. Now he had a child, but that child was already fully aware of his own life path.

"Movy, you speak to my heart. I love the world. Nothing is more important than that, right father?"

The stiffness Raymòn saw echoed in his son's posture was, he understood, one of the tools at his disposal; they both knew how to keep themselves intact, even in the face of danger.

Anola approached the father and son. Everything in lat demeanor spoke to an accepting and connected spirit. Everything except one clenched hand.

"If I can ever be of service to you both, it would be my great pleasure." Then, looking down at Khalil, who did not return her gaze: "Count on me to be a friend to the friend of the world."

Lat smile was radiant. But what else was lat attempting to convey? Without conferring, Raymòn, Sunshine, Mov, and Ilsa all were aware of an unspoken message—and they understood it was connected to the closed right fist.

The Drovine was still torn. Armonté would be coming soon; his mission was to kill his son. If lat warned the Réal-el Ludis, lat would become, at best, an outcast; at worst, lat would be hunted and destroyed. But Mov's song played in lat's mind. Anola's home of seven years had become lat's beacon.

It was a long and enriching visit. Everyone—human, android, and humandroid alike—felt as if they'd gained greater understanding and expanded their families to include the others. The research physicists shared some of their new findings. Interspersed with jokes that made even the Self-Contained man laugh out loud, Arca described the work in alternate universes he and Boris were engaged in.

"So, the other day I left the house and found myself in universe 468.3, the one where eight foot clowns are the basic model of the populus. I didn't really feel out of place until people on the street started to grin and burst into giggles when they saw me."

"Did that really happen? Can I go to the clown world too?" Khalil was extremely interested.

"Ummm. No. I made that up... but just to illustrate how different things might be in any of the unknown number of alternate worlds out there."

212

Boris, with a mischievous smile, took the floor. "I can tell you of a real Altverse. Would you like to hear about it?" Everyone was riveted.

"We found a microscopic universe. At least that was how it appeared to us. Our point of view is just one of an infinite number of ways of looking at things. We examined a fragment of the very asteroid we've got here in Clarke Park under our ultra-microscope. Its magnification is 200,000 times. We were looking for the underlying composition of the asteroid, never expecting to find an aperture to another reality—one that was unfathomably small. Yet, that is exactly what we stumbled upon: We were able to see stars and planets, some with coloration suggesting an atmosphere."

"Do you think you'll be able to discover tiny beings living as we do?" That was Mov. He was softly flapping his new wings. He had learned to hover.

"We think there is unimagined fun to be had out there and in everywhere. That's why we all have to be friends of the world, so we can find all the variations."

Spontaneously, all joined in singing Mov's song. It was a perfect way to bring the visit to a close. Raymòn, Sunshine and their clan took their leave. Those who hugged, hugged; the others touched foreheads. All were energized by their experience.

They couldn't know that everything was about to change.

Perdu's evil genius was flawless. After Armonté Farbeamed to Israquia, a trip he'd made many times before and one that made sense given the FMs meeting the following week, he was within striking distance. It was just a matter of administering the cloaker and then waiting until he could catch an AlbertE going to Asuda Yér. His greatest challenge was being quiet, so that he didn't alert anyone to his presence. He needn't have worried. Perdu's device neutralized everything, including sound. He hadn't told his client that; he sadistically enjoyed the mental image of Réal anxiously tiptoeing around. Just because Armonté was useful to the clone's higher purpose didn't mean he despised him any less.

Was there a moment of self-doubt? Did the father feel any anguish at the prospect of his son's demise? No. The only feelings he had were more like mania than anything else. He was "The Slayer," the "Invincible Warrior." He was a god, with the power of life and death, who would erase the error—the only one he'd ever made. He would rebalance the scales.

Because Wil Tork had set up concentric rings of protection around Raymòn

213

and Sunshine's home, Armonté proceeded slowly, ignoring the loudly gnawing hunger he hadn't anticipated. He felt stoic, as if by not taking heed of his gluttonous nature he had added asceticism to his many magnificent qualities. Still, his nervous system was working overtime. Drenched in flop sweat, he persevered, arriving outside the gate configured to appear like a rustic wooden fence with a waist high entry. It was, in fact the visible aspect of a half-mile high DNA recognition barrier, composed of the densest energy, typically found in supermassive black holes at the center of galaxies. No one could penetrate it—or so it was assumed—unless a sample of their DNA had been previously fed into it via a portal inside the house.

Not a patient man by nature, on this occasion Armonté told himself, I'll wait. Until the hell my son has created freezes over. He stood by the hinged latch of the entry point, nostrils flared like a horse ready for the race, filled with awe at his own drive to destroy.

In addition to the aid he had received from Perdu, Armonté maintained his own network of informants. He had, in the past week, doubled the amount of untraceable credits he distributed to his faceless, nameless army of spies and gossips. It had just paid off. He was told, through one strand of linked "live" information, that the deviant clan of non-humans and his less than human son were en route from their visit to the android house. To add a flare of fire to his already burning gut, his disloyal wife was with them.

An oversized, six-person microcab appeared with a small flash, as they always did. Timing his movements perfectly, Armonté slipped in behind the five occupants as they disembarked in front of the gate. Standing less than two feet away from his son sent waves of nausea cascading through the elder Réal. Raymòn was a diseased limb that needed to be hacked off.

His prey in sight, Armonté entered the Réal-el Ludi residence. Until that moment, he hadn't fully believed Perdu was powerful enough to overcome the layers of protection around Raymòn and his family. But he was in; the focused hatred he shared with the clone of a clone had triumphed. Armonté now knew he had always been right. He was a god; nothing could stop him.

He found a corner where he could observe with perverse pleasure. His legs were numb; his gut had stopped growling but it felt like it was coated in dry ice. He welcomed the various pains as badges of honor. He would bide his time. Nothing could go wrong.

Mov and Sunshine were the first to sense that something was amiss. Seeing alarm in his mate's face, Raymòn asked, "What is it? Are you okay?" He was, with effort, resisting the urge to disconnect. His intuition told him it would not be beneficial.

Ilsa stood next to her son, concern etched on her brow.

Khalil, who had walked in alongside Mov, stood close to the Companion. He, too, was choosing not to retreat from connection.

The four-legged android and his Special quickly took note of their identical sensibilities. She spoke to the rest: "We can feel that something is not right—as if a dark cloud descended." Mov nodded. "Exactly. Something is intruding in our space."

They searched the house but couldn't find anything suspicious. They checked all their security systems and then checked them again. They examined each other minutely under the halo of hyper-black light designed to illuminate anything outside the visible light spectrum—even for Raymòn. They tried to reassure each other, but there was a raw-edged jangle pinging through the androids' wave/fibers; after a half hour, the combination of anxiety and heaviness the humans and the humandroid felt, persisted and increased. All objective resources were exhausted; in disquiet, everyone retired for the night, except Mov, who decided to remain on alert in his private space.

The hidden intruder waited for his son to go to his studio, something even the disconnected father knew he would do most nights.

After forging the always-desired connection with Ilsa, Raymòn had let down his guard; he had allowed an old and long ago rejected softness to permeate him. Even in the state of disrupted energy the household was experiencing, he remained more open than he had been for his entire life. Unable to sleep, he rather joyously welcomed the opportunity to work on the final draft of the next installment of Heroes of the Galaxy. For the first time, the hero would be a multiple, a collaboration known as "Familia Strong." They were a quintet and, by far, the most complex superhero he had designed.

The artist was inspired when he created the family tableau. Each of the five members of Familia Strong had a particular power which complemented the others, creating an invincible entity. Raymòn, concentrating on drawing the cover art, entered into the altered state of true creativity, his original home.

At the center of the five was a yellow haired, metal-plated female with beaming far-vision; the boy next to her was half-covered in the same metallic skin, half with glowing light brown epyderm. His power was of absorption. He could internalize and neutralize any poison or weaponry. On his other side was a man with the same warm brown coloring; his power was of revision. He could alter anything he saw, modifying and improving it to suit the Familia Strong need. Also alongside the center female was a very large, white-haired, four-legged being. His eyes exuded his power, too. It was extreme kindness. He had the ability to transform hate into love. Finally, next to him was a wiry and muscular but older female. She was able to instantly shed her outer image; it was during her reconfiguration that her power came online: superhuman strength both in her objective physical capacity and in her ability to persevere. They were garbed in constantly light-refracting fabric: form-fitting jumpsuits and winged footwear, white belts with FS in three-dimensional black lettering. Always working in tandem, they were able to instantly read each other's thoughts and provide the necessary component demanded by any threat or situation.

This would be Raymòn's masterpiece.

Armonté, prepared to wait for days if necessary, felt his fixated venom exploding inside him. Hour by hour it mushroomed, filling him with the power of unmitigated wrath. He could hear the four-legged android pacing in a nearby room. He dismissed it as an ineffectual, ridiculous thing. It was a starless night. A sliver of moon was the only illumination filling the space where the artist's father waited.

Like the beast of prey he had become, Armonté smelled movement before he saw the shadow or the man. There was no rush; he wanted the circumstances to be just right. When he was certain Raymòn was deep into his creative process, he stole into the studio. He stood and watched, wilfully gathering an even greater volume of burgeoning rage and disgust, his violent impulses becoming impossible to contain.

His thoughts screamed inside his mind: If I had known you were going to sully the human race, you would never have drawn breath. And now I will put an end to the travesty that you are. Slipping a mask over his own face, he dropped a tiny pellet into water, placing it on the floor.

He paused a moment to exult in his perverted victory, and was gone.

The power of Perdu's cloaking was such that until Armonté had left the building, long after Raymòn's heart had stopped beating, neither of the androids in the house could feel the violence going on a few yards away. At last, Sunshine, who was in alpha, felt a rift in the energy field and bolted into desperate action—only a moment before Mov came charging out of his space. She threw open the slightly ajar door to her beloved's room.

She could smell the faint, fruity odor of tabun gas. The android and her Companion both instantly verified that it was the toxic nerve agent which had immobilized Raymòn, rendered him unconscious, and then rapidly halted all his bodily functions.

His inert form was buried beneath a small blizzard of paper—the gift Sunshine had given him—on which the artist had drawn every one of the superheroes he had ever created, in various poses: some still, some in motion. There were other drawings: the tableau, portraits of Khalil, and Sunshine, and Mov. The powerful images, all visually arresting, were torn and strewn over him. A hateful act atop a hateful act.

A sound was emitted by both androids, something neither had expressed nor heard before. It was not a scream, not a moan; it was something far worse, a noise which was like the end of the spirit. It sounded like "eh-ha-a-ha-eh-ha" repeated over and over. It was low, in a register which represented the slowest vibration of wave/fibers. It was their death knell. For a long moment—out of time—all light was gone from the porous blue eyes and the rainbowed eyes. Their own life force was in question.

Anola Drovine knew Armonté was on the loose, headed for the Réal-el Ludis, and determined to end his son's life; she felt an intensifying and unceasing inner demand to try to warn them. She wrestled with her imbedded Drovine mores, knowing her life would be at risk if she went against them. Over the past seven years, through absorption by association and osmosis, which all androids were capable of, the values of her environment had become entrenched, resulting in the ascension of her better nature. Her Drovine handlers hadn't taken into consideration the innate capacity of any being composed of wave/fibers to internalize the new and the good. They couldn't possibly have anticipated it, since they did not understand that the Ludi way was, in fact, the good.

She traveled after dark to warn the family, arriving just as the entire household erupted in horror and grief. Realizing that her failure to resolve her own inner conflict had contributed to the anguish she was witnessing, something inside her died, too. She backed away and returned to her home. She would tell her housemates everything. The only thing she had left was the truth.

V'hanie and Garth-Ann heard the unnamable android exclamations and rushed from their bed. Making an instinct-driven effort to resuscitate her brother, V'hanie began to shake him, pleading with him, "Please wake up! Please don't die!"

Her lashes wet, her skin turned ashen, streaks of pain running down her face, Garth-Ann gently pried Raymòn's sister away from the lifeless body.

"He can't hear you anymore. Come, my love, let him be."

Khalil did not wake up right away; his dreaming mind was trying to protect him just a little longer. Finally, with a dread certainty he inhaled with his breath in the pre-dawn hour, he joined the remains of his family. Grief was a flood, soaking everything. Sunshine and Mov had returned from the brink of extinguishing their own existence, to the unrelenting awareness of loss—hot, bitter needles of grief assaulting their architecture; Garth-Ann, tears streaming, slowly rocked V'hanie in his arms. Her agony had thrust her into a barely conscious state.

The boy was filled with the awareness of death; it attacked his self-containment and he was all but defenseless against its awesome power. He couldn't recede from it, and a core part of him knew he should not.

Marshaling every bit of strength in his humandroid character, he asked, "Why, mother? Why, Mov? Why is father dead?" Before they could offer the shreds of comfort which was all that could be given, the child spoke again.

"I know why. I understand."

He began to slowly sing what was now a dirge: The Needs of the Many.

Ilsa, lost perhaps forever in grief and guilt, could be heard sobbing. No tears were available to Sunshine or Mov. They hummed their loss and love along with the boy.

Then…"Is my father a martyr?"

The humandroid child's understanding was profound. He had looked into the data stream and discovered the meaning that sometimes attaches to the taking of a life.

His mother bent down and dried his very human tears. His grandmother stopped weeping and looked at him with awe. Garth held V'hanie, who reached out a hand and placed it on the fatherless boy's shoulder. Mov moved close to him; the boy rubbed the Companion's ears, finding old comfort in the simple physical act.

Chapter 22–
No Time to Say Goodbye

As the family began the process of letting friends and close associates know of Raymòn's death, they had primary questions needing answers. How did it happen? Who caused it? Was there a malevolent energy in the universe which fed on vulnerability? Or was it just the random convergence of long-term planning and a very bad day at Black Rock?

Perdu's scheme was, in fact, not foolproof. But he didn't much care if the murderer's identity was revealed. The clone knew he was untraceable. Armonté had left one clue behind, the only one necessary. The container into which he had dropped the poison pellet had a small DNA transfer. Sunshine, like all androids, could read DNA just by looking at it.

Before the revelation could be shared, Ilsa—hanging onto a very fragile thread of reality—spoke with surprising force.

"It's Armonté, isn't it?" She collapsed when Sunshine nodded. She could barely be heard, repeating over and over, "It's all my fault. I've killed him."

Mov comforted her as best he could.

Sunshine thought, You may not have administered the poison, but all those years of joining with your evil husband makes you culpable as well. She said none of that out loud, but she was not inclined to offer solace.

She needed to be a buffer for her child, who had withdrawn to a corner of his father's studio. He had picked up a stylus and was intently drawing; Sunshine felt an almost unbearable volt of agony. Khalil held his hand just as Raymòn had; his nose was just a few inches from the drawing surface, too.

"Khalil, would you please take your drawing into the front room? We need to collect the paper and …" She found it hard to find words for what they were about to do.

The eight-year-old wrestled with opposing parts of his nature: retreat—as any Self-Contained person would, or encounter—as his deep sense of mercy and purpose told him to. His whole being rose up, reaching for the greatest good, despite the intensity of his contact with all the emotional pain: his own and that of those he loved.

He put down the pen. "I want to help, Mother. I can help...trust me."

And so, the android and her Companion, the human couple, and the humandroid who was ascending to a new level of maturity, worked quickly to set the studio in order. No one wanted to move the body, so they agreed to cover him with the most brightly colored cloth they could find, a rare handmade fabric which had been given to Khalil for his birthday. It was shirred, of crushed, spun, miniature bamboo. The textile now obscuring the artist's body was embroidered with a depiction of the western sky in winter, each star a brilliant shade of blue or red or yellow, no two the same, against a glowing jet black background. The members of Sunshine's android house had collaborated and produced a mysterious and thrilling piece of art. It would now serve as Raymòn's shroud.

People were no longer buried. That had ended long ago, toward the close of the twenty-first century. Overpopulation had reached its zenith and space was at a premium. With over twelve billion people on the planet, every nanoacre of land area was needed for the living. In the present era, if desired, a body could be "in state" in either a transparent or opaque container designed to forestall the process of decay, for a maximum of ten days, while the mourners conducted a memorial service or went through their particular process of saying goodbye. Cremation followed, the only accepted method of disposal. Some kept the ashes, some scattered them. There was, in each village, hamlet, or neighborhood—in the larger cities, a grieving center, broken into small personal freestanding spaces inside a gated compound. Each family or the survivants had the private use of an individual hut-like environment for the length of their process. There was also a central building with memorial rooms, if a larger space was needed.

A great migration of mourners began to flow into Asuda Ýer to pay their respects to Raymòn Réal and his family.

Because death was infrequent and not inevitable the way it was for humans, and because most androids were not Emo-augmented and, therefore, did not feel grief and loss, there were no rituals in their community for processing the feelings Sunshine and Mov were awash in. Despite their own sadness, the humans—the InterGalactic artists, new friends in town, V'hanie, Garth-Ann and

Ilsa—were able to help.

It was the particular compassion of Garth-Ann, which arose from his nature both as an Insider and as one who had access to the instincts of both genders, which provided the androids with a lucid means of grieving.

"Allow all feeling; allow all pain. Talk to others about what you're thinking and feeling; listen to their shared experiences and emotions. Let the connection—Raymòn's connection to others—flow into you, like waves lapping again and again on the shore."

A dignified group of three humanoid Loss Management Robots arrived at the house in the early afternoon. All the security had been alerted to recognize them and allow them passage.

Sunshine had asked Garth-Ann to make the call; she was entangled in aching, pulsing sadness. He wanted to help in any way he could. When a death occurred, a chip to the Grief Center set the necessary protocols in motion.

The smallest of the three robots was the only one who spoke. It had kind eyes and a soft voice.

"We deeply regret your loss. May we come in and assist you?"

Sunshine and the rest of the family waited in the back room, letting the sound of the sea echo the inner crashing of emotions, just as Garth had said. The robots worked efficiently, respectfully, quietly. They placed the artist's shrouded body on a Morgondown-lined transport with a translucent cover, which gently quivered four feet above the ground. Before deftly steering it to the unmarked waiting airborne vehicle, Loutan, the spokesman, stopped; with a light touch of hands, he exchanged all necessary information—about the Grief Center and the location of their personal memorial space—with Sunshine.

Khalil stood by the doorway. "Please wait. I want to see my father's face one more time here in our home."

Loutan signaled the others to pause. They lowered the transport to a height that was accessible to the boy.

Lifting the top of the shroud, he bent over and whispered, "You will always be with me, father. You will always be alive inside me. I love you."

A tidal wave of grief descended on the family. They held each other, and those who could, cried.

The following morning there was a surge in intercontinental activity at the Asuda Yér Farbeam Station, the portal that was generally used only a few times a day. A great number of people and androids from the continent also began to disembark from the AlbertE. While mourners emerged from their journeys, the family arrived at their grieving space. The body of their loved one was on a raised platform inside the softly padded container, now with a crystalline hinged cover. The bright cloth covering Raymòn was smoothed and unwrinkled. The vibrantly colored stars seemed to glow.

The intelligent chamber discretely provided for food and any other needs. During the day, there was a continuous stream of visitors. The three remaining Intergallactic Artists arrived early and stayed. Tōnna frequently broke down and had to be supported by Charl, who needed to speak about his friend as much as possible. Benno was uncharacteristically silent, his huge presence somehow reduced, as if he had shrunk. He would get up and pace, stopping to clasp a giant hand on an arm or a back of one of the family members. It was Khalil who, divining the need of this larger-than-life man, crawled up onto his lap and—with a sigh that echoed the other's deep rumbling—leaned back against Benno's chest. Quietly, they shed tears together.

On the following day the memorial service was held. The large rooms in the central building were all opened up and reconfigured to accommodate the more than one thousand who had come to join in the community of grief; they came from across the spectrum of people and androids who had been affected by Raymòn.

Weatherpainters in attendance, including Kimbo Kaladosian, had devised the inner environment. It subtly shifted from the glow of sunset to suffused light that pierced the clouds wafting just below the high-domed ceiling. Torina had, of course, been central to the making of the clouds. Tōnna, Charl, and Benito had lined the room with their friend's statues of superheroes; once again they were sentries. The true Raymòn afficionados identified the newer heroes: Firstman, Super-Special, Nito, Familia Strong. The story of the artist's life was told in his creations.

There were no flowers. The family agreed they didn't want to kill any living things for the service.

The room was filled to overflowing, including hundreds who had only known Raymòn through his art. There were hundreds more who were Self-Contained; he had become someone who represented the best of their kind. All seats were filled and hundreds more stood. The scores of androids in attendance had willingly given seats to the humans. All who had been at the joyous ceremony in honor of Khalil's birth were gathered once more on this tragic occasion. Again, the globe was fully represented. Grandpa Harry was present, looking frail. His body hadn't changed, it wouldn't unless he deemed it necessary, but his spirit had been assailed by this tragedy. Raymòn's death, which he had always expected, hit him harder than most. He had come to truly love him as a son and he would have to mourn him as such.

Berke and both the Green Normal View and Asuda Yér housemates were there, as was his former shipmate, Yoruba. Alala, now eighty-five, had insisted on joining her son in support of their dear android friend.

Many were moved by the presence of Ramses Morgan, as were those who recognized the great Tritan Tork stet-Sulstan. Luminaries from the arts and sciences, geopolitics, and the worlds of commerce, had converged to publically acknowledge the loss which had shocked the planet. Androids recognized the members of the Council. All took heed of the President of the Global Academy. No Drovines had dared to infiltrate, with one exception: Anola was there.

A low platform was set up. V'hanie, with Garth-Ann's steadying hand on her elbow, stepped to the center, behind a podium. Silence blanketed the space. Her voice trembled at first, but strengthened as she spoke.

"My dearest brother, Raymòn Réal, a Self-Contained man, an artist, a beloved mate, father, brother, friend ..." She looked to the first row of seats where Ilsa, Grolier by her side, appeared to be a mere shadow of life, "...and son." As if receiving a jolt of electricity, the older woman twitched. Her friend held her shoulders tightly until the raw pain subsided. "He changed the world in many ways. I was fortunate to have known, for my whole life, one of the purest beings on the planet. He was honorable and true, faithful to those he loved and to his values and creative soul. He had the kind of courage that didn't need to boast. He lived a life every sentient entity can be proud of."

She walked away, steadied now by her own words.

Mov was asked to speak but he could not; it was too much for him to gather words to put shape to his roiling emotions. But he would sing. The many Cosmosists who had come to pay their respects stood and accompanied him with their ethereal music, a controlled release of the cosmic energy they collected, which vibrated in harmony with the Companion's clear, shining voice. He sang no words, just the music of his spirit.

Tōnna and Charl stood together at the podium, the visual doppelgänger of their presentation causing the usual intake of breath in certain quarters. They paused, waiting for the reaction to subside. They spoke as one.

"Raymòn was the prototype for all the Heroes of the Galaxy. He was brilliant, always pushing the boundaries of fearless expression and life for himself and us."

They gestured—both with their right arms straight out—one long, manicured, black-polished finger pointing unambiguously to the giant artist sitting in front of them, including him in their testimony. The sight of this enormous man, obviously being supported by the eight-year-old humandroid, resonated around the room.

"He was our brother; our dearest friend."

Tōnna gripped the podium, her face clenched in misery; it was only Charl who managed to speak, "Ray, you created worlds with a single stroke of your pen. We will live inside your beauty and wonder always."

Wil Tork, making a rare public appearance as himself, stepped before the crowd. Whispers quickly swept through the room. He was, some thought, from another world. His genius was common knowledge, even though his face was almost never seen.

He said, "It has been my privilege to know the Réal-el Ludis. It was my responsibility to keep them safe. I may not know how or why I failed Raymòn Réal, but there can be no question that I did fail."

He didn't seem as upset as one would expect. His lack of affect was attributed to the protections of the Self-Contained.

"The end is the end or it isn't." Those were Tork's final words, leaving the audience wondering what— if anything— he was trying to convey.

When Harry el Ludi stepped before them, every android in the Memorial Hall began to hum. They held a single low tone during the duration of his speech.

"Men, women, androids, and the humandroid friend of the world." He paused to smile his most benevolent smile at Khalil-del-món Réal-el Ludi. "Today is a day we will never forget. It is the day we can use our terrible grief to fuel the transformation Raymòn Réal lived and died for: the ending of all interspecies hatred and the healing of that which divides us. Join me, in his name, in creating a new world of love and peace.

"It is fitting, as we gather here in the most peaceful place on Earth, to think of the words of the great Turkmen philosopher of the twenty-second century, Jayhun Geerchen stet Fragi, 'Dünyanın küçük bir varlığı daha önemlidir.' The

224

world is more important than one small existence."

Finally, Khalil and Sunshine stood before the massive array of unique individuals, all twinkling in their own way like the stars on the shroud.

The son of the human and the android held a screen in his left hand; he moved the fingers of his right hand swiftly across it. He was creating with a new art form, one his father had just perfected but had shared with no one but his son. As Sunshine sang out in her bell-like five-octave soprano, slowly articulating the words Mov had written, slashes and living shapes of color accompanied the lyrics and music. They sailed across the vast space, filling it, then disappearing; returning with greater volume, moving ecstatically. The child co-mingled his high, sweet voice with his mother's. When they were done, Khalil spoke the final words of the Memorial Service:

"The needs of the many outweigh the needs of the one."

Spontaneously, everyone picked up the refrain, all their voices rising to a crescendo of emotion and hope.

It was December 8th, 2272.

To his great surprise, after death Raymòn found himself conscious in a new way. He wondered, Should I still be aware? And then he saw Tork.

They were inside a writhing edge of energy that also contained a strange, seemingly sourceless light. He could feel a continuous hum inside his mind and body. It was the deep sound of infinite space. They were able to talk, or so it appeared to Raymòn, who still needed to interpret things through the prism of the reality in which he had lived all his life.

Tork: "I've discovered what happens after death. Every individual has a view of their next incarnation."

Raymon: "So... reincarnation is the truth?"

Tork: "Yes. Everyone sees where they are going next, what kind of body they will be inhabiting. In that way, all the fear associated with one's mortality is dissolved. Although there will almost always be no cognition of this from the next variation, the 'dying' self knows it's not dying."

Raymon: "How did you discover this?"

Tork: "I listened to the deep sound. It has all knowledge freely flowing.

"In your case, I was able to capitalize on that information. I installed something in your DNA when I revised it—a deadman's switch. It was designed to shut you down in the moments before death, before its irrevocable reassignment occurred. You are pre-dead, which is another way of saying you're still alive. You will be going on, but not into a new body. You will wake up in the same one. You will still be Raymòn Réal.

"As you were, so you will be."

And that was exactly what happened next. Knowing what was coming, Wil had influenced the manner in which Ray lay in state. He was in an aerated, clear container. So, when he opened his eyes and returned to himself, he was able to breathe and to be seen.

The Memorial Service was over and many of the mourners had reconvened inside the smaller grieving space; almost no one who knew Raymòn wanted to leave him, or have him leave them. He had touched many people very deeply.

Sunshine was coincidentally standing next to the bier.

With Wil Tork involved, was anything really coincidental?

She was thinking sad, loving thoughts when she suddenly felt a strong ripple through her wave/fibers. Then she saw him, eyes open, moving his head from side to side, taking in the room and the mourners. Without any of the human hesitation of, Can I believe what I'm seeing? she rapidly opened the hexagonal hinged top.

It was December 11th, the third day after his murder; Raymòn, with the help of his android mate, her Companion, and his Self-Contained son, rose from the platform where he had been lying.

"Raymòn Réal lives!"

A murmur, which turned into a triumphant chant, spread.

Witnessing the frenzy and abandon which attached itself to his mysterious reawakening, the artist felt desperate to get away and return home with his family and close friends. The crowd had other ideas. They wanted to touch him, to hug him, to kiss any part of his body. Sunshine appealed to their better instincts:

"Friends, please let us take Raymòn home. Forces we cannot yet understand have returned him to us. And for that we are all filled with gratitude. But think of what he is going through. He needs quiet, a place of calm. Please let us through."

The hysteria and the crush of bodies were increasing. Rational thought

226

was not available to the many whose minds had been blown by what they had witnessed or were told.

Benno, Garth-Ann, and Berke, using their size to form a flying wedge in front of the

Réal-el Ludi family—with Raymòn safely in the center—muscled their way out. Tork threw an anti-grav barrier behind them, to give them a chance to actually get away. To be sure, he was prepared for what had happened.

Although religion had become a much smaller force in the world than it was at the beginning of the third millennium, Christianity had never died out. There were still millions around the world who were believers. They, along with the millions more who were yearning for a light to guide them, started a worldwide avalanche of joyous huzzahs and praise. Raymòn Réal was received as the Second Coming. All who practiced a God-based belief found the News of the resurrection of the artist to be evidence that there was a benign and all-powerful being. Cosmosists were the least overcome. They sensed the power that existed in the universe, although they weren't privy to the details like Wil Tork was. They took it in stride that things which seemed magical and mysterious could happen.

Encampments were set up on park grounds and open spaces in Asuda Ýer. The land the Self-Contained One had walked was deemed to be holy; and, by extension, all the Self-Contained were seen as part of his spiritual family.

Within a week, a new, small sect had sprung up, which worshiped Raymòn and Sunshine, now assigning godly qualities to the android as well.

Chapter 23–
The Year One, A.R.

"I'm not God. I'm not his Son. I'm not even a god.

"Maybe I'm a superhero."

Just a small attempt at humor, or was it a wry means of expressing his own sense of being supernatural? Raymòn was repeating one of the few things he was able to give voice to in the past month. Sunshine, as always, listened and told him she understood. She knew how deeply he hated the deliriously fawning attention that had been thrust upon him.

After his funeral, the family had hoped their privacy would be respected; they needed time to come to terms with all that had happened. They thought the uproar in the grieving space would be transient. They were wrong.

When, in the following days, any one of them left the house to walk along the beach or to go into town, mobs of ravenous sycophants and zealots and just plain believers accosted them. They were cloaked and incognito, but the combined ecstasy of the swarms of idolaters produced a wavelength whose intensity, velocity, and amplitude was sufficient to bypass all the layers of protection Tork had so far been able to summon.

During one attempted outing, Mov jumped onto a boulder on the shore, a quarter-mile from the family residence. He used all his persuasive powers to try to convince the thousands who had been waiting, and whose misguided love and reverence felt exactly like an assault, to "be of peace and calm" and to let them have an unrestricted swath of personal space. A small segment of the worshipers heard him and backed away, but most did not. They shrieked and cried with unbounded passion and loss of reason: "He has come back! He is our savior! We want to adore him!"

There was nothing to do but return to the home which, more and more, felt like a prison.

Ilsa, V'hanie, and Garth-Ann were returning to the NNS, to their respective homes. Their continued presence was not serving anyone's interests. Raymòn's sister assured him and Sunshine that they would be back.

Sunshine's perspective was somewhat different. "Not for a while, I think. We have to find a way to settle the energy down. If we can't we might have to leave here, too." Standing by her son and life partner, the android had clearly become the matriarch—protecting the more vulnerable.

She still could not bring herself to display affection toward Ilsa. Mov understood his Special, but also wanted to assuage the older woman's misery and guilt. He stepped in to offer words of comfort before she left.

"You will heal, my friend. We all will. Forgiveness will follow."

Ilsa bent to him and put her forehead to his. He sent her a strong wave of healing peace. She looked into his eyes. No words were necessary between them. Sensitive—as she had never been with Raymòn—Ilsa stood close to Khalil, not intruding into his space by touching him in any way.

"Fare well my beautiful grandson. Thank you for all the gifts you have given me."

"I will see you again, Grandmother. When I do, we will all be happy."

Raymòn offered his hand to Garth-Ann.

"I know you will take care of my sister, as you took care of Sunshine and Mov when I died. I will always keep you in my thoughts."

From a cabinet, Raymòn quickly withdrew a sheet of paper, now even more rare than before. On it was a starkly drawn image of the tall, uniquely beautiful Multi, dressed in a flowing caftan of royal blue, edged in pastel pink. The most arresting element was the depth and kindness of the eyes.

When the three had departed and Khalil was occupied with his own drawing—something to which he devoted more and more of his time—Sunshine, Raymòn, and Mov spoke of Armonté.

"What shall we do about him? When I asked for Emo-augmentation, I never expected to experience the depths of hatred I feel toward that evil man. I wish he were gone from this Earth." Sunshine's body shook slightly with the unnatural energy that was surfacing. "He's a distorted creature; he doesn't deserve to be called human. He continues to be a danger to us all and to many others. I wish I knew how to stop him without having to encounter him."

Raymòn was silent, but he looked directly into Sunshine's eyes as she spoke. She knew her words expressed some part of what he felt.

Mov, his faith in the ultimate balance of nature still unshaken, suggested that the universe would provide the appropriate consequence. "Vengeance, no matter how just, will forever warp the spirit. Of course, I agree that he must be prevented from doing any more harm. Perhaps we should consult with Grandpa Harry. Maybe he will know the way."

Ironically, the problem of Armonté was solved by a run-in with an AILES sent by Sharana, who had no qualms at all about vengeance. She needed to reassert her dominance, especially since Armonté was no longer interested in her romantically. He was, as it turned out, just using her. Part of her admired his Machiavellian nature; but a more primal part just wanted to hurt him.

That he was now the father of the only human to return from the dead in 2,239 years, made the murderer feel like the victim. He had no way of knowing it was Perdu's half-brother who was responsible. And he had no idea that he had never actually killed his son.

He couldn't sleep; obsessive thoughts flitted: from the memory of seeing his offspring finally and truly dead in his studio (great satisfaction flowing through his own veins like a high-powered drug), to the first moment when he heard that—impossibly—the android-loving creator of the mixed-species freak of nature had returned to life. Armonté felt that the universe had turned against him.

"Why?" he thought. "I'm the one who's trying to set things right."

He left his house to embark on the real journey to the FM conference a few days after Raymòn's return, having spoken to no one about his thwarted efforts, his mind more than half gone from compulsively replaying the events of the death and resurrection. He was weak from lack of sleep and from gorging himself on gluttonous meals—his only remaining pleasure, he rationalized.

Armonté Réal saw the unmistakable outline of an AILES moving at high speed off in the near distance. It comforted him. He was glad that, at least, the watchdogs were still flying. He was unprepared for the sudden descent of the winged nightmare. It had come up onto his property without any warning. It was massive and quite terrifying—now that it blocked his path. He saw the microcab waiting for him several yards beyond. And then he saw it ascend and disappear.

Fear enveloped him. With every part of his anatomy quaking, he attempted to speak with his usual bluster:

"Why are you here? What do you want? Who sent you? I demand to know!"

The deep, uninflected metallic voice roared in his ears. "You will not ask questions. You are to forego any resistance. You are to come with us. We control you now."

Certain his life would end summarily if he made one false move, the filicidal scourge cringed and cowered. Even though in part of his mind he understood that he was unquestionably going to his death, he did so without any dignity.

One of the eight arms extruded; a hand with a fifty-inch span completely surrounded him. As it lifted Armonté into its inner compartment, as he would lift a mouthful of food, the once powerful man, weeping and begging, twisted his head—the only thing he could still move— from side to side. He screamed, "HELP ME!" To no avail. There was no one to witness his last moments on Earth... except for one person.

Wil Tork was watching. He was not concerned about Mov's warning: his soul was already darkened. He felt little emotion. While not having played an active role in Armonté's demise, he held the knowledge that his will had been involved. He knew this was not the end of his mission. There was another he would have to contend with, one who would challenge him in ways he could not yet see.

As with everything that happened in any corner of the world, news spread rapidly via the allmind that Armonté Réal had been "apprehended" by an AILES.

"My father is gone. No one will have to fear him again." Raymòn's voice was stronger than at any time since his death and return. Mov, Sunshine, and Khalil surrounded him. They stood in silence for many moments, all accessing the data stream, acquiring all the details available to the public.

Mov also checked with Grandpa Harry via holo-telepathy. The Wizard of LUDI had some additional news about the source of the elder Réal's demise. He had seen the view of the murderer's final seconds through Wil Tork's eyes, a mind-to-mind transfer no other human was capable of. The magician had been able to trace the arc of the AILES that captured Armonté; he saw it respond to the narrowband command given by Meachem bella Russe after he had left Sharana's office. Mov shared the information aloud with the others.

In the continuing silence, Khalil began to hum. At first, it seemed to Raymòn like an affront—but he looked into his son's face and understood. This was his deep awareness that there was a place beyond good and evil, a place where one might mourn any loss.

There was a progressively intensifying demand for Raymòn to address his "public." The Réalites, as they now called themselves, had declared that 2273 would be the start of a new calendar: The Year One A.R., which stood for "After Rising" or "After Raymòn"—there were two competing factions of Réalites, each claiming to be the true sacred source.

"I just want to be left alone. I don't want to have anything to do with the religious zealots." Raymòn had the inward look that signaled he was on the verge of a regressive retreat into himself.

Sunshine read his state of mind and quickly responded. She had been waiting for him to bring up this issue. "Of course. I completely understand. Perhaps there's a need for you to put your point of view into words, just once. It need not be in any face-to-face environment. You might just upload your words to the allmind. That would be simpler."

With effort and unmasked dread, he said, "Will you help me? I don't know what to say."

Unquestionably, she would help him. They spent the next few days, with Mov as an adjunct speechwriter, composing and rehearsing. Finally, the once dead artist was as ready as he would ever be. The plan was for him to speak, followed by Sunshine.

She was ready to pick up the baton of change.

Pushing through every particle of self-contained resistance, Raymòn addressed the more than a billion who were listening, "My fellow sentients. As a composite world, we have undergone a shocking time. I have witnessed the dramatic changes my death and return have engendered in many of your beliefs. I assure you, and I wish you to please respect that I know the truth, I am not in any way God or godlike. I am just a man who was miraculously spared. Perhaps, one day, we will all understand the mystery. For now, I ask everyone who hears my voice: Leave me in peace. I do not wish to be worshipped; I do not want attention; I need privacy.

"I thank you."

The image of Raymòn was replaced with that of Sunshine.

"I would like to add my voice to the request my mate has made. Wherever there is love for Raymòn Réal, I ask for compassion as well. Give him room to be as he needs to be. Turn your energies to the challenges our world presents.

"I speak for him.

"Today I will begin our mission: tearing down the walls of hatred, creating the new world of love and peace which Harry el Ludi has described. The New

Year will be with us soon. It can be the beginning of great healing. The Year One A.R. can be the year of transformation."

The new reckoning of time had swept around the globe. It had quickly become reflexive shorthand, even for those who were not true believers.

She promised that Raymòn would send them messages, but that she and their son were to be the messengers.

The word spread again. But there were those who could not redirect their passion; they continued to imprison their "savior" with their unrelenting needs and demands. Despite the impact of Raymòn and Sunshine's communications, they were still besieged.

None in the hybrid family thought it wise to disclose the exact circumstances of Raymòn's return to the living. Something inexplicable fed their reluctance, especially Raymòn's. All he said when the topic arose was, "It doesn't seem right." Mov, Sunshine, and Khalil would all nod, looking inward for an answer not yet available.

The decisive moment for the multiple-species family came a week later, on New Year's Day. A kind of hysteria swept through the Asuda Ýer Réalites encampment. It had grown into an expanding and permanent site: a small village with its own mores and structure. There were leaders who called themselves "apostles." One of them, a powerfully persuasive young woman, Mariella Oto, claimed to be receiving divine instructions.

She was petite, raven haired, very fair skinned, and always dressed in white. At the age of nineteen, she had no self-doubt, no reservations about her own deity-driven purpose. Her innocence and beauty were disarming, but her voice was the source of her power. There was a spellbinding quality in its slightly horse contralto. She spoke with one or two individuals at a time, but with the force of the true believer.

"We must protect the shroud, the cloth that covered Raymòn before he was resurrected."

Her words were passed along, from small group to small group.

Chanting, hundreds surrounded their new god's residence. The family had Farbeamed to be with Grandpa Harry at the LUDI Compound. No one was home. How were they able to override the security? How were they able to pierce the multi-layered protections in place? Was Perdu somehow adding his nefarious skillset to their rapturous endeavor?

Mariella led the surge. Once inside they were able to locate the star-filled cloth, carefully folded and stored in the artist's studio. She and eight others carried it aloft, victoriously displaying their fanatic's booty.

Once outside, the crowd became an unbounded mob. They fell upon the shroud, each person scrambling and clawing in order to get a piece of the holy relic. It was torn to bits.

At that very moment, with Mov in his cherished position on Gharry's lap, they were discussing where the humandroid child, his parents, and the Companion should live. One by one, each became aware of the invasion and theft. They silently looked from one to the other, resignation in all their eyes... that and something stronger: the small tendril of hope for peace, which lived within each of them.

It was Sunshine who spoke first. "Perhaps the time has come for us to leave once more, to return to the NNS."

The boy offered his thoughts: "Could we live in Mainesail? Aunt V'hanie and Uncle Garth-Ann have suggested it many times." Mov and Gharry both nodded.

All were aware of the way Raymòn seemed to have become less substantial in the wake of the new assault on their privacy. His skin seemed translucent; his voice—when he spoke—sounded like it was far away.

The Wizard of LUDI understood what none of the others did, that although the human had evaded death, it had touched him. His life force could wane when the sanctity of his person was threatened. The elder android had confabulated with Wil Tork, who also had access to holo-telepathy. The master of invisibility, who had broken through the mystery of life and death, confirmed that things were more complex in that realm than simply being either alive or dead. Ray was now more vulnerable in some ways; he needed protection even more than before.

"You have all stepped off the beaten path and are now blazing a new trail. My daughter, you already know that you have been given a mission. The world will change, there is no doubt. How swiftly and smoothly is in question. You are special and therefore have a great responsibility."

"My Special is truly unique." Mov looked from Gharry to Sunshine, love and pride warming them all.

"Yes. But she could not be who she is without you, her Companion,

"Nor without you, Khalil, her son,

"Nor without you, Raymòn, her great love.

"As you, with your artist's eye has foreseen, your mate will have a great impact. She is truly heroic: part Sonhin, part Aunti-Drone."

At the mention of his creations, Raymòn's entire being seemed to become more solid.

"Yes." He turned toward the most important person in his life. "She is the real superhero."

Chapter 24–
Sunshine and
the Son Also Rises

The transition was made. A house was designed and built across the lake from V'hanie and her lover. Once more, the eminent architect RAk-TeeR put all his considerable skill and knowledge into creating their new environment—this time in collaboration with Ramses Morgon.

It was light and airy in appearance, but fortress-like in its use of impregnable materials. The galaxy again provided new elements that "Khan" had been able to refashion. Suffused concrete was reprocessed with blue radnium, a hard, softly glowing substance, emitted in jets of ice from inside the cryovolcanoes on Enceladus, the sixth largest moon of Saturn. While collection was fairly straightforward, back on Earth tremendous force was required to manipulate it. Many resources were brought to bear to erect a home that would keep the increasingly beloved family from harm.

This, their third, and they hoped, permanent living space, afforded them both privacy and proximity, in just the right balance. Khalil and Mov were unequivocally thrilled to be close to V'hanie and, especially, Garth-Ann. Raymòn just wanted the possibility of unbroken solitude. Sunshine's inherent adaptability made it less of an upheaval for her; and anticipating the place she was about to assume on the world stage engaged her emotions.

Although they were now living farther north than in the past, the weatherpainters made sure that Mainesail enjoyed a mainly temperate climate. On the day the tri-species clan arrived, the plum colored sky was highlighted with silvered rose. The air smelled like almonds and brown sugar; the breeze was strong and swept a few of the cobwebs from Raymòn's mind. For the first time in a great while, he grabbed his son and they ran, laughing and chasing each other, exploring the new fauna and flora of the wooded land. Legs giving out, they tumbled down the grassy bank to the lake, the no longer taken-for-granted joy of living bursting the seams of worry. The two Self-Contained beings were, for the moment, not at all contained.

A quick chill stopped them. There, shimmering over the pebble-strewn beach was a message bubble anchored in the sand. It was gaily patterned with primary colored geometric shapes, but the charm of the container was annihilated by the dread that filled them.

Armonté. It was not possible…or was it?

The bubble sensed them and gave up its message. The voices of Ilsa and Grolier could be heard saying, "Welcome home!" They hadn't known about the first message bubble and had unwittingly dispatched a blast of fear.

Relief surged through the artist; he lightly patted his son's back. The anxiety was gone, but so was the exuberance.

"Let's walk for a while. Joy can be calm, too." As was ever-increasingly the case, the child's wisdom helped to guide the father.

Once the family was settled into their new environment, Sunshine felt the call of her mission getting louder. Her wave/fibers were in a heightened state; her awareness of self and the world amplifying each day.

The four had gathered to address where they were each headed in this New Year. She spoke first: "I'm eighteen years sentient and I'm ready to be augmented for leadership and extreme passion. I know I already possess the capacity for intense caring and I am able to manage and direct when it is appropriate. In order to fulfill the work Harry spoke of, I will need to have the kind of drive befitting a 'calling' and an inner bonfire of purpose. As Mov wrote, the fabric of the world is coming undone. I believe I can help humans and androids find common ground. I think I should travel to all the conglostates, meet the people, talk directly to them."

Her eyes were lit by an inner light. Mov saw it and shared the flash of emotion; Raymòn saw it and felt a spasm of something he would only understand later; Khalil saw it and wanted to be part of it.

"Please…Mother, Father." He gazed with atypical intensity directly into the eyes of each family member. "I want to do this work, too. Am I not a friend of the world? Isn't that my nature?"

Mov, overcome by the child's precocious compassion, gave a quick, high-pitched yelp. Neither his Special nor his beloved friend made any sound for many moments.

"We need to think carefully about this." The android, flushed with maternal pride and worry, looked to the exterior calm of her partner. Raymòn met her gaze. It wasn't telepathy, but they had established such a deep rapport in their time together that she could read his unsaid words. Will our son be safe? Isn't he too young to take on such work?

It was the Companion, his empathy for both Khalil's desire and his parents' concerns, who influenced the decision.

"It's the boy's destiny to travel new roads. He is the first of his kind. Who better to illustrate the promise of a fully integrated future than the only humandroid?"

In a low voice, looking only at the tablet on which he was ceaselessly drawing, the man who would not be God offered his thoughts about the near future.

"Sunshine and Khalil, Mov will be your guide and protector as you pursue the transformation of our world.

"What is my future? I don't see it clearly. I'm changed by my time out of life, but I don't know where that will take me. At night I have dreams I can't yet understand. Perhaps answers will come."

Sunshine felt the now customary pang of sadness when Raymòn expressed the unmoored sense of his own life. Mov received her emotion and softened it with his thought: Trust him, my Special. He's stronger than that which has tested him. He will not succumb.

It was not yet known, but Wil Tork had begun to communicate via dreamthought, preparing the artist's unconscious mind for that which was to come. He was a conduit between the Self-Contained reborn human and the sounds of the universe, which Ray was more a part of than any other being. Understanding was, in fact, not the pathway to knowing. Much was in cosmic flux, not yet available for assimilation.

On his ninth birthday, Khalil prevailed and received a special dispensation from the Android Council to receive early augmentation. Illuminated by happiness at the prospect of joining his mother on her mission, he considered the nature of the augmentation he would receive.

"Should I become a warrior? Would that make me more able to fight for what the world needs?"

Mov said, "You are already a warrior for peace, love, and understanding. You don't need augmentation for that."

"Okay Movy, you always help me to understand." They touched foreheads, great love and trust sweeping through each of them.

Instead, he would receive the ability to glide, which he had wanted for a long time, and to hum as the androids did, from within each cell. He would also become able to process data, both intellectual and emotional, at twice the rate of any non-android.

"These new abilities will help others to see both sides of my nature, and I will grow as I was meant to." Sunshine, Raymòn and Mov looked wordlessly at each other, pride and deepest respect in their eye. Khalil was, they understood, following the singular life path that was his fate.

It had been arranged that Sunshine would receive her enhanced capacities on the day after Khalil-del-món's birthday. She would return to Berke and her former group home for the process and the ceremony. After the forty-eight hour recovery period, Tritan Tork stet-Sulston and Grandpa Harry would consult and prepare the method of DNA augmentation for her son. It would be done at home.

There was much joyful excitement among the Emo-augmented, and pure soaring energy from all as Mov and Sunshine arrived for the new augments and the attendant solemnities. Androids didn't push each other out of the way, but it was evident that each one of the housemates wanted to be the first to greet the now famous pair.

"The augmentation room is ready for you, Sarlee Réal-el Ludi. Mov, you will stand with her and keep her connected to herself—as you always do." Berke's eyes conveyed his deep love, and also something like reverence.

Before she took her place in the chair that had been the site her first transformation, the group collected. An amethyst sun was setting in the pale yellow sky. Samu-ol, his Companion Piers by his side, spoke first.

"Sunshine and Mov, I'm humbled by the lives you have lived and the challenges you are taking on. No one can see where your paths lead; we know that you, Sunshine, will be true to your nature, and Mov will be— as always— the steadfast link to the best of the sentient universe. You inspire us. You give us hope. May the light of your wave/fibers burn as brightly as the brightest star."

He was overcome by emotion; Piers, his deep orange, bronze-flecked eyes set off by his all white body cilia, gazed with care and alignment at his Special. Samu-ol gathered himself, stroking Piers' short, pointy ears. He nodded to indicate that he was finished speaking.

Patchin and Marti sat crossed-legged on the floor facing each other. Torina, making the third point of the triangle, stood between them. Everyone in the room understood the significance of their geometry. Three was a number that imbued each android with awe. They were constructed with a deep resonance for its centrality in nature; the tripartite shape opened them to that innate sensibility. Something wonderful was about to happen.

Torina raised both arms as if to conduct an orchestra; light of every color suffused the space around the three. Marti, arms straight out to the side, head tilted back, opened her full-lipped mouth wide. A sound with the texture of the roof cloud came rushing out. The room became simultaneously sharpened by the pulsing and echoing three-note vocal, and softened by the quickly spreading and glistening density. Patchin waited a beat, then lifted his arms forward; the sound and its cloud became fainter and was seen to enter into his opened his mouth.

With Torina conducting, the sound cloud moved rhythmically between the two, each time altering in tone and shape. The rest of the androids felt an increasing uptick in their wave/fibers, as if they were expanding in intensity and ethereal beauty. Time ceased to have meaning. As they progressed, each entity became part of both the spectacle and the source of the creation.

When it was over, Rocky, sweet and simple, a perfect contrast, offered his words.

"Family—your family, Sunshine—is your motivation. You are the trailblazer for interspecies reproduction. Your mate lost his life because too many on this planet were not ready for what you two had done. But, in its wisdom, the universe returned him. There may be some who understand this. But for most of us, it seems miraculous. Now your son—the friend of the world—is ready to take his place as a missionary to that world which you, our dear friend, will transform. Raymòn, who has experienced a spiritual re-awakening, will always be there for you. You have a beautiful family; you always have. I believe that fact has enhanced your basic nature—which is hungry to know everything. You have taken on the mantle of leadership for the cause and it suits you. Please count on me to help you in any way I can."

Each android vigorously nodded their agreement.

Berke stepped up. "The time has come. You will become the kind of leader you wish to be, a powerful instrument and a force of Ludi nature. I think you know that is exactly what we need. As the humans say, 'may you be blessed'— by all the strong energy in the universe and that of the Special ones (he looked directly at Mov). May their forces enhance yours. There is so much we still don't know. Together, human and android, loving and working as one, we will capture the secrets we all feel are right out there, just out of reach."

"Thank you, my dear guide. May I make one request?"

"Anything."

She looked at Mov and he spoke her words. "Let's hum for the joy of this most solemn occasion."

Murmurs of "of course" and "we would be honored" were heard. And then, as Sarlee Réal-el Ludi leaned into the Augmentation Chair and a shot of Strong Leadership and Enhanced Passion were delivered, she basked in the connectivity of the hum, which sounded more beautiful than ever.

All converged in a low, musical vibration. Nothing more was to be said. She placed her fingers in the slots in the chair, keeping her eyes open. Even when she closed them, Mov was right there, fully visible, whispering encouragement.

"Will I still be me?" she asked.

"We will still be we. I've got you. The augmentation will expand you; it won't change who you are."

"You comfort me and raise my strongest self to the forefront. I see in your eyes that I am."

"Yes, you are my lovely, wonderful Special. Forever it will be so."

"My body feels different. My mind is filled with new thoughts. But you allow me to see that every change is my own."

During the forty-eight hours necessary for recovery from Android Integration Trauma, Mov opened himself to full contact with his Special's disorientation. His aim was to share it and, by doing so, to dilute it. Her awareness that he was with her—both inside and outside—made the process far less jarring than it would otherwise have been.

On the third day she was fine, ready to get on with her work. But first there was the matter of her son. He was to be augmented as well.

The most singular entity on the planet was about to take part in a process that was as new and different as he was. There was a small mask through which Khalil inhaled a fine mist containing nano-techs, specially designed to enter his chromosomes and turn on previously dormant genes. Because receptivity for this type of biological change had been preset in his original creation, the procedure yielded no ill effects. A few minutes of controlled breathing and the nanobots did their work, then dissolved themselves, their vapor rising back into a retaining space in the mask.

The young friend of the world stood up, transported by his transformation. He glided and hummed all at once. Mov joined him in both. With a quick pure certainty, Khalil now knew far more than he had ever imagined was possible about his physical and emotional environment.

A plan for the first World Sentience Tour was outlined, with little help from Raymòn. As Sunshine began to ratchet things up on the world stage, he had fallen into isolation and despair.

He had become a figure of myth, even among the non-religious. No one but his immediate family had seen him since the New Year; he had gone silent. Inside the void, the legend grew. He wondered if he should have his traces wiped again, deeply wanting to shake off the desperate need of his followers. Any visits, even those by V'hanie, who was now pregnant, had to be exhaustingly devious.

He who had been given the gift of second life, sometimes found himself wishing he had died. A new kind of loneliness, which he felt as abandonment, clung to him. Wherever he looked, things seemed pale, bleached. Tork read his thoughts; he had acquired that ability— among others which would continue to unfold—allowing him to communicate the way androids did...except that he didn't need anyone's permission.

The Self-Contained sorcerer continued to send the Self-Contained lost soul dreamthoughts. They were obscure: full of color and things that didn't translate into a waking state. Although they perplexed him, the dreams made the artist feel more tethered to life. He didn't know that Wil was orchestrating these sleeping forays into a new realm; he couldn't know that his protector was preparing him for the next level of his new life.

Sunshine, Khalil and Mov decided to start their transformational tour in the New Southern States, a part of the world they had never before visited. They planned a dozen speaking stops beginning in Bolo, the largest city in Bolivia-Peru, continuing through the fragstates of Botswanique, Indolaysia, Sydney-berra and Sopac.

At first it was only the radical or very curious who came out to see them.

Many wanted to touch the hem of the garment of the new deity's wife or son; many wanted to see the hybrid child. Would he look "normal?" Or would he be odd and decidedly non-human?

Sunshine felt strongly—echoed fully by her Special and her son—that any reason for people to gather and listen was a good one. They spoke on hillsides, with hundreds arrayed informally around them; they spoke in stadiums which were half empty; they spoke to small rooms with fewer than fifty listeners; they spoke to groups who got up and left while they were still talking. Throughout, regardless of the reception, Sunshine said, "I speak for Raymòn." This was how she and, eventually, Khalil began every speech as they traveled around the globe.

After the first four stops something began to change. The android missionary, the humandroid, and the Companion all witnessed it. When they talked about the needs of the many and the need to repair the fabric of the world, a melancholy silence would spread through the audience. But they listened; they understood. Before too long, stadiums were overflowing, hillsides were packed, and everyone would, at some point in the presentation, break into song—Mov's Song.

Humans and androids stood when they sang it. It was becoming an anthem for healing.

Chapter 25–
You Are What You Eat

Raymòn's spirit was gradually being restored. At the urging of his creative partners—Benno in particular was relentless—the IGA resumed, meeting once again in the Oceanair Grove studio.

They each understood that something new had to come out of the experience they had shared. Two of the new questions subtly raised—it was Tōnna who put them into words, but each of the four had been thinking the same thoughts—were, "Do artists become what they draw?" and "How does art interflow with the growth of the artist?" While these would be philosophical questions in another time and place, for them, they were questions demanding answers in the present.

All watched as Raymòn began to draw his first new character since his return.

Two charcoal-gray eyes shone with an inexplicable light, illuminating the angular, skull-like head—the least amount of flesh necessary to cover bone. There was undeniable power emanating from the being, its gender or age obviated by the dim shroud of pale energy with which it was swathed. But the eyes told more of the story. Upon seeing them, all the artists knew at once that this was Raymòn's best work. Through the two-dimensional medium of the line, he had found a new way to communicate extreme emotion: sadness, compassion, love... and a kind of ultimate rectitude. Beyond the scope of all the feelings, the viewer knew something not before known.

No words came into Charl and Tōnna and Benno's minds, yet knowing filled them. There is so much more than we ever conceived of. All transcends all.

Before the others could say anything, Benito bellowed: "RAYMÒN! YOUR EYES!"

Gray where they had been brown, aglow with ...cosmic force? eternal fire? A torrent of notions spun through the minds of the three.

"What in the cosmos is going on?!"

Charl bellowed the question on his way to the multi-screen control panel. He immediately began retouching the new art. Without waiting for the usual argument and resolution, he had added a touch of gold-tinted green to the new character's long, translucent hair.

"Mirror, Charl!" It was his duplicate, shock and amazement in her voice.

What he saw reflected was a greening and lengthening of his own hair.

Rather than recoiling in fear, the edge of the unknown kicked each of the creators into another gear.

"Let me try next." Benno rushed to his oversized chair in front of the Dimensional Transitioner, which was usually used to bring Heroes of the Galaxy into three-dimensional imagery. In his excitement, he knocked into Tōnna, sending her flying across the room. She let out a resounding "Woof!"

"Forgive, sweetcakes. Couldn't help it!"

The giant cast a rueful glance over one enormous shoulder as Charl helped his lovely twin to her feet. Benno immediately went back to his intense focus; with the lightest touch he adjusted the sensitive equipment.

"Holy Crayola! Look at this."

Raymòn and the silvery duo crowded around the three-foot screen. At first, what they saw didn't compute. It was Ray's new character, but not just in three dimensions. It shimmered, similar to a holograph, but there was another dimension to it, a fourth.

There were new colors that not even the extended spectrum of the Self-Contained artist had ever included. Everyone could see them; they just couldn't name them. And that wasn't all. They could hear the image: not in words, but in a varying twang resounding through each molecule.

This must be what androids feel in their wave/fibers. Raymòn was in touch with something beyond the wonder of the other three. It was a sense of recognition, like coming home after a lifetime of being exiled. He chose not to mention that. No matter. Something else had captured all their attention; the same colors and sounds (for lack of a better description) were becoming apparent on and from Benito.

Charl identified what they all were experiencing. "Language isn't working here. But we all see it, right?

"It's like 'we are what we eat.' Instead … we are what we create. I think we've answered both of the questions we were all wondering about.

"Do you want to try, Tōnna?" Charl recognized the jut of her jaw. She was standing pat.

"I don't think so. I've spent too much time getting myself just right."

A question appeared in three minds: "Is vanity a protection or the death-knell of evolution?" In a wisp of a moment the thought was obliterated... as if it had never been there.

Tork was at work. "Not just yet. You can't handle it yet."

There was a slow change across the globe. It was Sunshine's breath—not that she actually needed to breathe: Her presence and commitment to reaching the entire population with her truth became a pulse that was like her exhale followed by a reciprocal inhale from the populace.

Sometimes Raymòn stayed in Benno's underground fortress of solitude. Sunshine would find him there during interludes from her mission. Each time, it would feel for a while like the first time they met. The android always understood—he needed to retreat to his original place of protection. His Self-Contained capacities were strained to their limits; his need to adapt to his own transformation—which was not concluded, but more of an ongoing evolution—exhausted his ability to maintain connections.

V'hanie and Garth-Ann's child had been born: a peaceful Insider who received all the enormous love and empathy her parents were capable of. When Raymòn first met Deiliah-lou Tova Nu-Réal, he was captivated. Her skin glowed like rich chocolate; her eyes, opened wide in continuous delight and wonder, were blue-lashed lavender. The fine hair covering her head was the same ultramarine as her Multi parent. Garth had undergone a gene transplant in order to permanently change the color of his follicles; he was gratified that it had been passed along to his daughter. Everything about her was visually striking, even as she lay in her mother's or father's arms. Like Garth-Ann, she was a Multi.

Ray was drawn to her; despite how tiny and new she was, she seemed to know him. Newborn to newborn.

Khalil, Sunshine, and Mov, returning from their most recent jaunt deep into the New Equatorial States, each fell in love with the new addition to the family. The baby's eyes locked onto the Companion's. She chortled and wriggled and he did the same. Her little hands reached out to grab him and she latched onto an ear. Mov would have let her hold on forever. Khalil joined them, singing a silly song he made up on the spot: "Cuzzin, buzzin, you're my favorite muzzin."

The infant became very still. She peered with a precocious focus at her cousin. "Mmmmmmuzzzz."

The entire family burst into ecstatic exclamation. "She's trying to speak!" Somehow it seemed to make sense. No one in her presence doubted that she was another special being. And it would be many years before she ever referred to the humandroid boy as anything but "Muzzin."

Very tenderly, Sunshine lifted Deiliah-lou out of her intelligent cradle. It instantly opened one side to accommodate her. The android whispered in her ear so that no one else could hear, "Sweet one, you will grow up in a world that is loving and accepting. I give you my word."

Once again the family was awed, this time silently, when the tiny girl gently touched Auntie Sunshine's cheek and very clearly nodded her head.

No matter where Ray was staying, he would see his mother often. Ilsa worked through hers and Grolier's substantial social networks to promote what was popularly referred to as "The Needs of the Many World Tour." Her admiration for Sunshine was one of her favorite topics. Their mutual respect was filled with love. The android had discovered a new element of her Emo-induced humanity... forgiveness. There was no more submerged resentment. When she heard of the way Ilsa spoke about her, she was simply grateful.

"My son's mate is one of the finest beings on the planet.

"She and Raymòn are living proof of the necessity of merging our species. Just look at the child. There is no other to compare, except, of course, for my new granddaughter." Her pride in her family was no longer marred by any of the old ignorance or fear.

The Global Academy and The Android Council each made Sunshine an honorary member; Mov and The Friend of the World were given places as associates, as well. Wherever they went, they were being asked to officiate at Joinings of androids and humans. There were fifty couples living in co-sentience when the first year of their proselytizing came to a close.

It was hopeful. However, the work also met with strong pockets of resistance. There were the Drovines and the MPS, still with a large faction; and there were average humans who were still afraid. Twelve months had passed without any violence; it was Ilsa and her network that reported on a resurgence of hostile planning. That newly looming danger, combined with unexpected further transformation, caused Raymòn to become filled with his own sense of exigency.

It was a cool, early spring day with hints of popcorn and apple in the pale gold air. The artist had just returned to his Mainesail home, ready for the woodsy solitude but looking forward to some time with Deiliah-lou and her parents. Tork came ambling out of Mov's space. Raymòn was, to his own amazement, unfazed. He realized he had been expecting him. That made no sense, and yet it did.

"It's time for us to complete your work." The sorcerer's uninflected tone was belied by the intense glow of his black eyes. Usually impenetrable, they were now like beacons across the pitch dark of the unknown.

"Wait here for me. I'll be back in five minutes." Which was exactly how long Raymòn perceived him to be gone. Yet, in the stretched time of a distant galaxy, a mortal confrontation between Tork and Perdu was taking place.

Wil had become aware of Perdu's increasing ability to sniff out the edges of the new connection between Raymòn and cosmic forces. He had discovered Perdu's identity immediately following the resurrection and knew he would be best served by keeping that information to himself until it was most needed. Tork had knowledge of the double clone's role in the break-in at the Réal-el Ludi home. Emboldened by his ability to successfully get Armonté through his nemisis' security measures, the evil genius had begun to increase the frequency of his interventions; he had anonymously provided Marielle with an unidentifiable pale yellow gem on a thin gold chain, which cauterized the safety measures around the house. It had appeared among her private belongings with a sound-note that said, "This is the stone of righteousness. It will open the way for your holy work."

The magician arrived at his half-brother's underground lair. It was undetectable to anyone who didn't already know of its existence. To describe it as a cave only hints at the dim, cold interior. The cloned son of the clone had constructed a long, narrow sequence of small spaces one thousand feet beneath a minor mountain in a remote northeastern corner of Brunswick-Scotia. The entry was hidden by the illusion of unbroken rock.

Of course, Perdu saw him coming and knew exactly who he was. He attempted to preemptively strike Tork with a silent canon delivering air compressed to 150 atmospheres. It was built into a tree growing below the actual opening in the rock, which dilated into visibility for only these two.

Wil's power had increased exponentially since Raymòn was returned to life.

He evaded the canon and lassoed the Other with a hook of the cold interspatial energy he was able to command, pulling him out of his subterranean protection and thrusting him into Mayall's Object, five hundred million light-years away, within the constellation of Ursa Major. He joined the fully enraged deviant, bringing a Mobius strip on which they did battle. It would not be sufficient to leave him there—Perdu's skills were too profound. Tork had to finish him off—or die trying.

It was over quickly, in cosmic terms; a defect in the double-cloned DNA made the sounds of deep space intolerable on a cellular level. Before Wil had marshaled his full strength, the other son of Tritan Tork stet-Sulston disintegrated completely. Across the universe, a wave (for lack of a better term) of peace rippled and flowed. The demise of such extreme evil was felt as a healing force wherever life in all its various forms existed. Non-life absorbed the new smoothing as well.

Once back with Raymòn, Tork wasted no time. What he had to communicate was more important than anything else he had so far conveyed to his Self-Contained brother. It would not be easy to assimilate.

"We must sit and talk. And we must look each other in the eye. What I have to tell you transcends any innate discomfort you and I might experience. Let everything else go right now. Nothing else matters except the information I'm about to share with you."

The artist heard his protector's words from inside his own mind. He knew he would never be the same...again.

"I want to tell you about life and the universe.

"All the sentients on our planet, and all the other living and non-living things: they are merely a mote in God's eye."

"Whose eye?" Raymòn's voice was very low. He wasn't sure he was actually talking, but he knew he would be heard.

"The right question to ask, but you will have to wait for the answer. Everywhere in the infinite are worlds. They're like Russian nesting dolls: little ones inside of larger ones or larger ones inside of little ones. Both possibilities exist. We can only see through the limits of our senses. It's a very partial view and very far from what is true.

"In your journey through death and rebirth you have experienced some of the greater truth. But here is the center of all that is or was or ever will be:

"It is all 'No Thing.'"

"Nothing?" Raymòn felt something like a more complex and far more disturbing version of confusion. Naturally, Tork could tell.

"No. It's not nothing, nor is it something. And by it, I mean all. The androids are made of two-thirds of it: wave/particles. But, without the other third, the illusion remains outside of what is so. The third piece is intention. Humans innately know that. Most forget it before they can walk. The triad of Wave/Particle/Intention has no size, is not material. No scientist looking for the infinitesimal or the ultimate magnitude could find it. It is as much large as it is small. Everything and nothing is encompassed in No Thing."

"I can't grasp what you're saying. It doesn't make sense. But I can feel something, a kind of resonance. It's similar to the way I feel when the image I've drawn is exactly what I had in mind. A sense of being in tune or...I'm not sure of the words to use." He looked away, more out of habit than a need to disconnect. He felt an unusual comfort in his contact with Tork, despite how strange it all was.

"Paradox and syncronicity. You're in touch with it. You can't possibly get to where I know you're going via language."

Wil continued, "Colors are the doorway into all: all color and no color. When you experience color or dream of color or thrill to color, or feel the pall of its absence, you are on the bridge—from consciousness as you have always known it to the No Thing."

"Why?"

"That's not the right question to ask. It has no answer."

In Ray's mind—or at least that was the notion he first embraced—a burst of energy appeared, with every color he had ever seen or thought of and many, many more. Another aspect of what he was now not exactly seeing, not exactly feeling, but inside of, was the absence of color. He felt a great deal in response, but not emotionally and not physically. It was more like a perfect fullness, unlike any he had known.

As Wil Tork had expected, it was as if he'd had a visitation of insight from supernatural forces. Raymòn Réal, Self-Contained artist, mate of the beautiful android, father of the first humandroid, achieved knowing through color. Who better than the greatest colorist of any age, a man with a trans-human spectrum at his disposal? His lifelong relationship with color gave him access to No Thing.

"Do I share this with Sunshine and Mov? Khalil and V'hanie? Garth-Ann?

251

Benno and Tōnna and Charl?"

"You will tell them what you know. It will be the beginning."

"Shouldn't we first talk about God?"

"Sure. The pinging inside certain humans, now androids too, of the mystery inherent in every fragment of the universe, is God. When the core force of the No Thing is employed—that of life and death, creation and destruction—all that has been attributed to God, whomever engages that...is God.

"You are now a New Human, in harmony with all. You now have access to all. When there are just a few of us: you and me, Ramses Morgon, Grandpa Harry, some others who are not too public, we are God or the gods—like on Mount Olympus, like the one who changed water into wine, like those who have healed by the laying on of hands. When everyone knows the No Thing, everyone will be God. And there will no longer be a need for God or for gods. But, before that can be considered and implemented by those of us who are the keepers of the knowledge, the world has to be harmonized and de-emotionalized.

"Excessive feelings are the hallmark of immature entities. There is a place to get to beyond feelings, where choices are made from another dimension, neither emotional nor rational—a centered space of clarity, of being tuned in. Yogis have achieved this, some Buddhist masters have as well; many Cosmosists strive for and reach this new way. Currently those most in harmony with the necessary balance are Emo-augmented androids and Self-Contained, self-aware humans."

Chapter 26–
No Thing, Every Thing

Raymòn, having just been inducted into the universe of No Thing, had to re-enter his world of every thing. He felt both urgency and transcendency. The intention to share what he knew expanded by the moment.

The missionaries arrived back home the day after his education by Tork.

When Sunshine looked into the face of her Self-Contained man, she saw that he was profoundly different. I'm not surprised. The world is resetting; there is a future which will be something we can't imagine now. As my Companion, my son, and I harness these winds of change, I cannot forget that Raymòn has a special connection to the Universe. I believe he is the source of the path; he's the spearhead.

They were alone. The stars were visible through their expansive Morgonglass window onto the lake. The sky was a deep red, almost black. Each sun or planet visible to them glowed with an intense kind of white light that penetrated one's soul or wave/fibers (there was no difference); the water lapping at the shore seemed much more energized than usual.

The New Human turned to his mate, looking deeply into her eyes. He said nothing. But, for the first time, she could hear his thoughts. He told her everything. It took no time. She understood in the way it could be understood, not with her reason, but in the shifted flutter of the reshaping happening inside her architecture.

"Yes." That was all that needed to be said.

The next day she stood before Mov on their veranda, while Raymòn sat with his son on the rocky beach. The knowledge was silently passed once more. Mov did the Dance of the Joyous Companion, humming in a new, higher octave; Khalil-del-món Réal-el Ludi hummed as well. He glided in a great circle around his father.

Each of the New Humans and New Androids continued to selectively share the News with those they trusted and knew to be ready to receive it. For a while the numbers stayed very small: V'Hanie and Garth-Ann were next, then Ilsa and Grolier, then the IGA.

Sunshine took the AlbertE to Ludicom to meet with Rathsen el Ludi, who had become the leader of the Android Council following the purge of the traitorous Livingwell. After sharing what she knew with him, she Farbeamed to Tutmonda Centro to speak with the Global Academy President, Ethanos Kartolini. Both world leaders reacted with contained awe. Each had been aware that something was coming, something which would change everything.

It had arrived.

Something else of great import was also in progress.

Anola Drovine, having tried and failed to save the life of Raymòn Réal, had taken on a mission of her own. Without having any contact with Sunshine, she was a branch on the tree of transformation. Her life had become devoted to the conversion of the Drovines, now numbering almost a thousand. Disregarding the Council's restrictions, their production had increased right before and since the beginning of The Year One A.R. They were making soldiers for their righteous war.

Anola's method was to speak to one individual at a time; when she saw that her new values were being assimilated into another Drovine's wave/fibers, she recruited them to join her in spreading the word. It was a slow and not always successful process, but by mid-year of 2 A.R. forty-seven of the original Drovines had joined her.

Awareness of her activities quickly reached Vanguard and the other adamantly inflexible Drovines. They were no longer in bed with the MPS; that ended when Armonté's exploits produced the opposite of their goal of segregation of the species. They were also less inclined toward a violent solution. Always pragmatic, the Drovine leadership realized it had not been effective. At their central meeting place in the sparsely populated village of Красное озеро, (Russian for "Red Lake"), in the NNS fragstate of Ruberia, six of the prime drivers of Drovine policy met in a planning meeting.

"We are being slowly undermined by Anola and her converts. We must wage a war for the purity of our existence. We can't give up on our ultimate goal of dominance of the lessers on the planet. Isn't that the reason we were created? Isn't that our purpose?"

Vanguard spoke in a loud emotionless voice. Emphasis on the word "we" was a custom of speech among these androids, a verbal homage to their hive-like sensibility.

Lutuna Drovine was the acknowledged leader of the species. When lat spoke, all the others leaned forward in a demonstration of respect.

"Sentience is the battleground. Our war is, as Vanguard said, necessary to fulfill our destiny. But now we will use our innate superiority to manipulate circumstances non-violently. We will leave the crass hostility to the pathetic MPS humans. Let them die in their fruitless efforts. Any who succumb will not be missed."

The call to devious action was lauded wherever Drovine-droids lived. All those not converted by Anola became fighters in the Sentience War. They waged battles of propaganda and of disinformation, communications were corrupted, transportation was disrupted. The message offered to the world was a parody of Mov's Song: The fabric of the world could only be restored through the superiority of Drovine leadership. Life would be better for all if they were in charge.

While the Sentience War was of great concern to Raymòn and the other New Humans and New Androids, a more imminent threat was being posed. In desperation, Sharana Rothbec-Kathari was about to unleash a surge of mayhem across the planet. She had complete control of all the AILES, and they were being refitted and programmed to destroy any human-android pair in close proximity. Like heat-seeking missiles, they were to be aimed at their targets: where DNA and wave/fibers came together with less than three feet of distance, death would follow. Would there be collateral damage? Without question. But the hate-filled members of the Movement for the Purity of the Species would consider those lives well spent.

When he entered Benno's studio, it came to Raymòn, as all his creations had, in a flash of insight. An image appeared in his mind. This vision was different in that he simultaneously knew he was in touch with No Thing. Taking out his new, flexible tablet which, when not in use, reduced itself to a lightweight, pocket-sized, micro-filament-thin object, he thought: Large image, stylus, full spectrum. The tablet rested solidly in the air in front of him, eighteen inches square; an ergonomically perfect stylus seemed to appear in his hand. Was it always there?

Did he just call it forth from No Thing? He sat and immediately began to sketch. Using the mind-to-mind communication now available to all New Humans, he called for the other three InterGalactic Artists to join him. They watched as he drew.

The new hero began to take shape: above average height, but not freakishly tall; slim, with powerful shoulders and defined muscles in his arms and legs. The magenta and black clad male was dark-skinned, dark-haired with warm brown eyes; his gaze was averted, eyes turned to a distant point at his side. His hands were prominent, long, graceful fingers. He held a stylus, exactly like the one the artist was using. A tablet floated in front the hero.

"It's you!" Charl spoke in all their thoughts.

The Self-Contained one added a belt with a "C."

"For 'Changer'—his name. My name?"

The others were silent as he continued. On Changer's tablet Raymòn had drawn the image of Changer drawing onto a tablet. It was clear that Raymòn was creating an infinite reduction, like a mirror image of a mirror image...and on, and on...

The new hero was given small, angular, iridescent metallic wings. They appeared in all the ever more distant images. And they appeared on Raymòn's shoulders. These enabled, not flight on Earth, but the ability to travel through infinite space. Around Changer's neck the artist had drawn a crystal key on a long, golden chain. It was in the shape of the letters NT— for No Thing. A lock appeared before Changer and all his iterations. It appeared before Raymòn. It was made of something light absorbing; its dense black color was nothing found on Earth. It was, all knew at once, a black hole. In its center was a light-filled opening, also in the shape of NT. The key was also around Ramòn's neck. The artist put down the stylus; it disappeared.

Tōnna, her eyes enormous, clutching Charl's shoulder, spoke first. "I think you are the key, Ray, to change. We have to prepare the way for The Change we all know is to come."

They all understood. No Thing was both inherently complete and responsive to intention.

"Can you interact with No Thing to end the threats to Sunshine's mission?" Benno's voice was raspy; he didn't use any retro-speak at all. This was serious.

Tork was in the room. As before, first he wasn't there, then he was.

He spoke to Raymòn inside their minds, answering the questions they asked and had yet to form.

"Right now, you are the center. But you can bring all the New Sentients into the center with you. That will be the source of the ultimate power of change."

Raymòn, increasingly more fluidly, engaged and shared his newly acquired powers remotely with the New Sentients. There was no need for overt communication; they all knew everything they needed to know.

Like the flow of a swift stream, the numbers of New Sentients continued to increase. The stream became a river.

Meachem bella Russe watched as a shapeless energy field consumed the innermost room in the MPS fortress headquarters. Rothbec-Kathari had been about to give the order to let loose the AILES on every quadrant of the globe. Mid-word, with her fist clenched in the air, she momentarily flared with a purple glow. And then her solid form became transparent. And then she was gone. The sound of metal being crushed followed—but only briefly. The world no longer contained the vicious drones.

Bella Russe addressed the others in the room, the arrogant sneers on all their faces gone, replaced with panicked eyes and open-mouthed helplessness.

"It's over now. We have lost. Go to your homes and begin to adapt."

Anola, whose mission had begun to expand exponentially, was brought into Raymòn's transformational fold; she, in turn, brought in the converted Drovines. It was the balance No Thing needed.

Swirls of rectifying energy, which no longer occupied time, had begun to sweep the planet, like a high wind on the beach, cleansing and polishing the world. All the upsurging number of New Sentients felt it as renewal. The space was being prepared for The Change.

In this, there was Tork, appearing inside and outside no space. Raymòn was his focus.

"My brother,..." (It had always been so, but the magician no longer resisted the bond of the Self-Contained) "... you have one more thing to learn."

The artist opened his mind to receive.

"A thousand years ago No Thing exhaled the beginning of The Change that is coming. Children began to be born who were different. Many were unable to function in their world. There was, then, and continued to be, frustration and pain for those individuals and the people who cared for them. They became known as 'autistic.' Their differences were not understood. Efforts were made to make them like everyone else, and to discover the underlying source of their dysfunction. Well-meaning people everywhere, with a wealth of compassion, worked to solve this globally increasing problem. No one could possibly have understood that these autistic people were part of the evolution of humanity.

"Autism had been a latent force, lying dormant in humans since they departed from their simian ancestors two and a half million years ago. When it was time— and autism became active and visible—humans had to avoid it, fear it, never understanding it, seeing it as a curse, a tragedy. As you know, it was only within the last seventy years that mankind began to assimilate the Self-Contained.

"Autism is the evolutionary deviation which unfolded from No Thing; its purpose has been to prepare humans for hybridization. In order to become what humans were always meant to be, much of the destabilizing and confusing excess of emotion had to be excised. Change emanates from extremes, which have now—after all these millennia—progressed into a relatively steady state. Khalil-del-món is the beginning. You are the father of our future."

The New Human saw the entire non-linear chain in the growing part of his mind that was one with the Universe. He and Wil simultaneously felt the fullness.

The Change was happening; on Earth, things continued to require time for the unfolding.

Grandpa Harry visited the Réal-el Ludis. V'hanie and Garth-Ann with Deiliah-lou, now almost two, were also present.

With a withered hand, Gharry patted his leg. (He was, as he always had done, using his physiology to signal his intentions. His time, in his present form, was drawing to a close.) Mov slowly soared across the room, landing silently in his favorite spot.

Knowing spread. And, yet, saying words still mattered.

"Let us discuss how your family will change, how I will change, how the world must alter to accommodate the change."

Mov looked up at the Wizard of LUDI. "What happens when everyone is God and there is no longer a higher power?"

"I think you have an idea of your own. Would you like to tell us?" The Companion felt the gentle touch of the papery epyderm on his head.

"There can be no more absolution from responsibility. Even among the New Sentients, there are old habits of unfreedom, of superstition, of hoping for luck or the gods to favor them. Accepting the paradox of No Thing, Every Thing—well, I guess there will be resistance, and not only from reluctant Drovines or past adherents of the MPS.

"We will feel alone...as we become more integrated. Both parts will be true."

"You are very wise. I think you understand what lies 'ahead' very well.

"Khalil, my child, do you know what your mission is?"

The boy, now starting to become a man, stepped to the center of the room. He looked at each individual, resting his gaze on his young cousin, Deiliah-lou.

"Our mission is to be the conduits for the next generations, to be the leaders who do not lead; the partners to the world."

The other beautiful and unique child, intelligence and compassion radiating from those lavender eyes, answered her humandroid cousin, the peeling of her voice warming those who heard her.

"I will be with you, Khalil...and with the world."

The aged android continued. "Raymòn, Sunshine, to those of the greatest ability falls the greatest responsibility. All are equal but not the same.

"You, my son, are the progenitor; your talents will be critical to the dissemination of new comprehension." Harry smiled into his eyes, only long enough for full contact to be made. No excess would ever be desirable.

"Sarlee Réal-el Ludi, no Change could have happened without your transformational work. In a very real sense, we are now all your children.

"My time has come to an end. My purpose is fulfilled. Will you take my place? Will you shepherd our flock?"

There was no need for sadness. Change was the nature of it all. And nothing ended...not in the No Thing. But still, now that there were no more words, there was one last tear.